Hunting Barbara

Diana Leon Clark

Published by Diana Leon Clark, 2024.

To my daughter, who inspired this book, and to my readers everywhere. Where would I be without your encouragement and support?

Chapter One

"I, Barbara Baines Allen, swear that the evidence I shall give ..."
After completing her oath, Barbara calmly took her seat in the
witness chair and waited for the first question from Mitchell
Andrews, John Garcia's defense attorney.

"Dr. Allen, you are currently an assistant professor in the
sociology department at the University of San Diego, is this correct."

"I am, yes."

"It's my understanding that your field of expertise is familicide,
murders taking place in a family setting. I also believe you've done
considerable research on homicides within families on southwestern
Native American reservations. Would that also be correct?"

"It is."

"You have also been an expert witness in this area before in
both state and federal courts. Would you provide the jury with some
information about your background?"

Barbara briefly summarized her half-dozen court appearances
and her academic background, including her dissertation on the
increasing incidence of familicide on reservations in California,
Arizona, and Nevada.

"Dr. Allen, you have studied John William Garcia's file and sat
through the previous three days of testimony. What is your
professional opinion about the circumstances surrounding the death
of Sara Garcia and the injuries to her son, Samuel?"

Barbara gave the attorney a small, polite smile. "The facts, of
course, are not in dispute. John Garcia admits he killed Sara Garcia
and severely injured his son. But isolated facts taken out of context
seldom lead to truth or justice. That is why we have trials. To
understand what John did ..." Barbara used the man's first name
intentionally; her job here was to make the man sympathetic. "... you

1

would have to understand the world he occupies—the Fort Mohave Reservation."

Barbara painted a bleak picture. A man who'd led a blameless life and been gainfully employed for thirteen years lost first his job and then his self-respect, sinking into a world of drugs and alcohol. The beatings of his wife and son, which he admitted to, had been going on for almost two years.

"There is a record of five separate occasions when the tribal police went to the Garcia household," she continued, "and yet there was no intervention beyond two arrests long enough for John to dry out. The system failed him just as it failed his wife and child."

Mitch Andrews didn't interrupt his expert witness's testimony. He'd worked with Dr. Allen once before and trusted her. She was a defense attorney's dream witness—cool, competent, and easy on the eyes. *Maybe wet dream's more accurate*, he conceded in private amusement. The professor, despite her prim demeanor, was hot. He suspected half the jury was fantasizing about her right this minute.

Barbara finished with a brief history of research on familicide, made casual reference to the work of Dr. Laurence Trask, a noted authority and her former mentor, and put the death of Sara Garcia in perspective. That's what Mitch wanted—mitigating circumstances—and she'd delivered beautifully. Since Barbara Allen believed every word she said, the jury would, too.

"That will be all, Dr. Allen."

Now the federal prosecutor had his turn at bat, and Thomas Surbaugh was pissed. How had this woman turned a drunken bully who'd beaten his wife to death into someone the jury could sympathize with?

"Dr. Allen, I will concede your expertise; it is not in question. What I do question is your common sense. Can you actually be telling this courtroom, this sworn jury, John Garcia shouldn't be punished for beating his wife to death and maiming his three-year-old son?"

"That is neither my intent nor what I testified to today," she told him in a calm, professional voice. "I'm simply pointing out a simple truth; the events of May 12th did not happen in a vacuum. John Garcia was, and is, caught up in a system that destroyed his confidence in his manhood, his sense of family and community, and his self-respect.

"Neither the tribe nor the federal government did anything to help the Garcia family with predictable results. Should he be punished? This is for the jury to decide. But I can tell you that although this crime was preventable, it was inevitable without intervention. It is simple algebra: A + B = C."

Surbaugh's glare was indignant. "Math, you're giving me a lesson in arithmetic? A woman is dead, Ms. Allen, and a young boy barely past babyhood beaten almost to death. John Garcia had a choice that night, and he made it."

The federal prosecutor eyed the jury sternly. He'd made a dent in the professor's calm façade and her credibility with the seven men and five women who mattered most to him at the moment.

"Mr. Surbaugh, have you ever spent any real time on a reservation?"

Barbara kept her voice soft, her eyes more sympathetic than antagonistic as she directed her attention to the attorney. She already knew he had no experience with reservation life though she carefully didn't belabor the point.

"It is a world apart from anything you can imagine. The closest I can come to an analogy is a pressure cooker. Tribal traditions and expectations, the larger California community where John Garcia worked and sometimes lived, the limitations and poverty imposed by federal oversight—all of that came crashing down on one poor, overwhelmed man. It isn't a question of whether or not he should be punished but rather how much punishment is enough."

Thomas Surbaugh frowned and turned to the judge. "I ask that the witness's last statement be stricken, your honor. Ms. Allen was not responding to a direct question."

"Objection, your honor." Mitchell Andrews stood and faced the judge. "The witness was simply expanding on her response about the A + B = C, which he challenged."

"Objection noted; I'll allow her comments to stand, but please confine yourself to direct questioning, Dr. Allen."

Sitting quietly in the back of the courtroom, Supervisory Special Agent Luis Vallejo Séguin snorted in disgust. This damn woman was torpedoing the whole case. Oh, Garcia would be found guilty, all right. But they'd go soft on the bastard.

He'd spent over a month gathering the facts and considered this case as open and shut as they came. A drunk high on meth had beaten to death a thirty-three-year-old woman, who'd done everything she could to protect her child, and then turned on his own son before the tribal police intervened.

He hated these kinds of cases. Fort Mohave wasn't even in his jurisdiction. He'd been loaned out to the Los Angeles office because of his so-called expertise. This case turned out to be a colossal waste of his and the FBI's time.

Still, the woman was nice to look at if he had to spend an afternoon in the overheated First Street Courthouse. He'd always thought he went for the whole package, which in her case sure wasn't bad—tall, blond, slim yet rounded in the right places. But the woman's hair, even though she'd pulled it back in a prim knot, had him fantasizing.

He couldn't tell how long it was, but it definitely would fall somewhere well below her shoulders. It had a tawny blond color that made him think of mesquite honey. He'd give a week's pay to see it down, put his hands in it. *Not likely*, he decided. There is a fine line between cool and cold, and Dr. Allen struck him as someone who'd never allow herself to lose control or let anyone, any man, take it.

Although he waited around for the jury's deliberation, Luis Vallejo already knew the outcome. John Garcia would be found guilty, but he'd be given a few years and some court-mandated counseling. That meant he'd get soft time instead of the rough and ready justice of Mendota or Lompoc he deserved.

• • • •

Barbara left the courtroom without waiting for the verdict. She'd completed her job and didn't want to know the details. Why did they always call her in after the fact? That man didn't start life a violent, vicious killer. His wife's death should never have happened. She thought about it all the way back to San Diego. *What a tragic waste*, she grumbled, one she'd never get used to.

Most of her life, the part she cared about, occurred on campus. She loved teaching, felt most at home in her large, untidy office in Loma Hall. Nearly every one of her friends was a colleague. Some would call it a cloistered life, but it suited her.

Since the sky had darkened by the time she arrived in San Diego, Barbara headed for her small, cottage-style home in a regentrifying neighborhood on 10th Avenue. Taking the oversized pins out of her heavy hair with a sigh of relief, she shook her head and ran impatient fingers through honey-blond hair that fell almost to her waist. *I should cut it*, she considered once again, knowing perfectly well she wouldn't.

After putting her neat navy suit back on its padded hangers, Barbara grabbed the sweat pants and ragged sweater that were more to her liking. Time to figure out what was for supper. *Too late to cook*, she decided; *I'll just make a salad and eat a hard-boiled egg. A glass of wine might help wash away the taste of the courtroom.*

Barbara joined the faculty at the University of San Diego three years earlier after finishing her Ph.D. at the University of Arizona. Marveling once again at the minor miracle that took her from the heart of the Midwest, Bemidji, Minnesota, first to Tucson and then San Diego, Barbara acknowledged she could never go home again. A life without snow, and her parents' equally frigid disapproval, was just what she wanted.

Soon caught up in her classes and research, Barbara left all thoughts of her recent court appearance behind. It was the part of her job she liked least. In late October, she got a call from Efren Adamson. Would she have time to talk to him about a case on the Pala reservation? "It's right up your alley," the young attorney assured her.

Wilma Lopez, a tribal member who worked for the reservation's water department, killed her thirty-six-year-old husband, Roberto, two months earlier with a kitchen knife as he slept. Then, she'd calmly called the tribal police.

Her cousin, Roy Mendez, had been sent to bring Wilma in. She answered every question the tribal police asked, repeating everything for the FBI agents sent the next day to interview her. Wilma admitted she'd planned her husband's murder before entering their bedroom. "I did it for my boys," she told her interrogators. "Things couldn't go on this way."

Barbara didn't interrupt as Wilma Lopez, sitting stoically in her bright orange jail uniform, described the events leading to her husband's death. The Pala Reservation woman had already been convicted by a judge in the U.S. District Court. They were now in the sentencing phase of the trial.

Wilma's husband, Roberto, a former member of the Logan Heights gang in San Diego, had gotten tangled up with his old gang seven months earlier. When a drive-by shooting went bad, he'd fled back to the reservation for safety. That was six weeks before his murder and Wilma's arrest.

Once he reached the reservation, he'd insisted on moving back in with his wife, roughing her up when she'd begged him to seek treatment instead. Wilma didn't want any drugs or alcohol in the house because of the children.

"That's for me to say, not you, *mujer*," had been his response—delivered with a blow hard enough to leave a black eye troubling her coworkers.

"After less than a week, it became impossible," Wilma said wearily. "Roberto drank constantly, did meth and cocaine with a few friends as worthless as he was, and started hurting the kids. I didn't care so much about me, but I couldn't let him continue beating them, so, I killed him. I didn't know what else to do."

Wilma's quiet recital of events seemed eerily familiar, and Barbara regretted once again that there'd been no effective intervention though Wilma's boss at the water company did try several times to get her some help. Too little, too late—it was an old story.

• • • •

The courtroom on West Broadway felt familiar though not in a good way; it was Barbara's third visit to the federal building in downtown San Diego. She couldn't help wishing it could be her last. Still, she'd do her best for Wilma Lopez and her two small boys. Jailtime wouldn't do anything to solve that family's problems.

Once again, calm and neatly dressed with her hair in a thickly braided knot, Barbara provided the judge with a detailed background of similar cases. She made no overt effort to persuade him.

Instead, she gave a simple, almost dry recitation of facts—Roberto's gang affiliation, his history of drug and alcohol abuse, the physical and mental abuse he inflicted on his family. All of this led to the atmosphere of fear pervading the Lopez household.

"Wilma's options were limited, Judge Benson, and the reservation's resources are stretched thin. She saw no alternative. Sitting here, you and I could easily think of half-a-dozen better alternatives, but none of them existed in her world view.

"Instead, Wilma Lopez made the best decision she could for her children, accepting her arrest and punishment with grace and dignity. In my opinion, she's been punished enough—and so have her children."

Luis Vallejo found himself experiencing a serious case of *déjà vu*. Once again, the case fell to the FBI, and he'd drawn the short straw. At least, this trial had moved along quickly. He'd sat through the earlier hearing with Judge Benson, impressed with the prisoner's stoic demeanor. Wilma Lopez did the crime; now, she'd do her time.

Or would have if Ms. Gorgeous Hair hadn't shown up at the sentencing hearing. Now, he wasn't so sure. Judge Benson might be a pro, but that damned professor had a way of twisting things, making the assailant look like the victim.

Sure enough, the woman received a sentence of seven years and would be available for parole in just over two-and-a-half. *Shit, why bother at all*, Luis fumed. When he encountered Dr. Allen in the hallway a few minutes later, he couldn't resist reproaching her.

"How do you sleep nights?" Luis growled. "Roberto Lopez may have been a piece of shit, but he was still a human being. We have laws for a reason, Ms. Allen. Everyone is entitled to due process even scum like Roberto."

"It's Dr. Allen, Mr. ...?"

"Vallejo, Supervisory Special Agent Luis Vallejo Séguin if we're going to trade titles here."

"I'd say it's a pleasure to meet you, but we both know it's not. I did my job, Supervisory Special Agent Vallejo Séguin. My, that's quite a mouthful. It tires me out to say it, so I'll settle for *goodbye*. Don't feel too bad; I'm sure you did your best. I simply held better cards."

She walked away, leaving behind a whiff of subtle perfume that made Luis more enraged than entranced. He was beginning to understand why men beat women.

• • • •

Barbara left the world of the courtroom behind, determined to focus on the last three weeks of classes before Christmas Break—*Winter Recess*, she corrected. *Best to follow conventions even in your thoughts.*

Although she enjoyed teaching, Barbara felt ready for a few weeks off. She'd attend a few parties, take in a gallery show or two, and sleep in late as many mornings as she could. In between, she'd work on her lectures for the spring semester.

Getting into the spirit of the season on December 23rd, Barbara chose a silky, emerald green dress that skimmed a figure not yet damaged by the wonderfully decadent holiday food and drink she so enjoyed. Lifting her heavy hair, she pondered—*up or down?*

Up, she decided, *but sexy casual.* Looping lengths around a small knot, she smiled her approval at the results. Then, she added a jeweled hairclip. *If I've done it right*, she teased herself, *it will look like that one pin holds everything in place. Bad Barbara.*

Chapter Two

The small gallery at the Spanish Village Art Center in Balboa Park felt overcrowded to Barbara, almost claustrophobic, but she persevered. Opportunities to see the collected work of Rodolfo Saenz came rarely, and he was a particular favorite.

Holding her glass of white wine high to protect it from the milling crowd, Barbara came face to face with someone she'd never imagined seeing at an art gallery—Special Agent Vallejo something. No, *Supervisory* Special Agent, she remembered with sudden annoyance.

"Well, well, Dr. Allen," Luis Vallejo almost purred, "I guess San Diego really is a small pond. I had no idea Latino artists were an interest of yours."

"Since you know almost nothing about me, I can't imagine why you're surprised. To be honest, I wouldn't have expected to find you at a gallery opening, either. Is the artist a cousin of yours or something? I know how large these Hispanic families can be."

Her own rudeness both surprised and annoyed Barbara. It was a trait she disliked in others and never allowed herself to practice—well, almost never.

Luis Vallejo's boom of laughter surprised her. "A hit," he teased. "How can a woman who looks as soft and approachable as you do tonight be such a porcupine? That's quite a dress, by the way."

Noticing how dense the crowd around them had grown, Agent Vallejo guided her into a small hallway. "There, that's better. No, Rodolfo isn't part of my family, just a friend and an artist I admire."

Embarrassed by her earlier behavior, Barbara relented. "A friend, really? You're very lucky. He's one of the city's most talented artists."

"He is, and if you can wait until the crowd thins a bit, I'll introduce you—but fair warning. Unlike me, Rodolfo enjoys flirting with beautiful women. Don't take a thing he says seriously."

"You prefer the celibate life, Supervisory Special Agent Vallejo?" Barbara gave the almost-too-handsome agent a thoughtful look. "Somehow, that surprises me."

Luis Vallejo's face reddened as he came close to choking on the wine he'd swallowed. "It's quite a leap from *I'm not a fan of flirting* to living a monkish existence," he rasped out. "How do you know I'm not married? Not everyone wears a ring," he informed her, his voice now cool, though Barbara noted the heat in his eyes with a certain satisfaction.

The small, rather superior smile she gave him irritated Luis. The woman might be a knockout, *God, her hair*, but she lacked manners, and he might have been married. She couldn't possibly know.

"No," she informed him, "there's no Mrs. Supervisory Special Agent, I'd bet my career on it."

"Please, that *Supervisory Agent* thing is getting old. It's Luis. And if you've no objection, I'll introduce you to Rodolfo as Barbara. No, I'm not married—now or ever. You aren't, either. Ever been?"

"No, I came close once, but our careers took different paths."

Once the crowd thinned, Luis introduced Barbara to Rodolfo Saenz. His friend didn't disappoint.

"Damn, Luis, I thought we were friends. How long have you kept this extraordinary woman from me? Don't think I didn't notice you secreting her away in that hallway. Two centuries ago, I'd have challenged you. I still might."

Luis grinned at the woman who'd torpedoed two of his cases. "I warned you." Putting his hand on Barbara's arm with a light but somehow possessive touch, he smiled at his friend. "Ms. Allen and I are merely professional colleagues of a sort, Rodolfo."

"You can't be an FBI agent!" the artist objected.

"A professor, actually. Luis and I have encountered each other several times in courtrooms." She leaned closer to the artist and whispered: "I don't think he likes me."

"My dear, I have been watching the two of you for a while and have a different perspective. I think Luis likes you more than he'd admit to even his closest friend, and that is both shocking and something to celebrate. Luis lives a monk's life. I complain of it often."

His choice of words made Barbara choke back laughter as Luis Vallejo's cheeks reddened again. The embarrassed agent decided it was time to bring their conversation to a close.

"I'm afraid I have another appointment," Luis informed them, "but I congratulate you, Rodolfo—a wonderful show. I'll leave Ms. Allen, Dr. Allen, in your capable hands. If you'll excuse me ..."

Rodolfo Saenz watched his friend hurry away, surprise written on his thin, expressive face. "Luis is not usually so abrupt. I think we made him uncomfortable. How well do you know my friend? He is admirable, is he not? Handsome, too, damn him."

Barbara took her time answering. What could she say that wouldn't be rude or an obvious lie? With his wavy brown hair, whiskey-colored eyes, and damn-near-perfect body, Luis Vallejo was *muy hombre* all right, just not the kind of man she admired.

"Yes, he's handsome, but I find him a bit spoiled. And my heart isn't likely to be stolen by an FBI agent. I prefer a different type of man."

"An artist like me, perhaps?" Rodolfo's dark eyes were mischievous. "Alas, I'm married."

They chatted about the opening and Rodolfo's work for a few moments and then drifted apart. Barbara left the gallery and drove aimlessly for a few minutes. Somehow, the holiday spirit she'd started the night with had vanished. She felt alone.

Surrendering to a strange restlessness, Barbara stopped at an upscale bar. She'd chosen one close enough she could walk home if she did something stupid like drink too much, not that she'd be that dumb.

She sat at a small table, ordered a martini, something she almost never drank, and looked around—big mistake. A tall, rather good-looking man in a navy suit locked eyes with her and left his group.

"May I join you?" he asked politely. "I think you might be the best Christmas present I've ever gotten."

He wasn't drunk, Barbara decided, but definitely on his way.

"I'm Wayne Jefferson and I'd love to know your name. Is it Angel, by any chance?"

Barbara couldn't help laughing. He was a little drunker than she'd realized. "Not even close, it's Barbara, but I'm really not looking for company. I just stopped by for a quick drink."

"My good luck. By the way, I don't live far from here in case you're interested."

Barbara sighed. This was why she hated going into a bar alone.

"I'm afraid I'm not. I enjoyed meeting you, Mr. Jefferson, and hope you have a pleasant evening, but it's time for me to go home—alone."

When she picked up her small purse to signal her departure, the man frowned in confusion, leading Barbara to suspect her lack of interest wasn't a frequent event in his life. *High-powered lawyer or someone in finance?* she wondered. He was almost certainly one or the other.

"You don't mean that." He put his hand on her shoulder, forcing her to stay seated. "You're not just beautiful, you're f-fascinating." He slurred the word. "I want to know more about you."

"The first thing you might want to know is that the lady is taken."

Barbara's eyes went wide as Luis Vallejo suddenly appeared at her table, his face and stance stern, even intimidating. How did he know she'd come here?

"I think that's for Angel to decide."

He's already forgotten my name, Barbara thought in amusement. She patted Wayne Jefferson's hand and smiled gently. "It was nice to meet you, Wayne, but my date is the jealous type; it might be best for you to rejoin your friends."

As the disappointed lawyer/financier walked back to his table, Barbara gave Luis a stern look of her own.

"Don't insult my intelligence by telling me you wandered into this particular bar by accident. Did you wait for me outside the gallery? I find this a little creepy, Agent Vallejo. Why are you following me?"

Without asking permission, Luis slid into the seat Wayne Jefferson vacated. "I'm an FBI agent, Dr. Allen; I'm merely concerned for your safety."

He took in her skeptical glare and gave her a sheepish smile. "Okay, I wanted to know where you live or maybe how you live. I wasn't stalking you, but the minute you got out of the car in the bar's parking lot, I knew my instincts were correct and that I'd made the right decision in following you. Have you any idea how dumb this was—going into a bar alone looking like you do?"

"I'm sure there's a compliment in there somewhere, but flattery doesn't interest me at the moment. Your behavior does. Have I exchanged one problem for another?"

Luis smiled again, this time a slow, rather lovely smile, Barbara thought, one that reached his gold-brown eyes and warmed them.

"I guess that depends on how you define *problem*. The short answer is *no*; I'm not interested in forcing myself on you. And while I find you attractive, you're not my type. So, perhaps I'm nothing more than curious."

Then, he gave her a frustrated look. "The long answer is more complicated. I've never done this before—follow someone without a professional reason. And I have no idea why I wanted to know where you live. I've already told you you're attractive, but so are lots of women. And I'm guessing an hour's conversation would reveal to both of us just how incompatible we are. So, we're back to curiosity. There's something about you that intrigues me."

"Well, since you're here, let's see just how incompatible we are. I think we should start with women's rights. That ought to prove enlightening. Why don't you order both of us a drink?"

It was closer to two hours than one before they parted, and both found their conversation stimulating and somewhat surprising. Barbara made it clear she saw Luis as a traditional Latino male, one deeply imbued with *machismo*. "You're a cop on top of that, which tells me almost everything I need to know about you."

Luis had made some judgments, as well. He saw her as a ball-busting woman, a deceptively pretty package but cold underneath. Dr. Allen was smart and knew it. She might swim in other ponds, but she'd pick an academic for serious romance. Characteristically, he shared almost none of his insight with her.

Their conversation veered from topic to topic—art, music, the state of the world. As the night wore on, they discovered surprising similarities and vast differences in their personalities and philosophies.

Barbara's biggest surprises were Luis's quick intelligence and a much broader education than she would have guessed. She found him impressive and, under the influence of a second martini, a compelling male, even *hot*, a word she despised.

Luis discovered something the sociology professor kept deeply hidden under a brisk, professional façade. Barbara Allen was Midwestern to her core, much more naïve and trusting than he would have guessed. The old-fashioned word *nice* described her best despite her tart tongue.

As he walked her to her car, Luis touched the glittery pin in her hair. "I'd love to pull that pretty, little bauble out and see your hair come tumbling down."

Barbara slid into the driver's seat and started the engine. Then, she gave him her intriguing, small smile. "That is a privilege that has to be earned, Agent Vallejo."

"Luis," he corrected.

"Are you going to follow me home?" she challenged.

"I am but don't take it personally. You've had two drinks, and San Diego can be a dangerous city."

On those words, he turned toward his own car and never looked back. Barbara tried to spot his dark-colored BMW following her on the way to 10th Avenue but saw nothing. He was either very good, or he hadn't bothered to follow her. She was betting on good.

Chapter Three

"**I** know I'm going to regret this ..." The voice on the other end of the phone was male, more baritone than tenor, but somehow hesitant. Barbara hazarded a guess.

"Just what is it you think you'll regret, Agent Vallejo?"

It had been five days since he'd followed her home—if he'd followed her home. She hadn't expected a call after that much time, especially one coming on a Sunday morning.

"If I'm still Agent Vallejo, I think there's no point in continuing our conversation." Barbara could hear the irritation in his voice.

"Luis," she couldn't entirely disguise her amusement, "I'm as intrigued and confused as you seem to be about what might or might not be between us, but I wasn't trying to insult you. You are an FBI agent. Since I'm pretty sure this isn't a business call, you must have something else in mind. Might I inquire what that something else is?"

"There's a place I know on India Street that serves great breakfast chimichangas. They're not for the faint of heart."

"El Indio," Barbara guessed. "It's a favorite of mine, as well. I think we'd better split the order. I remember how big they are."

Invitation offered and accepted, the two of them agreed Luis would come by for her in an hour. After she hung up, however, Barbara had a change of heart. Her reluctance wasn't about seeing Luis Vallejo; he'd been on her mind for days. But public meetings wouldn't get to the heart of things quickly enough. She wanted this attraction, or whatever it was, over.

Throwing together a quick breakfast casserole, Barbara put it in the oven then hurried to take off her sweats, choosing tan, fitted pants and a light-blue cashmere sweater. It took her just ten minutes to pull her hair into a long ponytail, which she wrapped in a loose knot, and swipe on mascara and lip gloss.

17

The doorbell rang right on time, and if Luis seemed surprised by the change of plans, there was pleasure in his eyes as well.

"You cook?"

"Occasionally, though I'm no Julia Childs. It's a little early for beer, but I've made a pitcher of mimosas if that isn't too sissy for you."

"Even a manly man drinks orange juice," he teased her. "Why the change in plans?"

Barbara shrugged a shoulder. "I can't understand this attraction—for lack of another word," she added when his golden eyes warmed. "I'm thinking we need some *alone time*. You should know that I'm not a promiscuous person, Luis. Even though I might be wrong, I don't think you are, either, but we're hurtling toward a physical relationship unless one of us develops a little common sense."

Barbara suddenly moved toward Luis, confronting him, her nose mere inches from his. "I dreaded the idea you might call at the same time I stayed close to the phone, which makes no sense. And I'm pretty sure it's a call you didn't want to make. I heard the reluctance in your voice."

"Don't you think this is a serious and somewhat premature conversation for a Sunday breakfast? If whatever is between us is physical, just that and nothing more, we'll figure it out, probably by having sex. If it's something different, something stronger, we'll figure this out, too. So, what's bothering you?"

"You, you're what's bothering me. What do you want, Luis?"

"Well, breakfast for starters. I think whatever's in your oven might be done. It smells delicious."

While Luis poured them second glasses of mimosa, Barbara took the potato, egg, and ham dish from the oven and got the mixed fruit she'd prepared out of the refrigerator.

After one bite into the fruit combo, he grinned. "Tequila, lime, and honey dressing—just like my mom's. You're definitely looking for the way to my heart as well as my body."

There was that ego again. It was one of the things worrying her. "We're oil and water, Luis."

Luis shook his head, his brown eyes merry with challenge. "I'm thinking more like tequila and lime—two things that might not seem to go together but do. I get why you're uncomfortable about us, though we don't know enough about each other to be an *us*, yet. Can't we simply take our time and see what unfolds? Our drunk friend was right the other night, by the way. You are a fascinating woman."

"Luis, I'm everything you disapprove of in a female—overeducated, though there is no such thing, financially independent, and sure to be on the other side of almost any social issue you can name."

"All true, I guess, but so what? I could name a dozen attributes of yours I do admire, not all of them physical. I'm not looking for a clone, Barbara, something who thinks and behaves like me. Are you? Is that the problem between us you see as insurmountable?"

She stared at him, startled into momentary silence. "I don't know; I never thought about it this way. Oh, my God, I must be a terribly shallow person."

Luis laughed—a throw-your-head-back, hearty laugh that surprised Barbara even as it caused warm tremors somewhere south of her stomach. "No, you're not." He surprised her by touching her cheek gently. "I think you're quite special."

He pulled her to her feet. "Let's change the pace a little. I want a kiss, Barbara Allen, just a nice, friendly kiss, and then I'll leave you to your thoughts and the dishes. I'm not up to that much domesticity quite yet."

He leaned into her space, watching for her reaction and liking what Barbara's face revealed. Their kiss moved beyond friendly in nanoseconds. Luis opened his mouth part way, intrigued when she touched his tongue with hers and then pulled back. *Barbara Allen,* Luis decided, *has commitment issues.*

She'd wondered how his kiss would taste and feel for weeks. It first crossed her mind when he'd confronted her outside the courtroom. He had such nice lips, well-shaped and firm.

As their kiss deepened, Luis didn't think at all; he simply enjoyed the sensation and her response. *Maybe not so cold* was his first coherent thought as he closed her door behind him.

• • • •

Luis's call late on a Saturday afternoon surprised and then annoyed Barbara. "I'm sure you've already made plans ..."

Didn't the man have any manners? Did he think she'd sit around all week waiting for his call? Or was he even more arrogant than that? Did he dare to assume she'd change her plans to suit him?

"I don't, actually, other than to catch up on some paperwork. It's been a busy week, and I'm tired."

She wouldn't lie, but she had no intention of seeing him, either.

"Great, I'll be over at 6:30 with a six-pack and a pizza. Let me guess—black olives and mushrooms. I'd better make that two pizzas. I give great foot massages, by the way; you'll feel like a new woman."

He hung up so quickly Barbara had no chance to argue. He'd done that on purpose. *Well, he'll have to take me as I am,* she grumbled. *I'm not changing out of my jeans for Mr. FBI.*

She did pull off her sweatshirt, however, exchanging it first for a loose-fitting, flowered top. Then, she thought about how quick he'd be to get his hands under that top. A stretchy red V-neck she could tuck in seemed a safer choice even if it did accentuate what she saw as a too-abundant chest.

He rang the doorbell at 6:30, dropped a friendly kiss on her lips, and headed for the kitchen. Thinking Luis was far too comfortable in her house and with her, Barbara didn't follow him. He was back in less than a minute with two bottles and a glass. How had he found her opener and a glass so quickly?

"I take you for the classy type," he teased as he poured her beer into a glass. When she didn't take it immediately, he set it on her coffee table. "Wow, I love your sweater—or, rather, I love seeing you in it. You've got great legs, too—long and lean. A very nice package, Dr. Allen."

"Am I supposed to feel flattered and fall into your arms?" she challenged him.

"No, that comes later, after the foot massage I promised you. For now, I think we should eat while the pizza's hot. I'll get plates while you put on some music."

Her choice surprised him—an older Spanish singer/songwriter, Luis Eduardo Aute. At his raised eyebrow, she couldn't help laughing.

"I'm not culturally illiterate, Luis, and I thought you'd find the choice appropriate. The man has the most seductive voice and lyrics I've ever heard."

"Entirely appropriate," he agreed. "Which of us is to do the seducing?"

"I think we should postpone that discussion until after we eat."

Luis gave her a long, lingering look. "I think we should put the pizza in the oven on low. Anything else would be a waste of that man's talent."

Without even asking, he whisked the pizza out from under her nose and headed for the kitchen. As soon as he returned, he sat on her sofa, patting the place next to him.

"Sit sideways and prop your feet against my leg. The massage will probably make you sleepy. I won't mind. I'm not going anywhere."

He meant it; he intended to massage her feet even before they ate. *Thank God, I washed them.*

It was relaxing, Barbara had to admit. Luis didn't say a word, just began giving her feet gentle little touches that increased in intensity as he moved up and kneaded her calves. The man and the music had an almost hypnotic effect on her, and she felt herself letting go. This felt as close to heaven as life got.

The next thing she knew, it was 9:40, and Luis was munching pizza as he sat on the chair across from the sofa she'd been sleeping on.

"Why didn't you wake me up?"

He shrugged a careless shoulder. "You warned me you were tired before I invited myself over. I enjoyed watching you, by the way. You're a sound sleeper, and you don't snore or drool. I consider those good things to know. Are ready for some pizza?"

"I don't usually eat this late at night."

"Make an exception; I don't want your stomach growling when we share our next kiss. I'd just as soon you focus on a different kind of hunger."

"Are you so sure there will be a next kiss?"

He didn't answer her, contenting himself with a smug smile. "I'll go get your pizza. It's a little dried out but edible."

He did kiss her again, though Luis surprised her by making it a *goodnight* one. This time, he pulled her against him so closely she could feel what turned out to be an incredibly fit body from breastbone to thigh—and then, as the kiss deepened, something else.

Luis didn't move away; nor did he pull her closer to his obvious arousal. Instead, he slid his hands into her hair, which she'd piled loosely on top of her head, and pulled out one of her oversized pins.

"Just one tonight, *Bebe*, and I intend to keep it."

"Baby?" Barbara's eyes narrowed. "I'm no one's baby, Luis Vallejo."

"I was speaking in Spanish; I sometimes do that, you know."

"It means the same thing."

"It's for your name—Barbara Baines, two B's."

"That's not what everyone would think."

"No one's ever going to hear it. We'll keep that endearment private—just between us when we make love."

"If we make love, you mean."

His breath came out in an amused puff. "I mean *when*. But I'm in no hurry. Seduction is a slow dance." He kissed her again, more in affection than desire, she noted in annoyance. "I'll call you."

He didn't, which both hurt and surprised her as day followed day with no communication. They hadn't known each other very long, and she'd expected things to end badly further down the road. But this sudden abandonment of an intriguing relationship felt abrupt and bewildering.

It's for the best, she assured herself. *Luis Vallejo Séguin is someone who'd never fit into my life.* Still, she'd been a little out of sorts on Valentine's Day and the two weeks after. Then, she made up her mind to forget him, reluctantly accepting a date with a new professor in the political science department.

When Barbara arrived home late in the afternoon of her scheduled and already dreaded date, she found a single rose on her doorstep. *How,* she wondered, *did Peter Evans find out where I live since we agreed to meet on campus?* The idea he'd gone looking for her address made her a little uncomfortable, Still, it was a nice gesture, quite promising.

Standing there, idly twirling the rose, Barbara felt rather than heard Luis behind her. She knew it was him before she even turned around. He created a unique kind of electricity in the air.

"Am I forgiven?"

She saw only his eyes at first. There was tenderness there, as well as regret. Then, she took in the black sling cradling his left arm.

"Someone shot you?" Somehow, she knew Luis didn't fall or get a normal injury.

"It isn't serious, a simple through-and-through. I got careless."

"I thought federal agents were investigators, not street cops."

"They are, unless they're undercover, which is how this happened and why I fell off your radar. I can't say much, and I don't like to talk about my work, but I'm assigned to gang activity in San Diego, Barbara. Nowadays, it's mostly drugs and prostitution. Since there's big money involved, it can get a little hairy."

He touched the rose she held in her hand. "I'm sorry I couldn't be there for Valentine's Day. Do you suppose we could discuss this inside?"

"I have a date, Luis. I'm supposed to meet him in less than an hour."

"Then, I guess I'd better let you get ready."

He turned and walked away. She'd disappointed him, Barbara realized. *I sat at home sulking while Luis was recovering from a bullet wound. Maybe it's just as well things happened this way. I don't think I could live with the anxiety of life with an FBI agent.*

There'd be no more waiting for his calls, she knew, because they'd never come. He'd move on and so would she. In fact, she was moving on right now—to Dr. Peter Evans.

Chapter Four

Barbara glanced at the man sitting next to her and repressed a sigh. The newest hire in the political science department of the University of San Diego was amusing, moderately good looking—though not in Luis's league, and as bored as she was.

Both knew the lecture they attended together would be their first and last date though they might someday be friends. Despite the many things they had in common, there were no tingles on either side.

As the weeks after her date with Peter Evans passed, Barbara thought about Luis Vallejo more than she wanted to and increasingly regretted the abrupt end to their relationship. She'd hurt him, and that knowledge added guilt to her frustration and an odd loneliness. *It'll pass*, she assured herself, *and it's best this way. Sex would never have been enough for me, and that seems to be all we have in common.*

When nearly two months went by and she couldn't stop thinking about the hurt expression in Luis's eyes, Barbara shocked herself by calling the main FBI office and asking for Supervisory Special Agent Luis Vallejo. She took pride in her research skills but hadn't been able to find a cellphone number or private address for Luis.

The receptionist transferred the call to Luis's cell phone, and he answered with a curt "Vallejo here."

"I'm sorry to call you at work, but you're a hard man to reach. I hope I'm not catching you in the middle of something—like a gang war. At least I don't hear any shooting."

Although he'd been sitting at his desk, Luis stood up and walked to the window when he realized who was calling. The surprise on his face alerted the other man in his small office.

When Luis jerked his head, indicating he'd like his partner to put some distance between them, Senior Special Agent Philip Reed simply grinned and stood his ground. This call was obviously personal; Luis never got calls like that.

Turning his back and keeping his voice low, Luis went straight to the heart of it. "If this isn't a business call, it should end right now, Barbara."

"It isn't, and it will. I've got your cellphone number now. I'll call tonight at ten. If that's a problem, you can call me earlier. We need to talk, Luis."

• • • •

"Barbara? There's a Barbara in your life? You've been holding out on your partner, Luis." Reed's voice was full of amusement. "Does this explain why you've been such a bastard for the last couple of months? Which of you got dumped?"

"Neither, not that it's any of your business. I just found myself in a relationship that was never going to work out."

"Yet she called and you salivated. It doesn't seem over to me. Is she hot?"

"She's a sociology professor. Does that sound *hot* to you? And even if she is, we live in different worlds. I have no idea why she called and wish to hell she hadn't. And this is quite enough conversation about Barbara Allen. We have a court appointment to get ready for, remember?"

The incident leading to the bullet hole in Luis's arm had finally come up for a hearing. The guy would do time, but he was small potatoes. Jaime Moreno would leave Mendota or one of California's state prisons with full status as a Sureño gang member and an opportunity to wreak more havoc before being blown away on some street corner. *Sometimes*, Luis grumbled, *my work seems pointless.*

• • • •

The knock on Luis's door a little before ten startled him, and he picked his gun up off the coffee table. Peering through the peephole, he saw Barbara staring at the door and licking her lips. A nervous gesture from Ms. Gorgeous Hair? Opening the door slightly, he challenged her.

"How did you get my address?"

"One piece of evidence always leads to another." She gave him a small smile Luis already thought of as distinctly hers, informing him in a smug voice, "You aren't the only one with good detecting skills." She walked past him without an invitation and looked around his small, barebones apartment. "It looks like you."

"What are doing here, Barbara? What do you want?"

"To apologize, mostly. I know I hurt your feelings when I accepted Dr. Evan's invitation to attend a lecture." She paused, biting her lip. "You hadn't called, and I thought you'd changed your mind about seeing me. I'm sorry."

"No apology needed." Luis gave her a cool look. "We don't know each other well enough for hurt feelings, Barbara. You were, and are, perfectly free to build any kind of social life you want. And I assume the guy you saw that night fits into your life better than I do."

"*Easier* is a more accurate descriptor. For some reason, *better* seems to belong to you."

"You shouldn't have come here."

"I know. Do you want me to leave?"

"No."

They stood there, staring at each other until Barbara looked away and sighed. Then, she touched his cheek as gently as he'd once touched hers.

"I'm afraid, Luis. You're outside anything I've experienced or ever expected to experience."

"I'm a pretty ordinary man, Barbara, but, if you find any comfort in it, you knock me off balance, too. I wouldn't call it fear exactly, more like gut-shot."

Her burst of laughter surprised both of them. "Gut-shot? Luis, what are we doing—acting like teenagers instead of completely adult professionals with an inexplicable but intense attraction to each other? Why don't I spend the night so we can put this behind us?"

He'd been hoping for just that since she'd appeared at his door—all warmth and temptation. Then, perversely, he changed his mind. She thought it was physical, this pull between them; he already knew it was something else.

"No, I want something different for our first time. Note this, Dr. Allen—first time, which implies there will be a second time and more after that. I won't kiss you tonight; it's too risky this close to my bedroom. But I will walk you to your car. What is today? Tuesday? Okay, I'll call you Thursday night. Keep Friday and Saturday nights open, maybe Sunday morning, too."

Their weekend never happened. Luis got word from his partner on Wednesday morning that they were on their way to San Bernardino. Gang violence had escalated over the last two weeks, and they'd been tasked with helping the local police find the problem and fix it. He made a reluctant call to Barbara.

"I have to go out of town, and I've no idea how long I'll be gone. This doesn't happen often, Barbara, but it is part of my job. You have no idea how sorry I am."

"Is it dangerous?"

"No, more like a business negotiation. I'll call you when I'm back. It might be a while. Don't give up on me."

• • • •

Luis was content to let his partner drive back to San Diego. It had been a long, tiring three weeks. One of L.A.'s gangs, North

Hollywood, had attempted to move in on a rival gang's drug business in San Bernardino, earning the ire of the Mexican Mafia. It took time and patience to learn what was happening.

Eventually, the two sides worked it out without an all-out war or overt FBI intervention, but Luis suspected things to flare up again before long. The amount of money involved staggered the imagination.

Agreeing to meet first thing the next morning to finish their reports, the partners went their separate ways—Phil home to his wife, Allison, and their twin boys and Luis to an empty apartment. *It's too late to call Barbara,* Luis decided, and he was bone tired. *I'll call her late tomorrow afternoon,* he decided before sleep claimed him. *Maybe we can meet for dinner or drinks.*

Barbara was apologetic when he called. "Oh, Luis, I'm so sorry, but I teach a night class on Thursdays, and I'm usually pretty wiped out afterward. What about this weekend?"

"Weekends are good; I'll make a dinner reservation for Friday. Do you trust me?"

Luis couldn't see the amusement that lit her green-gold eyes as she held her cellphone, but he sensed it in her voice. "Not one damn bit—but I'm flexible where food is concerned. Casual or dressy?"

"You pick, but keep your hairstyle simple. I have plans."

"Casual then. See you on Friday unless your partner calls."

"He'd better not," Luis growled.

• • • •

Barbara glanced in the mirror when the doorbell to her little house sounded at 7:30. She'd chosen copper-colored slacks, very fitted, and a matching scoop-necked sweater. Her hair was piled casually on her head, a few copper pins holding it in place.

"Wow!" was his greeting, and he pulled her close for a warm kiss.

"Wow yourself," she said as their lips parted a short distance. "You do casual very well—much better than your usual FBI black."

He wore dark jeans, nicely fitted ones, and paired them with a Henley sweater matching his light-brown eyes. Barbara suspected that wherever they went for dinner, the eyes of every female in the place would follow him. Luis Vallejo Séguin was intriguingly, dangerously male.

"We have reservations at a new restaurant named, of all things, Cattle Call. Their steaks are fabulous, and I've been told their seafood's good, as well. I suspect you're more the Shrimp Scampi type."

True, she thought, but he didn't need to know that. Barbara had no intention of behaving predictably around Luis Vallejo. The man was a short-term itch she intended to relieve in the next few hours.

Halfway through a filet rare enough to nauseate her, she gave up pretending. His eyes amused, Luis called the waiter over and ordered a crab salad, light on the dressing, for her.

"We might not agree on the subject of meat," he told her, forking the remains of her filet onto his plate, "but I'm confident we'll be very compatible when it comes to dessert."

"Chocolate Suicide Cake?" she suggested.

Luis shook his head slowly. "Sex, Barbara Baines Allen, lots of sex, though I have no objection to some cake first."

She made coffee when he brought her home, but both cups sat untouched. He fingered one of her copper pins, a question in his eyes. "May I?"

She nodded, not surprised when he didn't stop at one. He groaned as he fisted a handful then buried his face in the tawny mass.

"You do have a thing for hair," Barbara teased him.

"Just yours," he admitted, "just you."

Barbara thought she was prepared for his kiss. They'd done this before, after all. From the first sizzling second, however, she knew he'd been holding back.

She didn't even remember getting to her bedroom, but a moment of clarity came as he pulled her sweater over her head. Again, he gave her a questioning look. "You're sure?"

"No, but it's what I want, even need. You still frighten me, Luis. I'm not used to feeling so out of control."

"Tonight, *Bebe*, let me help you let go."

She should have objected to his endearment, if that's what it was, but she chose to relieve him of his sweater instead. Luis unhooked her bra and touched a breast lightly. "Everything about you is perfect."

He kissed her then, a slow, gentle kiss that promised more. "Make love with me, Barbara; I want to make you happy and convince you how unimportant control is when it's right between two people."

Using nothing more than his hands, wonderfully gifted and gentle hands, he took her over the edge, holding her tenderly as she climaxed. Then, he took her there again, this time inside her.

The descent from something close to heaven was abrupt when Luis swore softly. "Damn, no condom. I've never forgotten before. Now would be a good time to tell me you're on the pill."

His eyes were worried. Hers were not though she hadn't thought about protection, either. "You're safe, Luis."

"It isn't me I'm worried about. I'm sorry, Barbara. No man should be so irresponsible. I don't think I've ever wanted someone so much I lost track of something that important. We'll remember next time—say in the next half-hour or so, once I recover."

She laughed and kissed him again, running her hand over his chest. Barbara found it a very nice chest—broad, lightly fuzzed, with small, dark nipples already erect from her exploration.

"Barbara, in the name of full disclosure, I have to say I don't have a whole lot of self-control around you. Maybe I was hasty in asking you to trust me."

She let her hand slide lower, wrapping it around his growing member. "Oddly enough, I do trust you, Luis. And I'm a good judge of character. I also don't think it's going to be another thirty minutes before we need that condom."

They made love several more times, slept a little, and made a decision to shower together as dawn brought a rosy glow to Barbara's east-facing bedroom. Luis had promised his partner he'd meet him at eight.

"I don't want to leave you," he admitted. "The more we do this, the more I'm going to want you. I'd say it's been too long a hiatus for me, but that's not what's happening here."

"I make a very good casserole, a meat-eater's delight. Come back around 6:30—and plan on spending the night. I'm curious to see if you can top last night."

"A challenge," he grinned, "I intend to rise to the occasion, Barbara Allen." He laughed as he realized what he'd said. "You know what I mean."

"I think it works on both levels."

Luis grinned again. "Damn straight." I'll see you tonight, then." He gave her a smug look. "You might want to take a nap this afternoon."

Chapter Five

"You'll never know how sorry I am," a voice murmured softly in Barbara's ear. Although her heart took an uncomfortable bounce as she held her cell phone, Barbara said calmly, "I take it you won't be coming tonight."

"No, I'm in Los Angeles and have no idea what time I'll be able to return to San Diego. I truly am sorry, Barbara."

"Me, too," Barbara admitted.

"Think positive thoughts," Luis encouraged her. "If I get back early enough, I'll come knocking."

Just after dawn on Sunday morning, she heard him at her door. *What kind of idiot thinks I'd want his company this time of day when my hair's a mess, and I haven't even brushed my teeth?* she grumbled.

Luis, however, came bearing gifts—warm breakfast empanadas and hot coffee. He laughed, actually had the audacity to laugh, at her appearance in the tattered robe she'd thrown on as he kissed her tousled hair. "You have no idea how good you look to me right now. It must be love."

Although his words were casual, his eyes showed his seriousness. Then, giving her a wink, he told her: "We'd better eat while the food's still hot."

As soon as they'd eaten, Luis gave her sofa a longing glance. "I'll take a quick nap while you satisfy that feminine urge I sense to spiff yourself up. Then, I'm going to need a shower. I have my standards, too, and I'm not making love to a beautiful lady in yesterday's stink."

As his eyes closed and he curled himself more comfortably on her sofa, Barbara surprised herself by taking off her robe and covering Luis. He'd been up all night; she was sure of it—just as she had good reason to know he hadn't gotten that much sleep the night before.

Luis woke with a start before noon. Watching him from her favorite chair, Barbara suspected he didn't know where he was at first, but he got his bearings within seconds, giving her a rather cocky grin. "I'll grab that shower now. If you want me at my best, you might want to make a pot of coffee."

After a quick shower, Luis came out wearing nothing more than one of her favorite bath towels around his waist. Heading straight for the kitchen, the FBI agent downed two cups of coffee and then patted his knee. As she sat on his lap, her eyes wary, Barbara realized she hadn't done something like this since—come to think of it, she'd never sat in a man's lap. It felt oddly intimate.

Leaning back against his bare chest, she moaned when he kissed her neck. The sound of her murmuring made him smile.

"Barbara, if you still think this is about sex, you need to reconsider. Sex with you is wonderful, but it's not the big story going on between us. You told me a few days ago I frightened you. Well, that cuts both ways. I'm thirty-two years old, and this is the first time a woman has mattered to me—really mattered."

They spent most of Sunday afternoon in bed. Luis's expertise, she'd already learned, exceeded her. Although Luis was a confident, generous lover, she did notice something that amused her. He didn't want her on top when their lovemaking heated up. Somehow, they always wound up with him covering her.

His preference didn't surprise her; Barbara thought it said everything about Luis's strongly male approach to life and his rather dominant personality. Look how he'd already taken over her home.

If I had a dog, she found herself grumbling, *he'd be following Luis's commands by now, not mine.* Unlike her fictional dog, Barbara knew there were quarrels ahead. She had no intention of letting Luis run her life or their relationship. She'd worked too hard at building an independent life to turn traditional now.

As if he sensed her thoughts, Luis whispered in her ear: "We make an unlikely couple, but we are a couple, just the same. If you take it down to basics, Barbara, I doubt we're all that different. I'd like a loving relationship, children, time to enjoy a home and family, and a strong sexual connection. How is this different from what you want?"

"The devil's in the details, Luis. While I would like children and a good marriage, I can't see myself content with a life built solely around my family. I'm certain your family is traditional; mine was, as well. I made a decision as a very young woman to live a bigger life."

"Your work, you mean. I get that."

"It's more than having a career. You like to lead, Luis, make all the decisions—big and little. In fact, I'd call you a natural leader, and I admire your gifts in this area. But I'm not a follower. I've never thought of myself as a domineering person, but I'm fiercely independent."

"I'd never have guessed," he teased her, his eyes warm and amused. "Let's table this discussion until we've had a little more time together."

• • • •

Barbara had committed herself months earlier to presenting the keynote address at the annual meeting of a consortium of southern California's law enforcement agencies. The topic was dear to her heart: the intersect between Native American concepts of justice and U.S. law.

The conference room where Barbara made her speech was packed with curious, if sometimes skeptical, officers, and she did her best to answer the questions directed to her. Then, she returned to her room for a few minutes of peace and quiet. She always got butterflies after public speaking, never before.

Just as she put her keycard in the hotel-room door, she sensed the presence of someone behind her. Her heart skipped a beat before warm, familiar lips pressed against her neck. "You wowed them,

Bebe; I'm impressed. The men and women in that group are a hard sell."

"Luis, what are you doing here?"

My office sent me here. My SAC, Bill Kellerman, wants me and Phil *sensitized* to the Indian community." Luis's use of the word *Indian* was his swipe at political correctness.

"You knew you were coming and you didn't tell me?" she challenged him.

"I didn't want you to be nervous. I would have been if the situation had been reversed," he reassured her. "You were great. Even Phil said so—when he wasn't sleeping. As long as I'm here ..."

They parted reluctantly almost two hours later after following up on some good sex with a quick bite in the hotel's small café. Luis needed to go back to work, and Barbara had agreed to a 9:00 meeting with the Los Angeles police chief.

To kill some time, she wandered into the hotel's lounge and ordered a glass of Pinot Gris. Nodding her thanks to the bartender, she spotted a man approaching her in the bar's mirrored backsplash. Barbara recognized him; he'd asked her several insightful questions after her keynote address, and she suspected he wanted to continue their conversation.

Requesting permission with his eyes, he took the stool next to her. "We didn't get around to introductions earlier. I'm Davis Reynolds with the Department of Justice here in Los Angeles. Do you have time for a few more questions?"

They talked about Native American frustrations with the hybrid system of law imposed on them for a few minutes, but Barbara sensed he had something else on his mind. His interest seemed personal.

Davis Reynolds was a handsome man, early forties, perhaps. He had blond, curly hair and mesmerizing hazel eyes—*bedroom eyes*, her mother would have said. He appeared slightly taller than Luis—so, somewhere over six feet. He was also broader through the chest and elegantly dressed.

Their conversation was interrupted by a man, obviously a colleague, who stood in the doorway with several others. "Davis, are you ready for the meeting?"

Her companion nodded as he handed her his business card and leaned closer. "I don't know the name of the man who put that satisfied look in eyes a little earlier, Barbara Allen, but if it isn't a serious relationship, I promise you I'm better. I'd really love to hear from you."

He joined his friends, and Barbara dropped his card in her purse, thinking it might not be a good idea to leave a law enforcement specialist's card in such a public place. Then, she forgot all about him.

• • • •

Even though she understood Luis was a private man, one who rarely talked about his work or family, Barbara's frustration with their relationship grew as the weeks passed. She couldn't help resenting the way he kept her on the edge of his life. Even worse, she sensed their relationship was not moving forward or growing into a greater kind of intimacy. She needed that every bit as much as she craved their physical connection.

One night, her frustration bubbled over, and she asked him a question he couldn't or wouldn't answer.

"Luis, you know I'm estranged from my family and that they live far away. You, on the other hand, tell me you're emotionally close to your family and that most of them live nearby. Why haven't I met any of them?"

The silence between them grew, and Barbara sensed he'd given her an answer without saying a word. "You will when the time is right," he told her in aa clipped voice. "I don't like feeling pressured, Barbara. Let this go for now."

Well, she had her answer, one she'd anticipated from the beginning of their relationship. He intended to keep her right where she was—on the fringe of his life. She didn't matter to him, not really. This meant Barbara needed to share with Luis something she'd been considering for almost a month.

"I've decided to use this summer to complete an article I started almost a year ago. It deals with an infamous case of family annihilation in upstate New York. This means I'll be gone all of June, July, and most of August."

"I see." Luis's tone was cool. Barbara intended to punish him for their recent polite dispute; he sensed that instinctively and didn't much like it. "An important career move, I take it."

"This is what I do, Luis. You, of all people, should understand the demands of work."

Luis stared at her, his light brown eyes somehow turning darker with his resentment. "Believe me, I understand you perfectly. I guess there's nothing more to discuss. I'll miss you, Barbara."

It was a dismissal and not the way she thought their relationship would end. But she couldn't endure the way Luis compartmentalized his world. She occupied one box; his work was in another. His family, too, had a place of its own, separate from her.

I can't live this way, she decided, *and I won't*. She repeated that mantra over and over after Luis left and in the long nights that followed his abrupt departure.

• • • •

To distract herself from thinking about Luis, Barbara focused her energy on finishing out her semester and preparing for her trip to upstate New York. The early twentieth-century tragedy, though well-known, had confused scholars for years.

In the fall of 1928, Hiram Smith admitted freely he'd murdered his entire family and a handyman who tried to protect them, though he'd tried to destroy the evidence of his crime by setting his house on fire. What he wouldn't share with anyone was why. Two aspects of the old case interested her.

The first was Mr. Smith's steadfast refusal to explain why he'd done something so heinous when there'd been no indication of trouble in the family. She also wanted to know why he hadn't attempted suicide after murdering his family. More than eighty percent of male familicide perpetrators did.

The facts of the case were fairly well-known. Smith had been a well-respected and popular farmer and businessman in Lake Saranac, New York. One afternoon, he'd picked up an axe and gone inside his comfortable home to kill his wife.

When Scipio Fiske, a local handyman who worked part-time for Hiram, tried to stop him, Hiram murdered him, too. Then, he'd gone upstairs and killed his two daughters and an infant son with a kitchen knife.

Although he admitted the murders without any prompting, regretting only the death of his young son, Hiram offered no explanation. He just sat in his cell, humming to himself. When the court appointed an attorney, Smith refused to meet with him.

Despite all of her considerable skills and nearly three months of intense work, Barbara reached the end of her time in New York without being able to answer either question. All she could do is speculate, and what good did that do?

When Barbara returned to San Diego, arriving on August 21st, her first thoughts concerned Luis. They hadn't spoken, emailed, or sent texts in all those months, and she wondered briefly if he'd remember her return date and call. She'd already decided she wouldn't, no matter how tempted she found herself. What would be the point?

When Luis let weeks go by without calling or any other kind of contact, Barbara assured herself she felt more relief than hurt. Then, on Halloween, she found a card in her mailbox.

Now, I know witches are real was all it said, and although there was no signature, she knew who'd sent it. What surprised her was the pain she felt.

Chapter Six

As the winter recess approached and her classes wound down, Barbara had a disturbing dream about Hiram Smith. In her dream, he held a book, a Bible, and there was a small, secret smile on his face.

Barbara went through her notes on Smith's personal effects but couldn't find a reference to any type of book. Intrigued, she called the sheriff of Essex County. They'd become friends of a sort during the previous summer when she'd spent weeks going through his files of the 1928 case.

"Maybe one of the deputies back then lent him one of ours. We had, still have, a small bookcase for prisoners who want something to read."

"Could I go through them?"

"Sure, why not?" Lee Sanders hesitated a moment. "I could go through them for you to save you the trip. It's a bit nippy up here right now, and things are a little slow, so I've plenty of time on my hands."

Barbara repressed a small sigh. "Thank you, Lee, but a trip out of town sounds good right now. The holidays can be a depressing time for me, and I've no idea what I'm looking for. I'll see you in two weeks. You still owe me a dinner if I remember right."

It took less than two days to uncover the answer to both of her questions. The evidence had been there all along, but, ironically, no one thought to look in the right place.

The bookcase held three Bibles, two of them well-thumbed and relatively new. The third one, older and smaller, showed less signs of wear. She suspected it was a fundamentalist version, edited in ways she'd never detect or understand since she wasn't that familiar with the Bible.

The smaller book contained underlinings and penciled comments in tiny, hard-to-read handwriting. Sheriff Sanders thought the writing matched Smith's though an expert would have to determine that. There was also a long commentary on faithlessness and what the faithful owed their God, written on the only blank page at the back of the Bible.

Sitting in the county jail while awaiting trial, Hiram Smith had jotted down his initial jubilation when his wife, Elizabeth, left her Catholic faith and joined her husband's church. As they grew older, their children made a commitment of faith, as well.

His scribbled notes made it clear that, years later, she decided to return to her earlier faith, taking her children with her. In Hiram Smith's world, such an act of disloyalty to both man and God couldn't go unpunished.

Barbara knew now why he'd been so serene sitting in his jail cell and why he felt no remorse. He'd done his faith's bidding and secured his place in heaven. Since the people around him didn't matter in the grander scheme of things, he owed them no explanation.

The puzzle now unraveled, Barbara headed back to San Diego on December 22nd with a strong sense of satisfaction. She'd solved this longstanding mystery and found the evidence she needed to make her article useful to her peers.

The closer she got to home, however, the more depressed she became. Christmas was just days away, and Barbara would face it alone. It was the first time she'd experienced simple solitude as loneliness.

Although Barbara hadn't heard from Luis, never expected to, he haunted her thoughts and dreams as much as Hiram had. Even though she'd always expected their relationship to end badly, she missed Luis—physically and in other, subtler ways.

Promising herself she'd move on after the New Year, make a brand-new start, Barbara kept pushing back the date she'd officially declare Luis Vallejo part of her past. Then, she'd do her best to lock those memories away where they couldn't hurt her.

Valentine's Day was one marker; then, as it passed, she decided Spring Break would be the perfect time. She'd switch out purses and shoes, update her wardrobe and makeup, and make a conscious effort to find someone special. Focusing on the future would help her heal.

As she cleaned out the small, leather purse she'd used most of the previous fall, Barbara came across the card the Department of Justice lawyer had given her the night she made that keynote address. Looking at it made her laugh.

What balls, she thought, *men and their egos. "I'm better," indeed.* Still, Davis Reynolds had been genuinely interested in her presentation, and, unlike Luis, she'd found him sympathetic to the Native American community. Just as important, she'd liked the humor in his kind, hazel eyes. Maybe she should consider calling him.

No, she couldn't. It had been months, and he'd surely forgotten all about her. Besides, she'd never consider following up on such an inappropriate offer or request.

Barbara reminded herself she'd never behaved that way because it went against everything she believed. Dropping the card onto her dresser, she made a decision to ignore Davis Reynolds's invitation.

When the card was still there three weeks later after she'd picked it up at least a dozen times and given the Department of Justice lawyer more consideration than she believed he deserved, Barbara decided to give in to her impulse. What could it hurt? If he was in a relationship, uninterested, or didn't remember her, he'd tell her so.

• • • •

"Davis Reynolds here." His calm voice, as self-assured as she remembered, reinforced Barbara's fears she was making a mistake. When the line remained silent, he added: "How may I help you?"

Now, he sounded kind and supportive, as if he sensed the person on the other end of the line needed encouragement. Even if he was nothing more than a flirt, maybe even a married flirt, Davis Reynolds deserved better than a rude hang-up.

"It's Barbara Allen; I'm sorry it's taken so long for me to call. You probably don't even remember me."

"You make quite an impression, Dr. Allen. No, I haven't forgotten you. Is this a professional or personal call?"

"Personal, I guess."

"Then, I'm going to give you my private cell number, which is 213.334.1256, and make a request since I'm just about to go into a brief meeting. Will you call me back in an hour? Please do; I'd very much like to talk to you."

"I will." Barbara ended the call and gulped. *What now?* she wondered.

When she reached him exactly one hour later, Davis had left his office and was sitting at an outdoor café, a double expresso at his elbow. He felt nervous. *I'm never nervous,* he fretted, but it never occurred to him that Barbara Allen would call, especially after this much time.

He flushed every time he remembered what he'd whispered in her ear. *I'm better,* he muttered. *Jesus Christ, she's not the kind of woman you say something like that to. What possessed me to behave so stupidly?*

He answered her call on the first ring. "It's good to hear from you, Barbara. I wasn't kidding when I said you made an impression on me, one both personal and professional. I'm glad you called. Would you be open to our seeing each other? The logistics are a bit of a challenge since we live in different cities, but I get to San Diego frequently on business."

"Then, I hope you'll give me a call the next time you're in the city. It's easiest to reach me on my cell, but the university's sociology office during the day is a good alternative." She hesitated a moment. "I've never done anything like this before. I'm quite embarrassed."

"Please don't be; I'm delighted. You impressed me, and, I have to admit, intrigued me when I saw you at the conference. If it turns out we're destined to be friends rather than lovers, I will still consider myself lucky to know you. Thanks to you, I'm now looking forward to my next trip southward. That isn't usually the case."

Barbara's face was rosy when they ended their conversation. He'd probably call, but what must he think of her? He'd been kind to make his comment about friendship, smart, too. It gave him a neat way out of a relationship that might not go anywhere.

She liked his voice, warm and somehow intimate. *I made the right decision about calling him*, she decided. *My first impression of him was right on the money. Davis Reynolds is a good person.*

He didn't just strike her as someone kind and socially sensitive, however; he appealed to her as a man. Barbara sensed something solid about him, and even though he was older than Luis, he seemed to be a more modern male, one who'd be comfortable in a relationship with a professional woman.

Eight days later, she picked up her office phone to find Davis Reynolds on the line. "I called your office because I didn't want to disrupt you in class or a meeting. Are you free to talk now?"

"I am. Are you in San Diego?"

"Indeed, I am, and I'd like to see you if you have some free time today. I'm sorry about not giving you any advance notice."

"Don't worry about that. Tell me when you're free, and I'll decide whether it's better to meet me at home or my office."

"How about seven?"

"Then, at home would be best." She gave him her address and decided she'd go home as soon as her next class ended. Professor-plain wasn't the look she had in mind for tonight.

Davis arrived right on time, elegantly dressed and looking fine. His silver-gray suit was custom tailored, and he wore a cream-colored, French-cuffed shirt he'd paired with a cream, silver, and soft blue tie. What mattered more to her, however, is that his eyes were warm as he gave her a kiss that stayed inside the boundary of politeness but showed genuine pleasure in seeing her.

She'd chosen a wool crepe dress in bronze and kept the accessories simple. Since she couldn't decide if she wanted her hair up or down, Barbara compromised. She'd pulled the top sections back, looping the hair casually, and left the rest hanging straight down her back in case he wanted to play with it later.

It didn't take until later, he put his hands in her hair right away, fingering it gently. "You have amazing hair; I suppose you hear this all the time. But I noticed your eyes first—the way they light up when you're talking about something important to you. You're an intelligent woman, Barbara, and one passionate about your work. I find you very appealing."

She looked away shyly, pleased but embarrassed by his words. Then, she decided on a confession of her own. "What I noticed first was your knowledge of the Native American community and the sensitivity you showed in your questions both at the conference and in the bar. You have a strong aura of competency about you, too. I still sense that."

"God, please don't tell me I remind you of a favorite uncle; my ego can't take it."

Barbara laughed. "Not even close. I like the hum between us." Putting her hand on his arm, she whispered: "I don't have to tell you you're an attractive man, Davis. I'm sure you hear that every day."

"It only matters when I'm attracted back." A smile lit his hazel eyes. "I think it's time I told you where I'd like to take you tonight. Annabelle Lee is performing at Dizzy's, and she's one of my favorites—a nice blend of jazz and folk. Are you interested?"

"I rarely go to clubs or other music venues. I'm not sure why, but let me show you something, and the answer is a definite *yes*."

Barbara walked Davis over to her extensive music collected, sorted by type and era, which he found interesting. There were several albums by Annabelle Lee, including one he'd never seen.

After the concert, they returned to Barbara's house. Davis shook his head when she invited him inside. "It's late, and I know you have to teach tomorrow. May I show you my appreciation for a very pleasant evening with a kiss?" His eyes warmed. "I'd really like to."

She was already lifting her face. That hum between them had become a strong purr. Davis started slow, just a gentle brush of lips, before increasing the pressure and intensity as his large hands held her steady. It ended with both of them wanting more.

"May I take you to lunch tomorrow? I can meet you on campus if you're rushed for time." Davis's voice seemed a little unsteady, even breathy.

"I will be short on time, since I have classes at eleven and one, but I'd love to see you again before you leave."

Then, I'll meet you at your office at noon. If I can arrange it, I'd like to stay in the city overnight. There's another place I want to take you."

• • • •

Barbara noticed several of her colleagues, female ones, eying Davis as he approached her office. He did look spectacular in his navy suit, that beautifully cut red-blond hair shining with health. Everything about him said *yummy*, and she wondered how many women there'd been in Davis Reynold's life.

After their hastily consumed lunch at a campus eatery, Davis gave her a quick kiss goodbye, advising her to wear jeans and put her hair in a ponytail if she wanted to truly enjoy their night's adventure. That's all he'd tell her.

His brief instructions intrigued her, and she decided to follow his advice, dressing in black, tightly fitted jeans. She paired them with a black, V-necked sweater of the softest cashmere and tied a high ponytail with a red and black scarf.

Davis had dressed in jeans, too, and wore a black leather jacket over a silk T-shirt. "We're going somewhere I'm almost positive you've never been. It's a place called Full Contact Rock N' Roll, and the Legends, a local group, are playing tonight." Eying her high heels, he asked her: "Are those shoes comfortable enough for dancing? Maybe you'd better change."

Three hours later, they returned to Barbara's small home on 10th Avenue, tired because they'd stayed on the dance floor most of the night and full after the malt and French fries they'd shared. Barbara knew she'd probably regret that treat when she tried to button her clothes the next day.

This time, Davis came inside for a goodnight kiss but reminded her both of them had to work in the morning. Their kisses continued, however, and Barbara sensed he was as reluctant to part as she was.

"Davis, I know five dates is officially the magic number, but I don't think we need to be bound by other people's rules. We're adults, after all, and I don't know if I'll see you again. Stay with me tonight."

"We'll see each other again, Barbara, unless you block my number." The small lines around his eyes crinkled in amusement. "And I love that you think we're free to make our own rules. Here's the first one on my part—total honesty between us. I've kept my relationships with women casual for quite a long time, but I think we're headed for something different. So, my question is *do you feel ready for that?*"

Barbara looked long into Davis's eyes, silent for almost a full minute. Both sensed a third presence in the room. "Yes," she replied, "I think I am."

Chapter Seven

Certain something momentous was happening between them and needing time to absorb it, Barbara broke eye contact with Davis and asked him if he'd like a drink. She knew there'd be sex, but this felt like so much more.

When he didn't respond, she looked back at him. He was shaking his head slowly, something interesting in his eyes. "I want to remember every detail of our time together, Barbara. Let's start with a shared shower. All that dancing made me a little sweaty. The last thing I want to do is gross you out."

She leaned toward his chest and sniffed delicately, taking in his exotic, faintly musky scent. "A shower sounds wonderful, but I like your smell, Davis Reynolds. In fact, I like everything about you."

A sizzling kiss was his response before he turned her toward her bathroom, setting the shower temperature on the hot side. Davis spent the next few minutes undressing Barbara. He stopped for a nibble here and there, pinning up her hair before wrapping it in a towel to protect it from the water. Then, he stripped and pulled her into the shower.

They started at each other's shoulders, taking turns soaping each other before rubbing away any suds. Barbara used long, slow strokes down his firm belly before taking his penis into her hands. She fondled him for a brief moment and then washed away any soap. When she bent down and took him into her mouth, Davis's eyes closed for a moment of pure pleasure before he pulled her upright again. "Unfair," he told her quietly. "Let's wait until I can reciprocate."

Giving her a sudden grin, he turned off the hot water and hooted in laughter when Barbara gasped in outrage. He shut the cold water off, as well, and grabbed another towel to wrap around her. Pointing a finger toward her bed, he assured Barbara. "You'll be plenty warm in a moment."

"Such ego," she reproved.

"Think of it as a promise—my pledge to you."

Davis kept his word, drying off with quick strokes of the towel and joining her in bed. Barbara didn't think she'd ever been made love to so tenderly. He focused on learning what pleased her, how she liked to be touched, and where she was most sensitive.

"Davis, it isn't just about me. Let me give back a little."

"Next time," he insisted in a husky voice. "Right now, I want to please you, and believe me, I'm enjoying every minute of this."

She came once, twice, and was close to another orgasm when he finally relaxed inside her and released his seed into his condom. Both were drowsy, content to curl into each other, legs and arms entwined.

"Barbara ..." He didn't say anything more than her name. She didn't speak at all, just feathered kisses over his cheeks and chest. His hair there was red-gold, too. She found him utterly beautiful.

They made love once again that night. Half awake, she thought of Luis and his very different style of lovemaking. It surprised her that thinking about her former lover didn't make her sad.

In the morning, she awoke to find Davis examining her with those bewitching hazel eyes. "Much as I hate to, we have to get up and out of here. You have classes to teach, and I have an early morning flight. God, I hate leaving you after last night. It feels all wrong to put so many miles between us."

She touched his cheek with the back of her hand, loving the roughness of his red-gold beard. "That's part of the challenge of living in two different cities." When little frown lines appeared on his forehead, she gave him a hug. "We'll work it out. You've become important to me, Davis. I want you in my life."

He nodded. "I'll call you later this week or Monday at the latest. We'll plan a few days together. When's your first class?"

"At ten."

"Then, I'd better shower first. I have an 8:20 flight."

"How about if I make a pot of coffee and some eggs. I don't want to send you on your way hungry."

Davis's eyes gleamed with humor. "Sweetheart, there isn't a chance in the world I won't leave here with a hunger I can't satisfy when you're not around, but I appreciate the thought."

• • • •

As he'd promised, Davis called on Monday, asking if she could get away that weekend.

"I can," Barbara assured him. "Are you coming here, or would you prefer that I go to Los Angeles?"

"L.A. is best. Bring nothing but your oldest, most comfortable clothes and a bathing suit you don't mind ruining. Call and leave a message about your arrival time. I'll pick you up at the airport since it's on the way."

Judging by his instructions, Barbara knew their weekend would be casual. What she couldn't know was that he intended to take her camping in the mountains, where nights and mornings were chilly.

"You'll be okay. I threw in an extra sweatshirt for you. And you've got me. I'm very good at building fires." He gave her his version of a lecherous look. "Trust me, Barbara; I intend to keep you plenty warm."

Barbara eyed Davis thoughtfully. He was such a polished, self-assured man, but she sensed an entirely different, more adventurous side to him. Davis Reynolds struck her as someone who knew how to put work and everyday worries aside and simply enjoy life.

After their first night in his tent, she thought he'd made a wise decision about their weekend. They'd learn a lot about each other with this enforced intimacy. She doubted, however, she'd ever grow to love camping.

It occurred to her that Davis approached romance in a completely different way from Luis. Luis wanted to take things slowly and keep their relationship almost static. After almost a year together, she still hadn't grown close to him—not emotionally. Davis, on the other hand, wanted to move things along quickly.

He seemed to be a such an open man, one eager to share his thoughts and feelings with her. In that sense, she was much more comfortable with him than she'd been with Luis. *It doesn't matter*, Barbara reminded herself. *Luis isn't part of my life anymore.* After so many months of saying them, the words had begun to feel like a mantra.

She still missed Luis, but the sense of loss had faded. Davis wasn't a replacement. One man can never replace another. He was just a wonderful addition to her life, someone she might be able to build a life with if they could figure out this two-city thing.

On the way back to the airport Sunday night, Davis warned her it might be a while before they'd see one another again. "I've got a trip back to DOJ headquarters in D.C. coming up, and I have no idea how long I'll be there. Then, I'll have to deal with the work that's bound to pile up on my desk while I'm gone. Keep faith with me, Barbara. I'll return to San Diego as soon as I can. You have no idea how much I'll miss you."

When he'd been gone three weeks, it occurred to her Davis hadn't called at all and sent her a text only twice. At first, she didn't think much about it; after all, he'd warned her about his absence. Then, their time out of communication began to remind her of Luis's behavior. He'd also popped in and out of her life at his convenience. Was she now in the same of kind of relationship with Davis?

Don't be ridiculous, she chided herself. *Davis is a completely different kind of man, and I trust him to put our relationship first.*

Barbara acknowledged the differences between the two men but found their behavior strikingly similar. This made her wonder what she didn't know about the day-to-day life of Davis J. Reynolds. She wasn't even certain what he did for the DOJ beyond the fact that he'd mentioned being a lawyer.

• • • •

Intuiting some of Barbara's concerns about his long absence, Davis decided a face-to-face meeting might be better than a phone call. He'd fly down to San Diego and take her out to lunch.

When the sociology department's secretary called Barbara to tell her she had a visitor at the front desk, Davis was the last person she expected to see. She watched the secretary and several students and professors in the main office eye Davis curiously but decided against introductions. *I'll deal with the third degree later.* Right now, she needed to focus on Davis and his unexpected visit. They walked back to her office.

"Color me surprised," she told him with reserve in her voice. "How long have you been back in California?"

"Almost a week—but before you think I've neglected you on purpose, I'll try to explain. Our department is about to undergo some kind of audit, an internal investigation. There isn't much I can tell you except that I'm to be in charge of this operation. It will put a stress on our relationship, Barbara.

"I can't share much information, but I can tell you I'm going to be focused on my investigation. The last thing I want to do is put our relationship on hold for a while, but I don't have any choice, sweetheart." He'd offered up that last word tentatively.

After a mostly silent lunch, Davis took Barbara by the hand and suggested a walk around the campus. She watched his shoulders relax as they strolled. Then, he put an arm around her waist. "I think some of my happiest moments were on campus. There's such a sense of peace but with plenty of good energy. You'll lucky to occupy such a world."

As they approached the sociology building, he paused and grasped Barbara's shoulders. "Will you trust me, Barbara? Do you believe me when I say this assignment is temporary and that we will find a way to make our long-distance relationship work? It matters to me."

"We won't see each other at all?" she finally asked.

"Probably not. I'm going to give you a new cell number. Call me on that line for the next few weeks or, God forbid, months, but don't be surprised if I can't answer. I honestly don't know how long it will be. It would help if my weekends were free, but they're not."

There was little time to decide, but she sensed Davis had been honest with her about his situation and his feelings. She didn't want to lose him, and she did trust him.

"Okay, if this is what you need to do, then, I'll deal with it. Will you call me when you can? I'll miss you."

"Any opportunity I get, sweetheart." He bent his head and gave her a warm, lingering kiss that ended with sigh.

"I want so much more with you, but this will have to do for now. I haven't said it yet and hate saying it under such rushed circumstances, but you might as well know I love you, Barbara Allen. I think I knew how things would be for me the day we met. You're my *other,* and the greatest pleasure in my life is going to be proving this to you."

• • • •

Davis called regularly at first though she sensed his distraction. Then, the calls came with less frequency, and he often didn't answer her texts. Once again, his behavior reminded her of Luis.

The two men worked for the same organization, but she'd always assumed Davis was either a high-power lawyer or an administrator. Why would their behavior pattern be the same?

She went online to the DOJ website to see what she could learn by searching for his name. She found the information easily. He wasn't a lawyer, at least not a practicing one.

Davis J. Reynolds was a SAC, Special Agent in Charge, for the FBI's Public Corruption division. That meant he'd climbed higher on the bureaucratic ladder than Luis but still worked as an agent. How had she been stupid enough to get herself in the same situation twice? Suddenly, she felt a deep hatred for the FBI and everything and everyone connected to it.

His comment about his weekends not being free came back to her. Was Davis married, nothing more than a charming, hardcore cheater? He wore no ring, which meant little in today's world, but an out-of-town relationship would certainly be convenient if he did have a wife.

No amount of online looking would answer that question. She knew from experience the FBI protected their agents' privacy. After stewing about it for almost a week, Barbara did something she could never have imagined herself doing. She called a Los Angeles agency and requested the services of a private investigator. She needed to know more about Davis Reynolds.

It didn't take long. The agency's report was on her desk in just four days. Davis Justin Reynolds was 43 years old, held a degree in political science from the University of California, Berkeley, a Juris Doctor degree from Harvard, and a Doctorate of Juridical Science from UC, Berkeley in public law and regulation.

He lived in Palos Verdes Estates, married Valerie Anderson in 2010, and had two children—a daughter, Laura, and a son, Davis Reynolds, III. His wife died in 2019 after a fatal car crash involving a taxi.

Barbara glanced through the rest of the information, but none of it registered. Two emotions warred for control—sympathy for Davis's loss and guilt that she'd probed into his past. How could she justify doing such a thing?

One thing struck her as important. He had children, young children, and she'd had no idea. He'd never mentioned them, not once. Barbara struggled to get her emotions under control, trying to see things from Davis's point of view. Why should he share that information with her? They really didn't know each other all that well.

Maybe not in terms of time, she decided, *but we've gone past casual dating to a deeper relationship, and that was his choice more than mine. He should have told me about his children.*

On the other hand, Barbara knew she shouldn't have invaded his privacy. Davis deserved the opportunity to tell her in his own way.

And this new assignment, this investigation, had gotten in the way of their relationship, just as he'd warned her it would. She felt a sudden, strong urge to apologize. The man whose privacy she'd invaded so rudely deserved to know what she'd done.

Determined to confess her snooping, Barbara picked up her cell phone and punched in Davis's number, but a knock on her door forced her to end the call before it went through. As if her thoughts had transported him bodily, Davis stood on her doorstep, an expression she couldn't interpret shining from his warm hazel eyes.

Chapter Eight

"Davis!"

"It's nice to know you haven't forgotten me. May I come in?"

"Of course, I was just dialing your number."

A red-gold eyebrow went up, his left one, she noted with some absent part of her brain.

"Davis, I've done something inexcusable, and I need to apologize."

"Would that be for returning to the lost love I'm so curious about or hiring a private detective to check me out. I prefer the latter."

"You know?"

"About the lover? Only that he exists. About the detective, yes; he wasn't very discreet. I won't ask why you didn't approach me directly since I haven't exactly made myself available."

His eyes were smiling now. "If you have anything stronger than wine in the house, I'd love a stiff drink. It's been an interesting day."

"I've some good bourbon. Would that do?"

"Perfectly."

Davis settled on Barbara's sofa, drink in hand. He looked tired and tense, but his focus was on her. "What worries you, Barbara? Is it my work or my past?"

"Both, I think. It sounds like you might have some concerns, as well. You mentioned someone in my past, someone you suspect I loved. You're right; there is someone. He was—is—FBI, working out of San Diego. I met him in court, of all places. Our romance ended mostly because of the way he compartmentalized his life and the fact that he resisted moving our relationship forward in any meaningful way."

"And you think I'm the same kind of man."

"No, in most ways, you're very different, but I'm concerned that you didn't tell me you were an agent. I thought you worked for the legal division."

"Most of what I do is administrative, Barbara. That happens as you move up the chain of command. I haven't talked much about my work when I'm with you because we're just getting to know each other, and I want to spend our time together learning about you."

"I'm glad you do, mostly, but I'm not happy you didn't tell me about your children. I'm certain they're an important part of your life." She took his hand, sympathy in her eyes. "I'm so sorry about your wife. It must have been a terrible loss."

Davis didn't try to hide his pain. "It was and still is, Barbara. Valerie was a wonderful wife and mother. Over five years have passed, and I miss her every day. I suspect you're going through something fairly similar. It's hard to leave love behind."

"I'm learning not to think of it that way. Love shouldn't be forgotten or stored away in a closet somewhere. It should be celebrated and cherished. I'll always feel something for Luis—just as you will remember Valerie with tenderness for the rest of your life."

"Luis? That's his name?"

"Yes, Luis Vallejo. He's an FBI agent, too, assigned to gang activity in San Diego."

Davis's jaw dropped. "I'll be damned. I know him, Barbara. We've worked together several times. He's a bit of a rising star—the youngest SSA in southern California. He seems a little stern for someone like you."

"He is, I suppose. But we definitely found something in each other. It simply didn't work out. Tell me about your children."

"I should have mentioned them sooner; you're right about that. They're in Santa Barbara with my former mother-in-law at the moment. Things are unstable at work, and I can't give them the attention they need. They're better off out of it."

"How old are they?"

"My daughter is seven, almost eight, and the mirror image of Valerie. Davie turned five two months ago. He's all boy, but his personality is gentle, and he attaches deeply. I'm afraid my wife's death damaged him. She wasn't there when he needed her, and I didn't know how to fill that gap. I'll always regret what he lost."

"That isn't your wife's fault, Davis, or yours. I need to apologize to you for intruding into your private life. I panicked when I began feeling the same sense of isolation, of being pushed into a corner, that I felt with Luis. Can you forgive me?"

"I already have, sweetheart. I'm even glad you got curious since it led to a conversation about someone I sense you haven't entirely left behind. I meant what I said about honesty between us, Barbara. All good relationships require it."

"Is this why you're here—to clear up any misconceptions between us?"

"It is, and to invite you down to my beach house in Manzanillo, just the two of us. I need some R&R and your tender loving." Davis gave her a cheeky grin, his hazel eyes glinting. "In the spirit of total honesty, I have to say it's more about the loving part. I'm feeling needy."

"Nothing I like better than being needed," she teased back. "I'd love to spend a weekend with you in Manzanillo, maybe a day or two more if you can find the time. When?"

"This next weekend if you can. Pack light; all you really need is a couple of bathing suits and maybe a sundress in case we want to go out."

"Can you stay for dinner?"

Davis's expression turned wry. "Can't. I have a meeting at the FBI office here in San Diego. Your ex might be there. Should I say *hello* for you?"

"Let sleeping dogs lie, Davis Reynolds. Didn't anyone ever teach you that little bit of wisdom?"

He laughed and kissed her briefly. "Yes, ma'am. I'll call you tomorrow and arrange the details."

Putting his hands in her hair, Davis sighed softly. "You're very special to me, Barbara. It surprises me how fast that happened. Just as I didn't tell you about Laura and Davie, I haven't shared your existence with my children, either. Right now, I want it to be about us. The rest can come later. I'm feeling selfish about sharing you."

• • • •

They flew down in a small, private plane piloted by a friend of Davis's who also owned a beach house in Manzanillo. The Parkers, James and Louise, introduced themselves and promised they'd do their best to become invisible once everyone arrived at the famous beach town.

"It won't be easy," Louise warned Barbara, "since we only live three houses away. Still, Jim and I will do our best. God knows it's about time Davis found someone to spend time with besides his children," Louise teased her friend. "It's embarrassing to take him out in adult company. He still thinks fart jokes are funny."

Her comment made Barbara laugh before she added politely: "I hope we can spend some time together while we're here, Louise."

"No, we don't," Davis said rudely but with a big grin. "I hope to hell I don't see Jim's ugly face until we return to this airport. I have much better plans for the next few days."

As soon as they dropped their bags in the larger of the little cottage's bedrooms, Davis headed for the kitchen. "I make a great margarita, but there's a limit on one because I don't want you comatose tonight. I have plans, Barbara Allen."

When she came up behind him and wrapped her arms around his waist, Davis smiled and leaned back into her. "I like this," he told her in a soft voice. "You feel like home to me. I admire your name, too, very traditional." He gave her a sly smile. "I've always been a sucker for romance."

"A word of caution, Davis Reynolds. I may be a romantic like the tragic Barbara Allen, but I don't fancy either of us dying for love. That ballad breaks my heart."

"My sentiments entirely. "Bottoms up," he saluted her, handing her a glass. "And then we'll go see whose bottom is up."

"Davis!"

"Louise warned you I wasn't fit for adult company. It's been weeks, sweetheart, and I've missed you."

Barbara eyed Davis's bed suspiciously. "Are you sure it isn't full of bugs? How often do you get down here?"

"I'm sure. Bettina cleans everything once a week, and the house and grounds are sprayed regularly. Are all professors this finicky?"

"I wouldn't know. I just don't like the idea of little critters sucking my blood."

"How about bigger critters sucking your fingers and toes as well as other succulent parts?"

"Depends on the critter. Are you volunteering?"

"Hell, yes."

Davis scooped Barbara up, sat on the side of his bed, and proceeded to undress her slowly, giving her little licks and bites along the way. It wasn't long before he joined her under the light, colorful throw.

At first playful, Davis grew serious, even intense, as their lovemaking deepened. One coupling led to another as twilight turned to full dark, each one teaching Barbara something about the man who'd suddenly become so important to her.

Unlike Luis, Davis not only didn't mind her being on top when they made love, he seemed to enjoy it thoroughly. She found him an adventurous, uninhibited lover, one who combined a sense of fun with great tenderness. And stamina—the man definitely had stamina.

A long, loud growl brought their lovemaking to an end. Neither was certain whose stomach had protested.

"It's too late to eat a real supper," Barbara insisted. "I'd never be able to sleep."

"I'm good with some kind of snack."

"What about cheese, crackers, and a glass of wine?" she suggested.

"How about nachos and beer instead. It's one of my specialties."

"Nachos, it is."

Their four days passed in a blur of walks on the beach, playtime in the water, a little exploration of local shops, and a lot of time exploring each other. It wasn't just physical.

Davis told her about his life with Valerie—how they met, what drew him to her, and how she'd fit into his life. "You're nothing like her," he admitted, "which surprises me. I've always heard men tend to pick the same kind of woman."

Barbara didn't know what to say or how to interpret his words. When she got quiet, Davis took her hand, gave it a tender kiss, and held it against his heart.

"Maybe a man looks for different things in a companion as he matures. Do you remember me telling you that I saw you as my *other*? I meant it. I loved Valerie; she was a kind, gentle woman content to build her life around me and the children.

"But it's different with you. There's a stronger bond between us, a sense of emotional and intellectual connection Val and I never shared. I don't think I ever noticed that, at least, not consciously, until you came into my life."

"I feel it, too, that connection."

"Did you feel it with Luis?"

"In some ways, yes, there was a powerful pull between us. But we see life very differently. He is a traditional male, very Hispanic. I knew from the first we'd find a shared life difficult if not impossible."

"He was uncomfortable with your education and profession," Davis guessed, "and a bit intimidated by your independence."

"Maybe, I'm not sure. He didn't try to change me in any way, but he kept himself separate; I don't know how else to describe it. It doesn't matter anyway. Our goodbye was permanent and for the best."

"I wish I could be sure of that."

"Davis, what matters to us is that I'm sure. You make me happy in ways Luis never could, and you're such a complex, interesting man. There is the professional Davis Reynolds, who is competent, intelligent, and—elegant feels like the right word.

"Then, there is the private man, who thinks deeply and has a tender side. You're also funny and lighthearted, sexy, too."

"I like the sexy part. So, you think I'll do? Are we a couple now?"

He kept his tone light, almost teasing, but his eyes were serious.

"I'd say so. Will you be my sweetheart, Davis Reynolds?"

"I'll be your slave, Barbara Allen as well as your lover, your friend, and any other role you'd like to assign to me."

• • • •

The flight back to Los Angeles was filled with good-humored conversation from the Parkers and plans for the next trip.

"Louise and I are coming back in two weeks, Davis. Why don't you bring Barbara and the kids down, too? Lou and I can watch over them so you get some private time. We can even do a sleepover."

"Let me manage my own courting, Jim," Davis grumbled to his friend, but his eyes held amusement. "Actually, that sounds pretty good. Can you get away?" he asked Barbara.

"I can. It sounds like fun. Let's do a cookout on the beach. *Shrimp on the barbie*, as the Aussies would say."

• • • •

Two weeks later, six people boarded the plane instead of four. The two smallest soon starting giving Barbara a serious once-over. They had distinctly different styles of interrogation.

Laura asked their father's friend pointed questions—lots of them. How long had Barbara known her dad? Was she married? How did they meet? Had she ever been married? Did she like her dad? How much?

Davis's little girl didn't seem hostile, Barbara decided, merely concerned and perhaps a bit proprietary. Davie, on the other hand, looked for reassurance. Did she like children? Would Barbara send him and his sister away to school somewhere, so she and his father could be alone? Would she love her own babies more than them?

"Ah," said Barbara solemnly, "the wicked stepmother. I've read about her, too." She made a face. "I didn't like her much." Then, she touched Davie's tousled curls briefly. "No, I'd never do such a thing, and your dad would never allow it. I'm pretty sure I like children, Davie, but I haven't been around them all that much, and there's a lot I don't know. Perhaps you'd be willing to help me learn?"

Davis's young son, as blond and beautiful as his father, was silent for what seemed like an eternity. "I guess so, but Laura thinks we don't need you. And she can be pretty stubborn."

Laughter filled the small plane, but Barbara could see that Davis's daughter was embarrassed. "I think your sister is right to be concerned. Family is about the most important thing there is. This is what I do at work, Laura—study families."

Davis's daughter looked intrigued. "I didn't know anyone did that. Is it a real job?" she asked.

"It's called sociology, and yes, it's a real job."

Their three-day weekend passed quickly. By the end of it, Davis's children had accepted Barbara as part of their father's life. Both noticed a difference in him. He appeared more relaxed, happier, it seemed to them, when Barbara was around. He touched her a lot, and his eyes were softer somehow.

Davis surprised Barbara just before they began packing up. "Would you consider staying here in Manzanillo for a week or two with my rug rats instead of returning to California? It isn't about bonding, Barbara. I'm not testing you. Things are coming to a head in Los Angeles, and I'd feel more comfortable if all of you were safely away. I've talked to Jim and Louise, and they're willing to stay on."

"Davis, are you in danger?"

"There's no way of knowing. I don't think so, but I'm not willing to take any chances. All three of you are better out of it, and, in any case, I need to focus on my work. I know I'm asking a lot ..."

"It's summer, Davis. I don't have anything keeping me in San Diego. It'll be fun. What about your children? They don't know me all that well. Will this be okay with them?"

"Time on the beach and in the water—are you kidding?"

Davis knew his children. They whooped their approval, especially when the cottage next to theirs was occupied by a large and boisterous family from Las Vegas. Laura barely bothered to say goodbye to her father.

Davie, Barbara noticed, was less certain when the moment of parting came. His father picked him up, gave him a tender kiss on the cheek, and held him close for a long moment. "Take care of my girls," he whispered in his son's ear. "You're the man of the house while I'm gone."

It was exactly the right thing to say. Davie straightened in his father's arms. "I will. We won't go any farther than the Parker's house; I promise, unless Barbara says it's OK."

Chapter Nine

U ncomfortable at first about spending so much time alone with children she didn't know all that well, Barbara regretted agreeing to stay on in Manzanillo with Laura and Davie. It was a huge responsibility, and, despite Davis's reassurances, she did wonder if he was testing her. After two days, it didn't matter. She was having too much fun.

Barbara had been certain there'd be no time or opportunity to work on an article she'd brought along to polish. Davis's daughter, however, had other ideas.

"Daddy says grownups need time to concentrate. So, Davie and I will sit on the deck and do quiet things for one hour every morning. You can set the timer; that's what our dad does. Then, when Davie takes his afternoon nap, I can read while you work a little more. Is that fair?"

"More than fair, Laura; thank you. What would you most like to do while we're here?"

"My favorites are going to the *centro* to see the dancing fountain at night and visiting the archeology museum. Davie prefers playing on the beach and in the water, but he'll do anything you think might be interesting. Daddy says my brother's a pleaser at heart."

"Like his papa," Barbara responded with a smile that lit her eyes.

"You like my dad, don't you?"

"I do, very much. Is that okay with you?"

"Even if it wasn't, I'd still say *yes* because he likes you, too. Davie and I both noticed Daddy smiles more when he's with you—a happy kind of smile, not his polite one."

The three of them spent most of their time together on the beach, usually daring the shoreline waves to catch them and building sandcastles. Both Davie and Laura enjoyed playing all kinds of games with the children next door while Barbara kept an eye on them from Davis's deck.

Jim and Louise invited them down for dinner several times, using the pilot's dune buggy as an enticement for the children. Barbara worried Davis's friend would get bored driving them around, but Louise shook her head.

"Haven't you learned yet all men are nothing more than grownup boys with bigger toys? They love that shit."

She gave Barbara a sly look. "You sure made an impression on Davis. Those kids are his life; I'm surprised, frankly, he'd trust you with them. We've known Davis for years, and he's never let us keep Laura and Davie overnight."

"He has some heavy responsibilities at work right now, and I think he wanted them somewhere where they'd be safe and happy. This seemed like the right place, especially when you and Jim agreed to stay. Thank you for that."

"I suspect you're right about his preoccupation with his job. I'm just as certain he plans to make you a permanent part of his life. You're damn lucky if he does. I don't know a better man than Davis—and my God, he's so gorgeous."

"You won't get any argument from me."

• • • •

After a week of off-and-on pleading from Laura and Davie, Barbara agreed to a campout on the beach, certain that sand fleas would put an end to the festivities after a few hours. Instead, both children fell asleep after a serious fit of the giggles and slept soundly through the night. She managed a few hours, too, despite those flea bites.

Davis called the next day to tell them he'd be down for the weekend. He spoke with each of his children for a few minutes and seemed reluctant to end his call.

"It's been tense here," he told her. "I really need to get away, and I miss my rugrats. I hope they haven't been too much trouble."

"I've had fun, to tell you the truth, and I think they have, too. You haven't said anything about missing me."

"That goes without saying. I'm only half a person when you're not in my sightline. I'd say I find this a little scary, but it isn't. It feels fantastic."

"I miss you, too. See you tomorrow. Stay safe."

"I'm trying, sweetheart."

She replayed their conversation in her head after Davie and Laura were down for the night. His last comment worried her. *I can't just wait around for this assignment to be over*, she decided. *I need to know what's going on.* There'd been a tinge of fear in Davis's voice. The least she could do was let him share his worries with him.

• • • •

She was the bull in a mock reenactment of a bullfight with Davie. Head down, hands curled up in front of her ears for horns, she roared fiercely and looked over to see Davis watching her from the deck, an amused smile on his face.

Although dressed in a suit, he'd taken off his tie and unbuttoned both his jacket and his shirt. He looked tired to Barbara, closer to exhaustion. Still, he smiled.

"Davis!"

"Daddy!" preceded flip-flopped feet hurriedly slapping on sand.

In a practiced gesture, he scooped both of them up, one in each arm and planted noisy kisses on their cheeks. Then, he put them down, giving them a mock-stern look.

"Have you two behaved?" he challenged them.

"Of course," Laura told him in her oddly grownup voice.

"I've been especially good," Davie bragged to his father. "I didn't cry once." Then, he gave his father a worried look. "I did pull Laura's hair one time; she smooshed my castle."

"Sounds fair to me," he reassured his son. Then, he looked at Barbara. "You're still standing, even smiling, so, I assume it wasn't too bad."

"It was fun for the most part, but I'm as glad as they are to see you." She gave him a wifely eyeballing. "You look silly in that suit. Why don't you go put on more comfortable clothes, something you won't mind getting wet in."

"Walk me to the bedroom and keep me company while I change?" He waggled his red-blond eyebrows.

"In your dreams, who would keep Laura and Davie out of trouble?"

"We will," Jim Parker said as he and his wife walked up the beach toward them. "I saw you arrive and figured we'd say *hi*. We'll take the kids for some ice cream and a little playtime in the park across from the ice-cream store. Should take us at least forty minutes, I'm guessing, maybe even an hour."

"I owe you big time for this, Jim," Davis told at his neighbor, grinning broadly.

"Nah, I've been there when my kids were little." Jim took Davie's hand and asked him: "What will it be Davie—chocolate or strawberry?"

"Both," Davie announced, "I'm super hungry."

Everyone laughed as the group divided, the Parkers and Davis's children strolling down the beach while Davis and Barbara turned toward the cottage.

"You look tired. Are things going badly at work?"

"Later, I'm not wasting one of our forty minutes, Barbara. You look so damned good and a lot tanner. I'm guessing they didn't want to sit in the house and read all week."

"We can discuss that later, too. We have just forty minutes, after all."

Since the Parkers didn't return for almost an hour, Barbara had already started supper, and Davis was putting the finishing touches on a pitcher of margaritas, his tension gone. Once the pitcher was empty, the Parkers headed home, and two no-longer-hungry children cuddled on the sofa with their father.

She watched them surreptitiously as she finished assembling the shrimp tacos and salad she suspected only the adults would share. Davis was a wonderful father, which didn't surprise her, but she found his parenting more complicated than that. He'd had to be mother and father to Davie and Laura, all while doing work that might be mostly routine but could be dangerous, too.

She felt his vulnerability tonight, his worries for his children. Barbara knew he considered the two of them his greatest blessing rather than a burden, but it must be both. *I can lift that burden a little*, she mused. *And I want to.*

Davis caught her eye and smiled. "Is dinner almost ready? I'm starved."

"I'm putting it on the table as we speak." She turned to Davis's children. "Do either of you want a taco, or are you too full from all that ice-cream?"

Laura shook her head, but Davie considered it a little longer. "No," he finally said a little wistfully. "I think I'd throw up."

Both adults laughed, and Davis told his son: "Thanks for that lovely image when I'm sitting down to eat. Can you and your sister start getting ready for bed while Barbara and I eat? Then, I'll tell you a story about something that happened at work this week."

"Really?" Barbara whispered as the two little ones left the room. "You talk to them about your work?"

"I tell them stories, Barbara, to give them some idea, however fanciful and sanitized, about what their father does. They'd imagine worse if I didn't; and Laura is a worrier."

Both Davis and Barbara were surprised when Davie insisted on a story from Barbara, too, before he'd let them turn out the light. "Her stories are more fun, Daddy. She doesn't just tell us about her work. Tell my dad the one about Miranda and her magical sixth finger, and don't change any of the words this time," he instructed Barbara.

After lights out, Davis took Barbara out on the deck, waiting for his children to settle into sleep. Running his hand up and down her arm absently, he seemed miles away.

"Davis, I'm not one of your children; I don't want a sanitized account of what's going on in your office. You need to share your worries, and I need to hear them."

He nodded, but his expression was grim. "When I'm sure they're asleep."

Barbara went into the cottage and poured each of them a glass of wine. Then, she took a few pieces of Mexican chocolate and put them on a plate. The candy probably wouldn't sweeten Davis's tale any, but it might provide one small comfort.

He was sitting on the edge of the deck, his feet buried in the sand, when she returned. Barbara sat down beside him, putting an arm around his waist and resting her head on his shoulder.

"This feels wonderful," he told her. "You have no idea how happy it makes me to have you in my life. There're just aren't words to express how special you are.

She nodded, then gave him a small hip bump. "Quit stalling, Davis, and I want to hear everything."

"Okay, you asked for it. My visit to D.C. was a command performance. I had no idea why they sent for me until I got there. Neither did anyone in the L.A. office. Later, the AG put out a cover story to explain why I'd been called to Washington, but it was crap.

"Washington suspects—scratch that, has proof—my boss is working with the head of the Mexico Mafia and Mendota's warden to make sure the biggest drug shipments from Mexico get through to various locations in southern California without a hitch.

"Having a foot in the FBI and the warden in your pocket also helps streamline communications between Roberto Rodríguez Gonzales, who heads *La EME*, which is just another name for the mafia, and his lieutenants outside prison. He's a lifer, but it hasn't slowed him down a bit. With Ackerman, my boss, on board, it means the mafia's also privy to what the FBI knows."

"How could that happen, Davis? Why would someone who's built a successful career in law enforcement do such a thing?"

"Money's the short answer. You can't imagine how much. Forensic accountants have discovered at least three bank accounts Bob has opened under several different names in the Caymans and Curaçao. Lots of zeros in those accounts, sweetheart, more than he'd earn in ten lifetimes with the FBI."

"But if the director already knows about all this, why does he need you?"

"Because Washington isn't sure if Ackerman's working alone or if others in the L.A. office are helping him. This is what I've been working to uncover. I'm all but positive I've identified two men who are dirty, but there may be a third. I hope to hell not; Rick's been a close friend for years.

"Until now, Bob's managed to fly under the radar, but I'm pretty sure he suspects Washington is snooping around. He knows I'm the logical point man for an investigation but has no idea who I'm working with in the office or how much Washington knows. The answer to his first concern is no one. I just couldn't risk it, but he doesn't need to know that.

"Things are coming to a head, Barbara, and the next two or three weeks may well see indictments and arrests. That's what makes this such a dangerous time period. If I were to disappear, especially if they could get their hands on the evidence I've uncovered, it would at least slow down the investigation. Once those indictments go down, however, I'm no longer a threat to them. They'll have other problems."

"Can't you stay here until then?"

"No, I'm not done yet. I need to figure out if Rick Stevens is involved or not. That's the last missing piece."

"And then what?"

"We get married and live happily ever after if you're willing."

Davis's eyes were serious. "Please say *yes*, sweetheart. I don't think I could take hearing *it's too soon* or that you're not sure you love me."

"Not a chance in the world I'd say either one of those things, but I don't want a big, elaborate wedding, Davis—the smaller, the better. And sooner, rather than later.

"Any interest in getting an early start on that honeymoon once the kids are asleep?"

"Does a bear poop in the woods?"

"Did something that inelegant just come out of your lovely mouth, Barbara Allen?"

Her eyes challenged him. "Was I crystal clear?"

"Most definitely," he assured her, hugging Barbara to him. Then, he whispered in her ear: "I'm pretty sure the kids are asleep. Let's go take a peek."

On the way into the beach house, he halted briefly. "I want to show you something. This was here when I bought the place. I think my little Manzanillo cottage may have been used for smuggling."

He walked over to a bookcase and twisted what looked like an ordinary latch for a sliding glass door. A small space opened up—one barely big enough to step into. "I hope to God we never need it, but I'm glad it's there."

They entered Laura's and Davie's room, saw that his two children had settled down for the night, and headed for their own bedroom. Time for something a little less serious.

• • • •

Davis grunted when Davie bounced on his belly and shouted: "Get up, Daddy; I'm hungry, and Barbara's making pancakes. She knows how to make Mickey Mouse ones."

Laura was standing in the doorway. "They taste good, Daddy, honest. Did you get a good sleep?"

"The best," he told her with a wink. "Both of you head for the kitchen; I'll join you in a minute."

Davis didn't want them to know he was completely naked under the sheet that covered him and wondered if his kids could smell the subtle tang of good sex he and Barbara left behind. He certainly could.

She'd left her hair down, spilling almost to her waist. For some reason, Barbara seemed unconscious of her beauty or uninterested, he couldn't decide which, though he knew she was a little vain about her hair.

"Morning, Gorgeous. I think I'm ready for round two," he greeted her.

"What's round two, Daddy?" Davie asked him, his blue eyes curious.

"It means he's thinking about playing golf this morning," Laura told her little brother in a superior voice. "Maybe you'll make a hole-in-one today. You're really good at that, at least that's what Mr. Parker always says to Mrs. Parker when they talk about you. I don't even know what a hole-in-one is."

Barbara and Davis both choked on their coffee.

"Actually," Davis said as he recovered his voice, "I was thinking about a walk into *centro*. Is anyone interested in joining me?"

Everyone rushed off for shoes and sunhats of one type or another as soon as breakfast ended. They spent several hours shopping and visiting a small art gallery before a bored and hungry Davie insisted on eating.

"I didn't get even one shrimp taco last night. You ate every single one," he lectured his father.

"You were full of ice cream, remember?"

"Well, I'm not full now. Let's go eat."

After lunch, they returned to the cottage, where Davis insisted Davie nap while he cuddled up on the sofa with Laura for a serious discussion about the difference between dolphins and whales. When his daughter picked up a book and started reading, Davis retreated to their small deck, his toes once again buried in the sand.

Barbara joined him with two glasses of iced tea. "You seem more relaxed now."

"Good sex will do that for you," he grinned.

"Daddy, I'm up!" The words were followed by a startled expletive from Davis, as his son jumped on his back.

Davie turned innocent eyes on his father. "Can Laura and I bury you in the sand—please. Barbara lets us bury her if we put a towel down for her hair, and I never get sand in her eyes, do I, Barbara?"

"No, you don't. You're very careful." Then, she turned to Davis with a smile and whispered. "You might want to take a shower later or at least a swim. Sand finds its uncomfortable way into the smallest crevices."

Davis didn't say a word though he did stand up and grab his son's hand, his posture and expression that of a martyr. Later, he took Barbara's advice and went for a solitary swim. Barbara chuckled when she saw his suit floating beside him and the flash of a white fanny.

Afternoon slipped toward evening, and they all settled on the deck again to watch a spectacular sunset. Barbara sat close to Davis, her hand warm on his thigh.

The night was so quiet a slight metallic drone had Davis staring at the ocean. Then, he stood up, moving down towards the beach to get a better look. Suddenly, he turned toward Barbara.

"Take the kids inside, sweetheart. You know where to go."

Barbara could see a Zodiac rubber raft now with four men in it. It was making its way toward shore—toward them.

"Davis?"

Her lover's voice was deadly calm. "Take care of my babies, Barbara, and don't come out until you're sure it's safe."

He threw one agonized look at her before pulling a small gun out of his short's pocket. Then, he took off at a run for the water.

Chapter Ten

B arbara grabbed both Laura and Davie by the hand as they stared wide-eyed at their father's retreating figure. "We're going to play a game of hide and seek," she told them in a choked voice, "and I know just where to hide."

She ran into the cottage, stopped for a moment, then headed for the front door. Dropping Laura's hand briefly, she opened the door and threw one of her flip-flops toward the unpaved road. Leaving the door wide open, she led the children to the bookcase that disguised the small space Davis had shown her, twisted the small latch, and pulled both children into the small, dark space.

As Barbara closed the door behind her, she memorized the location of the small knob that would reopen it. Fighting tears and keeping her voice as calm as she could, she warned Davie and Laura they must be very quiet. "Your father is a good seeker, and I don't want him to find us."

"Why not?"

Barbara couldn't see Laura's eyes, but she heard the doubt in the little girl's voice and the beginnings of fear.

"Because your father promised me earlier this afternoon that he'd make hot chocolate for us later if he couldn't find us. It makes the game more fun. Let's be quieter than the tiniest, most timid mouse."

She waited for the sound of automatic weapons on the beach but could hear nothing but silence. Minutes passed, how many she couldn't begin to guess, but it felt like hours. Davie grew bored, and Barbara knew he wouldn't stay silent much longer.

Suddenly, the sliding glass door to the deck slid open, and she heard voices speaking in Spanish. Laura stiffened and felt for Barbara's hand. Davis's little girl didn't say a word, but Barbara felt teardrops on her arm as Laura pressed against her. Even though she was only seven, Laura understood this wasn't a game.

79

The men milled around, making random noises; then, she heard one of them say something about a *zapato*, a shoe. Certain they thought she'd fled out the door with Davie and Laura, Barbara swallowed in relief. Maybe they'd leave now.

They didn't. She could hear them searching for something as they knocked over chairs and tables, swearing in their frustration. Then, finally, it got silent.

"Can we come out now?" Davie whispered before Barbara slid her hand over his mouth. Instead of answering, Barbara picked him up and held his face against her cheek to quiet him.

Grief overwhelmed her fear as she held Davie's warm, little body against her. Biting her lip fiercely, Barbara fought for control.

There'd be time to grieve later when Laura and Davie were safe, and she already knew there'd be grieving to do. The three of them stayed silent for long, agonized minutes, all listening for the least little sound.

Finally, Barbara reached for the knob and opened the door. It was nearly dark now, and she couldn't hear any sound beyond the soft swoosh of the surf. She turned to Laura. "Do you know where your father keeps your passports?"

"He always puts them in there." Davis's daughter pointed to a small, overturned table.

"See if you can find yours and Davie's," Barbara instructed her. "Don't turn on any lights or make any noise. I'll be right back."

"Don't go outside, Barbara," Davie pleaded. "Wait for Daddy. I'm scared."

"I'm going to look for him on the beach," she reassured the little boy. "You and Laura wait here."

"Should I get Daddy's passport, too?" Laura asked, her eyes revealing a suspicion she couldn't yet articulate.

"I don't think he needs his right now, sweetheart. Don't go anywhere. Wait here with Davie. Then, we'll go visit the Parkers."

Although full dark had arrived, a crescent of pale moon silvered the beach. She searched for almost five minutes before she found Davis—half in and half out of the water. He'd fallen on his back, and several dark patches stained the front of his shirt and pants.

The men in the boat used knives; that's why she didn't hear any gunfire. *Why did he allow them to get so close?* Barbara wondered, Davis's pistol was gone, and she suspected he'd never had a chance to fire it. Did he recognize someone in the boat? Was it someone he trusted?

Barbara knelt down beside him, reaching out to put her hand against his heart as he'd once done in a tender moment. Tears ran down her cheeks in earnest now; she didn't care, didn't even notice.

"Oh, Davis. I never even got to tell you how much I love you. I wanted to save those words for a special occasion, and now, you'll never hear them. I'm so sorry." She straightened slowly. "I have to leave you, sweetheart. It isn't safe here, and I don't want Laura and Davie to see you like this."

She kissed his mouth, already slightly cool and metallic tasting, then stood. "I'll do my best for them, Davis—my last promise to you." Barbara hurried back to the cottage and led both children out the front door to the Parker's.

She didn't have to say anything; Davis's neighbors saw it in her face.

"You two look like you need something to drink and a cookie," Louise Parker told Davis's children. "Let's go to the kitchen."

Jim didn't waste any time. "Something's happened."

"They came by boat. I saw four of them, maybe five. Davis had a hand gun, but he never fired it; I have no idea why. He'd dead, Jim. I found him on the beach.

"The men in the boat searched for us, but Davis's cottage has a small panic room. Did you know that? Those men, Mexicans by the sound of them, were in a hurry, but they were definitely searching for something. They took my laptop. Davis didn't bring one, just a small tablet and his phone, which they took, as well."

She looked around. "I can't stay here. These men are professionals, which means they'll be looking for us. Whoever they are, they want something; I've no idea what. This means I'm putting you and Louise in danger. I think the best thing I can do is take a taxi to the airport and fly back to the U.S."

"Are you going to tell the FBI what happened to Davis? Maybe I should contact Davis's office by phone."

"No!" Barbara panicked. "That's not a good idea. I don't know much, but I do know Davis was investigating people in his own office. We wouldn't know who to trust. I'll fly to Arizona instead of California and talk to agents there or contact the local police. Would you call a taxi for me?"

"No, Lou and I will take you to the airport. That's the least we can do. Do you want us to keep the kids with us and fly back to California tomorrow? I know Davis has ... had ... a sister in L.A."

Barbara shook her head. "I promised Davis I'd keep them safe with me. That's my priority now. I'll deal with where they should go later. God, what a nightmare. We don't even have any luggage. I took nothing but my purse. Laura grabbed a book, and Davie wouldn't leave without his fuzzy bear. That's all they have, Jim. Those poor kids have lost both their father and mother. I can't imagine what's going to happen to them."

Her tears spilled over for a moment, but she pushed her grief away, focusing on what needed to happen next. "We'd better go; I want to leave before those men can make any organized effort to find us."

• • • •

Barbara would never remember the next hour—the drive to the airport, the rush to catch the last flight to Phoenix's Sky Harbor

Airport, and a hurried goodbye to Jim and Louise. Both children took refuge in silence, shell shocked and confused by the sudden changes in their lives.

The questions came once they were airborne. "Daddy's dead, isn't he?" Laura whispered to Barbara. "Those men killed him. Why?" The last word was a wail, both denial and a reluctant acceptance of her father's fate.

Barbara hugged Laura to her and tightened her hold on Davie, who sat silently in her lap. "Your father was a brave man, Laura, an important one, too. He knew things that some very bad people are trying to keep hidden. They won't succeed, sweetheart; I promise you the truth will come out."

"But Daddy will still be dead."

Barbara didn't know what to say, and what would words, however eloquent, mean to a little girl who'd lost both her mother and her father in the space of a few years? Davie and Laura were orphans. It was the first time the true horror of that word had any real meaning to her.

If this had happened just a few weeks or months later, she and Davis would have been married and his children safely hers. She wanted that for them and for Davis. Now, she'd have no say in what happened to them.

Davie fell asleep, still clutching his bear, but Laura sat, silent and stoic, her lips pressed tightly together. Keeping a comforting hand on Davis's little girl, Barbara used the time to organize her thoughts.

As soon as they landed and went through customs, she'd need to contact someone. The Phoenix police couldn't do anything. Davis's death happened in Mexico. She didn't trust the FBI, and no one in the military could help. Her mind refused to settle, and Barbara realized she couldn't make any rational decision while she was so tired and confused.

I'll sleep on it, she decided. Then, an image of Davis lying on that beach, forever sleeping, tormented her. She couldn't bear to think of him there all alone. Someone needed to care for him.

Much as she longed to be there for him, she knew it couldn't be her. His children needed her more. *Jim and Louise will do something*, Barbara assured herself and prayed it was true.

• • • •

Feeling a strong sense of relief they were back on U.S. soil, Barbara woke Davie, grabbed Laura's hand, and began the process of reentering the country. She didn't get far.

"Ms. Allen," a stern, middle-aged man took her elbow. "I would like to ask you a few questions. You and the children need to come with us."

"Only if you show me some credentials and explain what this is all about."

"As if you didn't know," a second man, younger than his partner, snapped at her. "We're FBI, Ms. Allen, and there's a BOLO on you. You're not being arrested, but that might come later. I suspect there'll be kidnapping charges if nothing else."

Kidnapping? That possibility had never occurred to her. "Are you from Los Angeles?" Barbara asked the first man. The idea she'd let Davis's children fall into the hands of men who might hurt them terrified her. She looked around the airport frantically. No one would help her. Who would believe her against the word of FBI agents?

"No, we're based in Phoenix. Will you come voluntarily to our headquarters, or do we have to go through the formalities of arrest?"

"I'll come with you as long as the children stay with me."

"Barbara?" Davie's blue eyes welled with tears. "You aren't going to leave us, are you?" He looked fearfully at the two men standing there. "Are these men bad, too?"

"No, sweetheart, they work for the FBI, just like your daddy. They simply need to ask us some questions."

The FBI building was larger than she'd expected and somewhat isolated in its location far north of the airport. She'd noted the address when they'd arrived, not that it mattered. It was a place she wanted desperately not to be.

The Phoenix agents led the three of them to a suite of offices, where a woman—a secretary or agent, Barbara had no idea—took Laura by the hand and approached Davie. His eyes wide, Davie screamed in fear.

"Please," Barbara begged the first agent, whose name she still didn't know. "Don't take them, at least not yet, not like this. Give me a few minutes."

She crouched down and held Davie close, reassuring him. Laura stood stock still next to the stranger who held her hand, her face expressionless. She was absolutely frozen until Barbara beckoned to her. "Come here, sweetheart, hold Davie's hand."

"Are they going to take us away from you, Barbara. Will we ever see you again? Is someone going to kill you, too?" Laura's fear gave her voice a high pitch.

Barbara saw the older agent wince. He had children. Somehow, that comforted her as nothing else could.

"No, of course not. They are here to find out what happened to your father. I'm sure your daddy told you stories about how they treat witnesses in the FBI. It's important they question people separately—to see how their information is the same and how it's different. That helps them solve the crime.

"Right now, you, Davie, and I are witnesses. We'll see each other very soon, right after they ask their questions. Tell the truth, both of you, and share everything you remember. Can you do that for me?"

Davis's daughter nodded. "Can Davie and I stay together. He's so scared."

The woman nodded and took both children by the hand. She gave each of them a reassuring smile, saying: "Before we ask our witnesses any questions, we usually get them something to eat or drink. Would you prefer ice cream or pizza?"

"Both," said Davie.

The normalness of his response put heart back in Barbara. "I knew you'd say that," she teased Davis's little boy. Giving each of them a kiss, she repeated her promise they'd see her soon.

As soon as the children left the room, Barbara turned to the agents. "What do you know about Davis Reynolds?"

The younger FBI agent's eyes narrowed. "That's not how this works. We ask questions; you answer them. I'll say this much; we know he's dead."

Barbara nodded. "I can tell you something about that. We were sitting on the back deck of Davis's cottage in Manzanillo when a small rubber boat, I think they're called Zodiacs, headed toward our beach. Davis asked me to take the children inside and hide."

She told them everything she knew, surprised by the resentment she sensed. She'd never actually seen an FBI interrogation, except on television and in the movies, but it seemed to her she was being treated more like a suspect than a witness.

Several hours passed with the agents asking variants of the same questions over and over again. She learned the agent's names. The older one was Miles Anderson and the younger one, James Baxter. They asked her about her relationship with Davis, her background, and what she knew about his work.

That last topic worried her. She suspected these men weren't involved in anything dirty, but bureaucracies have a life of their own. Anything she told them might, and probably would, get back to Davis's office in Los Angeles.

"Very little," she said finally. "I doubt the two of you are that different from Davis. I bet you don't talk much about your work at home, either."

The woman who'd taken Davis's children away earlier knocked lightly and entered the room. "The kids are asking to see Ms. Allen, and they're pretty insistent."

Agent Anderson smiled. "I don't see a problem. Bring them here. Then, take them to the guest suite. She can join them later."

A minute later, Barbara heard Laura and Davie running down the hallway. Laura stood close to the chair Barbara occupied, but Davie crawled into her lap.

"They like you," the younger agent commented, sounding somewhat surprised.

"I'm all they have right now." She put an arm around Laura. "I would have been their mother, well, stepmother, in a month or two. So, yes, we've gotten close."

She turned to Laura, giving her hand a light squeeze. "They're letting us stay in a suite, something like a hotel room, for a day or two, sweetheart, so we can rest. I'll join you there later. Why don't both of you take a bath and watch a little TV?"

"You're coming?" Davie asked, his eyes anxious.

"Absolutely. I'll be there in time for your bedtime stories, okay?"

"Okay," they both responded with a noticeable lack of enthusiasm.

"Barbara?" Laura added wistfully. "I wish Daddy was here."

"So do I, sweetheart. I wish that more than you can imagine."

Chapter Eleven

Agents Anderson and Baxter motioned her back into her chair as soon as the children left the room. Barbara complied though she couldn't imagine what more they could ask her. They'd been over everything at least twice. A sharp knock on the door brought another agent into the room—one she hadn't seen before.

The two men who'd questioned her earlier poured over the file the third agent handed them. The older one, Anderson, glanced at her once and went back to reading. Barbara jumped at a sudden, loud expletive from James Baxter.

"That sure changes things," he told his partner before swinging around to regard her angrily. "Let's talk a little more about that little hidey-hole in your boyfriend's beach house. Empty, you said—and the Mexicans were looking for something?"

"Yes," Barbara said, "to both."

"Not entirely empty, Ms. Allen. Our agents just reported back and guess what they found? Lot of baggies containing a fine, white powder. You a user?"

Barbara struggled to get past her shock. "There were no drugs in that hiding space or anywhere else in Davis's beach house. How'd they get there?"

"You didn't answer my question—you a user?" He grabbed her arm and turned it toward the light. Then, he tilted her chin to look up her nose.

Barbara batted his hand away. "Of course not. I'm a professor."

"You wouldn't be the first."

"This has to be some kind of mistake. Davis would never have anything to do with drugs, and neither would I. Someone else put them there."

"In a place no one knew about and the Mexicans apparently couldn't find. Seems doubtful. You and Reynolds have a fight? The kids said they never saw what happened. Did you kill your boyfriend, Ms. Allen, and steal his son and daughter?"

"Leaving a fortune in drugs behind?" Barbara challenged him. "Does that sound likely? And where's the logic in burdening myself with two children if I wanted the drugs? You've already learned Laura and Davie didn't see or know anything."

"Let's start over," Agent Anderson said calmly. "From what I see in that report, Washington asked the wrong man to lead the investigation. Reynolds should have been part of the investigation, not conducting it."

Barbara's cheeks reddened in anger, and her eyes narrowed. "That's not true. How stupid can you two be, not to mention monumentally unfair? Davis died trying to find the truth and get it back to Washington. This discussion is pointless. I have nothing more to tell you." Her voice roughened by her anger, she informed them brusquely: "I'd like to leave now. Where did you put Laura and Davie?"

"You won't be joining them, Ms. Allen, and don't give me any crap about what you promised them. You're now a suspect." Baxter's voice was cold, and Barbara realized he'd made up his mind about Davis and about her. "The agents who went down to Mexico to investigate are on their way here. They asked us to hold you and the kids."

Miles Anderson saw the anguish on Barbara's face and felt a stab of doubt. This woman didn't feel right for drug trafficking, and her concern for Davis Reynold's children was real. Still, she'd be safe enough here, and so would the kids while they sorted this out. Whether their dad was dirty or not, nothing good lay ahead for those two youngsters.

• • • •

Barbara wanted nothing more than to throw herself on the cot in her small cell and give way to tears—for Laura and Davie, for Davis, and for herself, but she couldn't. Davis would expect her to get his children out of FBI custody and keep them safe.

Think, Barbara. Who put those drugs there? It couldn't have been the men searching the cottage while she and the children were in hiding. The *why* seemed obvious once she thought about it—to frame Davis and cast suspicion on her. That would divert attention away from the men who killed him or at least ordered the hit. This made the *who* obvious, as well—the dirty FBI agents themselves.

Since the L.A. agents "found" the drugs after being told about the hidden space in Davis's cottage at some point, they were probably Ackerman's men. And now, they were on their way here. Maybe she needed to tell the Phoenix agents everything even if they didn't believe her. At the very least, there'd be some kind of record.

Exhausted by her lack of sleep and the trauma of dealing with Davis's death, Barbara reluctantly closed her eyes. The sound of the cell door opening woke her, and she sat up, smoothing her hair with her hands. *Why,* she wondered absently, *should I bother? My hair's the least of my worries.*

Three agents entered the small holding cell, but she had eyes for only one of them.

"Luis!"

"Barbara?" Luis gave her a stunned look. "You're the woman accused of killing Davis Reynolds and kidnapping his children?"

"Luis, you know that's not true. I'd never hurt anyone—least of all Davis. I'd say it's all a big mistake, but it's something even worse."

"But you were his lover, the woman in Manzanillo?"

"We planned to marry, yes. That part is true."

Agent Vallejo recovered quickly, ignoring his partner's curious look and turning to the senior agent from Phoenix. "I don't know how this mix-up occurred, but I'm familiar with Dr. Allen and seriously doubt she had anything to do with Davis Reynold's death. Something else is going on here."

"So, you know Ms. Allen. Should I be concerned about your connection to her?" Agent Anderson's eyes showed his suspicion. "You two are from San Diego and have no direct involvement in this case." Their clearance from D.C. was legit; he'd already checked on that, but he didn't know why they were here, and details like that bothered him.

Luis nodded briefly. "I do know her, yes; we were on the opposite sides of several court cases. I'd like to speak to her alone if I may."

The Phoenix agent shook his head. "Your partner can go or stay, but either Jim or I will keep you company," Miles Anderson told Luis. "You can conduct your interview here or in the office where we briefed you." He turned around and left the room.

Barbara took the same chair she occupied earlier; Luis and his partner sat facing her. Baxter, who'd been waiting in the hallway, stood with his back against the wall, a watchful expression in his dark, hostile eyes.

"What's going on? Barbara. How did you get involved in all this?" Luis's words seemed clipped and cold, and Barbara found his expression hard to read.

She gave him a short history of her relationship with Davis and his investigation of wrongdoing in his own office, omitting the specifics of why Davis had been given this responsibility and whom he'd targeted. Luis listened carefully, and she got the oddest feeling he already knew something about what Davis had been investigating.

"Luis, please, I need to see Laura and Davie. Those two children are coping with the death of their father, and now they're in a strange place with no familiar faces. They're desperately frightened. Please let me see them even if it's just for a few minutes."

Luis nodded and looked toward Special Agent Baxter. "Arrange it," he told him curtly. The authority in his voice surprised Barbara. Why would he be in charge here?

He turned to Barbara. "The kids will be here in a few minutes." Then, he lowered his voice, and his eyes took on that hardness again. "You sure didn't waste any time grieving for the end of our relationship, did you? Reynolds has, or had, the reputation of being quite the player, Barbara. I wouldn't have thought him your style. He was FBI, too, and I know you're not a fan."

Barbara maintained eye contact with her former lover. "Davis mentioned that he worked with you several times, but your description of him makes me doubt you knew him very well. He was extraordinary, Luis, the kindest man I ever met and devoted to his children."

"I take it you two discussed me at one time or another."

Barbara nodded. "Davis worried there was someone I hadn't left behind, at least not completely. I told him your name but not much else. I had no idea he was an agent when we met. Until a few weeks ago, I thought he worked for the Department of Justice as a lawyer."

Their tense confrontation was interrupted by a squeal of joy as Davie spotted her. Barbara pulled the little boy onto her lap and hugged him. Laura walked into the room warily before going to stand next to the only face in the room she knew.

"You didn't come," she chastised Barbara. "I kept promising Davie you would, but you never did."

"They wouldn't let me, Laura. I wanted to be with you two so badly." Barbara put her hand on Davis's daughter's cheek. "You are being very brave, sweetheart. Your father would be proud of you, of both of you."

The mention of her father brought a flood of tears. "I don't want Daddy to be dead, Barbara," Laura wailed. "I want him to come to Phoenix and take all of us home." Biting her lip, Davis's daughter looked at the men gathered in the room, her eyes infinitely sad. "They won't let us, will they? Davie and I don't even have a home now. We can't live there by ourselves."

Upset by his sister's tears, Davie began crying, too. Luis surprised Barbara by leaning over and taking the little boy from her lap. What surprised her more is that Davie didn't object to Luis holding him.

"Things are pretty tough right now, aren't they?" he asked Davie gently. "It will get better, I promise. Do you know how much you look like your dad? I bet you're strong and brave like he is, too. That's why you're taking such good care of your sister."

"You knew my daddy?" Davie's face puckered as he tried to control his tears.

"I did; we worked together, in fact."

"He was brave, wasn't he?" Davie said, tearing up again.

"Yes, he was. I know this is hard for you, Davie, but I need to ask Barbara some more questions, important ones. Could you take your sister back to your suite for a little while? I promise I'll bring Barbara to you in a few minutes."

Davie gave the only adult in the room who mattered to him an uncertain look. "Is he telling the truth, Barbara? Will you really come?"

"If Luis says he'll bring me to you, he will. He's one of the good guys, Davie—a friend of your father's."

Laura's sigh echoed in the silent room. "Come on, Davie. We can watch TV. Daddy won't mind." She stopped suddenly, swallowed, and corrected herself with a slight tremor. "I mean he wouldn't have minded." Taking her brother's hand, she led him out of the interrogation room.

Luis was silent for a moment before turning to Barbara. "They treat you like a mother. I can see the trust."

"I'm all they have, Luis."

"Let's get to those questions."

Luis and his partner had used some of the time Davis's children were in the room to look over the file agents Anderson and Baxter examined earlier. None of the information in that report squared with what Luis knew about Davis Reynolds.

He'd been surprised and a little confused almost a week earlier when he received a sealed letter inside a packet addressed to him. A short, handwritten note asked Luis to keep the letter sealed and safe until Reynolds either retrieved it in person or it became obvious he couldn't retrieve it.

Luis had followed the senior agent's wishes, showing the sealed envelope only to his partner. Now, he knew why Davis sent it to him. He couldn't trust anyone in his own office with the information, so he'd chosen the man Barbara had feelings for, someone she thought worthy of trust.

When the report of Davis Reynold's death in Mexico reached his office in San Diego, Luis opened the sealed envelope and quickly scanned the two-page summary of what Davis learned in his investigation. The report named Robert Ackerman and two other agents, John Nader and Bob Howard, as key players in something Davis called the Triad.

This previously unknown organization linked key officials in California's federal prison system, the Mexican Mafia, and the FBI in an alliance to control the flow of drugs from Mexico to southern California. Davis feared another agent, Richard Stevens, who headed cybercrimes, might be working with the Triad but hadn't turned up any solid proof.

Right after opening that letter, Luis contacted the Los Angeles FBI office requesting an update on Reynolds, telling the agent who took the call that he and Davis were close friends. Special Agent Randall Peters told him that two agents, Bob Howard and Richard Stevens, had already traveled to Manzanillo to look over the crime scene and retrieve Davis Reynold's body. The office would know more when they reported in.

These same two agents were now on their way to Phoenix, supposedly to return Barbara and Davis's children to Los Angeles for questioning. Instinct told Luis he couldn't let that happen. Somewhere, somehow, Barbara and Davis Reynolds' children would disappear while in FBI custody—probably under the cover of placing them in witness protection.

Barbara glanced at a silent, obviously distracted Luis. "Should we get started?" It was time, she decided, to share everything she knew.

He nodded, and Barbara began with the night on the back deck of Davis's cottage when he'd shared some of his investigation with her. She hadn't gotten more than a few words out before she felt Luis's shoe pressing against her foot.

When she continued speaking, he pressed down on her toes. It was a message; he didn't want her to say anything or at least anything important. Why? Was someone listening—someone he didn't trust?

Before she could interpret Luis's urgent message, the door opened, and two men she'd never seen before entered the room.

"I'm Stevens and he's Howard," the first man said to Luis. "Would you mind telling me just what the hell you and your partner are doing here?"

"Not a bit," Luis said calmly. "Davis Reynolds is a friend of mine, my best friend, as a matter of fact, and I wanted to know what happened to him. When I learned his kids and fiancée were here, I decided to speak with them. Washington okayed it, but I probably should have contacted the L.A. office. Sorry." He gave Barbara a cold look. "The information she might be involved in his death came later."

Just before the agents from California entered the room currently being used for an interrogation, Luis slipped his hotel key card out of his pocket and handed it to his partner. No one but Barbara seemed to notice.

Luis addressed the two newcomers. "I know you want to question her, but I promised Davis's kids she could spend a few minutes with them."

"Screw the kids," Agent Stevens yelled. "I've got some serious questions for this whore. Davis was my friend, too. Odd that he never mentioned you or her, for that matter."

Although Luis's eyes darkened, he kept his face expressionless. "I could say the same. Let me catch you up on what's been happening here—from my perspective, of course. I assume you've already spoken to agents Baxter and Anderson. Then, you can tell me how you managed to find those drugs in Davis's house in Manzanillo. You're going to have a hard time convincing me my friend knew about them. He was a pretty straight arrow."

"If you believe that, you didn't know him as well as you thought you did. Davis Reynolds was dirty, Vallejo." Bob Howard's tone was venomous. His glance slid over to Barbara. "You can bet that one knows a lot more than she's letting on."

Phil Reed stood up and turned to his partner. "I'll take her to Reynold's kids, Luis. Is twenty minutes enough time for your exchange of information with these gentlemen?"

"Should be," Luis agreed.

"That's all she gets, in any case." Stevens turned back to Luis. "Friend or no friend, I'd still like to know how you got authorization to come here, Vallejo. Reynolds is one of ours or used to be."

. . . .

Luis's partner returned in less than fifteen minutes, blood trickling through the handkerchief he held to his temple. "As soon as we walked in the room, she hit me with something she grabbed off the coffee table. Before my head cleared, she'd grabbed the kids and flown the coop. Talk about stupid security; there's an entrance onto the main street from the guest suite. I tried to find her, but she ghosted me."

"I doubt she'll get far," Luis told the agents from Los Angeles. "This isn't exactly a busy part of the city. She'll be easy to spot with two kids in tow, and I'm certain she won't leave them behind."

Giving Reed a considering look, Rick Stevens took control. "You stay here," he told Luis, "your partner, too. We don't need your kind of *help*. We'll work the area with the Phoenix agents. You better hope you're right, Vallejo. My boss isn't going to be happy."

"You okay?" Luis asked his partner when they were alone in the room.

"Yeah, it's just a little pizza goop diluted with coffee—fools 'em every time." I gave her your key card, room number, and money for a cab. I also warned her to go a few blocks away before catching one and to go at least a block past our hotel before she has him pull over. They might be able to trace the cab, but it will take a while, and they won't have any idea where she went from there."

"Thanks. I take it you caught our colleagues' names, too. Something stinks, Phil, and Barbara's right in the middle of whatever's going on. Once we make sure she and the kids are safe, I think it's best if we head back to San Diego. I don't particularly want to answer their questions, and there isn't much more we can do here. I'm pretty confident they'll be glad to see our backs."

"Stevens and Howard are going to be suspicious, Luis. It's not supposed to be that easy to escape FBI custody."

"Yup, there isn't much I can do about that, but when they verify our authorization from Washington and we mind our own business after returning to San Diego, they'll forget about us. Those two have bigger worries."

Luis told the secretary at the front desk they planned to head back to San Diego since there was nothing more they could accomplish here, and it wasn't their case. As he and his partner got into the rental and headed to their hotel to pick up their clothes, Luis asked Phil Reed for one last favor.

"I'll drive our rental back to San Diego, but I want you to make a little side trip. Hand me your cellphone. If someone checks, they'll have no way of knowing you're not in the car with me. I have a cousin in San Bernardino. Actually, he has a ranch just outside the city. Take Barbara and Davis's little boy and girl there. I've got some dots to connect."

Phil Reed nodded, amusement in his eyes. "You believe her, I take it, even though she screwed you over pretty good."

"I screwed myself, Phil, and the lady was smart enough to move on."

Luis returned to his hotel room and knocked lightly. "It's me, Barbara." Once inside his room, he told Barbara and Davis's children about his plans for them, warning his former lover: "Howard and Stevens are going to keep looking until they find you or whatever it is they're looking for. You don't have any idea?"

"Not a clue. I don't have anything, Luis. I've looked through my purse several times. There's nothing. We left Manzanillo in a hurry and didn't take anything with us. Whatever it is, it must be back at beach house, or the men in that boat found it."

"Phil will be here in a few minutes; he's gone to get a car. As soon as he texts me, I want you to take the kids and disappear out the side door at end of the hallway. He'll meet you there."

"I can't stay hidden forever, Luis."

"I know, *Bebe*, but I'm afraid it's going to feel that way. Right now, staying invisible is the only thing keeping you and those kids safe."

Chapter Twelve

P hil's text came less than ten minutes later. As soon as everyone piled into a white, mid-sized Toyota, Luis's partner pointed the car he'd stolen from a nearby parking lot toward California.

"With any luck, we have a few hours before anyone notices it's gone," he told Barbara, raising his eyebrows and giving her a small smile. Then, his curiosity overcame his manners. "Are you at all surprised Luis put his career, and mine, by the way, on the line for you?"

"No, I'm not, and I doubt you are, either. Luis operates under a rigid code of ethics. His feelings for me, whatever they are, change nothing."

Luis's partner snorted in amusement. "I'm pretty sure you're overestimating his honor and underestimating his hormones."

Barbara gave a small shrug. "On a different note, I haven't a thing to wear other than what I have on and neither do Davie and Laura. I'm also beginning to stink."

"We'll make a stop in Blythe," he assured her. "Can't do much about the smell right now." Then, he laughed. "Don't worry; you're fine."

Giving Davis's daughter a thoughtful look in his rearview mirror, Phil Reed added. "This might be overkill, but hair grows back quickly. Everyone interested in locating you is looking for a woman dragging around a little boy and half-grown girl. What if a woman with two young boys shows up at the ranch? That's not what the Mexican Mafia or anyone in law enforcement is looking for."

Barbara turned to look at Laura in the back seat. "How about it, Laura? You want to masquerade as a boy for a little while?" She knew Davis's very bright little daughter was listening to everything she and Phil said. "Would you let me cut your hair?"

Laura's hazel eyes narrowed. "Why can't Davie be a girl?"

"He's not quite old enough to pretend, Laura," Barbara said gently.

Davis's daughter gave that some thought. "Okay, it might be fun to see if I can fool everybody. Do I have to wear boy's underwear, too?"

Her obvious concern made Barbara laugh. "You'll be going undercover, like your dad did sometimes. I bet he told you stories about that."

A quick stop at a Walmart supercenter in Parker, Arizona, for some much-needed supplies and they were on their way. Phil wanted to dump the car in Los Angeles before a BOLO went out. He planned to leave it at a shopping center close to the airport.

The sign, Séguin Enterprises, was right where Luis said it would be, and they followed a long dirt road to a large, comfortable-looking hacienda, where cars, trucks, and jeeps were parked haphazardly.

They'd just pulled in when a tall man with serious, dark eyes walked up to the driver's side of the car. "I'm Ramón Séguin; I take it you're Luis's partner. How worried should I be about my family's safety?"

Giving Luis's cousin a nod, Phil Reed acknowledged the rancher's abrupt greeting. "Short-term, I think it's safe enough. Long-term, maybe not so much. You need to take that up with your cousin."

Séguin turned his attention to Barbara. "Are my children safe around you, Miss ...? I'm afraid I don't remember your name though Luis mentioned it."

"It's Barbara Allen, and the only answer I can give you is 'I hope so.' I'm not sure what's safe anymore. I apologize for Luis involving you, but I can't tell you how grateful I am. Let me introduce you to Laura, who's now officially Lorenzo, and Davie, or David to outsiders."

Barbara helped Davie search for his bear, which had slipped under some packages, and then helped him out of the sedan. "They're witnesses to a federal agent's death and the reason Luis enlisted your help. I intend to do everything I can to keep them safe. Their father is a hero, and, like their daddy, they've been incredibly brave."

Ramón's eyes softened as he bent down to speak to Davie and Laura. "I think you're going to like living at the ranch, especially if you like horses. I have a boy who's seven, too. We call him J.R. My daughter, Lucia, is four. They're out in the barn right now, playing with a new batch of kittens. Would you like to meet them?"

Laura nodded solemnly, but Davie balked, pushing his head against Barbara's leg.

"It's okay, David," she reassured him, reminding him of his new name by giving it a Spanish inflection. "I'll join you in a few minutes. I need to talk to *Señor* Séguin and Luis's partner."

Ramón signaled to a ranch hand and pointed toward the barn. Davis's two children followed the man slowly. Although Davie gave Barbara a concerned look, he straightened his small shoulders and continued toward the kittens.

"They'll be fine," Ramón assured her. "Luis didn't have time to say much beyond the fact that you're a college professor who's gotten mixed up in the murder of this Davis Reynolds by one of the worst drug cartels in California and Mexico. He told me that both corrupt FBI officials and the Mexican mafia think you've got something they want. Luis has no idea what. Do you?"

Barbara shook her head. "Whatever they want, I don't have it. We fled with nothing, *Señor* Séguin. I took my purse—that's it. I've been through it nearly a dozen times by now. There's nothing."

Phil Reed, impatient to be on the road and concerned about Ramón Séguin's ability to keep Barbara and Davis Reynolds' children safe, added:

"It doesn't matter what they're looking for or if she does or doesn't have it. They're looking, and, sooner or later, someone's going to figure out where she is. She needs to be gone by then.

"In the meantime," he turned to Barbara, "I want you to keep a low profile and talk to no one. Don't use your phone or your credit cards or reveal your identity to anyone. In fact, don't leave the ranch if you can help it.

"Keep them close," he advised Ramón. "I wouldn't talk to Luis on your regular phones. Buy a burner, and have someone in the family give Luis the number. It might be an overabundance of caution, but there's no way of knowing how wide a net they'll spread. Get that phone right away; I'm sure he'll want to call soon."

• • • •

With those sage words, Reed stepped on the gas, leaving a dusty trail behind him. Ramón looked Barbara over in silence then seemed to make up his mind. "Come inside and meet Alicia. My wife's the only one besides me who knows your real identity. It needs to stay that way. I'm the worrier in the family, Barbara Allen. Allie thinks Luis is a hero and loves the idea of helping him by hiding you and the dead agent's kids."

Ramón winced before shaking his head. "Sorry, that wasn't very sensitive. He was your fiancé, wasn't he? This must be incredibly hard for you, losing someone you loved and having your life upended like this. Luis was right to help you. I don't know how long you'll be here, but while you are, please consider us family."

Barbara simply nodded and followed him inside.

Alicia Sepulveda de Séguin was her husband's polar opposite—short, plump, and cheerful.

"You're so beautiful; no wonder Luis took you under his wing." She spoke over her shoulder. "You can go, Ramón. There's nothing you can do for this lady. I'm guessing she needs a bath, a change of clothes, and a chance to settle in. Any questions can wait."

Giving Barbara a sardonic smile and touching his wife's hair affectionately, Ramón left the two women without a word. Alicia watched him head toward the barn, a warmth in her eyes that told Barbara everything about Luis's cousin and his wife.

"He's very handsome, your husband."

"All the Séguin men have high looks. But it's what's inside that counts. They are beautiful there, too. Ramón may grumble, but you couldn't be in safer hands. Your children are in the barn with mine?"

"Laura and Davie aren't my children, Mrs. Séguin. I wish they were. Davis and I had planned to marry, but before we could, he died in Mexico, murdered by the cartel. I'm not sure what will happen to his children ultimately. I doubt I'll have any say in the matter."

"God's will," Alicia said serenely. "Luis will make certain they're safe and happy. He's much like Ramón. The two of them have a certain magic with children. It's the only time they're comfortable showing their hearts—except in bed, of course—though I can't speak for Luis about that."

Barbara's blush made Alicia curious. Did Luis have some kind of relationship with this tall, grieving woman? *Unlikely*, she decided.

A long, hot soak and some clean clothes restored much of Barbara's confidence. She felt ready to sit down with Ramón Séguin and work through a short-term solution to her problem, one that didn't include going into witness protection.

She'd worked too long and hard to sacrifice her education and training. In a little over seven weeks, classes would be starting up again. Luis needed to wrap things up by then. Even then, close to two months in seclusion felt like an eternity.

Although Ramón didn't say anything to Barbara, he wanted a quick resolution, too. These three strangers endangered his family. As he encountered his ranch hands one by one, he focused on floating a story about Barbara and the children that explained their presence at the *hacienda*.

Bonnie Sue was the Anglo wife of one of the Séguin cousins living outside San Marcos, Texas. Miguel, her husband and a former SEAL, suffered from PTSD. When he began mistreating her and the children, she fled to California. They'd be here until the rest of the family could get Miguel into treatment.

"If anyone shows up looking for her," he warned his ranch hands, "don't let on she and the boys are here. Miguel Antonio always had a bad temper and a strong sense of ownership. I'm guessing he won't quit until he finds them. Unfortunately, the family can't force him to get treatment—at least not until he does something bad."

• • • •

Within days, Barbara and Davis's children settled into a comfortable routine at the ranch. She stopped trying to keep Laura and Davie near her. It wasn't possible or necessary. Everyone on the ranch looked out for them, and Ramón was always nearby. Alicia hadn't exaggerated her husband's protective nature.

With less responsibility for the children's safety, Barbara began fretting about her own life. She missed her little house in Old Town and her friends at the university. Most of all, she grieved for Davis. They'd known each other such a short time, but he'd opened his heart to her so completely that time didn't seem to matter. In private moments, Barbara gave herself permission to mourn her lover and friend.

Isolation gradually bolstered her confidence that things were returning to normal. *By now,* she assured herself, *everyone must realize I don't have anything of Davis's or know anything about his investigation. They probably aren't even looking for me.*

In a brief telephone conversation, Luis dispelled this comfortable but unrealistic illusion. "They're looking, Barbara. Stay put and stay hidden. Ramón tells me you're worried about your job. Let that go for now, and don't even think about contacting anyone at the university. If it starts to look like you'll still be in hiding when classes start, I'll let your bosses know enough about your situation so they can make short-term plans. You don't need to worry; they can't fire you. There are laws that protect witnesses in federal custody."

As the days passed, Barbara found herself spending more time with Alicia than Ramón, which surprised her. On the surface, they had nothing in common. But Barbara found the woman's calm, family-centered life instructive, even inspiring. Underneath all that feminine fluff was a real, working brain, one that focused on very different things from hers.

"My husband thinks you knew Luis before this all happened. Is he right?" The question came as the two women prepared lunch for the family, which now included Barbara and Davis's children, as well as nearly a dozen ranch hands. Barbara hesitated before answering Alicia's question.

"We encountered each other in the courts several times," she finally said. "I testified as an expert witness in several of Luis's cases." She gave Alicia an amused look. "I don't think he appreciated my point of view."

Alicia shook her head. "No, I don't think that's what Ramón meant. It's more personal. Ramón thinks Luis is angry with you—the kind of anger masking hurt."

"Our relationship did get personal briefly, but we couldn't make it work. Our values and experiences are too different."

"Yet he has gone out of his way to help you and the children of a man you say you love but whom he must see as a rival. I don't think he's left his feelings for you behind."

"I did love Davis, Alicia; I still do. In some ways, he had the same protective instincts as Luis, but he was a far more open man. I needed that."

"What do you know about Luis, really? How can you judge him if you never met his family? You didn't, did you?"

"He wouldn't allow it. That was a huge part of our problem."

"Maybe they wouldn't allow it. Did you ever consider this? Or maybe he was trying to protect you from their rejection."

Barbara sighed. "It doesn't matter, Alicia. We couldn't make it work. Davis had nothing to do with our failed relationship. He didn't come into my life until months after Luis and I called it quits. You're right about Luis's anger. I felt it, too, when we encountered each other in Phoenix. But his emotions don't matter, either. Luis has a job to do, and he'll do it. His feelings are irrelevant."

Alicia let the matter drop, but Ramón brought it up less than a week later. The two of them enjoyed some alone time riding through the vineyard on horseback, something he invited her to do almost every afternoon.

"Alicia tells me you and Luis were lovers before this Davis Reynolds came along. It probably isn't any of my business, but what made you move on to another man? I'm certain you're the one who chose to end the relationship. It still isn't over from my cousin's perspective, or you wouldn't be here."

"I never told Alicia we were lovers—though it's true. Your cousin is a wonderful man, but Luis couldn't find a way to fit me into his life. I needed more from our relationship than he could offer, so our lives separated. Eventually, I met Davis. I don't regret my love for either man, Ramón."

They rode on in silence for a while, each occupied by thoughts neither wanted to share. Barbara took in the rich smells—horses and the ripening grapes—and gradually relaxed as they rode through the fields. She'd never experienced or imagined this kind of lifestyle, but she understood its appeal.

Ramón seemed reluctant to drop the subject of her relationship with Luis. "My aunt spoke of you once, at least, I think it was you.

She complained Luis had taken up with some Anglo woman. *Tía* Amparo is a woman of strong convictions and an over-abundance of family pride. She's had Luis's future all mapped out for him for years. It didn't include the FBI or someone like you."

"I understand something about family expectations, Ramón. Maybe joining the FBI used up all of Luis's independent streak. And, in any case, I would never want to create a wedge between Luis and his family. All of you are very important to him. I didn't have to meet any of you to know that."

Ramón grew silent again and then offered up another thought. "Disappointing family is difficult. Maybe Luis needed more time."

"It doesn't matter. I met Davis, and that changed everything. And now, all I care about is keeping his children safe. I could never have imagined it, Ramón, but I've come to not just care about but to love Laura and Davie, and giving them up to someone else will be the hardest thing I'll ever have to do."

Ramón nodded but didn't speak. His thoughts focused mostly on his younger cousin, whom he'd always admired, and on what Ramón needed to do to keep his family safe.

Barbara's mind refused to settle on anything. She couldn't think about Luis and didn't want to. He was part of her past. She had no future, at least not one that included a tall man with beautifully cut red-blond hair and warm, hazel eyes.

Chapter Thirteen

"But Barbara, I have to go back to school. It's the law, and besides, I want to. Davie needs to start kindergarten, too." Laura's little-girl voice was patient but determined. Barbara knew exactly how Davis's daughter felt.

She'd begun to grow restless, too. After all, they couldn't hide at the ranch forever, and her university classes would be starting soon in San Diego. She needed to be there.

All of them needed to resume a normal life. That probably meant Davie and Laura would go live with their aunt, the one who liked being an aunt rather than a mother, according to Davie.

During her five weeks at Ramón's ranch, Barbara spoke by phone with Luis several more times, usually at the tail end of his conversations with Ramón. They were brief, awkward discussions that went little beyond his descriptions of what Ackerman and the men he'd corrupted were up to.

Earlier in August, Luis had flown to Washington, D.C. to discuss Davis's investigation with the FBI's deputy director, handing over the investigative summary the L.A. SAC for public corruption left in his care.

Deputy Director Adam Pulaski listened to Luis's explanation of what he'd learned in Phoenix, his decision to hide Ms. Allen and Reynolds' children, and his growing conviction that Ackerman had ordered the hit on Reynolds. Grim-faced, the D.D. asked him to assume Davis's secret duties but to keep his investigation low key and focused mainly on Richard Stevens. "Watch your back," he warned Luis. "I don't want to lose another agent."

Luis didn't mention any of this to Barbara. What he did tell her was how intense the search had become on both official and unofficial levels. So far, no one had come up with any leads on her whereabouts, but it was now an active kidnapping case for the FBI, at least officially. For now, she was to stay hidden, which meant no school for Laura and Davie.

"Will this ever end, Luis? Am I going to wind up in jail for kidnapping?"

"It'll end when we bust up the Triad, Barbara, and you don't need to worry about being charged with anything. Washington knows why you've kept Davis's kids with you. How's Davie doing?"

She heard the tenderness in Luis's voice. For some reason, her former lover been drawn to Davis's little boy and vice-versa. She understood Davie's need for a strong male figure but wondered why Luis felt such an attraction. In the end, it didn't matter. Luis wouldn't have any more say in the children's future than she would.

"He's doing surprisingly well. I think having J.R. and Lucia to play with and the amount of time Ramón spends with him are easing him through the worst of it. Laura is having a harder time even though she tries to hide it."

"I should be there."

Barbara heard the worry in Luis's voice, and it surprised her. Davis's children weren't his responsibility. "You can't do everything, Luis, and, right now, I want you to focus on ending all this. The children need to settle into their new life, and I need to return to mine."

"How are you doing, Barbara—really doing?"

She thought about lying to him, but why should she? "It's like I'm living in suspended animation. Nothing feels real, and each new day brings me no closer to resolution."

Barbara was silent a moment. "I'm lonely, Luis—the deep, soul-sucking kind of loneliness that makes you wonder how you're going to survive all those empty years ahead."

"I should be there," he said, once again, and Barbara wondered what odd gene made Luis Vallejo take on responsibilities that weren't his. Maybe that's why he'd joined the FBI. But even Luis couldn't fix everything and everyone.

"I'll be fine," she promised him. "Time does heal; it isn't just a cliché. In the meantime, I've got Laura and Davie to worry about."

• • • •

Luis used work as a distraction from his own worries and found plenty to keep him busy. He had his regular responsibilities involving gang activities in San Diego as well as events on the nearby La Posta, Campo, and Capitán Grande reservations, where L.A. gangs were recruiting. He also surreptitiously monitored events in the Los Angeles FBI office.

Phil had managed to tap Ackerman's desk phone, but the Los Angeles ADIC rarely used it for anything but routine business. It would be another week or so before they'd get permission to access cellphone calls either to or from Ackerman, Howard, and Nader. The higher ups had decided against monitoring Richard Stevens. The evidence against him was slight and mostly circumstantial.

When his worries about Barbara, Davie, and Laura wouldn't go away despite Ramón's reassurances that everything was fine, Luis decided to take two days off from work to join in the family's annual *Día de Santiago* celebration.

The Séguin family traced their roots back to Galicia, Spain, and, like others in San Bernardino, continued to honor an important Spanish tradition every August 25th. Luis often came to take part in the mass at Saint James Catholic Church in San Bernardino and the two-mile walk to the old churchyard. Then, everyone returned to the ranch for a loud, alcohol-fueled celebration.

After Luis pulled onto the driveway leading to his cousin's ranch, he stopped the car briefly to look around. He'd spent half his summers here as a teen, working under his Uncle Martin's watchful eye. He liked the life and admired his uncle, but his strongest family roots were urban, and the idea of serving a larger purpose appealed to him more than ranching or viticulture.

He continued up the long, dusty road, nervous about spending time with a woman he couldn't seem to let go of, and pulled in next to Ramón's battered pickup. Davie spotted him first.

Luis had barely gotten out of his car when Davis's son barreled into him, wrapping his arms around his leg. "You did come! J.R. promised me you would. Can you stay with us, please? I missed you."

"Just for a day or two. Are you liking ranch life, Dav ...David?" he remembered.

"I am now. Are you going to ride a horse? J.R. says you're the best rider in the family except for his dad. Can I ride with you?"

"Yes, and yes, but I need to talk to Barbara first."

"You mean *Bonnie Sue*. That's her new name. We all have new names, but mine's almost the same. You'll be surprised when you see Laura. She's *Lorenzo* now. That's so we can fool everyone, but you won't be fooled. She's still bossy, old Laura."

When Davie continued to cling, Luis swung him up and settled him on his shoulders. "You're my scout," he told his young admirer. "Can you see *Bonnie Sue* anywhere? Is she hiding in a haystack or maybe in the tackroom under some straw?"

"No, silly, she's in the house, probably the kitchen. She drinks a lot of coffee. Did you know that? Daddy says she has coffee instead of blood in her veins."

Luis couldn't see Davie's suddenly troubled eyes, but he felt the tension in the young boy's body. "I think your dad was right about Barbara," he told Davie in a gentle voice. "Your father was a smart man, Davie."

"I know. Laura and I talk about him every day. Sometimes, I get sad watching J.R. and Lucia with their mom and dad. I guess that's because I miss him so much. I don't really miss my mother because I didn't know her long enough to remember her, but Laura says Daddy gave us a big enough love for both parents."

Davie's next words made Luis bite his lip. "But my daddy's dead, Luis. Who will love us now?"

"Well, I know one person," Luis told the little boy. "I had a visit from your Aunt Monica, and she's worried about you."

Davie's hands, tangled in Luis's hair, trembled. "Laura says she's got enough love to be an aunt but not a mother. I don't think she wants us to live with her."

Luis silently agreed. "Well, we can sort this that out later. I am sure she's anxious to see the two of you safely home. It may be a while, Davie. We have to catch the bad guys first."

"I know," Davie said calmly, "but you will. Barbara—I mean *Bonnie Sue*—says you're like my dad, which means you're a good guy. Maybe you even have superpowers."

His words made Luis laugh. "No superpowers, Davie; that's for sure. I'm more stubborn than anything. I don't quit until I get the job done. Your dad was the same."

When she heard Luis's voice outside the kitchen, Barbara looked up from the huge pile of potatoes she was peeling. The sense of relief washing over her surprised her.

"Does your sudden appearance mean the *all clear* has sounded?" she greeted him, her eyes hopeful. "Can we go home?"

Luis shook his head. "Sorry, no change there. I'm just here to celebrate one of our oldest family traditions." Lifting Davie off his shoulders, he added. "And to see this guy, of course."

He turned to Davis's son. "We'll go for that ride later; I promise. Why don't you go join the other kids now, so I can talk to Bonnie Sue?"

"Okay, I'll be in the barn. We have kittens; they're getting bigger every day, like us. That's what Ramón says."

As Davie ran off, Barbara gave Luis an approving smile. "He likes you a lot. Alicia tells me you have the same kind of magic with children Ramón has. It's a shame you have none of your own."

"Well, that takes having a woman in your life, and my magic doesn't extend quite so far. You know my failings better than anyone."

Barbara laced her fingers through his briefly. "Oh, I don't know; you have your moments."

Alicia chose that moment to enter her domain. "Luis, finally. We need to leave for the church soon. You and Ramón are going on horseback. The rest of us will go by car. I think six or seven of the men are planning to join you two. The other hands will take a Jeep."

"Okay, I think I'll take Davie with me on Ajax. He'll get a kick out of being in a parade."

"Is that safe?" Barbara objected. "I haven't let either one of them leave the ranch."

"It's normal behavior, *Bonnie Sue*," he teased. It would look odd if our visiting cousin and her children stayed behind. Besides, I can keep an eye on him more easily this way. We'll put Laura—Lorenzo," he corrected himself, "and J.R. on a mare Ramón can pony."

Barbara took one last, nervous look at Laura and Davie. It was just the second time she'd left the ranch since her arrival. At first, she felt almost panicky when they rode away, but her fears eased when Alicia joined her.

By the time the Séguin men arrived at the church with Laura and Davie, she'd relaxed enough to be curious about events going on around her. After the mass, she'd join the congregation in the walk to the cemetery while the men rode ahead.

Davis's children were once again out of her sightline again as she walked alongside Alicia. Horses, she quickly learned, move faster than people on foot. She'd have worried more if Luis wasn't with Davis's children. *It's odd*, she mused, *that trust used to be such an issue in our relationship. When it comes to keeping us safe, I don't doubt him at all.*

As soon as everyone returned to the ranch, Luis and Ramón closeted themselves briefly in Ramón's small office. Luis didn't have much to share with his cousin. Everything about the investigation had stalled. However, he'd learned from several different sources that Ackerman recently sent out feelers about Barbara and Davis's children.

The Los Angeles ADIC used the usual police and FBI channels to search for them but didn't stop with that. Luis listened in on taped conversations in which Ackerman encouraged Roberto Rodríguez, who ran *La EME* out of the federal correctional institution in Mendota, and several *Sureño* gang leaders to put the word out that the sociology professor and the two kids with her represented a dangerous loose end. Finding them remained priority one, he told the gang leaders.

"Are they watching you?" Ramón wanted to know.

"No, they sniffed around for a while after Phil and I made our trip to Phoenix, but it didn't last. That's why I felt safe coming here for the holiday, and it isn't anything that should ring the Triad's alarm bells. I come almost every year."

"What's next?"

"We wait for a move, a mistake. It'll happen, but I hate playing defense."

"I don't think Barbara's going to like your news. That woman wants her life back."

"I know, but she wants those kids safe even more. She'll behave."

Ramón laughed abruptly. "She doesn't exactly have a history of minding you from what I heard."

Luis's suddenly narrowed eyes didn't go unnoticed by his cousin. "Don't bother giving me the stink eye; Alicia's the one who wormed your sad history out of Barbara. My wife's a little pissed at you for letting her go."

"Old news, Ramón. Both of us have moved on."

"Maybe, maybe not. In your case, I've got my doubts."

"Let's focus on our real problems. So far, we've been lucky, but luck can change. I want you to keep your eyes and ears open. If anyone, and I mean anyone, no matter how well you know them, starts asking questions about Barbara and the kids, I need to hear about it right away. *La EME* has long tentacles, and people do things for family they might not otherwise consider."

As twilight brought an end to the barbeque, Barbara rounded up Laura and Davie for much-needed baths. When Davie objected, saying he wanted to stay with Luis, Ramón's wife intervened in her calm, no-nonsense way.

"You'll see Luis in the morning, David." Then, she turned to Barbara. "I'll take them upstairs. You and Luis have a lot to talk about."

Luis moved forward and offered his hand to Barbara. "There's still a little light. Let's take a walk. We need to go over a few things." Pulling her to her feet, he pointed to a path leading to the nearby Santa Ana River.

As they walked, Luis gave her basically the same summary he'd given Ramón about the investigation and the hunt for her and Davis's children. That brought him to Monica Reynolds and her surprise visit to his office.

"I'd talked to her a couple of times by phone, so I had some idea of what she's like, but seeing her made it ten times clearer. She's one of those ball-busting female execs they like to make movies about. If you think that's *machismo* talking, you're wrong.

"For starters, Davis's sister thinks you're a kidnapper and probably a murderer to boot. According to her, the FBI isn't doing enough to find you, and she intends to take it up the chain of command and then make sure they throw the book at you."

"Not my biggest fan, huh? I can't blame her, Luis. Look at it from her perspective. Her only brother is dead, his children are missing, and nothing seems to be happening. I'd be pissed, too."

"I'd give her a pass on this, but she's Davie's and Laura's aunt, Barbara, and I don't think she has any intention of making those kids part of her life. Those two have been through a lot and deserve better than an indifferent aunt and aging grandparents. What they need most is lots of love and someone to reassure them they have a place in this world and people they can count on."

"I don't disagree, Luis, but one thing at a time. Right now, I just want this over, and it sounds like that's not going to happen for a while. Classes at USD start in less than three weeks. If I'm not there, they'll hire someone else. I can't let that happen. Teaching there isn't just my job; it's my life."

"I know that better than most, *Bebe*," he said dryly. Then, noticing her discomfort at his use of her nickname, he apologized. "Sorry, it slipped out. The university will probably have to fill your slot temporarily, but I'm pretty sure I can protect your position long-term. The law's on your side, and you can return to teaching as soon as things are settled. Will you trust me on this?"

"Do I have any choice?"

"No, I guess you don't.

"Then, I suppose I'll have to. Should we be heading back? I usually tuck both of them in and read them a story this time of day. They need those kinds of rituals right now."

Luis grinned. "I'm still adjusting to this new image of you as Mother Hen—or is it Goose?" His warm eyes showed his amusement and a certain curiosity.

"This isn't something I chose, Luis. Life forced it on me." She paused, gave him a wry smile, and shook her head. "Actually, that's not true. I'd already fallen in love with them before any of this happened."

"Davis Reynolds was a package deal, I take it."

"I'd made up my mind about him before he told me about his children, but they made him more, not less, attractive."

"He was a good-looking guy and charismatic. I guess I can see what attracted you."

"Neither of those things mattered to me, Luis. Davis was interested in my work on familicide and shared my belief our indigenous citizens deserve better. He was also the kindest man I've ever met. When you add in the fact that he had a wonderful, even surprising, sense of fun, you get some idea of why he appealed to me."

"An improvement on me in every way. I'm sorry you lost him, Barbara. I mean that. The more I learn about Davis, the more I respect him."

"Luis, I didn't see him as an improvement on you or a replacement. You were no longer part of my life, and this was as much your decision as mine. Davis came along and made a place for himself in a surprisingly short time. I'll remember him as a wonderful gift for the brief months I shared my life with him and will always wish we'd been given more time. How about you? Anyone new in your life?"

"No, I'm not ready for romance. I messed things up with you, Barbara, by not keeping my priorities straight. I should have put you first, centered my life around our relationship, but I didn't. Instead, I tried to keep all the balls in the air. Turns out, I bobbled one, the only one that really mattered."

Luis stopped walking and gave Barbara a long, thoughtful look. "In a way, I'm glad life brought you back to me, even if only in a professional way. Seeing you, accepting your relationship with Davis, is making me a better person. That's just one more thing I need to thank you for. You've been a gift to me, *Bebe*, and I'm grateful."

He gave her a gentle hug, kissed her forehead, and turned her toward his cousin's home. He'd done it! He'd put their relationship, the little that remained, on a comfortable track. Barbara had no way of knowing how much seeing her reopened old wounds or that he was dealing rather unsuccessfully with his own grief.

Chapter Fourteen

Before it was fully morning, Luis sensed rather than heard Davie's headlong rush for his bed. Still, the impact of a determined little boy landing on his chest made him cough and then glance at the clock. Five A.M. Davie was an early riser.

"I'm up, I'm awake," he grumbled. "I suppose you're ready for a ride on Ajax."

"No," Davie told him, "I want my own horse."

"That will happen, *chico*—but not today. Ramón will decide when you're ready. His daddy didn't let me ride alone until I'd had my seventh birthday. Uncle Martin was right, even though, like you, I felt ready sooner. Those legs of yours need to grow a bit."

"Okay, I guess. Do we have to have breakfast first?"

Luis thought longingly of coffee but shook his head. "Nope, go get some clothes on. We'll go out the side door and be gone before they miss us."

Taking a trail that looped around the ranch, Luis let Davie settle back against him, his small hands light on the reins. Davis's little boy, excited and talkative at first, began to rest more heavily against Luis as his hold on the reins grew slack. The rhythmic rocking was doing its work. Davie, however, didn't go easily.

"Can't you live here with us?" he asked sleepily. "Ramón won't mind. He likes you, and, besides, you're his cousin."

"I have a job to do, Davie. If I don't find and arrest the bad guys, you'll have to stay here forever, so will Barbara."

"*Bonnie Sue*," the little boy corrected with a yawn, "but Ramón told us to call her *Mamá*. It's part of our pretending. I don't care if we have to stay. I like it here." His voice trailed off, and Luis used his knees to turn Ajax toward the barn.

Ramón was waiting outside the big gelding's stall. He took a sleeping Davie from Luis and headed for the house. "You better fix things with Barbara," his cousin threw over his shoulder. "I'm pretty sure this little guy has decided you're his new dad."

I wish it could be that simple, Luis thought to himself. He sensed Davie's attachment, could even explain it. What he didn't understand was his own feelings for Davis Reynolds' little boy, a pull he'd felt right from the first.

• • • •

Barbara saw Luis only from a distance that morning, his last at the ranch. She'd spotted him leaving the barn on horseback, heading toward a small rise, and felt a flutter of ... something; she wasn't sure what. Alicia gave her a curious glance and said she doubted Luis would be back before noon.

"Luis likes his alone time. That's when he thinks things through. Here comes Ramón with a sound-asleep Davie. The little guy going to need some breakfast and another bath when he wakes up. I'll bet he's pretty stinky." Then, she laughed. "The same might be true for Luis. Davie must have gotten him up at the butt-crack of dawn."

Since Laura had hidden herself away in Ramón's library with a stack of books, Barbara decided to busy herself with lunch preparations. She still didn't feel entirely comfortable in the kitchen, but time on the ranch had improved her skills. It was one of the few things she could do to make herself useful. Not only that, keeping busy helped with her grief.

She was thinking about Davis so intensely that her sudden awareness of a male presence behind her made her gasp and turn—half believing she'd find Davis standing there. The moment she recognized Luis, Barbara burst into tears, adding humiliation to her sudden, overwhelming grief.

Covering her mouth with her hand, Barbara tried to stifle her sobs; she never cried, at least not in front of anyone.

Uncertain what upset her, Luis pulled her into his arms and held her as she wept. "Is this about Davis?" he finally asked her, realizing he had no idea how to comfort her and maybe no right.

"Yes—and Davie and Laura. What's going to happen to them, Luis?"

"I don't know; I wish I did. At least they're safe for the time being with Ramón and Alicia. Unfortunately, they're a little less safe every day. We need to wrap up this investigation, get Stevens to compromise himself some way. That's the last missing piece, which reminds me of something important. I want you to meet me at the barn right after lunch. Wear comfortable clothing."

That *something important* became obvious when Barbara spotted the gun in Luis's hand.

"Luis, no. I don't like guns and know absolutely nothing about them."

"You're going to learn. We'll start today, and Ramón will continue the lessons after I'm gone. This particular weapon is a Glock .40 millimeter, the first one issued to me. It's solid, simple, and reliable. I hope you never need it, Barbara, but I don't want to learn the hard way that you did. Before you say *no*, I want you to remember one thing. You're the last line of defense for Davie and Laura."

Damn, Luis was right. What she'd never do for herself—carry a gun and use it—she wouldn't hesitate to do for Davis's children. She'd promised their father she'd do her best to keep them safe.

"Okay," Barbara agreed reluctantly, "don't laugh at my efforts, and stand where you'll be safe. I make no guarantees."

By the end of her first lesson, Barbara was more comfortable with the weapon, and her shots were getting closer to the target, even hitting it occasionally. Ramón would make sure she improved.

Luis ended their time together with another walk along the river. "Keep your eyes open, Barbara, and make sure Davie and Laura stay close to you or Ramón at all times. I know they like to run free, but it isn't safe."

"Do you know something I don't?"

"Not anything solid, but we know they're looking. Right now, the ranch isn't on their radar, but one chance incident could change that. So, be careful."

He touched her cheek briefly. "I'd tell you not to worry, but hypocrisy is not my style. I'll be worrying right along with you. They're good kids, but it isn't just them; I'd like to think you'll be around to inspire all those future scholars."

"I'll do my best."

"You don't know how to do anything but your best," he teased her. "And your best is pretty damn impressive."

Minutes before Luis left for San Diego, Davis's daughter surprised him by taking his hand and leading him into Ramón's library, closing the door behind her. It was the first time he'd been alone with Laura.

"What is it, sweetheart?" he asked, going down on one knee so they'd be on eye level. "What's worrying you?"

"It's Davie. The only night he hasn't cried himself to sleep since Daddy died was last night. Davie's so little yet, only five, Luis—is it all right if I call you that?"

"Your brother does, so, of course, you can. In fact, I'd like that. Are you afraid he'll cry again tonight because I'm not here?"

"Yes."

"Laura, I have a job to do; I can't stay. And, once things are settled, I won't be part of Davie's life anymore or yours. Barbara will return to her life, too. The people who get to decide what happens to you will do what they think best, and I doubt they'll listen to us. I wish things could be different, but they're not."

"You could adopt us—you and Barbara," she insisted.

"Barbara and I aren't a couple, sweetheart. She loved your Daddy and still does. I know you need a new family, and I'd like nothing more in the world than to give you and Davie that. It just isn't possible."

"Daddy always said all things were possible if you wished hard enough and got off your lazy butt," she added artlessly.

"Maybe he's right, Laura. But, in the meantime, take good care of your brother and mind Barbara and Ramón."

"I will, Alicia, too. Can you come back?"

"Not right away but soon, I hope." He touched her boyishly short, red-blond curls tenderly. "You'll be in my thoughts, Laura. You have your father's strength, his kindness, too. Barbara saw this before I did."

He stood and opened the door to the library, hoping she hadn't seen the sheen of tears in his eyes. To make sure no one else did, he shouldered his overnight bag and walked out to his car.

• • • •

Two weeks passed, and Luis was no closer to putting Stevens on the *definitely dirty* list than he'd been when he started. That meant he had to speak with the chairman, or, in this case, chairwoman, of Barbara's department. They'd need to find someone to take over her classes on a temporary basis.

Dr. Rinzler, chairperson of the University of San Diego's sociology department, was less than cooperative. "I don't see why she couldn't have notified me sooner. It will be almost impossible to find someone at this late date."

"She wasn't, and isn't, allowed to contact you, Dr. Rinzler."

"Is she in a witness protection program?"

"Not yet."

"What does that mean?"

"Technically, she's a fugitive, but the FBI has already established her innocence, and Washington knows where she is. Right now, hiding is the safest thing for her." Luis's half-truths didn't bother him, mostly because they were rooted in reality.

"This is most unusual. Perhaps the simplest and best thing for the university to do is terminate her."

"You'll put yourself in legal peril if you do and risk a lot of bad press. We're talking months here, not years. Just do a temporary hire and clear it with your dean."

When she reluctantly agreed, Luis said a silent prayer of thanks and returned to his office. He'd promised Barbara he'd keep her job safe. Seeing to her personal safety, however, mattered a lot more to him.

After Luis Vallejo left her office, Margaret Rinzler decided she needed something for her files, a letter making Luis's informal request official. She sent her request to the FBI at the San Diego address Luis had given her.

Since Barbara Allen's name was associated with an open case originating in the L A. office, the clerk who received the request forwarded a copy to the Los Angeles ADIC, Robert Ackerman.

Once it landed on his desk with a handwritten request from his secretary asking him how he wanted it handled, Ackerman realized three things: Luis Vallejo had involved himself in Barbara Allen's life in an unorthodox way, and the San Diego-based supervisory special agent almost certainly knew where Barbara Allen and Davis Reynolds' children were hiding. That led directly to a suspicion their escape from FBI custody in Phoenix didn't happen by accident.

What he didn't know was Vallejo's level of involvement. Nor did he have any idea how far up (and down) the FBI's chain of command any investigation of what happened to Allen and Reynolds went. Was Vallejo a loose cannon acting alone or, more likely, with his partner, or had Washington authorized his recent behavior?

Why Vallejo, he wondered. *What is his connection to Davis Reynolds?*

Robert James Ackerman, the Los Angeles ADIC, was a tall, dark-haired man with cold, blue-gray eyes partially obscured by metal-rimmed glasses and an intimidating personality. At fifty-five, he'd reached the goal he'd set on his twenty-fifth birthday—Assistant Director in Charge of a major city. It annoyed him somewhat that he'd wound up in Los Angeles. A Virginian by birth, he preferred the East Coast.

Until Davis Reynolds' death in Manzanillo, a death Ackerman orchestrated, the SAC handling public corruption cases served as Robert's second-in-command, at least on paper. Since Ackerman neither liked nor trusted Davis, he'd relied on John Nader to perform this role in an unofficial capacity.

Although Nader had been in the FBI as long as his boss, he hadn't climbed any higher than special agent. Several accusations of excessive force and an ethics violation guaranteed that. His political fortunes had risen, however, when he was assigned to the L.A. office and caught the eye of his current boss.

Concerned about Luis Vallejo, Ackerman buzzed Nader and suggested they meet at Trotter's, a popular bar just down the street, at 6:30.

"Anyone else?" his subordinate asked.

"No, not yet. I want to run a couple of ideas by you first."

"Shit!" was Nader's first reaction when Ackerman told him about Vallejo's recent visit to the University of San Diego. "We sniffed around him earlier after that Phoenix fiasco but came up empty. You think he has the woman and Reynolds' kids?"

"I'd bet my badge on it. Maybe not in his custody, but he knows where they are. Vallejo's a problem but less of one now that we know about him. I'm more worried about what I don't know. We're in big trouble if he's found that flash drive. I want you to do some digging.

See if you can find any connection between Vallejo and Reynolds and how Barbara Allen figures in all this.

"I don't know Luis Vallejo personally," he continued, "but everything in his file suggests he's a by-the-book, straight-arrow type. Another Reynolds. Maybe they worked together."

"Easy enough to find out. What do you want to do about Vallejo?"

Bob Ackerman shrugged. "Nothing other than keep an eye on him until he leads us to those witnesses and that damn flash drive. I want him monitored electronically twenty-four/seven. Make that Howard's priority. While you take care of all this, I'm going to find out if he's working with Washington or on his own. We don't have a lot of time, John."

"I get that, but I also think Pulaski's going to sit tight until he has everything he needs to make an air-tight case. Our deputy director is as anal as they come. If he had the goods, we wouldn't be sitting here."

"Tropical or mountains?" Nader asked his boss, mostly teasing but also a little curious about where Bob planned to go.

"You'll never know. Invite Howard and Stevens to your cabin this weekend. Let them know about Vallejo's curiosity. I want Rick to monitor him every way he can. Anytime that bastard touches a smartphone, a computer, or anything electronic, I want to know about it. Have Howard sweep your cabin, too—just in case. I don't want any surprises."

Chapter Fifteen

L uis Vallejo wasn't an easy man to track electronically. He seldom used his cell phone, sent out almost no emails, and spent little time in his office, which one of Bob Howard's more questionable P.I. friends had managed to bug over the weekend.

Tailing him proved equally unproductive. He followed his usual routine—the courts, private meetups with snitches and the young men he used as go-betweens when he needed to communicate with local San Diego gang leaders, and meetings with his partner and supervisors.

After two weeks of unproductive surveillance, John Nader decided to pursue a different course. He went over what he knew about the man. One obvious fact stood out for him. Vallejo was Hispanic, and everyone knows how tight family connections are among Latinos.

If Vallejo was hiding Barbara Allen and Davis Reynolds' kids and hadn't put them in witness protection, he'd probably put them with one of his relatives. Certain he'd decided on the best approach, Nader asked Bob Howard to do a simple, online search. "Build a goddamned family tree, and I'll shake it until the professor and those brats fall out."

It didn't take Howard long. Nader started first with Luis's immediate family. His father, Jorge Antonio Vallejo Insula, was a retired financial planner and a man of some importance in the local Hispanic community.

The elder Vallejo's wife, Amparo Séguin de Vallejo, was nothing more than a housewife with maids to oversee. She seemed to do little more than shop, gossip with a few, equally old friends, and visit her children and grandchildren.

An unauthorized search of their house turned up nothing of interest. Professor Allen and the kids weren't there. A few discreet inquiries in the neighborhood led Nader to conclude they'd probably never been hidden there. *Señora* Vallejo had a reputation for being notoriously anti-Anglo.

Luis's siblings, both younger, didn't seem to share their mother's prejudice though both had married within the Latino community. Several days of surveillance showed him Luis hadn't hidden the three with the younger Vallejos, either.

Since Luis's brother and sister both had small children, Nader doubted from the first that the agent would risk hiding Barbara and Davis's children there. That meant he and Howard needed to expand the search.

Bob Howard, the canniest tech guy in the Triad, agreed to focus on the extended Vallejo family. In addition to three uncles and an aunt, he counted some fifteen cousins somewhere in the vicinity. "This could take a while," he grumbled to his colleague, "unless we get lucky."

John Nader glanced at the diagram showing the Séguin side of the family. It was nearly as complex as the one showing the interconnections between the Vallejos. The top boxes contained the names of two brothers and a sister—all still alive and close to their oldest sister, Luis's mother.

He found eleven direct descendants, as well. Most of the family was scattered across southern California with the largest concentration in San Bernardino. *That*, Nader decided, *is where I'll start*.

• • • •

Several of the addresses appeared to be inside the city's limits. Many of the younger generation, however, lived on four different ranches outside San Bernardino. It seemed more likely Luis would choose to hide Barbara Allen and the children on one of those properties.

Although Martín Séguin owned the largest of the Séguin ranches, he no longer lived on the property or took any active role in its management. That fell to his oldest son, Ramón.

The second largest ranch was managed and co-owned by Ramón's cousin, Antonio. A third ranch, just five miles from Antonio's property, was owned by Antonio's father, Melchior Séguin, but managed by a second son, Alejandro.

He located a fourth Séguin ranch over fifty miles from San Bernardino. Nader decided he'd check it out later if he didn't locate Dr. Allen and the children on any of the ranches closer to town. Then, he'd look into the married daughters and their husbands.

Local feed stores near the various Séguin properties should have been fonts of information on the comings and goings of the family since the owners kept close tabs on their neighbors and best customers. Unfortunately, they also clammed up after Nader's second or third question. Personal loyalty trumped nosy newcomer even when the FBI agent reluctantly showed his badge.

It irritated Nader that he had little to show for almost three days of searching. Then, a chance encounter in a small café proved useful. The waitress remembered seeing a woman she didn't recognize with Ramón Séguin's wife in church, but she didn't know about any kids.

As Nader was about to leave the café, Molly, the waitress he'd chatted up, signaled for him to wait. One of Ramón's ranch hands had just entered the restaurant, asking for coffee and pie.

"He'll know about any possible children staying at the ranch," Molly assured the FBI agent. Enrique Solis did. He also remembered Ramón's instructions about anyone asking questions about his guests.

"Nobody there but family," he calmly told the man who said he was an FBI agent. "It's a working ranch in the midst of our busiest season. *Señor* Séguin hasn't got time to be entertaining guests."

"But—" Molly objected.

"No buts, Missy," Enrique told the waitress in his sternest voice. "I live and work on the property. There's nobody there but family." "Immediate family?" Nader challenged. "Ever been around these old families?" the ranch hand snorted. "Everyone's immediate and that's all the answer you're going to get, badge or no badge."

Special Agent Nader left the café with an overwhelming itch to approach Ramón Séguin. He'd do it first thing in the morning and with a warrant if Ackerman decided he needed to get one.

• • • •

Enrique Solis made the trip back to the ranch right after he left the café, abandoning the errand that brought him to town. *Señor* Séguin would want to know about the FBI agent right away.

Why are the Anglo woman and her two boys any of the FBI's concern? he wondered. *Are they looking for Ramón's cousin?*

"Did the man give you a name, Enrique?" Ramón wanted to know.

"I reckon he did, but damned if I can remember it. Unless I misread him, you'll be hearing it soon enough, probably tomorrow. You going to get that pretty little lady and her two boys out of here?"

"I think I'd better. It might not be my cousin or one of his equally crazy friends, but I can't think of a single reason the FBI would get involved in something like this. It's awfully easy to buy a fake badge online these days, so I'm not taking any chances. Thanks, Enrique. Your paycheck is now a little fatter."

"That's not why I did it," Ramón's longtime employee objected.

Ramón gave him one of his rare smiles. "I know that, but it's one more way of saying *gracias*."

Luis's cousin used the time it took to walk from the equipment shed to his house to think about relocating Barbara and the two children she was determined to protect. If the FBI or whoever was looking had decided to focus on Luis's family, passing her and the children off to one of his siblings or cousins didn't seem like a good idea.

Then, he thought about Felipe, his wife's former brother-in-law. The connection was there but tenuous—several name changes away from Séguin. And Felipe had a small cabin tucked away on Big Bear Lake. This might be the best place to take Barbara and the children. On the other hand, the cabin was fairly isolated, and he saw Barbara as an urban creature. She might not be comfortable in wilderness country.

It didn't matter; this needed to be a short-term solution with Luis responsible for making the next move. He'd let his cousin know about the bogus or real FBI agent nosing around and tell him where he'd hidden Barbara as soon as he took them to safety and returned to the ranch.

"Clean your boots; I just mopped the floor" greeted him as he walked through the kitchen door. After following his wife's grumpy command, Ramón kissed the top of her head and let his hand curve around one cheek of her fanny. "Anything for you, *mi amor*," he whispered huskily. Then, his face took on a worried look. "Where are Barbara and the children?"

"In the library. She insists they read or do puzzles this time of day. No lazy brains on her watch. J.R. and Lucia are in there, too."

"We need to get her out of here; the FBI or someone else maybe even worse is snooping around the area. I'm pretty sure they'll show up here tomorrow. I think I'll take Barbara and the kids to Felipe's cabin. I doubt an FBI search, or any other kind, would turn up such a remote connection. I hope to God I'm right."

"For how long?" Alicia asked, and Ramón saw the concern in her eyes.

"Until Luis finds another place to hide her. They can't come back here."

"Ever?"

Ramón shook his head. "Not until everything's settled, and I doubt Luis or Barbara will have any connection with Reynolds' children by then. Would you go up and help Barbara pack? I want to be out of here in less than thirty minutes."

• • • •

The four of them were on the road less than twenty minutes later after one, short holdup. Davie insisted on going back for his bear, which Barbara had forgotten to pack. She had, Barbara reassured Laura, remembered the book the little girl left in the library, the book Laura was reading the day her father died.

The rush out the door made long goodbyes impossible, which proved to be easier on everyone. Although it was less than forty miles to the cabin via CA330-N, the winding, hilly road made speeding impossible. Ramón used the time to fill Barbara in on the details of Enrique's encounter with the FBI agent.

"There's no way of knowing if it was Ackerman or one of his *compadres* or a legitimate agent just doing his job. In either case, it doesn't matter, Barbara. You need to stay hidden."

"I know. Does this cabin have electricity?" she asked hopefully.

Ramón gave her an evil grin. "It doesn't even have a bathroom—inside, anyway. The stove's a wood burner, and there's a couple of kerosene lamps. Think of it as an adventure. I'll give you a couple of quick lessons before I leave."

"How long will we be there?"

"Until Luis can make better arrangements. It isn't a place you can stay for more than a week or two. It's too isolated. We'll stop and get groceries on the way, but anything you need after that will mean a hike of nearly five miles."

Barbara gave him a mischievous smile. "Maybe we should stay a little longer. I can walk off some of those pounds your wife's cooking added."

Ramón's eyes traveled lazily over her trim frame. "No harm done," he assured her.

• • • •

The cabin was little more than a wooden shack. While it would keep out the rain and its only door had a lock that bolted, no one in their right mind could call it secure.

Luis needs to come sooner rather than later, Ramón decided. Even with a gun she now knew how to handle, Barbara would never be able to defend herself or Reynolds' children from the kind of men hunting her.

They went over the basics of managing the cabin while Laura and Davie explored the area outside. Both children cast longing looks at the lake less than 200 yards from the cabin but knew they couldn't go that far away on their own. Barbara would simply scold, but Ramón might spank.

Davis's children had no way of knowing Luis's cousin was all bark and no bite. Those stern eyes and commanding voice made prudence the better choice. He'd always relied on the same technique with his own children.

Before leaving, he took pity on Laura and Davie, walking them down to the lake for a quick wading adventure that included tiny minnows nibbling on their toes and the sudden sight of a box turtle appearing in front of them. *This place is even better than the ranch*, the two children decided separately. Davie grinned at his sister. "I like it here even if Barbara seems worried, Uncle Ramón, too."

Ramón's last act before he left was handing Barbara a cellphone, one of a cache he'd purchased earlier, with instructions to call him, and no one else, if she had an emergency of some kind.

"The best communication is no communication," he warned her. "I know that living without internet and other instant connection to the outside world isn't easy, but doing without it makes you safer."

"We'll be fine. Give Luis the number. Then, I'll know it can only be one of two people if the phone rings and both are my heroes." She gave him a peck on his cheek that made him blush.

"Cellphone service is spotty here," he warned her. "Leave the phone off to preserve the battery and walk up the hill once or twice a day to check for messages. It might not work at the cabin."

"We'll be fine," she reassured Ramón once again, "if I don't manage to burn down the cabin cooking our breakfast."

•   •   •   •

Brave words, Barbara, she mocked herself after Ramón left. Being abandoned in the woods with the overwhelming responsibility of keeping Davis's kids safe terrified her. In the daylight, strange sounds seemed manageable. In the dark, she knew it would be an entirely different story.

I wish Luis was here. I bet he knows everything about living like this, Barbara couldn't help grumbling. It wasn't just his knowledge she craved or even the certainty that he'd protect her and the children. It was the comfort of a warm, male presence she'd miss most.

Ramón called his cousin the moment he returned to his ranch, catching him at a bad moment. Luis was standing over the body of one his more reliable sources, a small-time dealer named Benny Gonzales. San Diego Homicide Detective Ramsey Ellerson had contacted him after talking to Benny's wife.

More angry than grieving, Rosa Gonzales wanted justice for her husband and a little money from Luis. "Just to tide me over," she told him. Then, she planned to return to Sonora with their two kids. It wasn't safe in the U.S. these days.

"You're sure no one followed you?" was Luis's first question to Ramón.

"Yeah, I'm sure. I didn't spot a single car on the road after we reached County Road 18. It's pretty lonely country. I think you should get her out of there as soon as possible. She isn't the self-reliant type."

Luis snorted. "You don't know her like I do. Barbara might hate every minute she's there, but she'll cope fine. I've only been to Felipe's cabin once, but it's in a gorgeous area. The kids will love it."

"Water, rocks, and dirt—what else do *chicos* need?" Ramón laughed. "But I think Barbara's tastes run more to hot water, electricity, and modern communication."

"She'll be a good sport, but I don't like the area's isolation, and I like the possibility that the FBI is poking around even less. Was it Ackerman's doing or someone out of a different office."

"I have no idea, Luis. If I get a visit tomorrow, I'll catch the name and pass it on to you. It almost doesn't matter. She can't be found by anyone."

"It matters; I'd rather see her arrested than killed. Christ, what a mess and Davie and Laura right in the middle of it."

"They're making the best of it, and both of them trust Barbara to keep them safe. I almost hate to see this case resolved. Those two little ones have no place to go from what Davie tells me."

"We'll see about that," Luis growled. "I think Davis's sister will consider any solution that protects her reputation and doesn't involve her having to take them under her wing."

Chapter Sixteen

Since darkness fell quickly after Ramón left, Barbara lit two kerosene lamps and settled both Laura and Davie on the rather ratty-looking sofa, hoping no mice had made a home for themselves in the cushions.

"You can read to Davie while I cook," she told Laura.

"Pick the one about Matthew Pepper and his talking dog," Davie insisted, which made Laura groaned theatrically. Davie always chose this story.

While Laura hunted for the pages he wanted, Davie turned his attention to Barbara. "What are you cooking for dinner?" Food was always uppermost on Davis's son's mind.

"Spaghetti and salad," she told him, then added: "We'll eat the salad as a first course."

Barbara had long since learned that Davie wouldn't eat more than a bite or two of vegetables if heartier fare was available.

"Okay," he said unenthusiastically, "don't put any onions in it."

"Or garlic," Laura added, "I'm allergic."

Barbara ignored their instructions since she'd spent enough time cooking for them to know the difference between their preferences and their allergies, which were nonexistent, according to Davis. Instead, she pulverized the onion and garlic, adding olive oil, parsley, and a small amount of tarragon to disguise the odor and taste.

As soon as the dishes were done, both children wanted to explore the cabin's loft, where they'd sleep tonight. Barbara let them bounce on the mattresses spread across the loft's floor for a few minutes then covered two of the mattresses with the clean sheets Ramón had pulled out of a small closet.

"I'll sleep on the small bed downstairs," she told them.

With little to do, they all agreed on an early bedtime. Barbara grabbled the flashlight sitting on the counter and marched them out to the small shack serving as a bathroom. "Get your business done now; we don't want to encounter a bear or bobcat in the middle of the night," she instructed them.

"There's bears here? Cool," Davie enthused.

Once back inside the cabin, Barbara bolted the cabin door, had the two children wash their face and hands, helped them climb the ladder to the loft, and kissed them good night.

Laura grabbed her hand as Barbara turned to head down the ladder. "We'll be safe here?" she whispered.

Although tempted to reassure her, Barbara wouldn't lie to Davis's daughter. "I don't know, sweetheart, but I think we'll be safe for a little while, and I don't think we'll be here all that long."

"Did you bring your gun?"

"Yes, I did. It's loaded, Laura, because it has to be. I don't want you or Davie going anywhere near it. It's my most important rule."

"We won't. Daddy was strict about that, too. I don't like them much—guns. If I could make the rules, there wouldn't be any."

"I feel the same way, Laura."

Davis's daughter wouldn't let go of her hand. "Barbara, I don't want to live with Aunt Monica. Can't we stay with you? I'll take care of Davie; we won't be much trouble, honest."

"You're no trouble, sweetheart. I'd keep you with me forever if I could. But it won't be up to me. Your grandparents, Aunt Monica, and probably some judges and lawyers will decide where you're going to live. I'll try to get custody, but I can't promise."

"You really will try?" Laura asked.

"As hard as I can; I can't imagine living my life without you and Davie. Your daddy wanted us to be a family. I do, too." She kissed Laura's forehead again and reached over to pat Davie's thigh.

Once she climbed down the ladder, made up her bed, and turned down the kerosene lamp, Barbara thought about what she'd just said. She meant every word of it.

Davie and Laura needed her, deserved to live with someone who loved them, had loved their father. *Too bad, the courts won't care about either of those things* was her last thought before succumbing to sleep.

• • • •

Warrant in hand, John Nader strode up to the barn, wondering which of the men standing there was Ramón Séguin—if any of them. "I'm FBI Special Agent John Nader, and I'm looking for the owner of this ranch."

"I'm Ramón Séguin," a tall, middle-aged man said. "What can I do to help you?"

"I have a warrant to search your property."

"For what?" Séguin asked.

"It's not a what but a who," John Nader answered. "We're looking for a woman, an Anglo woman, and two children."

"Plenty of those in California. I take it you're looking for my cousin Miguel's wife and kids. Why?" Ramón's face showed his confusion and a hint of suspicion. "They're not here anymore. I heard someone was nosing around and sent them away. Enrique told me yesterday you're FBI though I've yet to see a badge. What would you want with Bonnie Sue?"

"Who's Bonnie Sue? I'm looking for Dr. Barbara Allen and two children, a boy and a girl, belonging to one of our agents. When he was killed in Mexico, Barbara Allen kidnapped his children. If you're mixed up in this, you're in big trouble."

Ramón shook his head. "If you really are with the FBI, someone in your office screwed up colossally. Bonnie Sue has two boys—Lorenzo and David, and she's never been to Mexico. She's just scared spitless because her husband's bat-shit crazy. That's why she was hiding out with us."

"Where is she now?"

"I honestly don't know. We thought it would be safer that way. I took her to the bus station last night, but I didn't go in with her, so I've no idea which bus she took or for what part of the country."

"And I should believe you because ...?" Nader all but growled.

"You don't need to believe me, not that I give a shit. Call the Hays County sheriff in Texas. He'll tell you about Miguel's battle with PTSD and the restraining order Bonnie Sue filed. Call my cousin's dad in Austin; you'll hear substantially the same thing. Hell, if you can find him, ask Miguel himself."

"I still want to look around."

"Go ahead, but I'm telling you straight up they're not here."

Less than twenty minutes later, Nader pulled out of the ranch's long driveway and headed back to San Bernardino. He'd check out Séguin's story, but why would the man lie and then give him a story so easy to check on?

Not only did Séguin have small children to protect, but several employees confirmed the rancher's insistence that the children were both boys. It looked like a dead end, but Barbara Allen was still out there somewhere.

• • • •

"Aw, do I have to take a nap? I'd rather stay here and play in the water some more. Maybe we can catch another fish in the pail."

Davie's woeful tone would melt a harder heart than Barbara's, but she knew the cranky pants lurking inside an overtired Davis Reynolds, III.

"We'll come back here later this afternoon," she assured him. "Then, I'll make you and Laura bug sandwiches for dinner."

"You mean *big*, not *bug*," Laura corrected.

"Nope, I mean *bug*—the wiggly, squiggly kind."

"For reals?" Davie asked, his eyes huge.

"I won't be joining you for dinner," Laura said primly. "I'm not hungry, so I'll just have a glass of milk."

Barbara laughed and pulled on one of Laura's short curls. "No sillies, they're just hamburger patties I shape and decorate like bugs for the fun of it—very creepy but delicious." Then, she gave them a stern look. "If you two don't stop eating up everything in the icebox, however, it may come to that."

"Ramón said we could always hike back to the store," Laura reminded Barbara.

"It's nearly five miles, sweetheart, and I doubt Davie's little legs can cover that kind of distance. We're talking ten miles up and back."

"I'm going to be as tall as my dad, and I'll have very long legs," Davie informed her in a disapproving tone.

"I'm sure you will," Barbara responded, her eyes amused. "You are your dad's son in every way, so you're going to be tall and gorgeous, but you've got some growing to do first. Let's make our groceries last as long as we can. I suppose you'd like some Kraft's mac and cheese with those hamburgers."

"Yes, please," they echoed each other though Davie's voice was more enthusiastic.

"Deal, but now, I want *you*," she pointed to Davie, "to take a nap. Laura can read for a little bit while I gather a few berries I found close to the cabin. If I find enough of them, I'll make berry shortcakes tonight."

• • • •

Their days at the cabin had a sameness and simplicity that should have made Barbara restless but didn't. The seclusion bothering her at first now seemed reassuring.

She hadn't heard anything from either Luis or Ramón though she checked the cellphone regularly. She never saw any messages, but she knew the signal strength from a nearby hill was good.

Barbara chose to interpret their silence as good news. Soon, however, the phone's battery would die. That worried her. Maybe she could recharge it at the store.

The three of them explored the area around the cabin thoroughly, coming across animal tracks Barbara didn't recognize. The width of the tracks, however, suggested the animals approximated the size of big dogs. Barbara hoped the animals, whatever they might be, were friendly.

When they stumbled onto a small cave that showed no signs of occupation, Barbara designated it a safe zone. If someone showed up at the cabin while the children played outside, they were to run into the bushes and then hide here. She'd come for them when the danger passed.

"What if you don't come?" worrywart Laura wanted to know.

"Then, follow the road to the store and ask for help," she told them. "If you hear a car coming, hide in the bushes along the road until it's gone. Right now, we can't trust anyone."

To keep Laura and Davie occupied, Barbara insisted they help her with chores, even the icky ones like servicing the outhouse. She also sat them down after lunch every day to do lessons of some kind, everything from geography to arithmetic. Then, they went outside for some hands-on work in geology or biology. Their favorite time, however, was spent in or near the lake.

When they'd been there for almost a week, Barbara decided they had to make the long trip to the small store catering to campers and local cabin owners. This presented a problem.

Davie wasn't up to a trip both ways the same day; Laura might find it too taxing, as well. Although Barbara could manage it easily enough, she didn't dare leave them behind for almost a whole day—so what was the answer?

I'll worry about it tomorrow, she decided. Maybe Luis or Ramón would come for them by then. If not, she'd probably hike to one of the nearby cabins. If the owners were there, she'd ask for help getting groceries. If the cabin appeared vacant, she'd break in and help herself to whatever she could find. Ramón could make things right later.

One more road down the path to jail, she chided herself, but what choice did she have? Davie's and Laura's needs came first.

· · · ·

It took two extra stories to get her overly tired children settled that night. The full moon filled their small cabin with an eerie light that seemed to make Davis's children restless.

Barbara noticed more animal sounds, as well. She wondered if she, too, would find it hard to sleep with bright moonlight coming through the cabin window and the animals outside the cabin all stirred up.

The silence from the loft told her the kids had surrendered to sleep. Within minutes, she'd turned down the kerosene lamp and relaxed into a lazy kind of pre-sleep, aware of things but comfortably unconcerned. The last thing she noticed was the soft hoot of an owl as a shadow passed across the kitchen window, blocking the moon's light.

A shadow! Barbara came instantly awake. The only things she could think of tall enough to cast a shadow at that height were a bear on its hindlegs or a man. This couldn't be good. She needed to get her gun. Slipping out of the small bed, she padded noiselessly across the cabin floor toward the drawer where she'd stored Luis's Glock.

Turning at a small sound she didn't recognize at first, Barbara watched the cabin's door handle jiggle back and forth. Not a bear, then. The bolt held, however, and that small noise ceased. Gun in hand, she waited anxiously, trying to keep an eye on both the door and the kitchen window.

A soft knock on the cabin door startled her. It occurred to her that the person trying to get in might be Ramón or Luis. While she debated whether or not to ask who was there, she heard someone cough.

"Damn night air isn't good for anyone," an unfamiliar voice grumbled as Barbara's fears escalated. "Don't be scared," the voice said. "Luis sent me—says it's time for you and the young 'uns to go."

"How do I know you telling the truth?" Barbara challenged. "I'm not opening the door until I'm satisfied it's safe, and I have a gun."

"I know that, ma'am, Luis's old Glock. He told me he'd given it to you but said you couldn't shoot worth a damn. That's why I'm still outside. I don't relish getting shot. It hurts just as bad whether it's on purpose or accidently.

He coughed again. "If it's all the same to you, I'd like to get the hell out of this damp. Luis gave me a word, said you'd know he sent me. I feel like a damn fool saying it, but he told me to call you *Baby*."

Relieved but a little embarrassed, Barbara threw back the bolt and opened the cabin door. No one could know about Luis's private name for her unless he shared it. Motioning the stranger in, she lit one of the lamps, keeping the flame low.

The man facing her was probably in his early seventies with wise eyes and a full head of white hair. He seemed more amused than anything, but a remnant of authority hinted at his past.

"You worked with Luis," she guessed.

"Trained him, actually," the man admitted. "Name's Jim Corelle. "Hear you got yourself in a speck of trouble. The kids in the loft?"

"Yes. Why did Luis send you, Mr. Corelle? No offense but I'm sure you must be retired by now."

"You'd have to ask him; I sure as hell didn't volunteer. I'm guessing I had two things he wanted—a plane for a quick getaway and a safe place to put you and the kids."

Barbara gave him a measuring look and then smiled. "I think there's a third thing you're overlooking. He obviously trusts you. Will you help me, Mr. Corelle? Will you keep Laura and Davie safely hidden until Luis figures all this out?"

"That I will, but I wish you'd call me *Jim*. Don't much care for the *Mister* business, and I left *Special Agent* behind years ago. You're Barbara, he tells me. Let's get the kids up and packed. If you don't mind, we'll spend a few hours at a hotel somewhere before we head for the airport. A flight leaving during daylight hours attracts less attention at a small airport. I suppose we could stay here, but it's safer to leave the area if anyone's on to you.

"You own an airplane?"

"I do, a 182 Cessna Skylane, best four-seater ever built."

"Where are we going?"

"If I told you, I'd have to shoot you." Looking at her startled expression, Jim Corelle laughed gustily. "Castle Rock, Colorado. I own a small trailer park there. It'll be your new home for a while."

Chapter Seventeen

In the morning, they left the motel outside Big Bear Lake Village, where they'd spent the rest of the night, and headed for a nearby airport. Twenty minutes later, they were airborne and on their way to another small airport—this one at Reed Hollow Ranch in Douglas County, Colorado. Once they landed, the former FBI agent pointed to a battered Jeep.

The first thing on everyone's agenda was lunch. They'd landed well past noon, and Davie kept complaining about starving. Jim Corelle chose a small Mexican restaurant near Franktown and greeted the owner by name.

"*Hola*, Ricardo, I'd like you to meet my niece, Cindy, and her two young 'uns—Chrissy and Douglas. They'll be staying with me for a while."

"You'll be welcome," Ricardo said politely. "Your usual?" he asked his friend.

"Yup, but you can bring menus for Cindy and the kids. Double the portions for this little guy. He's way past hungry. Start them off with a little *horchata*."

Jim had briefed the three of them on their new names and backstories on the flight over. *Cindy*, newly divorced, was his brother's youngest daughter. She'd been living in Las Vegas but wanted something better, more grounded in traditional values, for her children.

The short drive from Franktown to the small trailer park Jim owned was silent. Davie had fallen asleep almost immediately after polishing off his lunch, and Laura busied herself taking in the local scenery.

Barbara focused on the fact that they'd had to relocated three times in less than two months. It wasn't simply a matter of worrying about her safety and the children's; she missed her old life and wondered if she'd ever set foot on the University of San Diego's campus again.

Jim finally broke the silence. "The mobile home you'll be using is pretty new—three bedroom, two baths. It should be comfortable enough even though the rooms are a little small. You can use my Jeep when you want to shop for groceries and other necessities. I'd stick close to home as much as you can—just to be on the safe side."

Thinking the children needed friends their own age, Barbara asked about putting Laura and Davie in school. Castle Rock was a long way from California, and no one had any idea where she'd gone.

"Not a good idea," Jim warned her. "Without school records, the school board won't admit them. If you'd gone into witness protection, the marshals would provide them but you're not. You're safer homeschooling them. Say it's for religious reasons. That's fairly common here."

Davie woke up when they pulled into Jim's carport, announcing he had to pee. "Your new home is right across the street, the tan-colored one," the former agent told them. "I'll go get the key. It's furnished right down to pots and pans."

He looked at the small duffle bags they'd brought with them. "I'd recommend a run to Target in the next day or two for some more clothes."

"No money," Barbara objected, "I can't even buy groceries."

"Luis already took care of that. To make it easier for you, I'll get some prepaid credit cards you can use. Cash is good, too. Don't skimp. My former partner can afford it."

"Will he get reimbursed?"

Jim snorted. "Well, maybe someday if pigs take up flying. Doesn't matter. I take it this is personal with him."

Seeing Barbara's unhappy face, Jim put a gnarled hand on her shoulder. "It won't be forever, Dr. Allen, just until the investigation wraps up and the trial is over."

"That could be months."

"Might go another six or eight," he agreed, or it could break much faster with confessions that guarantee a speedy trial. Since you're kind of stuck, you might as well use your time here to help those kids heal. Right now, you're about the best medicine I can think of."

Davie and Laura spent the next half-hour checking out their new home, arguing over who got the bigger bedroom and which living room chair each wanted to claim. Barbara settled the issue by putting Laura's meager belongings in the larger of the two bedrooms on the kitchen side of their trailer and Davie's in the other. Seniority had its privileges.

Food would be their first priority, and Jim knocked on their door just as Barbara was wondering how to make a dinner with bare cupboards.

"Ready to do a little shopping? There's a King Sooper's not too far from here." He looked Barbara over. "You do cook?"

"Enough to keep us from starving, but I'm no Martha Stewart. Keep an eye on Davie while we shop. Junk food's his favorite."

Two hours later, they returned to Jim's trailer park, the jeep completely filled with basic kitchen supplies, fresh food, and everything Barbara needed to stock her pantry. To Davie's disgust, almost everything was healthy.

While Barbara put away their groceries, Laura and Davie turned on the television and surfed the channels. Life here, she realized, where they were confined mostly to a smallish mobile home, would be very different from what Davie and Laura experienced at the ranch or the small cabin they'd hidden in briefly.

If she wasn't careful, Davis's children would spend far too much time in front of the television or playing games on the old computer sitting on the kitchen counter. She didn't want that.

Several days later, one of her neighbors, a tall Mexican-American man in his early thirties, noticed the pretty woman with two, bored children and offered some advice. Her children needed to find some friends their own age.

Jesús Mendoza Galán ran a small afterschool program in a nearby church. He'd be happy to take Chrissy and Douglas with him, watch over them, and return them safe and sound Monday through Friday. "They'll enjoy being with other children, Cindy—that's your name, isn't it?"

He knew from Jim the woman's religious convictions encouraged homeschooling, but too much protection from society led to isolation, which wasn't a good thing.

"Jim told me a little bit about you, just a little," he reassured her when he saw the alarm in her eyes. "I think you made a wise choice, coming here to Castle Rock. And your uncle's a good man. He'll help you get a fresh start."

"Why did you ask him about me?" Barbara challenged him and relaxed her guard a bit when she saw Jesús blush and look down.

"Mostly curiosity," he told her. "You don't look like you belong here. I mean that in a good way. I know something about starting over, so if I can help in any way, I'd consider it an honor." He blushed again. "No hidden agenda, I promise. I think Jim will vouch for me. I've known him almost five years."

"I'll think about it, *Señor* Mendoza, and I appreciate your concern."

Jesús gave her a look of surprise. "You know something of my culture. Most people would call me Mr. Galán."

"A little. I lived in Tucson for a while and studied Spanish in school. Most of it didn't stick, but I remember some things." Barbara held Jesús's gaze longer than was polite in either culture, measuring him. "Actually, I don't have to think about it. I think your program would be good for Chrissy and Doug, and I wouldn't mind a few hours to myself."

Jesús's smile, broad and genuine, made his thin face almost attractive. "Why don't I come over after dinner and ask them if they'd like to visit my program? You're welcome to visit, too."

After asking for and getting Jim's okay and accompanying Laura and Davie once to check things out, Barbara sent Davis's children off with Jesús every day. She was certain she'd relish the time alone; instead, she began to spend most of it talking to Jim Corelle.

She found him an interesting man. He'd joined the FBI in his late twenties, worked all over the United States, and retired when he turned sixty-seven.

His last stint as a supervisory special agent brought him to San Diego and a rookie agent named Luis Vallejo Séguin. "He's the best I ever worked with, smart, dedicated, and quick on his feet."

"What does that mean—quick on his feet?"

"Luis excelled at undercover work. It's the most challenging job at Justice; things can go wrong a dozen different ways. The quicker you react, the longer you stay alive. But it isn't just that. Luis has a feel for people, can sense which guy he can flip and which one he shouldn't turn his back on."

"How long were you partners?"

"Almost five years. I think I would have hung on longer, but Phil Reed came along. He wanted to partner with Luis in the worst way. That man had a serious case of hero worship. Luis was ready to mentor and more than ready to move up to supervisory special agent. About that time, my sister died and left me this trailer park. I decided to simplify my life."

"Any regrets?"

"Life's full of them, but nothing keeping me up at night."

"Luis must respect you as well as trust you if he asked you to watch over Laura and Davie—Davie, especially."

"I think they were add-ons," Jim said dryly. "Luis didn't say anything personal about you, but I sensed something in what he didn't say. You and my ex-partner have a history?"

"We do. Unfortunately, our approaches to life are very different, and we couldn't make things work. I began a relationship with Davis Reynolds, which brought Laura and Davie into my life. Someone in one cartel or another had Davis killed, and here we are."

Jim Corelle's eyes hardened. "Luis gave me a heads up. It isn't just the cartels after you. The Mexican Mafia and their affiliated gangs have also been sniffing around. And he tells me some dirty agents in L.A. are hunting, too. Distance helps, Barbara, but not as much as you'd like to think. We can't make any mistakes. Every one of these groups can cast a wide net."

"But I have Luis and you."

Jim laughed. "Yeah, that definitely tilts the odds in your favor."

• • • •

Supervisory Special Agent Luis Vallejo was having a bad day; they'd all been bad lately. He'd been able to piece a few things together in the last week from the tapped offices and phone lines of Ackerman, Howard, and Nader, but there were no game-changers.

Ackerman was too smart for that. All of them used burner phones and discussed serious business outside their offices. Who didn't these tech-savvy days?

Deputy Director Pulaski wanted to know why Ackerman hadn't taken the money, which the FBI accounting task force discovered but left untouched, and run when he almost certainly knew Washington had at least started an investigation. Luis drew a blank.

Both men suspected Ackerman knew Davis Reynolds wasn't the type of agent to go Lone Ranger. That meant he also knew those at the top planned to comb the bushes, looking for evidence against him.

Luis needed to wrap things up. Pulaski wanted firm evidence either clearing Stevens or confirming his guilt. He wanted the same thing.

Unfortunately, wanting and getting aren't identical. Until something broke or someone made a mistake, the investigation was on pause. Luis decided he'd be more useful focusing on his obligations to the San Diego office. An uptick in gang activity in City Heights had Phil preoccupied and overworked.

A telephone call from the warden at Lompoc caught Luis by surprise. A high-profile prisoner, one of *La EME*'s top lieutenants, had gotten into a scuffle with a fellow prisoner earlier in the week, knifing him and one of the guards who tried to break up the fight. It was his third strike, and the head of Lompoc Prison wanted him gone.

Warden Hirschberger had arranged a transfer for Chuey Corrales to ADX Florence, a supermax prison in southern Colorado, where he'd do solitary 22 hours a day. The warden wanted Luis to accompany the transfer team.

"Chuey Corrales," Luis laughed, "now, there's a name that brings back memories. I busted him, you know, over four years ago. He wasn't happy with me then, and I doubt he'll enjoy catching up with me."

"He's a slippery son of a bitch, Vallejo. You know this *La EME* bunch better than anyone. We'll use a couple of air marshals and regular Federal Bureau of Prisons transportation staff, but I'd like you to ride along and brief Max Schneider personally."

"When's the transfer?"

"A week from Tuesday. He'll go by van to LAX. You can meet the plane there. We'll arrange for a commercial flight back to San Diego or L.A., your choice."

On the way home to his small apartment in Torrey Park, Luis thought about his upcoming trip to Colorado. He'd been careful to avoid any kind of contact with Barbara or Jim to keep them safe, but this felt like too good an opportunity to pass up.

He'd noticed a tail from time to time but doubted Ackerman had him followed 24/7. The L.A. ADIC didn't have the resources. Most of the surveillance had to be electronic. Luis swept his car twice a day but hadn't found a tracker. They probably used his phone.

He patted one of his favorite devices, a small flip phone he'd "borrowed" from an old evidence file, one with no GPS. It was his *go to* when he didn't want to be followed. To confuse Ackerman and his cronies, Luis often had Phil carry his "official" phone as his partner went about his duties—just two agents doing their job.

Although he'd be careful and keep his visit short, Luis decided to make a short side trip to Castle Rock. Even if someone from the L.A. office followed him, a visit to his old partner wouldn't seem unusual.

Thinking about Davie's excitement at seeing him made Luis smile, and Luis knew he'd be excited. He had no idea why he'd been drawn to Davis Reynolds' little boy, but the bond was real and mutual.

That brought his thinking to both Laura and Barbara. *I stand a better chance at building a relationship with Davie's sister than I do with Barbara,* he admitted to himself. Still, he couldn't help hoping his former lover would be at least a little glad to see him.

Chapter Eighteen

Luis watched Chuey Corrales's eyes narrow as he spotted him board the small jet that would take them to the airport in Colorado Springs. "Miss me?" Luis couldn't resist taunting the man who'd come close to killing his partner.

At first, the *La EME* lieutenant didn't respond; then, he growled: "Who the hell thought we needed you on this flight?"

"I'm bringing your report card and some sage advice to your new warden. Your days as a player are over, Chuey. They'll record everything you say and examine every orifice every day. This place will make Lompoc look like a country club. You're going to get downright homesick for your old prison."

"You wish. Watch your back, Vallejo. You've managed to piss off some pretty important people."

"And how would you know?"

"Word gets around. I got nothing more to say to you." Contradicting what he'd just said, Corrales added. "Some of my homies think you walk on water as Feds go; I know better. Don't matter anyway. If I put out the word, you'll be dead. Shit, your own mother might take the contract. I hear you're messing around outside *La Raza*."

Luis simply smiled and settled in for the flight. In a few hours, he'd be seeing Barbara and the children, thanks to Chuey Corrales.

• • • •

Barbara watched Jesús bundle Laura and Davie into his car for the short ride to the Baptist church. He tested their seat buckles, smiled, and gave them a thumbs up. At first, it struck her as strange a Hispanic male would run an afterschool program. Just thinking

153

about Luis doing something like that tickled her. Then, she chided herself.

She was showing a stupid prejudice—actually, several of them. Jesús, though he'd never said a word about his past, was a man in some kind of recovery. Her professional training taught her that. If he found the work therapeutic and did it well, who was she to argue?

When she mentioned her curiosity to Jim, he gave her a steely look. "Jesús is a good man, Barbara. After a couple of false starts, he's put together a life that suits him. The school isn't his day job, you know. What they pay him would barely cover his rent here. He's an artist, a damned good one."

They went their separate ways then, each a little uncomfortable with the other. Jim had some errands to run, and Barbara wanted to do a little online research. Maybe she'd Google Jesús's name to see what kind of art he did.

She'd just opened up her laptop when a knock at her front door interrupted her. With Jesús and Jim gone, she couldn't think of anyone who'd come to her trailer. After a brief hesitation, she went to the drawer where she kept her gun and took it with her to the door.

"Luis!"

His eyes brimming with amusement, Luis leaned against her front doorjamb. "Since I'm in the neighborhood, I thought I'd drop by. I checked at Jim's place first, but he isn't home. The guy next door told me where you lived."

He reached out and took her hand holding the gun behind her back. "That's a rookie's trick, but I'm glad you're being careful. Where are Davie and Laura?"

"They're in a local afterschool program run by one of my neighbors. Jim was okay with it. Why are you here, Luis? What's changed?"

"Not much, actually. I'm supervising a prison transfer from Lompoc to Florence. Since it's so close, I thought I'd see how you're doing."

"When's your flight back to California?"

"A little after nine tomorrow morning. I'll bunk with Jim tonight. Would it be too rude to invite myself to dinner? I remember Jim's cooking."

Barbara laughed. "He usually goes out for dinner if I don't ask him over. The man eats nothing but Mexican food if left to his own devices. That can't be healthy."

"A little fattening maybe, but not unhealthy otherwise. My mother would give you a lecture about traditional Mexican cuisine."

He looked around her small trailer. "This must feel confining after living at the ranch. Ramón and Alicia are missing you, by the way. I get an earful every time I call."

"It's harder on Laura and Davie than me. My biggest problem is boredom. I want to go home, Luis. I need my life back."

"I know you do, *Bebe*," Luis replied, his voice soft with sympathy.

"You shouldn't call me that. Things have changed between us."

Although he started to object, Luis decided to remain silent. Barbara wasn't ready to hear what he needed to say. She might never be ready to deal with his feelings, and the last thing he wanted was her pity.

"When will they be home?" he finally asked her.

"Another hour and a half. Davie will be thrilled to see you. I'd better get all my questions in before he arrives. I doubt he'll let you out of his sight until bedtime. Would you like something to drink? I have beer, wine, and some bourbon."

"A beer would be great and maybe some chips to go with it since I missed lunch."

They were sitting at the table, discussing Luis's frustrations with the little progress he'd made building a case against Stevens, when the front door opened. Laura walked in first, her brother trailing behind her.

"Luis, you're here?" she said, surprise in her eyes.

Davie's blazed with joy. "You're here! Can we go home now? Can I live with you? Aunt Monica won't mind."

Luis got up from the table, swooping Davie up for a manly bear hug. "I am here, but, as usual, I can't stay. You can't go home yet, either, but I'm working on it, Davie, or should I call you Douglas?" he teased lightly.

Davie was surprisingly matter-of-fact. "It's Douglas here, but I want to be Davie again or Davis—that's my real name. Do you have to leave? We have just three bedrooms, but you could sleep with Barbara; she has the biggest bed."

The eye contact between Luis and Barbara was instantaneous, and neither blushed at their memories. After a few heartbeats, Barbara turned her attention to Davie, explaining why Luis wouldn't be staying with them.

"Luis is best friends with Jim, Davie. They'll want to spend a little time together. He'll stay for dinner, however, so you'll have lots of time with him. Why don't you go change your clothes?"

Luis put Davie down and placed a hand gently on Laura's head. "I missed you," he said softly. "Colorado is a long way from California, but Barbara tells me you're taking good care of Davie."

Laura gave him a solemn look but didn't say anything. Since her little brother would only agree to change into more comfortable clothes if Luis went with him, Luis took his hand and squeezed. Davie held on as if he feared Luis would disappear if he let go.

"I can show you my room. It's smaller than Laura's but closer to the bathroom. I've got a cool Avenger's poster. Fat Man says it's okay here, but I like the ranch better."

"Fat Man?" Luis mouthed to Barbara.

"His bear."

Luis nodded, a little mystified, and followed Davie off to his room.

Laura stayed behind with Barbara, her hazel eyes thoughtful.

"Nothing's changed, has it?"

"Not yet, but it will, Laura. Luis is very good at his job, and there are a lot of good men and women helping him. I'm sure things will change for us soon because I'm like your dad. I believe the good guys win in the end."

"Too late for Daddy," she said softly.

Barbara voice thickened with grief. "Yes, too late for him but not too late for you and Davie. That's what would matter to your father. He cared more about your future than his."

Laura's eyes shimmered with tears. "I'm worried Davie will forget him, Barbara. He's just five, and I can see already that he's letting Luis take Daddy's place. It hurts my feelings."

"Oh, sweetheart. We won't let that happen. Right now, Davie is lonely for your father and feeling a little lost. Luis's presence comforts him, but he knows who his father is and what a good man he was. He won't forget; I promise."

She put her arms around Laura and pulled her close. "One person can't replace another or make you lose happy memories of someone you love. But your heart, and Davie's, too, is big enough to love lots of people, Laura. Each of them will have their own special place in your heart and memories. Never feel disloyal because you add someone you care about to your life."

Barbara went into the trailer's tiny kitchen, pulling a pork roast and vegetables she'd prepped earlier out of the refrigerator to begin tonight's dinner. It quickly became a noisy affair after Jim joined them, surprised but pleased by Luis's visit. The retired agent passed on the wine but was comfortable enough in Barbara's kitchen to make himself a bourbon and water.

After dinner, the two men went out on the front porch for a private conversation. When Jesús wandered by, Jim introduced him to Luis, and the three men conversed about sports, ranching, and other things none of them particularly cared about.

Davie joined them as soon as he'd finished his chores and stood next to Luis in a proprietary way that wasn't lost on Jesús. The artist wondered briefly if Luis might be Cindy's ex. If so, why did he come here? Neither Cindy nor Jim seemed upset to see him, and Doug was openly pleased.

Jesús had always assumed the relationship between Cindy and her husband ended in discord. Maybe not. Or this guy might not be an ex-anything. Maybe he caused the divorce.

That impression deepened the next morning as Jesús watched Luis walk the short distance from Jim's trailer to Cindy's to say goodbye. Whoever the man was, Jesús noticed that he focused first on the children and tried to keep his goodbyes light even though Doug clung to him.

Picking up a camera, Jesús snapped several pictures—including one where Luis gave Cindy a kiss on the cheek. He'd taken a number of photographs of his neighbor already. She had an interesting quality he'd like to capture on canvas though he almost never did portraits.

· · · ·

Barbara watched Luis climb into his rental, keeping a polite smile on her face and waving goodbye casually as he began the drive to the Colorado Springs airport. The last thing she wanted was for him to see how hard she found it to let him go. He represented a tenuous connection to her life in California, but it was more than that. She felt safer with him around.

He'd stayed with her last night past midnight. They'd shared the sofa and the last of the wine, talking more about personal things than they did about Luis's investigations. He was curious about her relationship with Davis. How did it get so serious so fast?

"I'm not sure I can explain what happened between us, Luis. We just knew. Davis felt it first, called me *his other half.* I think he'd made up his mind about me even before we made love."

For the briefest instant, she saw pain in Luis's eyes. Then, he gave her a gentle smile. "That's when you knew?"

"No, my feelings came on more gradually. I wish you'd known him better, Luis. He had an unusual capacity for joy. I think you'd have liked him."

"Doubtful, *Bebe.* You're expecting too much from me. No man wants to appreciate the finer qualities of the other man in his woman's life."

"I am not your woman, Luis. I never was."

He reached out and touched her hair, stroking it idly. "No, I suppose not. That was my dream, not yours."

Chapter Nineteen

S anto Fuentes inhaled deeply, releasing the cigarette smoke almost lovingly as he sat on the front steps of his cousin's trailer. He hadn't called Jesús ahead of time because his cousin would find it harder to turn him away face to face. On the other hand, the personal approach hadn't worked with his mother or his sisters—bitches, all of them.

He'd left prison life yesterday after a warning not to contact any *Sureño* gang members. His parole board made it part of the conditions for his parole from ADX Florence. Now, he needed a place to land while he put his life back together again. He'd served nine years of a twelve-year-sentence for interstate kidnapping.

A bum rap, he groused. All he did was take his girlfriend across the state line to Los Alamos, New Mexico. They were on their way to his grandparents' home in Mexico, but Rosario needed a little convincing. After a slap or two, she'd quieted down, and then the damned Feds showed up.

I must have been born under an unlucky star, he grumbled as he lit another cigarette. As if FCI Florence, the federal medium-security prison he'd been sent to, wasn't bad enough, he'd been transferred to ADX supermax when he got into a scuffle with the scumbag who'd moved in with Rosario after he went to prison. The loser had shown up at Florence a year-and-a-half after he did when a drug deal went sour.

What the hell was I supposed to do—have a drink with the bastard and discuss Rosario's talents in bed? Screw that and screw him. Santo suddenly laughed. *Well, I guess I did in a way.* He'd stolen a small screwdriver from woodshop and stabbed Carlos Montero in the ass. Unfortunately, the *cabrón* didn't die.

They'd transferred Santo first to a different building, and things went okay until a guard began hassling him. It was petty stuff, taking his cigarettes or serving him dinner last, but the lack of respect ate at him. He'd led *Los Sureños* on Denver's West Side for over five years. That meant something.

One day, he'd let his temper get the best of him, jumping the guard, Dwayne Brown, and pummeling him pretty good before two other guards pulled him off and put him in solitary. From there, he'd been transferred to ADX supermax for the rest of his time in prison. Since there wasn't much of an alternative, he'd become a model prisoner.

Now he was out but not exactly free. They'd watch him like a hawk for the next two years and forced him to wear an ankle bracelet.

No contact with *Los Sureños*; they'd stressed that part of the deal. What the hell did they expect him to do with his time? Before he left prison, his parole officer said he'd hook him up with a parts dealer. Santo could deliver mufflers, struts, and other dumbass stuff all over greater Denver. The job included a broken-down van and paid minimum wage. He'd been better off in prison. Well, almost.

Now, he'd been released and needed a place to stay. Jesús's trailer struck him as perfect. Santo knew his cousin had gotten religion, left gang life behind, and started painting artsy-fartsy pictures, of all goddamned things. What kind of man does that?

When Jesús pulled into his driveway, Santo stomped out his cigarette and pasted a big smile on his face. Show time.

"Jesús, damn, man, it's wonderful to see you. *Mamá* and my sisters tell me you're doing great, so I couldn't wait to see for myself. You and me have a lot in common, *primo*. It took me a little longer than you, but I finally figured out that gang life was killing me. One of the priests at Florence helped me turn my life around and urged the board to grant me early parole.

"Now, I've got a job, and I'm ready to start over. I was hoping you'd let me stay here for a few weeks, just long enough I can put some money together for a place closer to work."

Santo gave his cousin another warm smile. The dumb shit was buying this.

"I'm glad you're out, Santo. Nine years is a long time. You'll find lots of things changed."

"TVs are bigger, that's for sure. I won't be here much, Jesús. I'll be working six days a week, and the padre arranged for me to do some straight talking to kids at Coronado High School. Imagine me being a counselor."

Jesús eyed his cousin with troubled eyes. Santo sounded like he intended to make a real stab at rehabilitation, but his aunt and cousins didn't think he'd changed very much.

Err on the side of generosity; that's what the Good Book said. Although Jesús wasn't particularly religious, he did believe the New Testament provided a solid path for living a good life.

"I only have two bedrooms, Santo, and one is set up as my studio."

"All I need is a single bed and a small chest of drawers, Jesús. I'll be gone all day, so just leave your art stuff where it is."

"All right, I guess your being here will work. No drugs, Santos. I mean it."

"I left all that shit behind, Jesús. I'm not allowed to have any contact with *Sureños* or any other gang members, either, but it doesn't matter. I don't want anything to do with them. I'm starting over."

Jesús motioned him into the house. "I have to leave in a few minutes for my afterschool program. I'll unload these groceries and then take off. You can settle in while I'm gone."

Santo watched from the porch as his cousin went two doors down and knocked on a trailer door. A classy-looking blond with two kids stood there talking to Jesús for a while. Then, his cousin and the babe's two kids got in the car and drove away.

Way to go, primo, Santo grinned. *I wouldn't have guessed this dump of a trailer park would attract someone like her. Hope you don't mind being cut out, Jesús; nine years is a long time, and I'm horny as hell.*

No point in wasting a nice afternoon, he decided, making the short walk to Barbara's trailer. She'd already turned to go inside. *Not yet, mujer,* Santo instructed the woman silently, *not without me.*

Barbara eyed the man approaching her with a sense of discomfort. From his rather shabby clothing to the tats covering his neck and arms, he had *gang member* written all over him. What was he doing at Jesús's house?

"Is there some way I can help you?" she asked him politely, wishing Jim would look out his front window and see them.

"I sure hope so. I just moved in with my cousin and don't know anyone in Castle Rock. Jesús suggested I make friends with the folks here in the park, so I thought I'd start with you. My name is Santo—Santo Fuentes."

"Mine is Cindy Corelle. The man who owns the park and lives right across the street is my uncle. He's retired from the FBI."

"Is that a fact? Might be why Jesús likes living here, makes him feel safe. Retired you say, must be an old guy."

"Don't let him hear you say that," Barbara laughed. "And I pity the man who underestimates him."

Hoping she'd said enough to warn off Jesús's cousin, Barbara turned toward her open door, saying: "Welcome to the neighborhood, Santo. I'm sure I'll be seeing you around from time to time. Please excuse me now; I've got some cupcakes in the oven."

"You and my cousin got a thing?"

"A thing? Do you mean are we dating? No, Mr. Fuentes, we're not. I'm already married."

The news surprised Santo, and he wondered if her husband was home. Barbara took advantage of his hesitation and closed the door behind her, flipping the lock as quickly as she could.

Santo Fuentes did more than make her nervous; he frightened her though she knew better than to let him see that. Jesús's cousin struck her as the kind of man who'd feed on fear, grow bolder.

I think I'll ask Jesús to hint him away, Barbara decided. Then, she sighed. Santo Fuentes didn't look or act like a man who'd take a hint.

He didn't. Over the next few days, his advances became cruder and more insistent. Fortunately, he was gone most of the day, returning just before or after Jesús took Davie and Laura off to school.

Jesús had spoken to him twice when Barbara complained, but nothing changed. His cousin also let it slip that Cindy's husband wasn't around.

Santo suspected trouble in her marriage and that the man lived some distance away. He'd seen the photographs Jesús took of Barbara and wondered idly if she knew her neighbor was taking pictures of her.

The man kissing her cheek in one of the photos was probably her husband. Good-looking dude. It didn't matter. He wouldn't interfere, and the little honey two doors down deserved some down and dirty.

Jim began walking across the street to Barbara's trailer once Jesús left with Laura and Davie. He enjoyed his conversations with her, but his gregarious nature didn't bring him to Barbara's door.

He'd spotted Santo talking to her on the front porch one afternoon and took in his "niece's" defensive posture. Although she downplayed her concerns when he questioned her, Jim sensed Barbara's discomfort with Jesús's new roommate. It seemed like a good idea to stay close when the kids left for school.

The third time he spotted Santo on her front porch, he'd crossed the street and interrupted Santo's courting if that's what the ex-con wanted to call it. The two men looked each other over, decided on mutual dislike, and squared off with chilly politeness.

"Uncle Jim" had the last word, telling Santo that Jesús's rental contract had a clause protecting his right to approve anyone moving into the park. "I'm sure you understand why. I run a clean, drug-free park."

Despite Jesús's stern admonitions and Jim's vigilance, Santo decided to make his move when he saw Barbara carry a load of laundry across to the small self-service washer and dryer area. He'd had time to learn more about Cindy and read her as the type who wouldn't fight back. She had *spoiled little princess* written all over her.

The only men who'd pay any attention to what he'd do to the princess didn't matter, and they certainly didn't pose a threat. *An old man and a wimp*, he jeered, and, in any case, he'd be gone before either one of them learned what happened. He'd endured enough of his holier-than-thou cousin. Santo packed his small suitcase and stowed it in the van. Now, it was time for a little fun.

"You've been avoiding me."

Barbara dropped the basket when she heard Santo coming up behind her and turned to face him. "Yes, I have. Since you don't seem to understand subtle messages, Mr. Fuentes, I'll be more direct. I'm not interested in you, so you're wasting your time."

Santo grinned. Maybe there was more to her than he'd thought. Good, he liked a little heat in his women.

"You think I give a shit about what you think or want? It's what I want that counts, *chica*, and today that's you. If we walk across the street to Jesús's trailer, we can do it nice and comfortable in his bed. Otherwise, I'll take you here on the floor. It's going to happen either way."

Barbara stood motionless, either frozen with fear or considering her options. Santo wasn't sure. He reached out and grabbed her arm. His aggression galvanized Barbara. Pulling her arm free with a surprising strength, she pushed him off-balance and sprinted for the door.

Santo caught her in less than three steps, grabbing her long ponytail and halting her progress. "I think I'll do you from behind—less chance you'll scratch the shit out of me that way. Pull your shorts down, and then put your arms against this table to brace yourself." When Barbara just stood there, he growled: "If you don't do as I say, I'll cut them off of you."

Barbara heard the metallic click of his switchblade.

Jim's voice broke their stalemate. "If you plan to leave with your balls intact, I suggest you walk across to your cousin's trailer and get in that piece-of-shit van. I'm only going to make this offer once."

Santo turned around. "You got a gun, old man? If you don't, I'm going to cut you bad. Then, I'm going to finish my business with your niece."

"You're not a serious enough threat to require a gun, Fuentes. I read you as a street punk. Without your gang ..." Jim shrugged his shoulders.

"I've done hard time—ADX Florence, asswipe. No one disrespects me."

To Barbara's eyes, the knife in Santo's hand seemed huge, and Santo's fluid movements showed he knew how to use it.

"Go back to your trailer, Barbara, and lock yourself in. Then, call 911."

She noticed Jim had called her *Barbara* in front of Santos. *Stress*, she thought, wondering why her mind wanted to focus on something so inconsequential.

"You take one step, I'll gut him," Santo warned her. "If you stand here nice and quiet, I'll won't hurt him bad, nothing more than make sure he's in no shape to stop me from enjoying you."

Barbara stayed stock still, eyes wide with fear but unwilling to risk Jim's life.

"That's a good girl. Now, get rid of your pants. We'll let your uncle watch."

Her slow, reluctant movements caught Santo's attention as he took in her long legs, a mistake Jim took advantage of. Luis's mentor was surprisingly fast, but Santo was younger and more agile. Barbara heard Jim's hiss as the knife slid up his forearm.

"Santo, what the hell!"

Jesús stormed into the small laundry room, eyes glittering in anger. "*Tía* Mariana is right; you're nothing more than *inmundicia*, filth. No one's safe with you outside prison. You just cut a cop, *cabrón*, a Fed. They'll lock you away 'til you're an old man, and I'm glad."

"I'm still the one with the knife, *primo*."

"Gun trumps knife, Santo," Jesús said, taking a good-sized Sig Sauer out of his pocket. "I left school early because I sensed you were up to something—all jumpy but with that small, smug grin I remember from the old days. I thought it was drugs; it never occurred to me you'd go after Cindy. Rape is low even for you."

"You won't kill your own cousin."

Jesús shook his head, his eyes showing a deep sadness. "No, I guess I can't. That doesn't mean I won't shoot you. Legs first, the knees, probably. That'll stop you quickest. Usually messes you up for life, however. Then, your shoulders—maybe the right one, so I don't hit your heart by accident."

Jim had been maneuvering inch by inch to Santo's right. Barbara watched his slow movements but had no idea what he was planning. In one quick movement, the retired agent grabbed an iron sitting on the counter, bringing it down on Santo's neck in a hard blow designed to incapacitate, maybe even kill.

"Wow!" she exhaled. Then, she moved toward Jim. "Are you okay? How badly are you hurt?"

"It'll need stitches, but I'll be fine. Call 911, Jesús. And then hand me the phone. I'm going to call the warden at Florence.

Jesús found some clothesline, using it to tie his cousin's wrists and feet. Santo, who appeared unconscious, didn't resist, but his cousin didn't take any chances. Neither did the 911 responders.

Jim was taken to Castle Rock Adventist Hospital, and Santo Fuentes went to the county jail, where he'd be examined by a doctor and then held in isolation. His parole officer had been notified, but Jesús's cousin was heading back to Florence.

On his way to the hospital, Jim thought seriously about calling his former partner then decided against it. Luis couldn't do a damn thing from California. Nor did he need to do anything. Barbara was safe, and Santo Fuentes was in jail. All he'd accomplish by calling is making his friend worry.

Chapter Twenty

F BI Deputy Director Adam Pulaski picked up the telephone and made his decision official. He'd appointed Wilma Blankenship the new SAC overseeing public corruption for Los Angeles. She'd replace Davis Reynolds, which felt a bit like throwing the lamb in with the wolves.

Not that Wilma was an innocent. She'd been in the FBI over twenty years, serving with distinction in Rhode Island and then Chicago. What made Pulaski uneasy was his decision to keep her in the dark about the ongoing investigation of her new office.

He'd done it to protect her. The FBI's deputy director didn't want Ackerman getting suspicious enough, or nervous enough, to make an aggressive move against Wilma before they could arrest him. He also thought she needed time to get up to speed.

If the Los Angeles assistant director in charge decided Wilma knew nothing about the Triad, he'd marginalize her and leave her alone. That seemed best for now.

ADIC Robert Ackerman thanked the deputy director for making the transfer bringing his office up to full staffing and ended the call from Washington. *Shit! What was Pulaski up to now? And why a woman? More importantly, how much did she know?*

Ms. Blankenship would arrive in less than a week. He'd need another week or two after that to figure out how much she knew and what her instructions were. This put a decision about how to deal with her too damn close to the arrival of the next shipment of fentanyl and marijuana from Mexico. At least, he'd have an opportunity to read her before the big one.

Curious, he pulled up her file. Just what kind of agent did Pulaski intend to send his way? She was career, twenty-two years in the field. Her last position, Supervisory Special Agent for violent crimes out of Chicago, meant the woman was no lightweight.

Until she arrived and he had a chance to read her, all he could do is watch and wait. He hated waiting, especially now when the next six-to-eight weeks would be critical. After that, he'd be gone. So would his reputation, but what had his awards and reputation ever done for him?

• • • •

Wilma Blankenship walked through the glass doors of her new office with an eagerness that surprised her. She found California, with its sunny, mild climate, a welcome change from dreary Chicago. And public corruption usually meant mostly administrative duties. She welcomed this change, too. Violent crimes had worn her down over the last few years.

ADIC Ackerman looked like his dossier read, Wilma decided. Tall, dark-haired, hard blue-gray eyes behind wire-rimmed glasses, he was all business and cool to the point of being cold. I don't think we'll be *besties*, she acknowledged privately, *but I'm certain he's good at his job or he wouldn't be here, and that's what matters.*

"I'll have you spend the first week going over Reynold's files on any open cases. You might want to review some of the closed ones, as well. Davis was competent and thorough. I expect the same level of professionalism from you. I doubt you'll disappoint me. You have a good reputation, Ms. Blankenship."

"Wilma, please. If you don't mind, I'd like to get started right away. If someone will show me to my office, I'll put a few things away and start pulling files."

"No rush, there's nothing pending that's high profile or urgent." The ADIC watched the woman's eyes as he carried on a mostly one-way conversation. Nothing, no response of any kind. Either Blankenship was a damned good actress or she had no knowledge of Washington's investigation. In a week or two, he'd know which, and then he'd deal with her.

"I scheduled a short meeting for later this afternoon. I'd like to introduce you to the senior staff. Four o'clock—main briefing room. Welcome aboard, Agent Blankenship, Wilma."

He hadn't told her what to call him. No problem, he'd be ADIC Ackerman when she referred to him and *Mr. Ackerman* or *sir*, when she addressed him directly. Rank has its privileges, after all.

A quick readthrough of Reynolds' pending cases told Wilma that Ackerman's earlier comments about Reynolds' cases rang true. None of the investigations seemed high profile or critical. Somehow, that surprised her. There'd been something odd in Deputy Director Pulaski's voice when he offered her the position.

Davis Reynolds, her predecessor, was something of a mystery. The word spread after his death he'd been involved with the Mexican Mafia. Why the hit then? And none of this fit his history. He'd been a golden boy, well respected, even liked, by the agents she'd talked to. It would be interesting to get his fellow agents' perspective later today.

The briefing room was full when she and Robert Ackerman walked in together. Wilma read most of their expressions as welcoming and curious, a normal reaction to a new face. Slowly, as they introduced themselves and explained their various roles, she began to sort them out.

One of the lowest ranking agents, Special Agent John Nader, did the most talking. He seemed on the short side for an FBI agent, stocky, too. His disheveled, mostly gray hair was thinning, and his cold blue-gray eyes resembled the ADIC's. Wilma found something about him off-putting. Maybe, it was his foul mouth.

The SAC for terrorism, Mike Douglas, was a tall, open-faced man in his mid-forties. He'd come late and chosen a seat next to Wilma, greeting her warmly. "It's nice to have a woman onboard," he told her. "If you're free, maybe we can meet for a drink after work.

I'm married, so no hanky-panky, but I like being on good terms with my colleagues."

Two of the SACs, Rick Stevens and James Dudley, remained silent and seemed to be reserving judgment. Wilma wondered if that was their normal response to meeting someone new or if it meant something else—perhaps a resentment caused by their earlier closeness to Reynolds.

Three days into her new appointment, Wilma knew something was wrong in the Los Angeles office. She'd been through all of Reynolds' open cases several times and a dozen earlier cases, all now closed. Nothing there accounted for what happened to the SAC she'd replaced.

Wilma couldn't be certain, but the files she'd examined seemed thinner than they should be, as if someone had gone through them, pulling out anything sensitive. She considered the possibility Davis Reynolds had been sleep-walking through his work. It seemed unlikely, given what she'd heard about him.

The staff she'd met appeared divided about her predecessor. Ackerman didn't confide in her, so she had no idea what he thought of Reynolds other than his earlier remarks about competence. Nader clearly hated him, making several pointed comments about his incompetence and bad attitude. Rick Stevens called him "dirty" but refused to elaborate, saying the man had been a friend of his.

James Dudley, the SAC for white-collar crimes, worked with Reynolds frequently, he'd told Wilma, and trusted him completely. "Davis was the best SAC I ever worked with—the best agent, period. I don't care what Ackerman says, or any of the rest of them, he was an honest cop."

Mike Douglas, who'd taken her out for a drink after her first day, agreed with Dudley. "We didn't work together often because terrorism isn't his field, but you get a feel for people in this business. Davis was one of the good guys."

••••

Scuttlebutt about the new SAC handling public corruption in Los Angeles filtered down to the San Diego office and Luis Vallejo. He immediately put in a call to Adam Pulaski. How much did the new SAC know?

"Not a damn thing, Vallejo. Wilma's no virgin, but bringing her into this mess at such a late date seems like a bad idea."

"What if Ackerman decides she's been fully briefed? You've set her up to be blindsided."

"I'm guessing that won't happen. If you want Blankenship safe, my advice is stay away from her. If Ackerman or any of his cohorts hear about a meet between the two of you, they'll all assume she's a danger to them and act accordingly."

Luis thought about Pulaski's warning for a few days, no more certain than Pulaski which path was safer for Wilma Blankenship. In any case, he didn't intend to ignore the wishes of the deputy director. Then, he got a phone call.

"I found your name and number written on the back of the mat on Davis Reynolds' desk, which is my desk now. My name is Wilma Blankenship, and curiosity is my abiding sin."

"I know who you are, Ms. Blankenship. Are you calling from the office phone?"

"No, my cell. Why? Is that a problem?"

"I'm not sure. Let's play it safe. Buy another phone—a prepaid one your office doesn't know about. Call me away from your office when you've done that." Luis ended the call, wondering if she'd follow his instructions.

Less than half-an-hour later, he got a second call.

"This better be worth the price of a second phone," Wilma warned him, only half teasing.

"We won't be using up many of your minutes. Let me ask you a question. What do you know about Davis Reynolds?"

"Only what I've been told, and I've heard contradictory things."

There was dead air for a moment; then, Luis Vallejo asked the new SAC an odd question. "Are you the type of person who winds up putting her hand in the hive because the honey's worth the stings?"

"Curiouser and curiouser, I feel a bit like Alice encountering Wonderland. Yes, I suppose I am."

"Then, we need to meet, Ms. Blankenship—somewhere private and at a time when your absence wouldn't be noticed in the office."

"You're FBI, too, I take it. Were you and Reynolds working a case together?"

"No, though we did work together several times. Let's just say I inherited a case from him."

All right, tomorrow's Saturday. I plan to do some shopping at a mall near my townhouse. Why don't we meet at the Los Angeles Mall in front of Bed, Bath, and Beyond, at 2:00? Is that private enough?"

"Should be. I'll see you there. Look for a Hispanic male in his mid-thirties. I'll be in jeans and a UC, San Diego sweatshirt."

• • • •

"You left *good-looking* out of your descriptor," Wilma told the tall federal agent who'd walked up to her with no hesitation. It didn't surprise her that he spotted her so quickly. In or out of her classic FBI suits, she looked like what she was—a middle-aged cop.

Wilma found the small smile he gave her telling. Luis Vallejo wasn't a man who needed to be told about his good looks. Nor did he particularly care. He focused entirely on her and looked like a man on a mission.

"I asked you earlier what you knew about Davis Reynolds, and your answer indicated you hadn't learned much. It might be smarter, and certainly safer, if you kept it that way." Luis's eyes and tone of voice warned her of his seriousness.

"Would knowing more about him impact the way I do my job?"

"Absolutely."

"Then, say on."

They'd taken seats in the back of a small café serving Mexican food. Both ordered coffee and nothing else. This didn't qualify as a social occasion. Then, Wilma took the lead.

"Why did Davis Reynolds have your name and number written on the bottom of his desk mat, Agent Vallejo?"

"I'm not sure. He contacted me just before he died, sent me a package for safe keeping. It surprised me, to be frank. We didn't know each other all that well, though I'd worked with him briefly on several cases. I think he chose me for two reasons: he had no idea which agents in his office he could trust, and we shared an acquaintance whose judgment he felt he could rely on."

"What was in that package?"

Luis gave Wilma one last thoughtful look and decided. "Some instructions for me and a summary of his investigation of people in his own office. Davis was building a case against your new ADIC and some of the men in the Los Angeles office. Washington suspected they were part of something Davis called the Triad. It's a partnership of prison officials, *La EME* and their subordinates, and a few corrupt agents designed to keep drugs flowing into southern California."

"Wow! I guess it's no surprise there's nothing in his files. If Washington knows, why didn't Washington brief me? It's not exactly a vote of confidence that Pulaski left me in the dark."

"He wanted to keep you safe and decided ignorance was bliss. You should know things are at a critical stage. He's hoping the case will break in the next few weeks. I don't think it's a reflection of his respect for you."

Wilma's stony expression said more clearly than words what she thought of Pulaski's protective but dismissive behavior. Then, she gave Luis a penetrating look.

"Why are you telling me this? I'm guessing he told you not to."

"A couple of reasons. You asked, for starters, and I don't trust Ackerman. He's likely to assume the worst about you and act accordingly. You need to know that. I also think you can be useful. It's hard to read what's happening in your office from San Diego."

"You want me to poke around."

"No, I don't. I want you to go about your daily routine as if we never met. What you can do is observe the dynamics of the office—who's in and out of Ackerman's office, and how those men, and they will be men, interact with each other. I'm particularly interested in Rick Stevens."

"You think he's dirty?"

"I know he is; I just don't have the proof Washington needs. No heroics, Ms. Blankenship. Ackerman's dangerous and probably a little desperate. He knows things are about to unravel. Frankly, I'm surprised he's still going through the motions and taking such a big risk. I'd like to know why."

"Does he know about you?"

"Yup, and I'm sure there's some surveillance, but I wasn't followed today. My partner is carrying my usual cellphone, which shows that we're somewhere in downtown San Diego. Phil will drop the phone by my apartment later. And I'll be home for the day. Don't you love GPS?"

"So, I'm to watch the comings and goings of my colleagues and keep you informed. Anything else?"

"Get to know your fellow agents, Ms. Blankenship. I'd rather call you *Wilma* if you don't mind. I'm not big on formality."

"Works for me, and you're *Luis*. Am I looking for possible suspects or allies?"

"How about both? Any ideas so far?"

"You haven't mentioned his name, but I'd put John Nader at the top of the list of suspects—mostly because I don't like the man, and he's thick as thieves with Ackerman."

"You'd be right. Watch your back, Wilma. I'd rather see the bureau lose some useful information than a good agent." With that, Luis stood and left his new confidante sitting there.

Chapter Twenty-One

Jim Corelle pulled into the large guest parking lot of the Florence prison complex and locked his Jeep, not that it was worth stealing. He'd gotten an earful and a request from his friend, Ricardo Sanchez, who owned a restaurant in Franktown.

Ricardo's older brother, Tomás, had requested compassionate release from ADX Florence. A gangbanger who'd made his first kill at thirteen, Tomás had moved up the ranks, graduating from petty drug deals and prostitution to running one of the biggest drug networks in Colorado.

Fifteen years ago, he'd been busted. Now, Tomás was in the last stages of stomach cancer and wanted to die with his family around him. Ricardo had asked Jim to come to the hearing and support his older brother's release.

A hell-raiser at first, which explained why he'd been transferred to ADX Florence, he'd settled into late middle age and then a long bout with cancer. All the fight and braggadocio were gone. Tomás Sanchez wanted nothing more than to die in peace and with a little dignity—as much as cancer would allow.

Jim entered the facility, feeling the same sense of hopelessness and anger prison always gave him. What a waste of life. Why couldn't humanity do better?

As he walked down the hallway, he glanced out the window into one of the small exercise yards. *Two hours a day out of solitary*, Jim thought, watching the men below, *which is two hours more than most of them deserve.*

His eyes widened in surprise as he spotted the only two men he knew in the entire Florence system, Chuey Corrales and Santo Fuentes, standing close together. What were the chances of that? Then, after glaring at Santo for a few seconds and fingering the long scar on his arm, he walked on.

Santo noted Jim's presence before the con standing next to him did. *What the fuck is a retired FBI agent doing here?* he wondered idly. Then, his anger overtook curiosity. "I should have finished you off when I slid that knife into you," he shouted at Jim's image as he began jogging the perimeter of the exercise yard.

"You know that *pendejo?*" a gruff voice asked. "What's he doing in Colorado?"

"Owns a trailer park in Castle Rock. He's ex-FBI."

Chuey Corrales jogged next to Santo for the brief time the two guards would allow cons to spend time together. "The old bastard and his partner, a Mex like you and me, busted my ass. Then, to add insult to injury, Vallejo, his old partner, showed up as part of my escort team to Florence. Too bad you didn't kill Corelle. He must have more lives than a cat. I damn near got him, too."

With that, Chuey stopped jogging and began doing jumping jacks and toe touches. Their time in the yard was finite, and seeing Corelle gave him a rush of adrenaline he needed to work off.

Santo went back into his cell and picked at the boring lunch awaiting him. He didn't know the prisoner he'd conversed with in the exercise yard, but he found the man's anger interesting.

For some reason, his thoughts turned to the Hispanic-looking man in the photograph with Cindy Corelle. It didn't strike him as likely, but what if the man in the picture was Corelle's old partner? Then, he shrugged. What difference did it make?

Santo's exercise period didn't coincide with Chuey's until two weeks later. The younger man had almost forgotten about the photograph until seeing Chuey reminded him.

"My cousin has some pictures of a babe who lives in the park with her two kids. In one of them, a *Latino* brother is kissing her. I wonder if that might be Corelle's partner. You said he visited Colorado recently because he was one of the cops who brought you here."

"A woman with kids—two of them, you fucking kidding me?" Chuey Corrales's eyes glittered with excitement. Even in Lompoc, the word had filtered down from Roberto Rodríguez about the left-over business from Manzanillo.

"I need to see that photo," he told Santo.

"Sure, I'll just ask the warden for a day-pass," Santo joked, "no problem."

"Hey, you two, less conversation and more exercise," one of the guards yelled, "or exercise time is over."

The two prisoners separated, knowing they probably wouldn't see each other for several weeks. Still, they'd be scheduled together again sometime, and if life in supermax taught you anything, it was the virtue of patience.

Santo looked forward to payback for Corelle and the retired agent's spoiled niece. The details of what that payback might look like eluded him. Chuey saw it differently. He'd earn points with Roberto if he could hand him the woman and kids they'd been searching for in California. Favors were as good as gold. He considered it a longshot, but, hell, what did he have to lose?

Chuey Corrales couldn't be sure of anything, however, until he saw the photo. Santo could give him the address of that trailer park, but that left him with two problems—how to find someone to steal that photograph and how to smuggle it into ADX Florence.

The answer came to him two days later as he exercised in the small square the guards usually took him to. Congratulations were going around to the thin, dark man he knew as Antonio Rivas—a *Sureño* who'd done hard time for killing a Fed in Littleton over fifteen years ago. He was about to be released.

"Tony, you interested in a job?" Chuey asked the lucky about-to-be-released prisoner.

"How much risk?" was the man's cautious answer.

"Very low but big bucks and the undying gratitude of *La EME's jefe* in Mendota. You interested?"

"Maybe, what do I have to do?"

"Steal a photograph from a guy's trailer. I don't know the specific address right now, but I'll have it in a week or so. When are they springing you?"

"Ten days. Can you have the address by then? And how will I get it to you. I doubt they'll let me visit you for old time's sake."

"You married?"

"Not anymore. They gave me twenty years, too much for Sarita. Got a girlfriend, though. Some women get off on the whole prison thing. Maritchu's been visiting regularly for the last five years."

"Well, she can visit me—show me a picture of my nephew, who's getting married to a *Blanca*, more's the pity."

"How much?"

"A couple of thousand and a little fentanyl to sweeten the deal. I'll arrange it with one of my lieutenants on the outside."

Six days later, Chuey had the address and information about when Jesús would be gone. He passed the details along to Rivas and then waited for his visitor. The guards wouldn't allow him to keep the photo, or even touch it, but they'd let him look at it if it didn't appear suspicious.

If the man in that photograph proved to be Luis Vallejo, he'd have Rivas send the photograph to one of his "cousins" in Los Angeles. From there, someone could take it to Roberto Rodríguez, who'd decide if the woman in the photo was the right one. If she was the one Roberto wanted, disposing of her would be someone else's problem.

• • • •

Maritchu Morales was a small woman of mostly indigenous descent. She eyed Chuey with suspicion. "I don't like talking to you," she told him bluntly. "Antonio is out now, and I don't want him coming back here. This will be the last time he does anything for you."

Chuey didn't acknowledge her comments in any way. All he cared about was that photograph. "You got my picture?" he wanted to know.

"*Sí,* but we'd better talk a little more first. I don't want the guards thinking there's something important about this photo. I've already had to explain why I want to show it to you once."

He knew Antonio's woman was right, a short visit spent looking at a photograph would make the guards suspicious. They'd set it up as a visit from a family member, someone he had history with. But what the hell could he discuss with someone he didn't know?

"How's Tony doing?"

"He's good, seeing old friends. He tells me he's not interested in getting back in the business, that things have changed too much. But I don't think he's telling me the truth."

"You got a problem with him rejoining his brothers?"

Maritchu gave him a hard look. "That's none of your business." Then, she shrugged. "He's a man; he'll do as he pleases. I think it's time to show you the photo now."

It took only one, brief glance. Vallejo, no doubt. He spent more time examining the woman in the photograph. *Damn shame she has to die,* he thought. *She's a real looker,* but if this woman turned out to be the one Roberto was looking for, she'd be dead soon and probably not nearly so pretty.

• • • •

Jesús Mendoza opened the door to his trailer after walking Doug and Chrissy over to Cindy's. His mind turned to dinner—specifically what he could find to fix. His refrigerator was almost bare, but he didn't want to go out again.

Eggs, it would have to be eggs and toast with the last of his salsa. That would hold him until tomorrow. He gave a small, contented sigh. Jesús liked coming home to an empty place, felt real relief to have his cousin gone. It had been weeks now, and he still found himself looking for the beat-up van whenever he came home.

Thinking about Santo made him glance into his studio, which had served as his cousin's room those brief few weeks. Then, pleased to see it still empty, he continued on to his own bedroom.

Something niggled at him, but he couldn't identify what bothered him. Walking back to his second bedroom, he looked around but saw nothing missing or out of place. Still, he had a weird feeling something wasn't right. The anomaly hit him as he reentered his kitchen.

One of the photographs sitting on the small, cluttered desk where he kept his art supplies was wrong. He walked back to his studio and picked up a small, framed shot of one of his paintings. It should have been a photo of Cindy and the man who'd visited her recently.

He remembered sliding it into the frame months ago. Going over to a pile of photos, he went through them carefully but saw nothing missing or out of place. It was just that one photograph, but who'd taken it and why?

There had to be something important about this particular picture. Someone had come into his place and taken it and nothing else. Who would know about it? He couldn't think of anyone besides Santo, but how could have been him? Dinner forgotten, he headed for Jim's doublewide. They needed to think about this.

"You're sure you put it in the frame?" Jim asked his friend.

"I am," Jesús insisted, "and even if I didn't, it would be in that stack of photos and it's not."

"Why were you taking pictures of Cindy?" Jim's scowl showed his displeasure and a growing concern.

"I wanted to paint her. I've finished several sketches to see how I want to approach the painting. You'll welcome to look at them."

"No, that's okay, Jesús. I'm sorry if I sounded suspicious. But if you're right about the photo, and if Santo is the only one who knew it was there, the obvious question is why did he want it enough to go to the trouble of having someone steal it."

Jesús gave him a worried look. "There's another important question. Why did he want that photograph specifically? I have several of Cindy alone. If my cousin has some sort of weird fixation on her, wouldn't he have wanted one of just her?"

"I have no idea, but I'm guessing it's something else entirely. When I spotted Santo in the exercise yard, he was standing next to a con named Chuey Corrales. Did Santo ever mention him?"

Jesús shook his head. "There's some kind of connection between Cindy's friend and this man?"

"There's bad blood, but it might be something even worse. It's possible Corrales isn't interested in Luis at all; he might be after Cindy and the kids."

"Her husband is that powerful, his connections reach this far from Las Vegas? I take it the man who was here a few weeks ago isn't him."

Jim gave his friend and tenant a thoughtful look but wasn't sure what he wanted to tell Jesús about Barbara's background. Would silence or sharing her background with the young artist make her safer?

"I'm probably worrying for nothing, and I sure as Hell don't want my niece frightened; she's been through enough. Keep this to yourself, will you?"

"Sure," Jesús reassured Jim, "but I think we'd better keep an eye on Cindy and the kids just in case."

"The more I think about it, the more I'm convinced it's about my ex-partner. That's who Luis is, Jesús. He and Cindy have a history, but

Chuey Corrales might not be focused on Cindy at all. He hates Luis and might be trying to arrange a hit. I think I'd better call Luis and give him a head's up."

• • • •

"You think it's possible Corrales has made the connection between Barbara and me—that he's figured out that she's the missing woman from Manzanillo?"

"I don't fucking know, Luis, but it's possible. You might be the target, but we can't ignore *what if*. What if Corrales knows about Barbara Allen? There's a lot of dots we haven't connected, but I don't like coincidences. Santo Fuentes almost certainly arranged for the photo's theft. He either wanted it for his own sick reasons involving Barbara, or he's said something that helped Corrales make the connection between you bringing him to Florence and your visit here. Santos knows I'm a former FBI agent.

"It isn't a giant leap from you to Barbara," he continued. "Ackerman knows about you, and I'm pretty sure he thinks you've hidden her somewhere. He wants her and the kids dead. By now, he's got *La EME* and its various subordinates looking, too. You see where I'm going with this?"

Sitting at his desk in San Diego, Luis frowned in frustration. "I can't simply wait around to see what happens next. If the Triad knows about Barbara, they'll come after her. If they don't know, but they're keeping some kind of electronic surveillance on me in case I make a stupid move, I could lead them right to her."

Jim heard the worry in Luis's voice. "Two words, buddy—Nancy Tyler."

"Nancy? You think I should take Barbara and the kids there?"

"No, I think I should take them there. No one's following me."

Luis was tempted. Nancy Tyler ran operations in San Diego when he and Jim first partnered. She'd retired and moved to Denver, where she had family. But she was in her 70's now; he wasn't comfortable intruding on her safe world.

"No, I'm coming to Colorado. I suspect we're ahead of them, Jim, thanks to your friend, Jesús. We can decide what to do when I get there. In the meantime, keep your guns loaded and clue in Jesús. I think he'll prove helpful."

Chapter Twenty-Two

Jesús listened intently as Jim summarized events in Manzanillo and described what had happened since. A sudden, unexpected wave of resentment toward his cousin almost overwhelmed him. Wherever Santo went, trouble always followed. As if nearly raping Cindy wasn't enough, his *primo* brought trouble to her door again. Her name is Barbara, he reminded himself.

Although Jesús didn't know Luis well enough to care what happened to the FBI agent, the person he'd known as Cindy was special to him. He understood his cousin's attraction, but he'd grown up with Santo, knew how his cousin thought. That intimate knowledge made him doubt Santo had some kind of pathetic crush on her. He saw women as disposable items.

No, stealing that photo was someone else's idea. It might be either a personal vendetta by this Chuey Corrales person against Luis Vallejo, or someone wanted to hurt Cindy. He still found it hard to think of her as Barbara.

In either case, a kind woman and the FBI agent's children she'd committed herself to protecting faced an unknown danger. Jesús's immediate impulse was to hide her away at one of Denver's hundreds of motels. Then, she and the children should go into witness protection. It saddened him, however, that he'd never see any of them again. He'd begun to see the three of them as an important part of his day.

It frustrated Jesús when Jim agreed they'd be safer in a hotel but insisted on keeping his promise to Luis. Jim's loyalty to his partner seemed to be overriding his concern for Cindy and the children, and Jesús found that unacceptable. Nor did he understand why Luis thought it necessary to handle her transfer to WITSEC personally.

• • • •

Antonio Rivas frowned in concentration as he listened once more to the second-hand message from one of Chuey Corrales's confederates. He was to watch the woman in the photograph he'd stolen and learn her routine. Evidently, she lived in the same park as Santo's cousin.

He could do that. The money would be welcome and the risk minimal. Keeping an eye on her, however, proved to be mind-numbingly boring.

"The *Blanca* almost never leaves the fricking trailer," he complained to his woman, "and when she does, it's usually to spend time with the guy who owns the park or to run a brief errand. I can't find any pattern."

He sent the information back to Corrales a few days later, using a reluctant Maritchu as the courier. His next set of instructions came back the same day, and he didn't like the news. He was to hire someone trustworthy and experienced to help him carry out a hit on the woman and kids.

Antonio Rivas didn't want to go back to Florence. What he'd done for Corrales up to now qualified as smalltime and risk free. This job was different. If he didn't plan carefully, or if something he couldn't control happened, he'd be fucked. Still, Chuey didn't strike him as the kind of brother you said *no* to.

The sudden appearance of two *Sureños* out of L.A. worried him, especially after they announced they'd take the lead in planning and executing the hit. The head of California's *La EME* didn't intend to take any chances. He wanted this woman gone—the kids, too. Then, they needed to search the trailer thoroughly for a flash drive.

Before the two men from California showed up, Antonio had tapped Nacho Buñuel for the job. Even though his friend wasn't the brightest light in the room, he followed orders and had no hesitation when it came to killing innocents. He also knew how to keep his mouth shut.

Rivas decided that sometime in the midafternoon would be best for the hit, probably an hour or two before the kids went off to school. Although Corelle would be awake that time of day, he'd consider the chances of a daytime hit small, so he'd lower his guard. It also made escape easier. Nighttime traffic in Castle Rock and the surrounding area was too light to protect them once they left the park.

Guillermo Bequél, one of the men Roberto Rodríguez sent to the small Colorado town, disagreed. Daytime hits were too risky. He also disagreed with Rivas about the need to continue surveillance right up to the moment of the attack, insisting Rivas already knew her routine.

"It'll be best to hit them sometime after midnight," he insisted, "and I don't want any of us seen skulking around earlier. "Corelle's old, his skills rusty, but I think you're right about eliminating him first."

The second man Roberto Rodríguez sent to Castle Rock, Tigre Moreno, was a slight, nervous man who took his orders from Guillermo Bequél. Nacho, unlike Antonio, didn't care who was in charge. He simply wanted it done and the money in his pocket.

Rivas quietly acceded the decision-making to Bequél after making a decision of his own. Although he wouldn't say a word ahead of time, he intended to walk away from the job. Maritchu had it right. They needed to slip across the border and start over in Saltillo. A simple life in northern Mexico sounded a hell of a lot better than growing old in Florence or being dead.

• • • •

Luis drove his rental car into Castle Rock Manor just as it got dark. He stopped first at his former partner's trailer; Luis had a few hard questions for his friend. After sharing a drink with Jim, Luis crossed the small, private road and knocked on Barbara's door.

He'd been annoyed when Jim told him Jesús had taken it on himself to tell Barbara she was in danger. How would worrying her, and frightening the children if she shared the news with them, make Barbara and Davis's children any safer?

Luis changed his mind, however, after Davie proudly showed him the hidden space under the trailer Jesús made earlier in the day. At first, the excitement of seeing Luis made Davie forget his new playhouse under the bathroom floor. He sat close to Luis on the sofa, full of questions and hungry for attention.

Then, Davis's son remembered where he'd be sleeping that night and insisted on showing Luis. "This is where Jesús wants Laura and me to sleep at night," he said with touching enthusiasm. "Isn't it cool?" Giving Luis a regretful look, he added: "You're too big to sleep down here."

"It's okay, Davie; I'll stretch out on the sofa. But a secret room only stays secret if you remain quiet no matter what you hear going on up here. We're leaving tomorrow, so this will be your only night to enjoy it."

"We have to move again?" Laura asked. "Can't we go back to the ranch? I liked it there best."

"Not yet, Laura—but soon, I promise. Ramón and Alicia ask about you all the time."

"I'm big enough for my own horse now," she told him proudly. "Ramón said so." Then, the little girl glanced down at the small space that so intrigued Davie. "I don't like it down there much."

"It's just for this one night, Laura," Barbara reassured Davis's daughter. "Speaking of that, it's time for you and Davie to get ready for bed. We'll leave the trapdoor open until you're asleep, and you know how to open it if it's closed. I'll bet it's nice and cozy down there. Jesús did a good job. Not many kids have a hideaway like this."

"Because most kids don't need one," Laura said in that oddly mature tone she sometimes used. Then, she turned to her brother.

"Let's take a few books and a flashlight. Jesús says it's safe for us to read down here. No one can see if we have a light on."

She turned to Barbara. "You don't have to leave the door open. Davie and I aren't afraid of the dark."

Barbara didn't say anything until she'd poured a glass of Malbec for herself and retrieved a beer for Luis. Then, she seated herself next to him on the sofa. "Do you think Jesús is right to worry?" she asked in an anxious voice. "Are Laura and Davie in danger, more danger than before?"

"The danger's real enough, *Bebe*. I'm not sure about the timing or even the intended target. I'm hoping we're safe enough tonight, and you're leaving tomorrow. You do understand that WITSEC is absolutely essential now?"

"I suppose so. I'm tired of all this, Luis, and why won't you stop calling me *Bebe*?"

Luis grinned. "That still bothers you?"

"On more levels than you can imagine. Why are you here, anyway? Jim could have arranged for government protection. You didn't need to come all this way to hand us over in person. What if someone's following you or bugged something you always carry, like your badge or wallet?"

"Not much chance of electronic surveillance. I stripped and left everything—my watch, my phone, even my usual clothes—behind. Everything's new. Following me physically isn't that easy, either. I doubt Ackerman has the resources for a 24-hour tail."

"Still, you didn't need to come."

"There are all kinds of needs, Barbara." Luis wrapped a long arm around her, pulling her close to him on the sofa and fondling the nape of her neck. "I'm going to lose track of you soon. That scares the hell out of me."

"I'm still griev—"

Luis's lips against hers were soft but insistent. When he ended their kiss, he whispered against her cheek. "I've missed you, Barbara—physically, emotionally, pretty much every way there is to feel a void in your life."

"Please don't, Luis. I'm not ready, and we already know how this will end. We aren't right for each other."

"That's not true, Barbara. I think we're perfect for each other, and I believe we're right for Davie and Laura, too. It doesn't mean you wouldn't have built a good life with Davis or that I'll ever replace him as a father in their eyes. But he's gone, *querida*. Nothing can change this. Those kids need us, and I want you back in my life. Just think about it, okay?"

"Luis," she put her hand against his chest, pushing him away gently, "life is complicated. Even if we were a couple, it's doubtful we could get custody of Davie and Laura. Your work is dangerous, and I've been tainted by all that's happened. I doubt we'd be seen as desirable parents. And it isn't enough, anyway. I can't build a relationship with you because Laura and Davie need a family. It wouldn't work."

Luis smiled and stroked the tawny hair he found so entrancing. "Before you go into WITSEC and I lose track of you, I need to tell you how important you are to me. It has nothing to do with Laura and Davie. I love you, Barbara; I think I've loved you since we met accidentally at Rodolfo's opening."

"Love isn't enough, Luis. A marriage takes mutual respect, trust, and a whole host of things that aren't there for us."

"I think they are. Do you trust me, Barbara, to do my best to keep you safe?"

"Yes, of course I do."

"Do you believe me when I tell you that I see you as a capable, intelligent woman, one that I respect?"

"Yes, but—"

"Do you understand how much I regret losing you because I didn't share myself with you in important ways?"

"Yes, of course, I do, but Luis, nothing fundamental has changed. We come from different cultures, have conflicting expectations about relationships."

Luis sighed, giving Barbara's hair one more stroke before dropping his hand. "While you're in WITSEC, I want you to think about something. I'm not the only one who came up short, Barbara, though I'll admit the biggest mistakes were mine. From the first, you made assumptions about me because of my ethnicity, my job, and my personality. All those preconceptions colored how you saw me.

"I am a man first, Barbara. That comes before everything. I knew I'd found my mate almost immediately, and I'll admit it surprised me. You didn't fit my expectations, either. It took a while, longer than it should have, to get my priorities straight. In the process, I lost you.

"Life's given me a second chance, and I don't intend to lose it. You told me Davis knew there was someone in your life, someone you hadn't gotten over. He still took a chance on you, believed he could make you happy. It's no different for me. I love you, Barbara. I know you still love Davis; an important part of you will always love him."

Luis stroked her hair again, certain it was the only caress she'd allow. "I'm okay with that. But I also believe Davis was right. You never stopped loving me because you didn't know how. You still don't know how. I can't let go of you, either.

"Let's fight for our relationship, *Bebe*, and let's fight for Davie and Laura, not simply because we love them and not just because they need us. We're better together, all of us."

"You make it sound so easy."

Luis grinned. "There's nothing easy about you, Barbara Baines Allen, not one damned thing. It doesn't matter. Get some sleep now. We have plenty of time to think about us, about a life together, after all this winds down. If I'm lucky enough to be part of Davie's and Laura's lives, I have to be the man, the father, they need me to be. And I have every intention of being the man you need, too."

Luis leaned forward and kissed her cheek. "I'll walk you to your bedroom and finish locking up."

"It's only ten feet, Luis," she teased him.

"I know, but it gives me another excuse to kiss you."

After a quick kiss, he closed her bedroom door, double-locked the front door, and took a long look at the kitchen door, which opened onto a small deck. It wasn't the sturdiest of barriers, and the door opened inward, making it easier to break in.

After looking around the kitchen, he grabbed a few wooden utensils and went to work. It might not keep out a determined intruder, but it would definitely slow one down.

Satisfied, he stretched out on the sofa, covered himself with a light blanket, and settled into sleep. One of Luis's last thoughts was a deep regret he'd be sleeping on the sofa rather than sharing Barbara's bed. *Soon*, he promised himself. Although he missed their lovemaking, he longed for their emotional connection, that sense of belonging heart and soul, even more.

In the grander scheme of things, he grudgingly admitted, sex, or, rather, the lack of it, wasn't the biggest issue between them. They'd always gotten that part of their relationship right. But Barbara didn't feel ready for physical intimacy, and they had other issues to settle in the months ahead. In time, he'd convince her they belonged together. Any other end to their story was unthinkable.

He'd been sleeping almost an hour when he heard something that brought him out of REM sleep. It took a few, precious seconds to clear his head.

Slipping out of bed and grabbing his gun off the coffee table, Luis opened the door to Barbara's room. "We've got company; stay here," he whispered before leveling his gun at the front door.

Chapter Twenty-Three

Guillermo Bequél was pissed. Antonio Rivas had been a no-show at the trailer park; he didn't leave any message or give them any kind of warning. The bastard just walked away.

"We don't need him," he assured the others. "It doesn't take four men to take out one woman and two small kids."

After a few, quick modifications to their plan, he sent Nacho Buñuel across the street to take out a sleeping Jim Corelle. He and Tigre would enter Barbara's trailer from two different directions in the meantime and finish things there.

Guillermo had gone over Antonio's crude floorplan carefully, deciding he'd come in from the front of the trailer and head for Barbara's bedroom—only steps away. Tigre would use the side door, which put him closer to the kids. It didn't matter which one his friend killed first. Neither child represented any kind of threat.

The first hiccup to Guillermo's plan was the man now standing directly in front of him, Glock in hand and a hard, competent look in his eyes. The second was the sound of Tigre struggling to open a side door that refused to budge. The fool spent more time than he should have before retracing his footsteps to the front door.

Unaware of Luis's presence, Moreno walked into the trailer's small living room, eyes widening as he spotted a man holding a gun. "Christ," he muttered before bringing his own semi-automatic up reflexively, a second too late. Luis fired first, his two bullets hitting Tigre center mass. A low grunt was the only other sound in the dark living room before Bequél's partner went down.

Guillermo used those few confusing seconds to rush through Barbara's bedroom door, slamming her back against her bed and then grabbing her by the arm. His orders were clear, kill her, but Guillermo needed her alive right now. She was his ticket out of here.

"Back up," he told Luis, pinning Barbara against him with his left arm. The other hand held a gun. "Then, I want you to put your gun down nice and easy. If you don't, you'll be picking up pieces of your girlfriend with a tweezers."

"You'll be dead."

Guillermo shrugged. "Everyone dies sometime."

Even in the dim light of the moonlit trailer, Luis saw the resolution in the gang member's eyes. This guy wasn't bluffing. Putting a hand up in resignation, Luis moved toward the coffee table, placing his gun on the edge of the table's smooth surface. Just as he took his finger off the trigger, a nearby car alarm went off, and the park's floodlights brought sudden daylight to the immediate area.

The experienced hitman looked away for less than a second. Still, that distraction proved enough. Luis reached for his gun, firing almost blindly. A second shot from a few feet away followed his at almost the same time. *Jim,* Luis decided, grateful his partner figured things out and came to his rescue.

As Bequél crumpled to the floor, Luis heard a high-pitched wail—a sound he knew he'd relive in his dreams for years. *Barbara,* he panicked; either, he'd accidentally shot her or the man now bleeding out on the floor had.

But his former lover was rushing toward someone in the kitchen. It was Laura. Her eyes wide in shock, the little girl held Barbara's gun held tightly in tiny hands that shook wildly.

"It's okay, sweetheart," Barbara reassured Davis's daughter as she took her gun from Laura's stiffened fingers. "It's over, and we're all fine. You did a brave thing."

"I had to, Barbara. I know I'm not supposed to touch your gun, but he was going to shoot Luis. Please don't be mad at me. I couldn't stay down there even though I made Davie promise he would. Then, I got your gun out of the kitchen drawer. In the dark, no one even noticed me."

Sobbing now, Laura had begun to shake, as well, and Luis scooped her up and snuggled her close for a moment before carrying her over to a far wall. "Barbara's right; you did a very brave thing, Laura, but you didn't kill that man. I did." He pointed toward a small hole. "See, that's where your bullet went. You missed him, *hija*, but not by much."

A shadow in the doorway made Luis turn, a finger tightening on his gun's trigger.

"Jim," Barbara shouted in dismay. Blood streaked the old man's face, and one arm hung uselessly.

"I'm fine; most of the blood's from the other guy. Sorry it took me so long."

Luis was at his partner's side, easing him down on the sofa. "Call 911, Barbara, tell them we need at least three ambulances and several detectives."

He gave Jim a searching look. "I'll go check on the guy in your trailer. Any chance he's not down?"

"He's not just down, he's dead," Jesús said calmly from the doorway. "I think this party's over."

"You set off the car alarm and turned on the park lights?" Luis asked.

"I did. Hope it helped."

"It did. Thanks."

Luis covered the men who'd tried to kill them with sheets Barbara took out of the closet then walked over to small hiding place Jesús made for the children. Opening the small trapdoor, he pulled a silent Davie out and held him close.

"Your sister's a hero, Davie. She helped stop one of the bad men. You are, too, because you followed your orders. Sometimes, that is what heroes have to do. I'm proud of both of you. Now, I want you to go over to Jesús's trailer and wait there until the police officers come to talk to you."

He turned to Barbara. "You, too. Jesús can keep you company. Jim and I will wait here. It may be a while before they get to you, so sleep if you can, the kids, too."

Barbara grabbed a robe, belting it carelessly. Her hair had come out of its loose braid, but she barely noticed. Shock made her movements slow.

Luis gave her a brief hug. "*Querida*, I'll join you there as soon as I can. WITSEC will be here in a few hours, and you'll be out of danger. God's on our side, Barbara, or this would have ended very differently."

They all heard the far-off sound of a siren. Help was on its way. As soon as Jesús led his neighbors away, Luis turned to his partner. "How bad is it?"

"Hurts like Billy-be-Damned, but that's a good sign. It's pure, dumb luck it ended the way it did, Luis. I was older and slower than that asshole. Fortunately, I was also a bit smarter. Speaking of smart— you've got one brave and smart little girl there."

Luis nodded, his eyes full of pride. "Laura's definitely her father's daughter. She's got *cojones*, that one."

"Whose shot did the deed?" Jim asked his friend. "I heard you tell Laura she missed, but she didn't, did she?"

Luis shook his head. "I don't want her having to deal with that, Jim. It's better this way."

"The crime lab people are going to know."

"I'll talk to them. It doesn't matter, anyway. All three men are dead, and you know as well as I do that dead men tell no tales."

The park was suddenly alive with police cars and ambulances. Jesús had already sent his neighbors upset by the gunfire back to bed, but several came out again to watch a show more exciting than anything on TV.

Soon, there were half-a-dozen uniformed officers and several men in suits entering Barbara's trailer. One man took charge—sending Jim off with the paramedics and directing a team to gather evidence at the retired agent's home.

A little more than two hours later, the officers completed their investigation. The bodies were already on their way to Douglas County's morgue.

Luis's version of what happened would be the official, or public, version. The details of one kill shot would be buried deep in the files. No one saw any benefit in exposing a brave little girl to media attention and the nightmares sure to follow.

· · · ·

Once the initial phase of the investigation ended and the local police left, Luis walked two doors down to Jesús's place. The other two trailers were crime scenes, and none of them could stay there. Finding a motel seemed like too much work. Right now, Luis's priority was sleep; all of them needed to rest before the people from WITSEC arrived.

But, first, he told Jesús and Barbara that he needed to check on Jim one more time. After a quick visit to the hospital, he'd join everyone at Jesús's trailer for at least a couple hours of sleep. Barbara's friend could keep an eye on everyone in the meantime.

The artist and part-time afterschool director had already urged Barbara to take his bed since Laura and Davie immediately crashed in his second bedroom. "I'll be perfectly comfortable on the sofa," he assured her.

When Luis returned an hour later, Jesús suggested the agent share Barbara's bed. "She won't admit it, but I think she's having trouble coping with what happened tonight. Those kids are her world. Right now, she needs your comforting.

Too tired to argue or explain their relationship, Luis entered the room where Barbara was sleeping. He took off his belt and shoes but remained fully dressed. When he sat down on the bed, Barbara put her hand on his arm.

"Can't sleep?" he asked her.

"I don't want to close my eyes. I still see him, Luis. I can smell his sweat and feel his clammy hands on me. I don't think I'll ever stop being afraid."

"You will, *Bebe*, and it won't take very long. The next few hours will be the toughest. Let me hold you tonight and offer you any comfort I can. Things will start to look different in the morning."

"Why did they come, Luis? Why are we so important to them? I can't think of a single way we pose any threat."

"They believe you have something of Davis's—something that will reveal the relationship between *La EME* and Ackerman. At least, that's my best guess."

"I don't; we don't. Except for the clothes we had on, and I've been through those over and over, the only items that we took were my purse, Davie's bear, and Laura's book. That's it. I've looked everything over several times. There's nothing, Luis."

"Where's Laura's book?"

"Back in my trailer—in her room, I think. I've examined it page by page and found nothing."

"Did you look for a microdot?"

"I don't even know what that is."

"I'll check tomorrow. What about Davie's bear, Fat Man?"

"It's in the bed he's sharing with Laura. He won't go to sleep without it."

"I'll go get it. If Jesús isn't asleep, I'll ask him to put on a pot of coffee."

Luis was back in a few minutes, Davie's rather bedraggled fuzzy companion in his hand. "Jesús says he has a robe he never uses in his closet. You're welcome to wear it. It's warmer than the one you had on earlier. Let's go into the kitchen where the light's better."

Jesús poured everyone a cup of coffee and put a small sugar bowl and a carton of milk on the table. Then, he handed Luis a small pair of scissors, saying: "I'd better get my sewing kit. I don't want Davie coming unglued in the morning if he finds his bear in pieces."

Luis looked the bear over, squeezing it inch by inch, but found nothing. Barbara's eye was sharper. One of the bear's paws seemed slightly thicker than the other.

"Start here," she recommended.

Luis examined the seam and could see that a small tear had been carefully resewn. He picked up the scissors and made a new cut along the seam. When he'd made the hole large enough, he inserted his forefinger and probed inside. Something was there.

Jesús handed him a tweezers, prompting Luis to remember the larger thug's comments earlier that night about needing tweezers to pick up pieces of Barbara. He'd come so close to losing her. Bile backed up in his throat.

"I've got it," he told them and pulled out the smallest flash drive Barbara had ever seen.

"Got a computer, Jesús? I'd like to see what's on this drive."

"A laptop. It's pretty old."

"I don't think it matters. Would you get it please?"

Everyone stared at the small screen as a twenty-seven-page document loaded. Luis scrolled quickly through the pages. This was what everyone was looking for and what Adam Pulaski needed to complete his investigation.

Davie had it all along—damn! Luis felt an unexpected frisson of fear. Had Ackerman and *La EME* known about the flash drive hidden in Davie's bear? No wonder they'd risk anything to get it. WITSEC needed to arrive soon and take Barbara and the kids safely away.

"Well, now we know what they are looking for," Luis said softly. "I'll get it to the deputy director as soon as I can, just as soon as

WITSEC's come and gone. I don't think you'll need to stay in protective services all that long, Barbara. This will blow things wide open."

It was after four in the morning, and everyone needed some sleep. Luis, as usual, took charge. "The marshals are due sometime between eight and nine, which means we'll only get three hours or so of rest, but that's better than nothing. Let's go back to bed, Barbara." Luis turned to Jesús. "Make sure we're up by seven."

"I'll set my kitchen timer," Jesús told them. "I don't trust myself to wake up on my own. I'm not used to this much excitement."

Luis remained dressed but pulled Barbara close when they slid under the comforter. She wrapped her arms around him, nestled her head against his chest in a way that seemed so familiar to him, and quickly fell asleep as he stroked her back.

His eyes refused to close. Luis prided himself in his thought process, his ability to analyze things logically, but, tonight, ideas ping-ponged around in his brain. The three most important people in his life would be disappearing in a few hours, and he'd have no idea where they'd gone or for how long. He wasn't sure how he'd deal with that.

Morning came and with it, a soft knock on their bedroom door. They needed to get ready for the WITSEC team's arrival. Barbara would use the next few minutes to pack everything they'd be taking with them. It wasn't much.

Luis was sitting at the kitchen table with another, desperately needed cup of black coffee in hand when Davie came into the room. Without making a sound, the little boy slid into Luis's lap and leaned against his chest.

After a few minutes, Davis's son sighed. "Can't you come with us, Luis? What if the bad guys come back again?"

"They won't know where you are, Davie. These marshals are the best in the world at hiding people, so no one can find you."

"Not even you?" he asked, his eyes showing a new worry.

"Not even me, but it's only for a little while, I promise, a few months at most. Then, we'll all be together again."

Davie didn't say anything more as Luis stroked the boy's curly hair absentmindedly. A few minutes later, a brisk knock on Jesús's door brought the U.S. marshals into the room.

"Everyone ready?" a youngish woman asked. "It's time for goodbyes."

The finality of their separation hit Davis's daughter hardest. She'd been terrified the night before by the possibility Luis would die. It felt almost like losing her father again. In that terrible moment, she realized it wasn't just Davie who needed the tall, dark-eyed man who made her feel safe. Her sobs tore at everyone, Luis most of all.

His own eyes filled with tears as he hugged her close. "It's not for long, sweetheart; I promise. Then, we'll be together again—you and Davie, Barbara, and me. We're like a family. We are a family if that's what you want."

"What if they won't let us?" she sobbed.

"Then, I'll kidnap the three of you, and we'll go live on a tropical island someplace. You didn't hear a word of this," he said to the WITSEC officer standing there.

The man grinned. "Doesn't sound like a forced kidnapping to me."

Luis picked up Davie, who snuggled up against him. With his other arm around Laura, he gave Barbara a quick kiss on her cheek. "I'll see you as soon as they spring you," he assured her.

"That's not how Daddy kisses Barbara," Davie told Luis indignantly. "That's how you kiss old ladies."

"Or babies," Laura added.

"I can do better," he assured his critics, "but I need a little space."

Taking Barbara into his arms, Luis pulled her against him and gave her a real kiss, the one he'd longed to give her, as Davie, standing beside his sister, hooted his approval.

"Leave your doubts in whatever city they take you to, *Bebe*," he whispered in her ear. "I meant every word I said to Davie. We are a family, and you are my *mujer*."

Chapter Twenty-Four

"Flagstaff?" Barbara asked the woman sitting in the front passenger seat of the car. "We're going to Arizona?" She tried to remember what she knew about the small city—mountains and snow and not a lot else.

"It's a nice, quiet town with a big university. You'll be comfortable there. We have new papers for you, as well as a house and health and school records for the kids. In fact, you'll have everything you'll need for the next few months or years, depending on how things work out."

"Years?" Barbara's heart speeded up in panic. "You can't be serious; it couldn't possibly take years."

"Probably not, but you never know. It's best to be prepared." Roxanne Peterson gave the woman seated next to her a sympathetic look. "Let go over some of the details. Can you trust the kids to stick with their new identities? They're both pretty young."

"By now, they're experts," Barbara sighed. "This really sucks."

"All right, your name is Ellen Sinclair, and you're the wife of Staff Sergeant William Allen Sinclair, who is serving as an ordinance specialist in Iraq. You came to be closer to his family in Williams while he's deployed. Flagstaff probably won't be your long-term home. You're a social worker by profession, currently unemployed. Your children's names are Tiffany and Brent."

"A bit posh, don't you think for the kids of a social worker and a noncommissioned officer?" Barbara objected.

"Maybe you're the ambitious type," Roxanne laughed. "I like that you're getting into the spirit of your character. We have a resume and several pages of bio providing details of your imaginary life. Don't think you have to share everything with the first person you meet; that's a rookie mistake."

"Where are we living?"

"In a neighborhood called University Heights. It's not far from the college. I haven't seen any pictures, but I'm sure its comfortably middle class. Your kids will be going to a school called Manuel de Miguel Elementary."

Barbara glanced down at the sleeping children and sighed. "This isn't good for them—all this moving around. Just about the time they come to trust someone, we have to move on. These poor kids need their family, what's left of it."

Laura stirred against Barbara's side and opened her eyes. "You're our family," she whispered, "you and Luis. He promised."

"Luis?" Roxanne challenged Barbara. "Is he the FBI agent who handed you over to us?"

"Yes."

"You do know you can't contact him, right? You're fully sequestered, which means not even the FBI can know where you are. They have to go through WITSEC. My partner and I are your only contacts from here on in. Feel free to make friends, both you and the children, but no one is to know anything about your past."

"I understand." Barbara stroked Laura's arm. "She means you, too, Laura."

"My name is Tiffany," Davis's daughter corrected her. "That name stinks, by the way. I sound like a real snot."

Roxanne laughed. "People will judge you more by how you behave than by your name, Miss Tiffany, and you're not a snot, more like a smart ass."

The drive from Castle Rock to Albuquerque's airport took just over six hours. From here, they'd take a short flight to Flagstaff. Although the two marshals would be on the plane with them, they'd sit in a separate section. Ellen Sinclair and her children would arrive alone and unremarked.

• • • •

"I like this backyard a lot," Davie enthused. "Look at all these trees. I bet I could climb to the tiptop of that one." He pointed to a fifty-foot pine.

"You'd better not," Barbara objected, only half teasing. "I'm afraid of heights."

"Are there bears here?" he asked hopefully.

"I don't think so, Brent."

Davie's new name didn't come naturally to Barbara, mostly because she didn't want it to. His name was Davis Justin Reynolds, III, and it was a name she treasured, one that deserved to be remembered and honored.

"Maybe we can ask the neighbors," Barbara offered a disappointed Davie. "By the way, both of you start school tomorrow. Are you ready for kindergarten?"

"I guess so. Tiffany is going to the same school, isn't she?"

Davie's willingness to call his sister *Tiffany* reminded Barbara that he wanted to do his best to adjust. She needed to do the same. So far, both children seemed to like it here. It helped that Flagstaff resembled Castle Rock in many ways including its weather. But there was no Jim Corelle and no Jesús Mendoza. She'd miss both of them. Davie, she knew, missed male companionship even more.

With no adults around to talk to or share her worries with, Barbara felt lonely, a little lost. It didn't entirely surprise her when she found herself on the south campus of Northern Arizona University the day after Davie and Laura started school.

Their absence gave her time to explore an environment that felt comfortably familiar. Within a few minutes, she'd located the sociology department.

Since she was supposed to be a social worker, it seemed relatively safe for her to enter the building and request a schedule of upcoming classes. Maybe she'd take a class or two. It might be fun to be a student again—to face the podium from the other side.

Those classes wouldn't start until January, however, and it was already November, which made it too late to enroll this semester. Surely, by January, Luis would be finished investigating. The trial might even be underway. *No*, she decided, *no classes at NAU*. That didn't mean she couldn't spend some time on campus. It felt as close to home as she could get.

By the early part of December, they'd settled into their community and their new lives. Laura was doing well in school and seemed to enjoy it, but Davie struggled. Barbara couldn't understand why. He was bright, already read a few words, and took an interest in everything. Not according to his teacher.

"Brent doesn't concentrate, won't sit in his seat for more than a few minutes, and disrupts other students. Perhaps he's not ready. You might want to consider another year of preschool," his teacher, Mrs. Michaels, told Barbara.

"My son did everything I asked of him this summer," Barbara objected. "I can't understand what's changed."

"Children behave differently with their parents," Renata Michaels told Barbara in a rather patronizing tone. "And if you're not trained as a teacher, you might not notice his lack of skills."

Her attitude convinced Barbara of two things: this teacher wasn't interested in helping Davie, and she'd already pegged him as "less than talented." A quick visit to the principal made it clear Davie wouldn't get the help he needed there, either, like placement in another classroom.

Determined to give Davie the academic start he deserved, Barbara spent the next two days asking around the neighborhood. It wasn't long before the same name came popping up—Mountain School, a charter school in the same neighborhood.

Small and progressive, it seemed a perfect place for Davie. Although Laura didn't want to leave her new friends behind, Barbara was nervous about splitting the children. Still, it seemed wrong to wrench Laura away from a situation she found comfortable.

Deciding she'd leave the decision to Davis's daughter, Barbara took both children to *test drive* the new school. They loved everything about it. "More fun," said Davie; Laura found it "more interesting."

Within a week, Barbara knew she'd found the right place for both of them. *Brent* made friends immediately with a boy who lived two doors down from them. His new teacher found the sweet, energetic boy with red-gold curls more than ready for school. "He's not just smart," she told Barbara, "Brent's a natural leader."

Tiffany, too, made new friends easily. Day by day, Davis's children eased their way into a new life. As much as that relieved Barbara, it also worried her. Flagstaff couldn't provide a long-time home for any of them. Both children needed continuity almost as much as they needed love. It worried her they'd be leaving again in a few weeks or months, once again abandoning new and fragile friendships.

And then what? she worried. Her mind seemed to do little but formulate questions. Would their Aunt Monica make a home for them, or would it be their aging grandparents? What if Laura and Davie became wards of the state? Would she and Luis be allowed to adopt them?

Stop, stop, stop, she told herself. *There is no "Luis and me" in this picture. He obviously thinks so, but what about my feelings for Davis? It might be best if I act alone, present my case as a solo parent to the children's relatives and the courts.*

She feared Luis's reaction to that, suspecting he'd oppose her and seek custody himself. It took her mere seconds to realize she couldn't do it—separate Luis from Davis's children.

It wasn't fair to Luis, and it wasn't what Laura and Davie wanted. Davis's children saw the two of them as a couple, a mom and dad. It was what Luis called *a package deal.* That scared her nearly as much as

Laura's and Davie's uncertain future. *How*, she wondered once again, *did I get myself into such a mess?*

• • • •

As soon as the WITSEC car pulled out of the trailer park in Castle Rock, Luis got in his rental and headed to the hospital. He wanted to check on Jim one more time and apologize for almost getting him killed.

"Most fun I've had in years, Luis, and I'm going to miss those young 'uns something fierce. You going to do right by them?"

Luis gave his former partner a hard look. "That's probably not up to me, Jim. Their situation is complicated."

"Doesn't look all that complicated from where I sit. Those two need new parents, and you and Barbara are nuts about them."

"But not about each other," Luis said, his tone wry.

"That's at least 50 percent not true—no, more like 75 percent. You're on board; a blind man could see how you feel. It's Barbara who's conflicted, and who could blame her after all she's been through? Hell, she's still going through a thoroughly messed up life. She needs time, Luis. Grieving is a hard, lonely process. With all that's happened, she hasn't had any real opportunity to put her relationship with this Reynolds guy in perspective."

"He was an exceptional man, Jim. The more I learn about him, the more impressed I am. How am I supposed to compete with a dead hero?"

"I don't doubt he was special for a minute; look at his kids. But don't sell yourself short. Davie and Laura don't. They're smart kids, and they've obviously made a decision about their future. Now, get this business finished and settle things with your young woman. I like her, by the way. She's got grit and smarts. You two should make some mighty fine babies."

Luis grinned. "I think so, too. Thank you, Jim, for everything. I'll let you know how things turn out."

"You'll do a hell of a lot better than this, Luis Vallejo. You'll invite me to your damned wedding."

Before leaving the hospital, Luis called ahead to Denver's international airport, booking a flight to Washington, D.C. The flash drive they'd found was burning a hole in his pocket, and by now, the hunt was on again for Barbara and probably for him.

He'd made a copy of Davis's flash drive and left it in Jim's trailer as a backup, a little insurance in case things didn't go well. Jim knew where to find it, but no one else would.

The FBI's deputy director all but grabbed the flash drive out of Luis's hand. "You're sure the data names Stevens, too?"

"It does. I've been through it a couple of times. Davis included some texts and emails I have no idea how he got his hands on. The man had serious skills. We lost a valuable asset in Manzanillo. Any chance we can go after the cartel members responsible?"

"Not likely. We haven't a clue who was in that zodiac. I'm betting Davis Reynolds knew at least one of them, however."

Deputy Director Pulaski had what he needed. Now, he intended to move on to the next phase of Operation Triad, as Davis had dubbed it. Pulaski sighed, regretting Davis Reynolds' death and the frustration he felt with Ackerman and his associates. He'd found this case more challenging and depressing than any he'd faced. Corrupt agents at this level didn't happen every day.

Neither he or anyone in the FBI could do much about Roberto Rodríguez. The man was already a lifer. Still, a transfer to ADX Florence might weaken his hold on trafficking and La EME's structure. The new warden at Mendota, whoever he or she might be, could get a better start at controlling the prison, too, if Roberto moved on.

In the meantime, Pulaski wanted to hold off arresting Ackerman and the others because of a new wrinkle in the case. Davis had learned about a drug shipment, a big one, scheduled to arrive in Los Angeles at an unknown date. Pulaski knew two things about the drug drop. It was coming soon and would probably contain the biggest supply of fentanyl ever brought to Los Angeles. He didn't want those drugs reaching the streets.

As tempting as he found it to concentrate on that, the deputy director kept his focus on the bigger picture. He was part of a cat-and-mouse game involving corrupt agents, the Tijuana cartel, *La EME*, and Mendota's warden as well as several key members of his staff at the prison and collaborators in the California state prison system. This meant a lot of moving parts and a good chance of things going wrong.

Eyes on the prize, he told himself. No matter what or who fell through the cracks, it wouldn't be Ackerman and the agents he'd corrupted. Bagging them remained priority one.

It wouldn't be easy, even with the information Luis Vallejo had provided. Ackerman was smart and well-connected. His position made it nearly impossible to work around him without tipping him off. He also knew his superiors had opened a file on him and that Luis Vallejo played a part in all of this. That probably took the ADIC from careful to damn-near paranoid.

After weighing the alternatives, Pulaski sent Vallejo back to San Diego with a tail, someone experienced enough that the San Diego agent wouldn't spot him. As things moved closer to resolution, Luis became more exposed, and Pulaski didn't want to lose another agent, especially one as street smart as Vallejo. Maybe he should it ease him out of the picture now.

• • • •

Roberto Rodríguez sat in Mendota's board room, listening in quiet fury as the second team he'd sent to Colorado gave their report. He'd lost his first, hand-picked team to a retired FBI agent in his seventies and a female college professor. He found it humiliating.

The two *Sureño* gang members he'd sent to Castle Rock and Florence when Bequél didn't report in didn't learn much. The operation involved four men—the two he'd sent and two chosen by Chuey Corrales. Three men were dead. The fourth man, someone named Antonio Rivas, had gone to ground. No one knew what happened to him.

Their sources seemed certain he hadn't been arrested, and there was no mention of him in the reports. So, where was he?

They'd also learned that someone in the trailer park, an artist, had tried to help the woman and the kids she guarded so ferociously. His help, evidently didn't go beyond offering his home for the night and building some kind of protective hidey-hole in Allen's trailer for the two kids. The guy seemed more the good Samaritan type than anything.

Other people in the park told them there'd been another man present, a Hispanic who didn't live there. No one seemed to know his name, but one woman insisted he'd been there at least once before.

That pretty much summarized what they knew. The retired agent was still in the hospital but would be released soon. The woman, Barbara Allen, and the two kids were gone. No one had any idea where.

The Denver and Colorado Springs airports had been dead ends, ditto the train station and the buses, which meant they probably left Castle Rock by car. Whose car and the direction they took were unknows at this point.

Now, Roberto wanted to talk to Ackerman, hoping his partner-in-crime might know more about what happened in Castle

Rock than he'd been able to learn. He wanted answers. More than that, he wanted assurances the upcoming shipment would be safe.

Chapter Twenty-Five

Wilma had followed Luis's instructions about not involving herself for weeks now, but her irritation was building. She watched Ackerman's cronies come and go from his office, saw them leave the building together, but she'd learned zilch. That needed to change.

The new SAC for public corruption was a bit of a tech junkie, one with a small, private collection of tools at her disposal. The time had come, she decided, to up her game. Smiling slightly, she fingered a small object in her pocket.

When Ackerman went into Nader's office, she headed for the woman's restroom, hastily keyed for her privacy the day after she arrived. Located in what had been a closet next to Nader's office, it was now accessible only from a different hallway. After locking the door, Wilma put a small voice amplifier against the wall. She'd missed the first part of their conversation.

"... eliminate any residual risk. We need to meet away from here, all of us. I know it's risky, but we've got a couple of issues that won't wait. One of them is dealing with Vallejo. He's messed in our pond one too many times. Let's not use your cabin for the meet. I'm concerned they may be watching it." The voice was Ackerman's.

"Okay, how about Tucchio's in Long Beach? It isn't one of our usual places."

"That'll work. Put the specifics on a paper and walk it around to Stevens and Howard. Then, shred it. I don't want anything discussed in the office."

"We'd know if they'd bugged us. Bobby checks every damn day," Nader objected. "You're being paranoid."

"I want that meet to happen tonight, John. Take care of it."

Wilma heard the door open and close, waited a few minutes, and then walked back to her desk. Picking up her purse, she told the receptionist she was taking her lunch break and had some errands she needed to run later.

Five blocks later, she stopped at a small café, took out the cell phone she kept in a hidden pocket of her purse, and punched in a number.

"Vallejo here."

"Luis, it's Wilma. I picked up some information you need to know. Ackerman plans to meet with his cohorts this evening. I have no idea when, but I do know where—a place called Tucchio's in Long Beach. You're on the agenda, and I think they're planning something ugly. They're really pissed about something."

"Yeah, Roberto Rodríguez sent some gang members after Barbara Allen when he figured out where she'd gone, but we got there first. She's in WITSEC now. They may not know I was involved, but they will eventually when the local feds send their reports up the chain of command."

Wilma sighed. "I'd love to spy on them personally, but they'd spot me right away. I don't have anyone here to turn to because I haven't had time to develop any kind of network yet. Any ideas?"

"Do you have access to the right kind of audio equipment—the type almost anyone could operate?"

"At my house, yes. You have someone in mind?"

"An old marine buddy, a lawyer. I'm sure he wouldn't mind a nice dinner out with his wife. Since we don't know the exact time, they may have to eat and drink their way through the entire menu. I'll have him call you on your burner sometime this afternoon to arrange a meet. It would be best if you weren't in the office when he called."

"You think they've bugged my office?"

"I doubt it, but why take chances? This sounds like it might be the break we're looking for, Wilma, so I'm going to fly up to Los Angeles. Let's meet at your house somewhere around midnight. What's your address?"

• • • •

Luis felt a familiar tingle as his excitement grew. This meet was important, or Ackerman wouldn't have taken the risk. Thinking of his upcoming call to a friend he hadn't seen in several years, Luis grinned in anticipation.

Alex Becker had worked in the Judge Advocates Corp with him for nearly four years. They'd formed a firm friendship which they'd maintained in a casual sort of way even though their lives took very different directions after their stint in the marines. Luis had joined the FBI and remained single while Alex had become a partner in his uncle's law firm, married a local girl, and fathered a son, Luis's godson.

The conversation went pretty much as Luis suspected it would. Alex was bored and more than ready for a little adventure. He and Ann Marie would arrive at the restaurant by six and stay until the job was done. Then, he'd take the information to Ms. Blankenship's house.

"Is she hot?" Alex wanted to know?

"That wouldn't be the descriptor I'd use. It doesn't matter anyway. You'll have your wife with you, remember?"

"I was merely curious. You're going to meet us later?"

"That's the plan. Watch that temper of yours, Alex. I don't care what you hear. You can't show any reaction to what they're saying and avoid eye contact with anyone in the group."

"Don't worry; I may not be a bigshot federal agent, but I can handle this. It's Ann Marie you need to worry about. She'd be more than happy to gut anyone who'd put the hurt on you."

"I do love your wife."

"It's mutual, which is why you don't get many invitations to Rancho Palos Verdes."

Luis decided against booking a flight ahead of time. Why give anyone a heads-up if he was being tailed? There would be plenty of seats on a Tuesday flight, and if he flew into Burbank, he could avoid a rental car by taking the light rail and then catching a cab to Wilma's.

He doubted Ackerman's surveillance was all that good. The ADIC might be high up in the command structure, but he wouldn't dare use FBI resources other than the few men he'd corrupted. Bureaucracies love their paperwork, and paperwork leaves a trail.

Luis's 7:35 flight landed at 8:15. He connected with the light rail and arrived at Wilma's small home in Westwood just after 9:30. Alex and Ann Marie hadn't arrived.

Wilma gave him a big smile as she ushered him into her living room. "It looks like you're finally going to catch a break, Luis."

"My second of the week and this one thanks to you."

Her left eyebrow rose fractionally. "What was the other one?"

"The one I mentioned earlier. *La EME* went after a woman and two kids in hiding, but I got there first. Right after that, I found a bit of evidence Davis Reynolds hid, one everyone and his uncle have been looking for. Now, the D.D. has it. We'll see the end of this case, from our side, anyway, sometime in the next two weeks; I'm sure of it."

"And then what?"

"A giant drug bust, a shakeup of California's state and federal prison system, the arrest of Ackerman and his buddies, and a big-assed series of trials that will dominate the headlines here for months."

"You're going to be a rock star in the FBI, Luis. You ready for that?"

"Not if I can help it; public grandstanding is not my style, and it would make me almost useless in undercover work. Besides, I have more personal goals in mind these days, Wilma. I want a life, a real life—wife and kids, that sort of thing."

The doorbell ended their discussion. Alex Becker strode into Wilma's townhouse, his eyes wide with excitement. Whatever he'd overheard, it must have been important. His wife's eyes, however, glittered in anger. Something had Ann Marie Becker pissed.

"Wait 'til you hear, Luis. More than half of what we taped concerns you," Alex informed his friend.

"These men are planning to kill you, Luis, as in bang, bang, dead," Ann Marie huffed. "Since it's obvious they're FBI and have powerful connections, you need to leave the country for a while. I have a good friend in Germany who can hide you."

"He's not going anywhere, Ann Marie. This is what he does." Alex gave his friend an envious look. "God, I wish I'd joined the FBI with you. This was the best night I've had in years."

Ann Marie Becker turned narrowed eyes on her husband. "Take that back. You have a son; you have a wife—me. I don't want to be a widow."

To punish her husband for even considering such a dangerous lifestyle, she added maliciously. "Though if something happened to you, I wouldn't mind swimming in Luis's pond if he'd leave the FBI."

Her words made Luis laugh even as he held up both hands in a peacemaking gesture. "She's kidding, Alex. Let's listen to the tape. I admit to some curiosity about what they've planned for me."

The tape went on for over an hour, and Alex was right; the bulk of the conversation was about Luis. After discussing several possibilities for disposing of him, Ackerman finally gave the task to Nader. The group initially considered using some of Roberto Rodríguez's men, but Ackerman wanted it done right. Finesse wasn't in *La EME*'s playbook.

The tape also revealed the date the drugs would arrive and where. The final pieces were falling into place. *Time to shut the Triad down and give Davis Reynolds the justice he deserved,* Luis thought in satisfaction

"Two things have to happen right away," Luis told his friends. "I need to speak with Pulaski, and Ackerman has to be monitored discreetly 24/7. Whatever else might happen," Luis promised them, "the ADIC is not going to slip away."

After sending Alex and his wife home with his thanks and a stern reminder not to discuss this with anyone, Luis sat down with Wilma. He needed her help, but there were limitations he'd insist on.

"None of these men are your problem, Wilma, and I don't want you trying to bird-dog them just to keep me safe. I'll deal with those bastards my own way. From what you tell me, Ackerman rarely leaves the office except for lengthy lunches during the day, but he's canny about electronic surveillance."

Wilma grinned. "Sometimes, the best tech is low-tech or even no-tech; nobody's looking for that these days. I'll keep my eyes open at headquarters, but we know pretty much everything now anyway including the timetable. We're simply stuck marking time because Pulaski's not going to do anything before that drug shipment arrives here in the States."

Wilma gave him her own stern look. "Even though you don't think so, the biggest problem at the moment is keeping you alive. Think Ackerman would believe you had a sudden yen for a vacation in Fiji?"

"I'm not going anywhere."

• • • •

His shoulders hunched in anger, Roberto Rodríguez frowned at Mendota's warden. Roger Delvecchio was delivering the news about Ackerman's plan to eliminate Luis Vallejo along with strongly worded instructions to stay out of it.

"Forget that shit! Vallejo's mine," *La EME*'s chief yelled at the warden. "I'm the one who lost two men in Colorado. I thought it fucking odd a woman and an old man aced out four *Sureños*. Now, you're telling me Luis Vallejo's got that damned professor and those kids hidden where I'll never find them. I owe that asshole big time. You tell Ackerman I'll take care of it. And believe me, there won't be any slipups."

Mendota's longtime warden reluctantly relayed Roberto's message to the Los Angeles ADIC, whose first reaction was anger.

"They've already fucked up once with him," he growled. But a cooler head made Robert Ackerman rethink his earlier pique.

Vallejo's work for the FBI involved gangs. If his murder looked like local gang retaliation, it would divert suspicion away from him. Right now, a diversion seemed like a good idea. "And if they fuck up," Ackerman told his second-in-command, "it isn't going to make much difference to us. We'll be gone."

• • • •

To make sure there were no mistakes this time, Roberto contacted his brother-in-law, Santiago Aguilar, who was serving twenty-to-life in California's Terminal Island facility. Santiago managed the loosely affiliated *Sureño* gang members in San Diego and North County, both inside and outside the prison system.

Although the message had to be delivered second hand, Roberto's instructions were clear enough. Santiago was to use one or two of his best men, make sure Vallejo's injuries were fatal, and carry out the hit within a week.

Roberto's brother-in-law thought about it for a while before selecting Martín Orozco Fierro to arrange and carry out the hit. The younger man, who'd moved up from San Diego's Logan Heights gang to full *Sureño* status at the age of nineteen, now managed most of the prostitution and gaming activities in the southernmost part of California even though he'd just turned thirty-five.

Martín's first task would be to gather as much information as he could on Luis Vallejo in the next twenty-four hours. Santiago chose Miguel Arête, whom everyone called *La Araña* or "the spider" because of his long, attenuated body type and his stealthy, predatory personality, to work with Orozco. Arête wouldn't quit until he'd finished the job.

The two men met at Martín's sprawling, hilltop home overlooking the ocean north of San Diego.

"Nice digs" Miguel commented. "You're pretty young to be living this large."

"Well, you know what they say about talent rising like a good bread. I've learned to work smart, Miguel, not just hard. That's one reason I'm not crazy about this assignment. I don't see how killing a Fed makes us any safer or richer."

Arête shrugged a shoulder. "It don't matter, smart boy. Santiago says put this dog down, he goes down. Personally, I like taking out a Fed—arrogant sons of bitches, all of them."

Chapter Twenty-Six

After dividing surveillance duties on Luis for the next twenty-four hours, the two *Sureños* parted. They'd pick the place and the time for the hit sometime in the next forty-eight hours. Martín paced the floor of his study, listening to the sounds of his family in other parts of the house.

Rosa was in the kitchen, preparing dinner. *Three maids and she still won't relinquish control of her kitchen*, he chuckled. He could hear his daughter, Iliana, practicing the piano in the family room. At twelve, she was the child he felt closest to. She'd been just three when he went to prison for the last time.

No more prison time Martín had promised himself in that jail cell. He couldn't leave the *Sureños*, no one did, but he'd been careful since his parole. In the last few years, he'd built what looked like a legitimate business. This job was likely to fuck that up. *Damn! Why did it have to be Luis Vallejo?*

The agent did him a favor almost a decade ago when Martín got busted on what could have been serious human-trafficking charges. Conviction would almost certainly have led to a long stint in San Pedro or Lompoc. Luis walked back the charges to *soliciting* and *arranging to solicit* and recommended to the judge that Martín serve his time in the county jail so he could see his kids on a regular basis.

Now, Santiago wanted him to kill the guy. Martín didn't consider it merely a matter of fair play. Killing a federal agent meant serious blowback, and the idea of taking out Vallejo, or trying to, made him nervous. The cop had proved to be both smart and lucky.

Nor was this his only concern. If he and Arête succeeded in eliminating him, Vallejo's replacement might be more aggressive, a real hard ass, which would complicate *Sureño* business. Most of the gang members he knew saw Luis as someone who'd listen and play fair even though he'd never roll over.

Santiago hadn't said much about why they wanted him dead and wouldn't welcome any questions. He'd simply expect his orders to be followed. Martín went over his dilemma from every angle, but the more he thought about it, the more he resisted killing Vallejo. It just didn't make sense.

Not killing him, however, came with its own set of problems. Martín considered Miguel Arête the first obstacle. He was good at what he did because he enjoyed his work. The little piss ant wasn't a shining light intellectually or ethically, but he'd die trying to do what Santiago wanted done.

The second problem, and in many ways the more worrisome one, was the consequences of failure. Neither Santiago nor his brother-in-law had forgiving personalities. Screwing up was not an option in their world, and if they were annoyed enough or caught a sniff of disloyalty, they might come after his family. *Shit!* Why couldn't he find any good answers here?

Martin thought about witness protection but didn't have anything to sweeten the deal. And he knew his Rosa. A life that didn't include three maids and a big, fancy house was no life at all.

Maybe it would be best to carry out his orders and deal with the consequences the best he could. Then, he changed his mind. *I've stayed alive and out of jail by following my instincts, and my gut's telling me to find a way out of this that doesn't include killing Vallejo.*

• • • •

Martín still hadn't come up with any kind of plan when he took over Vallejo's surveillance at four in the afternoon. Ten or twelve hours of sitting in his car should give him plenty of time to think.

Darkness descended and with it a plan, at least a half-assed one. He called Miguel, suggesting they meet in the morning. "I have an idea about where and when to make the hit."

After ending his surveillance, Martín treated himself to a good dinner before driving to Luis's apartment. He pulled into the far end of the parking area where the dim light didn't reach. Then, he waited.

Cars came and went, but none belonged to Luis Vallejo. At midnight, the dark BMW slid into its assigned slot. Martin watched the agent started up the stairs to his second-floor apartment—a surprisingly easy target. *I could piss Arête off by completing the job without him* flashed through his mind. Then, he heard a slight, metallic click.

"My gun's in my jacket pocket," the *Sureño* leader announced to the man standing behind him, "and it's not loaded. If I turn around, will I be looking at Luis Vallejo's partner?"

"Martín, is that you?" Luis asked as he approached his partner and the man standing next to him. The *Sureño* leader hadn't heard Luis cross the parking lot, his attention fixed on the man's partner.

"It is, and I'd like a slightly less public place to hold this discussion if you don't mind."

"My apartment, then. Phil will lead the way. I'll be right behind you."

As soon as he closed the door behind them, Phil Reed patted Martín down and confiscated his gun, which, as he'd promised earlier, wasn't loaded.

"You're getting careless, Reed," the *Sureño* told Luis's partner, showing him a narrow switchblade sheathed behind a broad silver buckle. "It's small but damn sharp. I tell you this as an act of friendship."

"I take it you're not here to kill me, so why are you here? Don't tell me you've moved into drugs or enforcement, Martín. I pegged you for smarter than that." Luis's tone was neither friendly nor unfriendly; instead, it was all business.

"Santiago Aguilar got orders to take you out and handed the assignment to me. I thought about it and decided it was bad for business, and, to be honest, I owe you."

"A gangbanger with a conscience, now I've seen everything," Phil Reed said snidely.

"You alone?" Luis wanted to know.

"I am tonight, but I won't be tomorrow or the next night. The bad news for you is that Santiago chose Miguel Arête as my partner in crime. You heard of him? He's damn good."

"*La Araña*, he is good, lucky, too. I've been trying to take him off the streets for three years. I'm flattered by Santiago's choice. What'd I do, by the way, to piss him off?"

"It's not him, it's Roberto Rodríguez, and I have no idea what his beef with you is."

"But I do," Luis grinned, glancing at his partner. "Let's focus on the more immediate concern. Since I'm pretty sure you don't have some kind of death wish, I assume you want to walk away from this with your skin intact."

"I do, and I'm not interested in looking over my shoulder for the rest of my life, so no witness protection."

"A screw-up this big will cost you, Martín. Your bosses aren't the forgiving type."

"I'm working on that."

"Your idea as good as mine?"

Martín Orozco gave the FBI agent a curious look. "Probably, but I'm listening."

"Arête is the key. He's not someone who can be bought or scared off, and he won't quit. Won't leave any witnesses, either, which is why Phil and I haven't been able to arrest him. On the other hand, putting him in prison doesn't strike me as such a hot idea, either. He's the perfect enforcer for someone like Aguilar or Rodríguez. However, like all of us, he has an Achilles heel."

"Such as?"

"His little girl is sick. If Rodríguez hears that unexplained money has flowed into Arête's account, he'd take a hard look at him if things go south. That might help you walk away without repercussions."

"It might but only if Miguel is dead."

"Phil and I can't go outside our directives, Martín. We can't let you kill him, either, not in cold blood."

"You won't have to. Miguel will be looking to kill you. Even Feds have the right to defend themselves. Tell me the rest of your plan."

Twenty minutes later, he nodded his approval. "You're taking a big chance, but I think it'll work. I like it."

Phil turned to his partner. "How fast can we arrange for a $200,000 deposit to Arête's account? The money can sit in there for up to three months, right?"

Luis nodded his head. "Yeah, but it could take a week or two before we get the cash. That's too long. Any suggestions?"

Martín shrugged his shoulders. "I'll have the money to you by tomorrow morning. Watch yourself, Vallejo. I can't guarantee things won't go south."

• • • •

Before the two *Sureños* met to finalize their plans in the morning, Phil Reed used a burner phone to let Martín know he'd chosen the spot for the attack on Luis—a small park near Scripps Mercy Hospital. Their attack would follow the staged drug bust they'd agreed to. What he didn't tell him was why he'd selected that particular spot.

The park was quiet, relatively empty that time of day, and close to medical services if anyone needed them. It was also a place where drug deals went down on an almost daily basis, an important part of their plan.

As Martín went over the details of the hit on Vallejo with Miguel Arête, he decided on a few changes to Luis's plan. He had to do something to convince Santiago he'd done his best to carry out Santiago's wishes.

Luis and Phil set things in motion and then went about their normal duties. When their day ended, Luis suggested dinner at Coasters—"just in case," he joked "One last, good meal."

During dinner, Luis suggested altering their plan, insisting Phil leave the park as soon as the sting went down. "You can fade into the background with the agents making the drug bust. That way, Arête will face only one target. He's lasted this long because he's a cautious man."

His partner flatly refused, insisting he didn't trust Martín Orozco despite Luis's confidence in the *Sureño*. It also left Luis too exposed. He'd be facing two gang members with no backup. "Let's stick to the original plan, Luis."

Both men were certain Miguel Arête would insist on making the kill shot himself. Martín was there for backup, which probably included taking out Reed.

Their plans complete, Luis gave his partner a reassuring pat on the shoulder. "Dinner's over; let's head for the park."

As Luis hoped, the staged drug bust went down without a hitch. Once the police officers left the area, Luis found himself tensing as he walked toward his car. He'd taken Martín at his word, and his instincts told him he'd made the right decision. A sudden thought, however, made Luis pause. *Had Davis Reynolds done the same thing that night on the beach in Manzanillo?*

Luis saw the man's shadow first then watched in surprise as Arête pitched forward, his gun discharging harmlessly. *Where the hell's Martín*, Luis wondered as he glanced around the park. Just as he spotted him, a second shot gave Luis an adrenaline rush.

It took him a few seconds to realize Phil was the one who'd fired. Martín, who'd materialized from behind a tree, collapsed a few feet from Arête. His howls made it obvious he wasn't dead or even seriously wounded.

"You shot me, you bastard," Martín snarled at Phil.

"Damn right, asshole, you targeted Luis. You're lucky I didn't kill you. I still might." Phil's chest was heaving, and Luis saw the hatred in his partner's eyes."

"I didn't intend to kill him if that's what you think. I simply wanted to put a bullet in him so it looked like I tried. One of you needs to shoot Miguel, too. A knife wound might trigger questions in people I don't want getting curious. So, do me a favor and lose the evidence or claim the knife as your own."

"Why should we believe you didn't intend to kill Luis?" Phil challenged Martín. "Give me one good reason."

Luis laughed, his eyes showing genuine amusement. "I can. I had every intention of giving Martín a souvenir of this night's work and for the same reason he decided to shoot me, to give him some credibility."

Phil cocked his head, listening. "I think I hear a siren, which means someone's reported gunfire. We'd better get Martín out of here if you don't want him arrested.

"I don't," Luis agreed. "You got a doc that will deal with your arm if we drop you at home or someplace safe?"

"My car's right over there. Since I need to be 'the one who got away,' I'll have to drive myself. What about my knife?"

"My knife," Luis corrected. "One more thing, Martín, Lourdes Arête still needs help. Any chance you don't need the money back?"

"No problem—I can't believe I just said that. While I'm at it, I'll keep an eye on her family, too. Her dad was a *hijo de puta,* but that's not on her or her *mamá.*"

As Martín walked away, Luis picked up the knife, wiped it against his pants, and replaced the *Sureno's* prints with his.

"As your partner, do I know you carry a non-regulation knife?" Phil teased Luis.

"Not a clue," Luis insisted before greeting the police officers approaching him and Phil cautiously.

"FBI," Luis told them. "I'll reach nice and slow for my credentials."

"What the hell happened?"

"We had a drug bust a little earlier this evening and thought we got them all. Evidently, two men held back and decided on a little revenge. They came after me and my partner."

"I see one man down. Where's the other one?"

"He got away, but Phil's pretty sure he shot him. You might want to check for blood in the grass."

"You think your man's dumb enough to head for that emergency room over there?" the second policemen asked.

Phil laughed. "He's dealing drugs, so he's not the brightest bulb on the tree. I'd sure as Hell check it out."

After the policemen took their statements, agents Vallejo and Reed headed home for the night. They'd have to fill out their own reports in the morning. Within minutes of their filing, Luis got a call from Adam Pulaski.

"I had a fucking tail on you for a week, Vallejo and nothing. He's back in Washington two days, and this goes down. You're one lucky son-of-a-bitch. But you've pressed your luck too far. I want you in Washington on the next plane."

"I'd rather not. This is my case, mine and Davis Reynolds. What if I make a counter-suggestion?"

"Go ahead; I'm listening."

"Wilma Blankenship is proving to be a good asset. What if I stay cooped up in her house while everyone thinks I've gone back to

Washington? Between us, we can be your eyes and ears in the L.A. office. Ackerman's bound to be hyper-vigilant right now, and he's a smart man. I don't want to spend the rest of my life chasing him down. Deal?"

"I guess so, but make sure you stay put. What about your partner?"

"He's got plenty to do in San Diego, and I don't think he's on the Triad's radar. It's me they want."

"Do you want me to notify Wilma Blankenship she's about to have a houseguest?"

"Nah, let me surprise her."

Chapter Twenty-Seven

"Somehow, I never saw myself as the cougar type," Wilma teased Luis. "How am I going to explain a hunky FBI agent hanging out in my townhouse to my friends?"

Although Luis grinned, he gave his associate a serious answer. "No one's supposed to know I'm here, Wilma, which means no explanations will be necessary. I'll monitor communications between Ackerman and the others the best I can from your townhouse while you keep an eye on them from your office.

"Don't expect anyone in that group to get careless," he warned her, "but wouldn't a screwup on their part be a nice bonus? We'd better call Pulaski and find out what he's got planned."

Wilma nodded and put her cell on speakerphone when the deputy director accepted her call.

"Wilma," he said cautiously, "good to hear your voice."

"She knows pretty much everything I know," Luis informed his boss. "I think it's time to speak freely."

"Everything except why you chose to sideline me on this," Wilma added grumpily. "I want to see something in writing on that."

Adam Pulaski's tone was mollifying. "The decision was mine, Wilma—and it doesn't indicate any lack of confidence in you. It was just too late in the game to bring in someone new."

"Except that's exactly what Luis did when I started snooping around. Let's change the subject for now, but I'll want a full explanation later. The good news is we know when the drugs are arriving, at least what day. We also know where. What we don't know is who is bringing them in or how."

"If it's coming into the port of Long Beach, it'll be commercial, probably container shipments," Luis guessed. "How will they get it past the dogs?"

They heard Pulaski's hesitation. "I'm not sure. Sometimes, the handlers are bribed to use dogs that haven't been trained. Another trick is rubbing something strong, like menthol, on the dog's noses to block their sense of smell. There are all kinds of ways of getting past security, especially if you're part of security."

"If it's containerized, and we know the pier it's arriving at, we could search every ship arriving that day," Wilma offered.

"Your plan won't work," Pulaski objected. "For one thing, I don't want anyone arrested at the docks. We need to find out where the drugs go for distribution after they arrive. And the fact we know the specific pier the ship will be docking at tells us port personnel are involved. Pier slots usually aren't assigned until arrival. That means we've got an additional problem. Any suggestions?"

"We have two more days," Luis told the others. "Let's use the time to consider every option we can think of, but as important as the drugs are, I don't want anyone doing anything to jeopardize nailing Ackerman and his associates. That's my priority."

"Agreed," the deputy director told them. "To make sure we're not distracted, or stretched too thin, I've already decided we're not moving forward on the cleanup of the state and federal prisons in southern California until the drug bust and the arrest of Ackerman and the others go down. We'll need a few days, anyway, to bring the state officials in on what's going on in their prisons. They aren't going to be happy."

After a short silence, Pulaski came back on the line. "Sorry about that, another call. We'll talk again later tonight," he promised. "I have to take this call."

Wilma put her cell on vibrate and glanced at Luis's small suitcase. The SSA packed light. "You've got your choice of two bedrooms, but I'm betting you'd prefer blue-gray to lilac," she teased him. "Dinner's at six if you'd like a short nap."

Adam Pulaski's phone call came just as Wilma and Luis finished dinner. "Everything's set. My alpha team will take point on identifying the ship and the container company being used. They'll also work with DEA officials to follow and arrest the gang members involved in bringing the drugs in and handling their distribution.

"I want you and Wilma to work with a second team. Your focus will be on arresting Ackerman, Nader, Stevens, and Howard. I've listed them by priority, but I want every one of those bastards. Any questions?"

"Tell me more about the timeline." Wilma managed to make it sound more like a request than an order but just barely. Her instinct for command amused Luis.

"Still in flux until we find out what ship the drugs are on. Your end of things needs to go down the minute those drug raids begin, so you're not going to get a lot of notice. SSA Burich and his team are arriving in L.A. tomorrow, Wilma. He'll swing by your place sometime around noon, so plan accordingly."

"You're staying in Washington?" Luis asked.

"Got to. I'm too visible for field work these days. If I show up in L.A., Ackerman will find out about it and smell a rat. We're getting close now, and I want a textbook performance out of everyone. Davis Reynolds deserves nothing less."

• • • •

Deputy Director Pulaski eyed the teams gathered in the conference room adjacent to his office sternly. They, in return, maintained a respectful silence.

"We're down to the wire on this, and I'm not sure who we can trust at the port in L.A., so discretion always. The DEA has its operatives in every container port in western Mexico gathering information on ships headed for Long Beach that are scheduled to arrive in California on December 23rd.

"We should have that information by tomorrow at the latest. I have no idea if we're looking at one ship or half-a-dozen likelies. Obviously, the number of ships will determine our strategy. You're on the next two flights to L.A. out of here. Margie has your packets—tickets, hotels, specific assignments—waiting for you. Get it right. We're doing this for Davis Reynolds."

The seven men and three women Pulaski was sending to California knew better than to discuss their upcoming operation on the plane or anywhere they could be overheard, but the need for secrecy increased their eagerness to meet with the team they'd been assigned to. This was huge, basically two operations in one. Each agent heading west believed he or she had been assigned to the more interesting and important task.

Once they landed, everyone went directly to their hotels and waited for their team leader to call a meeting. SSA Donald Evans, an internationally experienced agent, would lead the takedown of the drug peddlers planning to distribute the fentanyl.

Ned Burich, another veteran agent, headed the team working with Luis and Wilma. Burich wasn't sure how he felt about sharing his command, especially with agents he didn't know. On the other hand, he trusted the deputy director's judgment, and what choice did he have?

Deputy Director Pulaski's first call went to Don Evans.

"We've got solid information from our agents in Mexico. It looks like there are three possibilities out of Lazaro Cárdenas—the *Maya Maru*, a Dutch freighter, the *Maria Elena* out of Chile, and the *Benjamin Monroe* with U.S. registration. All are scheduled to arrive December 23rd. We won't know for certain which ship it is until they're assigned a pier. The one thing we're certain of is that the target ship will be berthed at Pier 7.

"The other two likely container ports, Manzanillo and Ensenada, don't show any ships arriving in Long Beach on the 23rd, so we can probably eliminate them unless something changes.

"We have a DEA agent at Lazaro Cárdenas who will identify the companies who've scheduled container space on all three ships. As soon as the ships arrive and get their pier designations, we'll know which freighter the drugs are on, the number of containers each company has, and the shipping ID numbers we're after."

Agent Evans frowned as he listened to his boss. "How do we get to these containers to plant tracking devices if we can't trust port personnel?"

"That's the stickiest part of the plan, but I think you'll like what we've come up with. I'll contact the city of Long Beach's fire marshal and the port's fire and security personnel right after the ship we're looking for docks. We'll inform them we have a report of illegal hazardous material arriving at the port. Since we aren't certain which ship contains the hazardous material, we'll need to search every ship arriving at Pier 7 within a certain time frame. We'll make the window small enough it won't include more than two or three ships.

"I want you to take charge personally of supervising the assignment of port personnel to various teams. Because we don't know who to trust, see that the port's personnel wind up searching the ships we aren't interested in. If that doesn't work, point them in the wrong direction once they board with you. Your team will find the suspect containers and tag them with the mini-trackers you'll find in your equipment.

"Just to make it interesting," Pulaski continued, "one of the other two ships will have at least one container of 'hazardous material' that will be removed before the ships near it can be offloaded. Finding HM should make any dock workers on the Mexican Mafia's payroll less suspicious. It will also slow down any offloading, giving you time to put the next part of the operation in place.

"Once you know how many containers you're tracking, put together teams to follow the drugs. I doubt they'll all go to the same location, so split your men into squads. The DEA will handle the raids, but I want at least one of your men assigned to each operation."

"Any idea what's coming in?"

"Fentanyl, for sure, lots of it. I'm guessing some meth, too. They pack small, which means we probably aren't looking at a large number of containers—three or four at most. They could spread the shipment out, but this increases the risk of detection and creates logistical problems."

"There are a lot of loose ends here, Adam."

"Not as many as you think. Timing is the trickiest part. We won't know which ship has the drugs until we know the pier assignments for the three ships. Then, the involvement of the fire marshal and port officials has to go down quickly. That's your job. But *no-warning* raids are more common than you'd think when hazardous materials are suspected.

"In the meantime, the DEA agent in Mexico will give us the company ID designations for whichever ship docks at Pier 7. Once you're on board, you can use the ship's manifest to target the areas where the containers we want to put trackers on are stored."

Supervisory Special Agent Evans frowned again. "At the risk of repeating myself, I'm still concerned that there are a lot of moving parts here."

"I put you in charge for a reason, Don. You can think on your feet. This is going to work. Thanks to you, those drugs are never going to hit the streets. Think of it as a Christmas present to all those who won't die and their loved ones."

Evans called his team together immediately after he hung up the phone. This was the hardest part of the operation for him—waiting for the information he needed to make the bust.

• • • •

"It's the *Maria Elena*, the Chilean ship," Pulaski told his Alpha team via speaker phone. "Only two companies are loading at Lazaro Cárdenas—Renfru Industries and Márquez Container Shipping. Renfru has 18 containers, all of them refrigerated cars with a cargo of seafood. Since the company ships regularly from Lazaro Cárdenas to Long Beach, I doubt it's them."

"What do we know about the other company?" Special Agent Douglas Fowler asked.

Pulaski answered after checking his notes. "They're a small operation, no more than three or four shipments a year, usually craft items and toys. They're loading three containers."

"Easy enough to check on both shipments," Evans assured his boss." It won't take us any longer than the teams searching the other ships. We've got all we need, so let's roll."

"Give Burich a heads-up now and a second call as soon as you start boarding the *Maria Elena*, Deputy Director Pulaski told the SSA. "Careful, Don. Messing with the Mexican Mafia isn't all fun and games."

"Says who?" his old friend challenged him.

Twenty-five minutes after Evans made the phone calls to the city fire marshal and the port's fire and security main office, the FBI agents met the city and port officials sent to Pier 7 in the port's main security facility. Evans quickly explained the situation.

Then, he broke his men, already augmented with DEA agents he didn't identify, into three teams that would search each of the ships for the suspicious containers. He added port security personnel and two specially trained firemen to each of the teams.

The next step was meeting with the captains of the three ships, getting a copy of each ship's cargo, and initiating the search. Their intel out of Lazaro Cárdenas proved solid. A quick search of the first Márquez container was all they needed. After placing the mini-trackers on each of the three containers, Evan's men and the

DEA agents moved on, continuing the search with the local officials who'd been sent to a different part of the ship.

The search ended when the team searching the freighter docked next to the *Maria Elena* spotted medical wastes, both radioactive and infectious, in a small container shipped out of Colombia. To Evan's amusement, the search team also found two containers on the same ship that were chock full of heroin bricks. He'd let the DEA deal with that.

Cargo off-loading, already on hold, would be delayed another two or three hours at the pier thanks to these discoveries. Evans used the time to organize the next part of the operation—following the containers and initiating the raids that would recover the drugs and bust the *Sureño* gang members set to distribute the fentanyl.

To Evan's surprise, all three containers were loaded onto trucks headed for the same address, which turned out to be a warehouse in Frogtown. As soon as he knew the bust was underway, Evans made a quick call to Ned Burich. Then, he clapped his hands in anticipation. They were down to the fun part.

Chapter Twenty-Eight

"**N**ice work, Don! I'll want to hear all the details later." Ned Burich gave Luis a thumbs-up as he ended his call from Donald Evans. "Our turn now," he told the man sitting across from him in Wilma's kitchen with a grin.

"They followed the drugs from the port to a warehouse here in Los Angeles. Even as we speak, they're planning a major raid with DEA. As soon as Pulaski approves, we're clear to take down Ackerman and the rest of them."

"I'll call Wilma and see if they're all in the office," Luis volunteered. "The last I heard, Ackerman still hadn't returned from lunch, but he's notorious for taking long lunches. While I'm on the phone with her, why don't you call Pulaski and see what he's thinking?"

• • • •

Deputy Director Pulaski's adrenaline was running high. One operation was about to end successfully, and a second one would soon be underway. The only fly in the ointment was Ackerman's absence from FBI headquarters.

He'd hoped to get all four men in one clean sweep, but they couldn't wait any longer. No one in the office apparently knew where the ADIC went for lunch or why he didn't return.

The auditing team, which monitored the off-shore accounts of both Ackerman and Nader, still hadn't figured out what Ackerman did with a big withdrawal from one of his accounts in the Cayman Islands.

The Los Angeles ADIC had the money wired to a bank in Santa Barbara and then transferred to his local account a day later. A few hours after that, he'd withdrawn the entire amount in cash.

The auditors couldn't find any trace of what he'd done with the money. Pulaski spent several days puzzling over it. Quick getaway money? *Unlikely,* he decided. *It isn't easy to cart around nearly $300,000 in cash.* Foreign bearer bonds were a possibility. Hell, it could be any of a dozen things.

He'd worked through a probabilities list. The first idea that came to him was the possibility Ackerman planned to use the money to fund his disappearance.

An RV made some sense if Ackerman intended to stay stateside, but Pulaski doubted a man as smart as Ackerman would consider staying in the United States. Buying a small plane seemed unlikely, as well.

Three-hundred thousand wasn't enough money for a plane big enough to fly any distance, and where could he go that didn't require a flight plan? Even more telling, as far as Pulaski could see from his file and some quiet sleuthing, Ackerman didn't know how to fly a plane.

Given Ackerman's location on the Pacific Ocean, a seaworthy boat seemed like a good bet, something small enough he could handle it himself and sturdy enough to take well out into the ocean. A boat was a wise choice for other reasons, as well.

With hundreds of marinas and maybe thousands of private docks along the southern California coastline, the FBI had no easy way of finding him. Even with the help of the coast guard, he'd be hard to apprehend once he left for Mexico. He could head for any number of Mexican ports—big or small.

That's as far as he'd gotten in his thinking, and it all remained conjecture. It was best for his men to make their move now. Once they arrested everyone else, he'd concentrate on finding Ackerman if he never showed up at the office.

• • • •

Wilma met the part of Burich's team assigned to her at 4:35 P.M. in a nearby cafe and went over the last-minute details of their plan. Only Stevens and Howard were in the office now. Nader left the office fifteen minutes earlier, just before she got Pulaski's *go* directive. Timing, so critical in any operation, didn't seem to be working in their favor.

The three agents assigned to her accompanied Wilma into FBI headquarters, where they arrested Stevens and Howard without incident. They didn't have to take them far. The FBI's holding cells were in another part of the building.

Neither Stevens nor Howard showed any interest in discussing their missing colleagues' locations; nor did they ask Wilma what they were being accused of when Wilma interviewed them individually. Both maintained a stony silence.

"That better change," Wilma informed each of them, because it looks like the two of you are left to face charges while Ackerman and Nader conveniently slip away. "First one to talk wins points," she warned them. "I wonder which one of you is smarter."

Now, she'd let them sweat a little. Wilma used some of that time to speak privately with Jim Dudley and Mike Douglas about Ackerman's corrupt involvement with the Mexican Mafia. Neither man had any idea where their ADIC went.

Douglas, in particular, seemed to be in shock. He couldn't imagine betrayal at this level. How had it happened, and why hadn't he seen it?

"Why did Washington tell you and not us?" he challenged Wilma. "Were we suspects, too?"

While Wilma oversaw the paperwork on the arrests of Howard and Stevens, Ned Burich and Luis divided the remaining four agents into two groups. Douglas Fowler and Rick Bitterman would join Ned in a search for the now-missing John Nader. Luis and the other two agents would begin the search for Ackerman—a daunting task since he had a six-hour head start on them.

Deputy Director Pulaski had already informed them of the money Ackerman had withdrawn from his account in the Caymans. Luis agreed a boat capable of taking Ackerman to Mexico was the most likely purchase. But where he'd hidden this boat and what destination in Mexico Ackerman selected would be anyone's guess.

Luis warned his deputy director Ackerman might have used the money to buy prepaid credit card under one or more false names. That meant they shouldn't put all their efforts in finding a boat. "The truth is beyond searching his home and talking to his wife, we have no idea where to begin."

Before they split into two teams, Luis and Ned discussed the possibility Nader could be on that boat, too, if there was a boat, or on his way to join Ackerman. Luis doubted it. The ADIC struck him as a lone wolf at heart, one who fundamentally didn't trust anyone. Nader was a follower who'd served his purpose. The ADIC's unofficial second-in-command would be on his own now, like Stevens and Howard.

With nowhere else to start, Special Agent Burich drove to Nader's home in the West Adams Boulevard neighborhood. Nader apparently lived well for an FBI agent. Since he'd been divorced over twenty years, Burich doubted Nader had married money, and they knew from his bio he hadn't inherited it. *Why, then*, he wondered, *hadn't Nader's affluent lifestyle raised any red flags?*

There was no car in the missing agent's driveway, and no one answered the door, which didn't surprise anyone on the team. A glimpse through the garage's side door's window showed only empty space. Their target was gone, just as they'd expected.

"Should we search inside?" Fowler asked.

Burich nodded. "It's probably a waste of time, but it might give us a clue about where he went. It's also the only way we can be sure he isn't here."

They announced themselves before making a forced entry that set off two separate alarm systems. Three locked suitcases sat in the hallway, partially hidden from view. That changed everything. Burich's voice was crisp with authority.

"Fowler and Jones, upstairs—and be careful. I'm sure he's carrying. "Rick, you and I will sweep this level. He's here somewhere."

"Where the hell are his cars?"

"No idea. We'll worry about that later. If it turns out he's not here, we'll hide our own vehicles and wait."

The agents who'd gone upstairs cleared the back two bedrooms before the nearest closet door in the third bedroom flew open. "Shit!" Doug Fowler's surprised expletive preceded two shots fired at almost the same time. Then, the agents searching downstairs heard him finish his sentence after a yelp of surprise. "You bastard, you barely missed me."

"We got him," Matt Jones shouted down the stairs, "but you'd better call the EMTs."

"How bad?" Burich asked his agents as he hurried into the third bedroom. After taking a quick look at Nader's arm, he teased the colleague who'd shot him. "Matt, you're losing your touch. It's barely a scratch. I doubt he'll even need to go to emergency. He deserved at least a muscle shot"

"You fired on a fellow agent," Nader growled at Matt Jones. "I'll have your badge. You can't just barge in here without a warrant. I don't even know why you're here."

"Those packed suitcases suggest something different," Burich scoffed. "I doubt you'll be suing anyone since we have a warrant. Where's your boss?"

"Somewhere you'll never find him," Nader said smugly. "Now, I want to call my lawyer."

"How you going to pay him?" Fowler asked, turning to Burich. "You want to tell him, Ned? Or should I?"

"Be my guest," the senior officer told him.

"All your money's gone, numbnuts. Washington seized everything about three hours ago. I doubt you've got enough in your accounts now to pay for cab fare to the airport."

Ned Burich turned to Fowler. "I want you and Matt to bring him to Wilshire when the medics are through with him. I'll take Bitterman with me. I doubt catching up to Ackerman will be as easy as nailing the other three. Luis Vallejo wants him bad, and it's personal with him, so I don't want him searching on his own."

· · · ·

Luis and the two agents assigned to him drove to Robert Ackerman's home in Sherman Oaks. It was a sprawling, comfortable-looking ranch house with a dark blue Mercedes convertible parked in the driveway.

Ackerman's wife, tall and sour-looking, didn't seem surprised to see them. "He's not here, and I doubt he's planning to return. What's he done?"

Despite his fear that he was wasting precious time, Luis answered her question civilly. "What makes you think your husband's done something?"

"Gee, I don't know—little things like finding the house unlocked when I got home, his safe in the study left wide open, and a few of his personal things missing, along with his luggage. I also noticed Bob's wedding ring, the one I bought for him with such high hopes, sitting on top of his dresser. Then, you guys show up. I haven't lived with an FBI agent all these years for nothing."

"Do you have any idea where your husband is, Mrs. Ackerman?"

"Hell would be my first choice. Thirty-two years of worrying he'd be killed gradually turning into a desperate hope he would. He stopped confiding in me years ago. No, I have no idea where Bob is. What's your name, by the way?"

"Sorry, I'm SSA Luis Vallejo out of San Diego."

"Did he take a woman with him?"

"Excuse me?" Luis's voice showed his surprise.

"That would actually make me feel better—the idea Bob cared enough for someone to run away from his responsibilities. He didn't, did he? What did he do? I think I deserve to know."

"He's had some illegal dealings with the Mexican Mafia."

"Drugs? That surprises me. He's spent most of his life trying to stop the flow up from first Colombia and then Mexico. I guess I didn't know him as well as I thought I did."

"You're sure you don't know where he went?"

"Not a clue. I doubt you'll find him. My husband may be a bastard, but he's a smart man."

"We think he bought a boat recently, maybe stashed it at a nearby marina. Did he tell you he was considering something like that?"

"No, he never mentioned anything about a boat. Bob's not into recreation of any kind. Besides, he can't swim."

Luis noticed a sudden change in Mrs. Ackerman's eyes. She'd remembered something. "You're sure?" he prompted her. "Your husband left you behind and expects you to clean up all the mess and face the embarrassment this is going to cause you all alone. I don't think you owe him any loyalty."

"There is something though I'm not sure it's important. The word *marina* caught my attention, that's all. I found a receipt for marine fuel in Bob's old khaki jacket six or seven days ago. I saved it because I thought he might need it for his expense account."

"Do you have the receipt?"

"No, I gave it to him that same day. I remember the name of the marina, however. One of my few gifts in life is an eidetic memory. He got the fuel at a place called the Sun Harbor Marina—Pt. Loma, I think."

Luis nodded in appreciation. "Thank you, Mrs. Ackerman. I wish I could do something to make your life easier in the weeks and months ahead. You don't deserve this; no one does."

"It's Rose, Agent Vallejo. I'll be okay. Actually, I'll probably be better than okay. I have a sister in Oklahoma I haven't seen in a while. I'll leave an address where I can be reached when you need me, but I think it's time to start over."

Luis nodded, putting his hand on Rose Ackerman's shoulder briefly. "One day at a time," he advised her. "And I think you should postpone leaving for a while. I don't have to tell you why."

• • • •

"You are one lucky son-of-a-bitch, Vallejo," Agent Burns told him as they drove toward San Diego. "Ackerman could have been anywhere. Now, after sweet-talking his wife, you make a few phone calls, *et voila*, you have the guy's slip number."

"Except the boat's not there, and I doubt Ackerman's planning on a return. It's a big ocean," Luis replied.

"The coast guard's on it. They've got helicopters up, too. They'll find him."

"He'll make for international waters," Agent Walters guessed. "Make's interdiction harder."

"I don't think so," Luis responded. "Ackerman isn't an experienced boatman. I think he'll hug the shoreline. He's got a bolt-hole somewhere in Mexico, probably on the Baja. If he reaches it, finding him will be a whole lot harder."

"Will the *Federales* cooperate?" Burns wanted to know.

"I think so," Luis told the agent. "The Mexican navy, too. We have a good chance of getting him even though I doubt he's in U.S. waters by now."

They pulled into the U.S. Coast Guard's sector headquarters across from San Diego's international airport. A Jayhawk helicopter was waiting.

"Thought you might like to be in on the fun," a young captain informed him. "An NSC, that's *national security cutter* for you landlubbers, spotted him about 75 miles north of Ensenada.

"We're following him at a distance, but I doubt he knows we've found him. Don't worry, our guys won't let him reach shore, but the Mexican navy will do the actual stop. It's their waters, after all. They may or may not turn him over to the cutter that's following him. Let's go catch some sky."

Following the young coast guard officer's advice, Luis and the two agents he'd brought with him boarded the Jayhawker and sat back to enjoy the ride. Luis noticed the pilot flew a southwesterly pattern to make certain he stayed in neutral airspace. They'd been in the air just forty-five minutes when the call came in.

The Mexican navy had intercepted Ackerman's boat, a Sea Ray Sundancer, about five nautical miles from Ensenada. They hailed him in both English and Spanish before sending over a small boarding party.

Before the zodiac reached Ackerman, his boat blew up, knocking two Mexican officers on the navy's small craft into the water. The debris field made it clear no one could have survived the explosion. The former Los Angeles ADIC was dead, probably from explosives he'd placed on board though the Mexican authorities might never know what caused the blast.

Chapter Twenty-Nine

"**W**ell shit, that's kind of anticlimactic," Burns grumbled. "Guess Ackerman didn't want to risk a Mexican prison."

Luis maintained a morose silence while Burns and Walters chatted with the pilot on the way back to San Diego. The ADIC's death left Luis oddly dissatisfied. How was that quick, nearly painless death any kind of punishment for what Ackerman had masterminded, including the murder of Davis Reynolds?

He wondered about Barbara's reaction to the news that the man who ordered Davis's death was dead himself? Would she be relieved Ackerman died before he could profit from Davis's death or share Luis's resentment he'd gotten off so easily?

The government would move to trial as soon as they could, Luis suspected. Both the DOJ and the California state government would want to put the embarrassment behind them. *La EME*, he knew from experience, would just move on, seeing this as one small battle in an ongoing but very lucrative war.

The three agents made the drive from San Diego to Los Angeles in silence, all of them tired to the bone. It was after midnight when they arrived at the hotel where the two agents were staying. Burich and Bitterman waited in the lobby, annoyed they'd missed the party.

Although Luis wanted to interview Nader and the others, he knew he needed sleep and a chance to assess how things went down. Besides, no one was going to let him near the disgraced agents at one in the morning.

Justice, such as it was, had been dispensed in Ackerman's case. Now, Luis wanted to know for certain which of the three remaining agents had carried out the murder of Davis Reynolds. He could at least offer Barbara that small bit of comfort.

When Luis arrived at the FBI's headquarters on Wilshire Boulevard at 7:15 the next morning, he couldn't believe Wilma got there first. He hadn't heard her move around her house at all. "I never left headquarters," she informed him. "By the way, Pulaski will be here in a couple of hours."

She gave Luis a long look. "If I'm the one who stayed up all night, why is it you're the one who looks like Hell?"

Luis grinned reluctantly. "I distinctly remember you telling me I'm hot."

"I'm not disputing that. You disappointed Ackerman took the easy way out?"

Luis's grin faded. "What do you think? Barbara and Davis's kids deserve better."

"I doubt she's focused on that, Luis. From what you've told me, which isn't much, I'm guessing Barbara Allen simply wants to get on with her life. Where do things stand between the two of you, by the way?"

Luis's suddenly wary expression made Wilma laugh out loud. "You needn't poker up; I haven't been prying. It's just obvious your feelings for her aren't entirely professional."

Luis frowned "I haven't seen the woman in over two months, Wilma. I have no idea where her head's at. Once the marshals tell her Ackerman's dead and she'll be returning to California, I suspect losing Laura and Davie will be her biggest concern."

"I thought she was eager to go back to teaching."

"She is, or was, but Davis's death, not to mention staying ahead of everyone chasing her, has changed Barbara in important ways. I saw that in Castle Rock. She dealt with losing Davis Reynolds and the stress of hiding from some very bad guys by protecting his children and seeing to their emotional needs. I'm worried about what happens when her stress and sense of responsibility fall away."

"See, this sounds like more than a professional concern."

"No comment."

"None needed," she informed him, her eyes full of sympathy. "Davis Reynolds was an impressive man, Luis; everyone says so, but you're not exactly chopped liver. If you want her, man up and don't take *no* for an answer."

"You haven't met Barbara. She isn't the type you can force into a relationship. Believe me, I've tried."

"Then, try something else. Find out what she needs, which isn't necessarily what she says she needs, and give it to her." Wilma gave him a wry smile. "With two failed marriages, I'm the last person who should be giving advice. So, on another topic, what's your next move?"

"I want to interview Nader, Stevens, and Howard. One of them will tell me who killed Davis. That's the only question that interests me. I'll leave the rest to you and Pulaski."

· · · ·

Luis met first with Nader in one of the FBI's interrogation rooms. He already suspected Nader hadn't killed Davis. An experienced agent like Davis Reynolds would never have allowed someone he knew to be dirty to get that close unless they were friends. Richard Stevens, Davis's longtime colleague, almost certainly did the deed.

What Nader could do is confirm two important facts for Luis—Stevens killed Davis, and Bob Ackerman ordered the hit. Ackerman's second-in-command made it clear from the first he had no intention of cooperating.

"You've got nothing to offer me, Vallejo. Shaving a few years off my sentence isn't going to make any difference to me. Whether I die in prison or come out an old man, who cares?"

"You're FBI, Nader. Where you're going, that's going to create a special kind of Hell for you. I can at least see you're sent where one of your fellow prisoners won't slit your throat in the middle of the night."

"Don't care about that, either. I'm just sorry Bob didn't make it. One of us should have profited from the risks we took."

Luis decided on a different tactic with Stevens and Howard—choosing to interview the two of them together. It was risky, but he needed to sow the seeds of distrust.

"You two do know Ackerman and Nader screwed you over, right?"

"That's not true," Howard objected. "If you're saying this because they left headquarters earlier, you're wrong. We'd agreed to leave at different times. This wasn't supposed to go down so fast, and all of us wanted to avoid attracting attention."

"I'm talking about the money they didn't bother to share with you. Why is it Nader and Ackerman had multiple off-shore accounts with big dollars in them? Neither of you did, and, believe me, we looked. I'm guessing you stashed your money somewhere, but I'm betting it doesn't resemble anything like the $25 million Ackerman socked away. Nader had a more modest $12 million."

"You're lying," Stevens told him calmly. "Nice try."

"I can prove what I'm saying easily enough. What's your take, a couple of million, maybe as much as five? Small potatoes. You were had, my friends. Nader's convinced me he didn't kill Reynolds though he did confirm that Ackerman ordered the hit. That leaves you two. I'm guessing it was you, Stevens."

"Guessing free, but it buys you nothing."

"True, but your silence puts Howard at risk for a murder charge. Killing a Fed is serious business. How about it, Howard? You want to go down as an accessory? Tell the truth, and I'll see you get a few perks like easier prison time and maybe a few years off your sentence."

"He can't prove anything, Bob, and Pulaski won't be bound by anything Vallejo promises either one of us."

"I'm not promising *you* anything except justice, Stevens. There is no *us* in this little adventure. Bob here knows he has nothing to gain by staying silent. If he's smart, more than just computer smart, he's going to make the best deal for himself he can."

"I didn't kill Davis Reynolds, and you've got nothing that says I did. I heard it was Mexicans," Howard growled.

"Three Mexicans and a gringo according to several different witnesses," Luis confirmed. "That means one of you is guilty of murder and the other one isn't. The federal death penalty's been reinstated for capital crimes, Howard. You willing to take the fall for Stevens?"

"I didn't kill Reynolds," Howard repeated. "How many times do I have to say it?"

• • • •

Luis decided it was time to separate the two men. "OK, we'll do it the hard way. The deals off the table, Agent Howard, as of midnight tonight. I'll make myself available until then. If you choose not to cooperate, I intend to make your list of charges as long as I can, and, believe me, accessory to murder will be on that list.

"Oh, by the way, we already know from your passport that you were in Mexico, no doubt helping Stevens stash drugs in Reynold's house. This means we have the option of turning you over to the Mexican authorities. I've heard bad things about their prisons. I'm sure you have, too. Maybe they'll let the two of you share the same cell."

Knowing Stevens would never confess even to spare his partner, Luis returned to the wing housing the FBI short-term prisoners shortly before 9 P.M. and requested Stevens be brought once again to an interrogation room. "Make sure Howard hears you retrieving him," he told the older of the two guards, "and that he overhears you telling Stevens he made a smart decision. Shut down any response he tries to make."

Luis acknowledged Stevens with a nod when he entered the interrogation room but didn't speak. Instead, he turned away and left Stevens alone in a locked room with a guard outside. Less than ten minutes later, another guard informed Luis that Howard wanted to speak with him.

"You guessed right, Vallejo," the computer whiz told Luis with a surly look. "Ackerman sent Stevens down to Manzanillo with orders to kill Davis because he was getting too close to finding out about the next drug shipment. I didn't have anything to do with it beyond rigging things to make Davis look guilty of dealing drugs. If that bastard said I did it or helped in any way, he's a goddamned liar."

"Did Stevens tell you anything about the murder?"

"No, not really—said he puked afterward. They actually were friends, you know."

"Anything else?"

"I don't know many details, but I do know the Mexicans in that boat with Stevens were members of the *Familia Michoacana*. I heard Ackerman making the arrangements on the phone."

Luis returned to the room holding Richard Stevens. The disgraced agent gave him a dirty look.

"I suppose Bob told you I was the man in that zodiac. He's a liar and so desperate to save his own skin I doubt anything he says will hold up as evidence in court."

"How'd you know it was a zodiac, Stevens? I never mentioned that little detail."

"I'm sure I heard it from someone, or maybe I just guessed. I can't be sure, of course, seeing as how I wasn't there."

"We'll see what the eyewitnesses say."

"There aren't any witnesses," Stevens told him smugly, "except for the kids and Reynolds' babe. And they had to be too far away ... at least that's what Howard told me," he added after a slight hesitation.

Luis gave Rick Stevens a feral smile. "Nice save, but it's one more nail in your coffin. You sure you don't want to brag about how you suckered your old friend and left him bleeding out on the beach?

"I didn't know Davis Reynolds all that well," Luis continued, "but I knew him well enough to know he gave you the benefit of the doubt. He paid a terrible price for that simple act of decency.

"Now, it's your turn to pay. I hope they fry your ass, but I also hope you make appeal after appeal, praying to God you can buy a little time until the day comes you realize time's up. I'll be there when it happens, Stevens, and I'll be smiling."

Luis drew his hand across his throat, indicating it was time to stop recording their conversation. Then, he turned and walked away. It took everything he had not to pound Richard Stevens senseless. Tears filled his eyes as he walked out into the cool night air.

Davis's death, however painful, happened fast. Barbara's suffering went on much longer, was still going on. Laura and Davie continued to suffer, too. There would be retribution but no real justice, not for them.

• • • •

Deputy Director Pulaski debriefed his team at the Los Angeles headquarters of the FBI, laying out the next phase of the operation. They'd be going after prison officials in both federal and California state prisons known to be corrupt.

Luis was thanked for his service and dismissed. He had no part in this investigation, and his ADIC in San Diego wanted Luis returned to his regular duties.

Investigating gang activities didn't interest Luis at the moment. He focused on one thing—Barbara Allen's return to California. He also wondered whether or not Laura and Davie would be sequestered with her until after she testified at the trial or if the authorities planned to turn them over to their aunt.

His first thought was to seek permission to visit them, either together or separately, when the three of them returned to southern California. Then, he thought of another possibility. Suspecting the marshals wouldn't break their rules, he decided on a different approach.

He'd get Deputy Director Pulaski, who owed him, to pressure WITSEC to keep the three of them together. Then, he'd ask his SAC to lend him to the marshal service for the month or more they'd be in hiding. He could be part of the security team.

"Are you fucking kidding me, Vallejo?" SAC William Kellerman growled. "Your partner's been holding down the fort for the better part of a year, and now you want time off?"

"It's only for a few months, Billy, and Phil's doing fine without me. I've been part of this case since Davis Reynolds died on that beach in Mexico. My testimony will be important in putting those three away and verifying their links to *La EME*. I can use this time to get ready for the trial."

"What makes you think the U.S. Marshals will let you bunk with an important witness. It isn't exactly protocol."

"I'm another set of eyes and an extra gun. Wherever Barbara Allen and those children are now, they're safe because no one's knows where to look for them. The U.S. is a damned big pond. That changes once the marshals bring them here to California. Don't forget, I'm a target, too. *La EME's* already made one try at me."

"So, you want to go hide like a scared little girl?" the SAC jeered.

"That's insulting, Billy, and sexist, too. Davis's daughter, Laura, is as brave as any of the agents I've worked with over the years and a hell of a lot smarter than most of them. She's eight and doing her best to cope with tragedy you can't even imagine. I want to be there for her and for Davis's son, too."

"And maybe rekindle an old romance, huh?" Bill Kellerman laughed at his favorite agent. "You needn't look so pissed; even SACs hear scuttlebutt from time to time. You really think this is important?"

"I do. If you can't see your way clear to doing this, Billy, I intend to tender my resignation today."

"Oh, for Christ's sake, Luis, don't be such a stiff-necked asshole. If and when Barbara Allen and the kids are relocated to this area, I'll see that you're temporarily assigned to their protection. You don't need to take a leave of absence. But you'll owe me, and I never forget a favor, at least not one owed to me."

Chapter Thirty

B arbara looked up, first in curiosity and then surprise, from the journal she was reading in Northern Arizona University's library. Roxanne Peterson, the agent responsible for protecting her, was standing there with a serious look on her face.

A sudden panic had Barbara scrambling to her feet. "Has something happened to Davie or Laura?"

"No, Scott has them. He picked them up at school a few minutes ago. I'm here to collect you. Just so you know, you're a hard person to track down. That means you have less than two hours to pack before we take you back to California."

"The FBI's ready for me to testify?" Barbara asked, her relief evident.

"No, not yet. But it's getting close enough the prosecutors want to go over the details of what you saw in Manzanillo and the attempt on your life in Castle Rock. They also need to prep you for the trial."

"Are we going to L.A.?" Another thought made her eyes widen in panic for a second time. "They're not going to separate me from Laura and Davie, are they?"

Roxanne put a reassuring hand on Barbara's shoulder. "The address they gave us is West Covina, and no, the kids are going to stay with you until the FBI assesses the danger they might or might not be in. They won't be testifying, at least, that's the scuttlebutt."

Laura was crying when Barbara entered the University Heights' home they'd lived in for the last two months. Davie sat listlessly near his sister, holding her hand. Davis's young son looked confused and defeated.

Laura turned desperate eyes on the woman she'd come to depend on. "I don't want to go, Barbara. I'll miss my friends. Why do we have to keep moving? Davie doesn't want to go, either. We like it here."

"Things are changing, sweetheart. The bad men who killed your father are in jail, and I need to testify against them. Then, you'll have a real home, a permanent home. No more moving."

"Will it be with Aunt Monica?" Davie asked.

"I don't know, but that's probably what will happen."

"Luis said we'd be a family," Laura objected, tears in her eyes. "He promised."

"He wants us to be a family, Laura; so do I, but I'm also sure the courts will be the ones to decide. I'll make you a promise, too, just like Luis did. The two of us will support whatever you and Davie choose about who you want to live with. But I want you to remember that the judges, your aunt, and your grandparents will do what they believe is best for you and Davie."

She tousled Laura's now much longer hair. "One good thing, for sure, will come out our return to California. You'll be able to see Luis again. At least, I think you will."

"Seems likely," Roxanne told her three charges, a small, secret smile on her face.

• • • •

By the time their SUV turned into the driveway of the suburban ranch home in West Covina that would be their next temporary stop, everyone was resigned to starting over. On the long trip from Flagstaff to L.A., Roxanne and Scott reassured Barbara and her charges they'd stay with them until Barbara's role in the trial was over. Then, of course, everything would change.

All of them spotted a familiar figure sitting on the front steps of the house immediately.

"Luis," Davie and Laura shouted in unison. "It's Luis!"

Both tumbled out of the car and ran toward the FBI agent. He scooped both of them up and planted kisses on their cheeks, reminding Barbara of Davis doing the same thing in Manzanillo.

Tears filled her eyes as she remembered the loving look on Davis's face. She saw that same expression now.

"They've missed you," Barbara told him in a quiet, controlled voice. She didn't want Luis to know how much she'd missed him.

"I thought they might have forgotten me by now. It's been two months."

"And seventeen days," Laura reminded him. "I've counted every one of them."

"Can you stay with us?" Davie asked. Those words had been part of nearly every conversation Luis shared with Davis's little boy. This time, the answer was different.

"Yes, I can—in fact, I have to. I'm part of your security team. I'll be staying here with you until the trial's over."

"For reals?" Davie challenged him.

"Yup, you may be sick of me before the trial's over."

Davie shook his head vehemently. "You can share my room if it's big enough unless you'd rather sleep with Barbara."

After a quick, amused look at Barbara, Luis responded courteously to Davie's offer. "The house is big enough we can all have our own rooms. But if you're ever scared, Davie, or even sad, you can bunk with me, OK?"

"OK, Laura, too?"

Luis smiled at Laura's vivid blush. "Somehow, I think she'd be more comfortable with Barbara."

Since their arrival a few hours earlier, Luis had devoted most of his attention to Davis's children. Now, he drew Barbara aside for a private moment. "We need to talk."

"Well, we should have plenty of opportunity if you're part of our security team," she said coolly.

"Don't, Barbara, don't push me away. There's so much I need to tell you."

"Personal or professional?"

"Both."

"Later, when Davie and Laura are asleep."

Davie, more emotionally open than his sister, came looking for Luis at that point and stayed within touching distance of him through dinner. They'd settled for delivery pizza since there were almost no groceries in the house. Tales of Flagstaff dominated Davie's conversation.

"I liked it there, Luis. We had big trees in our backyard, and it snowed a lot. School was cool, too. I can read by myself now, so Laura doesn't have to read stories to me anymore."

He'd exaggerated, but Barbara didn't correct him. Davie thrived in Flagstaff once she'd changed his school. It was the one thing she regretted—leaving the Mountain School behind. Both children had flourished there.

Finally, and with great resistance on Davie's part, Barbara got both Laura and Davie down for the night. The house seemed eerily quiet as she joined Luis in the living room. Roxanne and her partner were making a run for groceries. A brief, awkward silence descended as each waited for the other to speak.

Luis caved first. "Barbara, these last two months damn near made me crazy. You'll never know how hard I found it to have no idea where you'd gone or what was happening in your world. But I think we'll finally get justice for Davis. Ackerman's dead, but Stevens, Howard, and Nader will be spending a long time in jail. It was Stevens who killed Davis, by the way. He may get a capital sentence. I intend to do my best to see he does."

Barbara nodded, but her thoughts had nothing to do with justice. Davis was irretrievably gone. Putting those responsible for his death behind bars made no difference in her life. It didn't change anything for Laura and Davie, either. She doubted Luis would ever understand her feelings.

"You don't take any comfort in that, do you?" he said suddenly, his voice gentle. "It's different for me. I believe in justice—in balancing the scales. And putting those bastards in jail makes you and the kids safer. That's even more important."

Both returned to their earlier silence, and, again, Luis spoke first. "I wish I could bring him back to you, Barbara. You deserve to have the life you lost that day."

Barbara's mind followed another track. "Luis, the day I went into witness protection, you told me I bore some responsibility for our failed relationship. You said I allowed my prejudices to sabotage a love that should have flourished. I can't tell you how much your words hurt me. I live with them every day."

"I never intended to hurt you, Barbara."

"I know, Luis. You simply spoke the truth, and that's why I found your words so painful. I never saw myself as prejudiced. I thought I was behaving as a rational, informed professional would—making assessments on probable behavior and protecting myself against hurts to come if we moved forward."

"It's healthy to want to protect yourself, Barbara, from both physical and emotional danger. I understand why you did what you did."

"Don't try to excuse my behavior, Luis. Everything you said was true. I harmed both of us because I allowed statistics and my professional training to blind me to an important truth. You're a distinct, unique individual, one who deserves to be judged, or, rather, accepted, on your own merits. I'm truly sorry."

Luis's eyes showed regret. "The greater guilt is mine. I pretty much lived up to the cliché of both cop and traditional Hispanic male. Although my behavior didn't match what was in my heart, I kept my feelings private, which shows you how smart I am. You're an intelligent woman, Barbara, but you're not omniscient. You had no way of knowing my heart. I'm sorry, too."

"What's going to happen to Laura and Davie?" she asked, partly to change the emotional intensity in the room and equally because it was uppermost in her mind.

"I don't know, but I doubt we'll get a fair hearing. Their aunt will take them out of a sense of duty, but she doesn't want them. They'll grow up with nannies and private schools."

Barbara put her fingers over her mouth, deep in thought. "I promised Laura we'd support whatever choice the two of them made. Money can't replace love, Luis. I'm not sure how I'll get up in the morning if I know they're unhappy."

"Well, I did promise I'd kidnap the three of you. Are you interested in being a fugitive the rest of your life if things don't go our way?"

"We aren't a couple, Luis, and I doubt it would make much difference to the courts if we were."

"We aren't a couple yet," he corrected. "I haven't given up on us. And I'm spending the next couple of months with you, Laura, and Davie. Anything can happen in that much time."

"I don't think time is going to help me fall out of love with Davis Reynolds."

"I don't expect that to ever happen, *Bebe*. Laura and Davie are always going to love their daddy, too. That's the way it should be. But I also see their affection for me. I'm asking you to let those two incredibly wise children be your guide. They feel no need to choose between holding onto their memories of their father and building a relationship with me."

"You make it sound easier than it is."

"Nothing worthwhile comes easy, Barbara. In a few months, everything is going to change. The trial will be over. There's a high likelihood Davie and Laura will go to their aunt at least temporarily, and you'll be reinstated at the University of San Diego."

"That isn't enough for me anymore. I can't let them go, Luis; I just can't. Would you really take us out of the country?" Barbara wasn't sure if she was considering the option seriously or not.

"Yes," he said without hesitation, "if I'd exhausted every other option. I've changed, Barbara. Work isn't enough for me, either. But we're two smart people. Let's find a better solution."

"I suppose you think we should start by getting married as soon as I'm out of witness protection. I'm sure you believe that would make our case for keeping Davie and Laura stronger."

Luis shook his head, regret, once again, in his eyes. "I won't marry you, *Bebe*, not until I know for certain that you love me at least as much as you love Davis. I'm willing to share you with Davis and his children, *querida*, but I have to be an equal partner."

• • • •

As the weeks passed in isolation, Barbara and Luis sensed an unusual intimacy growing between them. It wasn't so much physical, at least not sexual, as emotional. Still, they sat close to each other and touched with growing frequency.

Luis returned to an earlier passion—brushing her hair and braiding it before she went to bed. He was a naturally affectionate male, Barbara realized, much as Davis had been—touching her hair or her cheek and pulling her to him for a hug when he saw sadness in her eyes.

Luis and Davis are very different men, Barbara acknowledged privately, *but I see similarities, too*. Both had strong protective instincts and a tender side. They shared a love for children and a talent for parenting. She'd seen that immediately in Davis but it took longer with Luis. There'd been no opportunity to observe him around children until Laura and Davie came into his life.

Both lived by a strict ethical code, and both were risk takers. That last trait worried her. Davis's death in Manzanillo made it essential his children never experience this kind of loss again.

She saw a need for stability as one of the main obstacles to a permanent relationship with Luis. Davie and Laura needed to know the adults in their lives would be there for them.

Although she longed to share her concerns with Luis, Barbara didn't know how to initiate this particular conversation. His work was as much a part of his identity as hers had always been for her. How could she ask him to give that up?

• • • •

Barbara suspected Luis would grow restive living as she had for more than six months now—isolated and housebound. Instead, he stayed busy on small projects both inside and outside their rented house.

"Mister Fixit," Roxanne called him, and the nickname seemed appropriate. Davie followed Luis everywhere, asking questions and imitating Luis's moves as the FBI agent fixed leaking faucets, unclogged toilets, and tackled their weed-filled backyard.

When a tiny, abandoned kitten wandered into their front yard, more dead than alive, Luis taught Laura how to care for it. "It needs more than food and water, Laura. It needs human warmth—to be held gently and frequently. This little one has had a rough start. More than anything, it needs to feel loved and safe."

"I can do that," she assured him solemnly.

Luis put his hand on her head, his eyes soft with affection. "Yes, you can, Laura. This kitten's luck changed today because it found you. Have you decided on a name?"

"Since I don't know if this is a boy kitty or a girl kitty, I think I'll call it Lucky. Is that an OK name?"

"It's perfect, sweetheart."

On April 17th, Barbara received word she'd be testifying in the first of three trials the following Tuesday. She felt ready. Luis had given her a clear picture of what the prosecutor wanted from her and the likely tactics of Nader's lawyer in the first of the three trials.

"I forgot you trained as a lawyer, Luis. Do you ever think about how different your life might have been if you'd opened a practice?"

"Too dull," he told her with a mischievous smile, "I need more excitement in my life. That's why I've always liked undercover work."

Those words rattled around her brain as she went into the courtroom. Over a week earlier, Luis had casually mentioned the attempt on his life in the park, glossing over the danger and making it sound almost humorous.

Luis is perfect for Laura and Davie in every way except one, she acknowledged with a sinking feeling. *But that one thing is critically important. Those two have had all the loss they can endure.*

I shouldn't be allowing Luis to get so close to them. No matter how much all of us want him to part of our future, it isn't possible. I need to find a way to ease him out of their lives.

Chapter Thirty-One

B arbara's role in the trials of John Nader and Robert Howard turned out to be relatively minor, mostly verifying what Davis told her about them and rehashing what she'd read on the flash drive Luis recovered in Castle Rock.

Richard Stevens' trial, on the other hand, was more complicated. For one thing, the prosecutor wanted Barbara to identify Stevens as one of the men in the zodiac.

"I can't say that with any certainty," she admitted when Stevens' lawyer pressed her. "The boat was too far away."

"Did he seem at all familiar when you encountered him in Phoenix?" David DeRosa, the U.S. district attorney asked Barbara, already knowing the answer but wanting to establish the connection in the jury's mind between Stevens' activities in Mexico and his subsequent appearance in Phoenix.

"No, he just seemed scary. Both he and his partner, Mr. Howard, seemed unprofessional to me. They showed too much anger and aggression for seasoned FBI agents. It also bothered me that someone who claimed to be a friend of Davis's showed no compassion at all for Davis's children."

When the last trial came to an end, Barbara wasn't sure her testimony made any real difference. The simple truth was she didn't know that much, had never come face-to-face with any of the men except for the two men who briefly interrogated her in Phoenix and the men involved in the attack in Castle Rock. Most of what she knew was hearsay.

"You're a more important witness than you think, Barbara," Wilma assured her over a glass of wine. "Your description of Davis facing those men alone on a Mexican beach, of having to hide in that small, dark space with his two frightened children, and describing how you fled with them afterward made what Stevens did more personal to the jury. That's huge."

"I'm just glad it's over. Will I be released from WITSEC soon?"

"Probably in a few days. You can contact your university any time you want after your release and start getting back to your real life."

"My real life," Barbara said softly. "I don't know what that is anymore, Wilma. The government's case against its corrupt agents might have come to a close, but a far more important trial, at least to me, awaits. I promised Laura and Davie theirs would be the deciding voice on their future. I have no idea how to keep my promise."

Wilma gave the woman sitting across from her a calculating look. "It seems to me Luis has a stake in this, too. Don't you think your case would be stronger if you two married?"

Barbara shook her head. "Luis told me several weeks ago he wouldn't marry me just to strengthen our position in court. I think he's right. Our shared love for Davie and Laura isn't a compelling enough reason to marry. More importantly, it isn't the right reason. There's this little thing called *love*."

Wilma rubbed her chin thoughtfully. "Don't you have feelings for him at all? Frankly, I find that hard to believe. Luis Vallejo isn't just hot; he's someone special, Barbara. You know this as well as I do. He's smart, gutsy, and tender-hearted. For whatever reason, he's chosen to love you every bit as much as he loves those kids, and I don't think time or distance is going to change how Luis feels. He's that type of man."

"I do have feelings for Luis, Wilma; I have since long before Davis came into my life. But you can care for someone and still know you can't build a life with them. Luis's work is dangerous, and Davis's children have already lost one father. They deserve something better than living with a daily fear they'll lose someone else they love."

"So, it's his work that's the problem?"

"Mostly."

"Have you discussed how you feel with him?"

Once again, Barbara shook her head. "I can't take his work away from him, Wilma. It's the most important thing in his life."

The FBI agent snorted. "If you believe this, you don't know Luis at all. He told me months ago that you and the children had become everything to him. I doubt he's given his work with gangs a single thought since he joined your security team. In fact, he threatened to quit the FBI if his SAC wouldn't get him assigned to your security detail."

"He hasn't said a word about any of that to me."

"Some men are talkers, while others are doers. Give me a doer every time. I've gotten to know Luis pretty well over these last months. He's not one to share his feelings with words; that's true. But it seems to me he shows you what's in his heart every single day."

Barbara set her empty wine glass on the table. "I know you mean well, Wilma, but I have to put Davie and Laura first. Unfortunately, what any of us want our future to look like might be irrelevant. Monica Reynolds is in the driver's seat."

When Roxanne told her the security team would be leaving in two days and she was free to return to her home in San Diego, Barbara had just one question. "What about Davie and Laura?"

"They're being released, too. I've been in touch with both Monica Reynolds and the children's grandparents. They've requested a meeting with you as quickly as it can be arranged. Luis insisted they include him."

Roxanne gave Barbara a sympathetic look. "None of them sounded too friendly. I think you've got your work cut out for you. Ms. Reynolds called you a child snatcher and implied you barely knew her brother or his children."

"I can disabuse her of those notions." Luis stood in the doorway of their safehouse, his whiskey-colored eyes dark with something—resentment or worry; Barbara couldn't be sure. "You ready to take on the enemy?" he asked Barbara.

"They aren't evil, Luis; these people are Laura's and Davie's family, what's left of it. I'm sure they want what's best for Davis's children."

"We're what's best for those two, and if they'll so damned concerned, why don't they want Davie and Laura to be there when we meet with them? I'm betting it's because they don't give a rat's ass what those two kids want. You've been Davie's and Laura's mother in every important way for nearly a year now. Nothing can undo that bond, and decent, loving people wouldn't even try."

· · · ·

As she and Luis entered the conference room in Monica's corporate headquarters in Santa Barbara, Barbara understood instantly why Monica Reynolds didn't want her brother's children present. She sat at a long table, a lawyer on either side of her. One represented Davis's estate, while the second was there, he informed them, to protect Monica's interests. Mr. and Mrs. Anderson had chosen to come without representation.

"So, you're Barbara Allen," Monica said snidely. "I've imagined what you looked like for over a year. I can see what attracted Davis. He always was a sucker for buxom blonds."

Ronald Anderson, whose daughter, Valerie, had light auburn hair and was on the petite side, urged civility on everyone's part. "I know this is difficult for all of us, but we're here to determine what is best for young Davis and Laura."

Luis interrupted her. "If that's the case, why aren't they here?"

"The reason we thought Davie and Laura shouldn't be here for this meeting," Nancy Anderson told him in a gentle voice, "is to urge Dr. Allen to do what the children can't—think beyond events this last year. I don't doubt that after all this time, they've become very attached to you, my dear, but children are resilient, and we have their futures to think about. I'm hoping you'll be willing to think of what's best for them long term."

"If you're as attached to them as you implied in your written response to our request for a meeting, you'll think beyond yourself and your own interests," Monica added. "That's what we're asking you to do, and we're prepared to fight you if we must. As I'm sure you've learned, our resources are considerable."

Luis held up a hand to halt Monica's comments. "I'm a little confused here. Let's back up and start over, and I'd like to know why Mr. Stranahan is here. Why is the presence of Davis Reynold's estate lawyer necessary?"

"We'll get to that," Monica continued.

"No, I'd like him to answer my question before we proceed," Luis responded.

Barbara had been quiet up to now, wondering why Luis was focusing on this lawyer. Now, she spoke in a quiet, calm voice. "I agree with Luis. Why are you here, Mr. Stranahan?"

"Because of certain provisions in Davis Reynolds" will."

"What provisions?"

"Let's get to those later," Mrs. Anderson urged. "We're here to decide what's best for my grandchildren, and all of us agreed months ago that they should make their home with us, my husband and me. Monica will play an active role in their lives, of course, but the nature of her work means she's out of the country frequently. If you'd like to visit with them from time to time, I'm sure that can be arranged."

"Before this discussion goes any farther," James Stranahan said, "I think Dr. Allen and Agent Vallejo should be informed of changes Davis made to his will less than a week before his death since they're pertinent to this discussion."

"I'm listening," Luis told the lawyer, his eyes intent.

"Davis told me quite a bit about you in our last discussion, Dr. Allen. He admired and trusted you. Had he survived, I'm confident Davis had every intention of marrying you. That's why he made you his primary beneficiary and named you as his children's guardian."

The silence greeting the lawyer's last words was so profound everyone heard Barbara's whispered "Me?"

Luis gripped her hand. "Of course, you. I should have guessed. A man as wise as Davis Reynolds wouldn't leave something so important to chance, given the danger he'd found himself in."

"We're prepared to fight," Monica insisted. "Those children belong in a certain milieu, one you could never provide. The Andersons and I can. Davis was under an incredible strain those last months. He couldn't think clearly."

"I'm sorry, Ms. Reynolds," James Stranahan said in a firm voice, "but I don't agree. Davis experienced stress, certainly, but he was looking forward to a life with Dr. Allen and very clear about his preferences.

"He knew how focused you are on the family business, and he trusted you with running the company, which is why he divided his half-interest between you and his children. You also hold their proxies until they reach their majority. Reynolds Relocation, Inc. belongs to you for all practical purposes."

"The rest of his assets he divided between his children and Dr. Allen, with her acting on their behalf until they reach the age of twenty-one. Davis trusted me to carry out his wishes, and I am obligated, both legally and ethically, to do just that. In my opinion, Dr. Allen's guardianship will stand up to any legal test."

The lawyer turned to Barbara. "Davis's estate has been probated. Because of your unusual circumstances, our office was unable to contact you. In the interim, we've prepared all the necessary papers and held them in trust. His estate, as of yesterday, is valued at something over sixteen million—not counting his children's share of Davis's company stock."

This time, Luis's low whistle broke the silence.

Barbara swallowed a sudden ball of fear. She'd had no idea Davis had this kind of money. It made her feel uncomfortable. Worse than that; it made her feel unprepared. Maybe Monica was right.

Luis entertained no such doubts. "Barbara's guardianship of Davie and Laura was Davis's choice, and everyone here needs to respect his decision. So, let's turn our eyes to what's next.

"I know Barbara wants Davie's and Laura's grandparents and their only aunt to be part of those kids' lives." Luis eyed each of them sternly. "She's stood up for you every time we've discussed what might happen even though she believes, as I do, and Davis obviously did, that they belong with her.

"Let's not put them through more trauma. They've lost the most important members of their family, their parents. Nothing can change this. But they have grandparents who love them and an aunt who wants the best possible future for them. Barbara, anything you want to add?"

"Only that Luis is right. I came here today prepared to beg or fight for keeping Davis's children with me because I couldn't imagine a life that didn't include them. The three of us have been through an experience I can't begin to describe. Thanks to Luis and the men and women of the FBI, we came through everything safely though not without harm.

"Now, Davie and Laura need to spend some time with family members they haven't seen in nearly a year. You'll find them changed—sadder in some ways and more grown up than any of us would wish. I'm asking you to share your love with them and your grief. Davis was their rock, a touchstone they'll never lose because I won't let that happen.

"I have no idea what kind of relationship with me you'll chose to have, but I hope it's a warm one. We all want the same thing—for those children to grow up safe and loved. This makes us a family."

• • • •

Monica suggested they meet again after everyone had an opportunity to absorb what happened. "And this time," she told them, "Davie and Laura should be part of the meeting."

She turned to Barbara. "I think you should know I'm still not convinced we're doing the right thing. Despite your kind words, you aren't family."

James Stranahan, strolled over to Luis, who was standing alone by the large window of the high rise. "How do you figure into all this?" he asked the FBI agent.

"I'm here to support Dr. Allen, and those two kids are pretty important to me, too."

"She's a wealthy woman now. A different kind of future awaits her."

"You don't know Barbara Allen. That money doesn't mean a damn thing to her. All she cares about is those kids."

"You really believe that, don't you? I find it quite touching. Money changes everything, Agent Vallejo. I'm afraid you're about to learn how true this is."

The lawyer walked away from Luis, pulling Barbara from her conversation with Ron and Nancy Anderson. "There's something more you need to know, Dr. Allen. Davis entrusted our office with a letter to you as a "just in case.""

"Do you have it here?" she asked the lawyer.

"No, and I can't give it to you quite yet. Davis's instructions were explicit. You were to receive the letter three months after you assumed guardianship of his children."

"I've played that role for more than half-a-year now, Mr. Stranahan."

"But not officially. I suspect this will happen after our next meeting. Make sure you leave your address and cell number with me. I'll give you a call in a day or two."

Barbara touched his sleeve. "Thank you, Mr. Stranahan, for everything. I had no idea Davis made me their guardian. He never mentioned it. I've agonized for months over the possibility I might lose those two. This is, without doubt, the second happiest day of my life. The day Davis asked me to marry him will always rank as number one."

"Call me *James*," he told her. "I think you'll do, Barbara Allen. I always knew Davis was a smart man. Now that I've met you, I'd go farther. I'd say Davis Reynolds was a wise man and a lucky one despite what happened to him."

Chapter Thirty-Two

L uis took Barbara's hand as they walked to his car. "Didn't see that coming," he told her. "Now, what?"

"We go tell Davie and Laura the good news. Then, we go back to San Diego. I suppose my first priority will be getting a bigger house, probably a three-bedroom."

Barbara gave him her small, intimate smile. "In some ways, I hate to say goodbye to that little house. It holds a lot of happy memories."

His eyes warmed. "Some of them the time I spent there, I hope." Then, he surprised her by shaking his head. "Three bedrooms won't be enough. I intend to make babies with you, Barbara Allen, two or three at least. We can discuss the exact number later."

"Luis—"

"No fears, Barbara, we survived the unthinkable—the likelihood Davie and Laura were lost to us forever. The rest is easy. We can take our time, work out anything that worries you."

"I wish it were that easy. So much money, Luis. I don't know a thing about managing funds or fiduciary responsibility."

"You'll learn, and I suspect James Stranahan will find someone to help you in the meantime."

Barbara's face clouded. "Oh, that reminds me. Mr. Stranahan said Davis left a letter for me, but I can't see it for another three months because Davis thought I'd need more time once I learned of my guardianship. At first, I was excited, but now I'm not sure I want to read his words. It will be like experiencing his death all over again."

"Davis wasn't a cruel man, Barbara. He'd never hurt you on purpose. I'm certain he hoped with all his heart you'd never have to read that letter. I also think he needed to say something that couldn't be said until the dust settled if he did die. And, I suspect it was something he thought you'd need to hear."

"I miss him so much, Luis. Will the pain ever go away?"

"I think so, little by little and in fits and starts. There's a saying in Spanish—'*No puedes vivir en mañana o ayer.*' You can't live in tomorrow or yesterday. Davis will always be an important part of your life, sweetheart; you're mothering his children, after all. He trusted you with everything important to him, and I believe you'll work through your pain by deserving his trust."

• • • •

"For reals? They promised we can stay with you?" Davie's eyes were anxious, as if such good news came with a catch. "But we're going to live in San Diego? Why not Flagstaff? I liked it there."

"Because my work, and Luis's, is in San Diego," Barbara told him. "And we don't have to hide anymore. That's why we went there, remember?"

"If Barbara wants to live in San Diego, that's where we'll go," Laura told her brother in a prim voice. "She's our guardian now, and we have to mind her."

Luis grinned as he picked up Laura and swung her around. She was his serious child, always on her dignity, and he wanted her to laugh more, to be the child she remained deep down.

"Luis, you're making me dizzy," she objected.

"I have a weakness for dizzy blonds," he teased her, throwing a warm look at Barbara.

"Is Luis going to live with us?" Davie wanted to know.

"Not right now. My house is too small." Barbara hoped that answer would buy her a little time.

"You can always buy a bigger one," Laura reminded her. "Luis will be lonely if he has to live all by himself."

"It's not forever," Luis reassured her. "It simply takes a while to sell one house and buy another. If my apartment wasn't even smaller than Barbara's house, all of you could live with me. In the meantime, be a little patient. Things will work out, and I'll be spending lots of time with you."

"That's what Daddy always said—that things will work out in time." Laura's expression grew sad. "I miss him so much, Luis. Why does death have to be forever?"

"That's a pretty big question for such a little girl, one even our philosophers haven't been able to answer."

"What's a philosfer?" Davie wanted to know.

"Someone who tries to answer life's *why* questions," Barbara told him.

"I've got lots of those," Davis's son informed her. "Can't Luis answer them?"

Luis's eyes brimmed with amusement. "Maybe a few of them, sport. But I've got a question for you first. Would you like to spend a few days at Ramón's ranch before we drive down to San Diego?"

"Could we?" Two pairs of eyes gazed earnestly at Barbara.

"If they'll have us," she assured them.

"I get to ride a horse all by myself," Laura bragged. "Uncle Ramón promised."

"Maybe I can, too." Davie hoped aloud. "He said I needed longer legs. They're longer now."

$\bullet\ \bullet\ \bullet\ \bullet$

"My goodness, they've changed so much," Alicia whispered to Barbara. "It's not just that they're older; they seem more confident, happier, too. When Luis told us Davis Reynolds made you their guardian, we were so grateful to God. Ramón and I feared we might never see them again. Now, they'll be part of our family."

"Luis and I have no plans to marry, Alicia, but I would like to keep you in Laura's and Davie's lives. I know Luis has feelings for me, and he's very attached to Davis's children, but his regard for me doesn't mean I return those feelings enough to marry him."

"Barbara Allen, that's the first lie I've ever heard you tell." Alicia's usually placid expression was gone. She'd gone rosy in her indignation. "I watched you with Luis here at the ranch and saw the sadness in your eyes when he left. I don't think you realize how often you two touched or how tenderly. Why do you deny what is so obvious to me and to Ramón, as well? We have talked of it many times."

"I'm still grieving for Davis, Alicia. Luis understands how I feel."

"Well, *claro*, of course, you are. I'm sure he was a fine man." Alicia's eyes turned kinder before her pragmatic nature prevailed. "But he's dead, and you are not. Nor is Luis. Life goes on and takes you with it. Do you think it's fair to keep Luis on the edge of your life, only sharing the children he loves as his own as you see fit? He is too much a man for that and too good a man, as well. Shame on you!"

Ramón's wife gave Barbara a sly look. "You think you know Luis, but not so much, I think. My husband, who is occasionally wise, understands that well. I think these next two days are going to open your eyes and your heart."

Alicia's comments were interrupted by the sudden appearance of Luis and Ramón, all four children in tow. "I promised them a ride, *querida*," Luis's cousin told his wife. "We will return in two hours, maybe less. I'm sure all of us will be very hungry."

Alicia gave him a pat. "What else is new? No matter, I'm sure Barbara hasn't forgotten how to make enchiladas and *arroz con frijoles*. We'll be ready."

The ranch house seemed quiet after the men and children left. Alicia, usually a chatty, even-tempered woman, went about her duties in stiff silence.

Barbara noticed but was too preoccupied with her own thoughts to care. Why did everyone champion Luis? First Wilma, then a phone call from Luis's partner, Phil Reed, and now Alicia. *Surely, I'm entitled to my own feelings,* she grumbled, *and how can any of them claim to know my heart better than I do?*

The sound of cars arriving, voices and slammed doors, interrupted her reverie. "Ah, they are here" Alicia said as she took off her apron and headed for the front door.

Before she could get there, the door burst open and more than a dozen men, women, and children walked in carrying food and suitcases. Alicia welcomed them with hugs and kisses.

Everyone's eyes were on Barbara, the only non-Hispanic in the room. "So, you are Barbara Allen, no? an elderly gray-haired woman asked her.

"*Tia* Amparo, this is Barbara, Luis's fiancée."

Barbara turned to object but was silenced by the sudden fury in the older woman's eyes. "We shall see. I know of you, Barbara Allen. You hurt my son once; I will not allow it to happen again. And to use his love for children to manipulate him—this does not speak well of you."

"Mamá, your manners." A handsome man a few years younger than Luis, spoke gently but in a firm voice to his mother. Then, he turned to Barbara. "I am Raúl, Luis's brother." He put an arm around the tall, dark-haired woman beside him. "And this is my wife, María Carmen."

A shorter, even younger version of Luis, this time a female, stepped forward. "I am Catarina Vallejo de Rodríguez, Luis's sister, and this is my husband, Arturo. I have been so curious to meet you. You are very beautiful, which does not surprise me. Luis has a discerning eye, but we seldom see that because my brother is a private man. You are just the second woman he has presented to his family. I was certain he'd marry the first."

"A fine Mexican young lady," Amparo Vallejo interjected. "Her father was the governor of Oaxaca. The de Lorcas are a very distinguished family, much like the Séguins and Vallejos."

A deep, male voice interrupted Amparo Vallejo's praise for Luis's earlier love. "I am certain this young woman, Barbara, is it not, is all she should be. Luis would not have chosen her otherwise." A tall, distinguished man smiled down at Barbara. "I am Jorge, Luis's father. You are looking a trifle overwhelmed, my dear. Please be at ease. It is merely our numbers that are intimidating.

"I would like to present my grandchildren," he continued, "but you couldn't possibly remember all of them, and there is time later for you to sort them out." He gave her a warm smile, Luis's smile. "I understand I am to gain two more. Children are always welcome in the Vallejo family." With a nod at Alicia, he added. "And the Séguin, of course."

His wife, Amparo, sniffed but didn't say anything more. Instead, she smiled brightly at Luis, who'd joined them, looking both thunderstruck and furious. Ramón handed the horses off to one of his hands and led the children inside.

"*Hijo*, we've come to meet this young *gringa* and the children Ramón tells us you are so fond of. *Tan blanco—so white*," she lamented as her gaze moved to Davie and Laura. "*Ni una palabra de español.*" Her easy dismissal and rudeness to Davie and Laura infuriated her son.

"They don't need to speak Spanish, *Mamá*, he informed her. "We get by just fine in English, a language you will confine yourself to today if you expect me to stay."

He turned to Ramón. "Was this your good idea?"

"It was, and I have no apology for you, Cousin. Barbara, Davie, and Laura are about to be part of our family. You know it, and I know it. I already consider them family, as do Alicia and our children. Yet you hide them away as if you're ashamed of your feelings for them. That needs to end."

Luis paled before flushing in anger. "Be careful, Ramón. Your words are very close to insulting."

Amparo gripped his son's shoulder possessively. "Is he right, Luis? Do you intend to make these strangers part of our family? I wish you would not."

Luis turned to his mother. "You speak plainly. I will, as well. It is not Barbara I'm ashamed of, nor is it Davie and Laura. It's you, *Mamá*, and your stupid prejudices. If your behavior forces me to choose, be assured I will choose them."

"Luis!" Luis's father's voice was stern but calm. "You speak passionately, as you should, in defense of those you love, but we are not your enemy. Amparo's views are well known, and we do not challenge them openly because she is family, and that is our way. This does not mean those ideas are shared."

He gave his wife an equally stern but loving look. "You will be silent the rest of today, *querida*, and you will keep your eyes open even as your lips remain shut. If it is in you, and I believe it is, you will keep your heart open as well. My son has made his choice, selected his *mujer* as is his right.

"I don't know you yet, Barbara Allen, but I know my son well. He is a wise young man, careful with his heart." Jorge Vallejo Insula turned to Davie and Laura, who stood close together in silence, confused by all the emotion around them.

"Ramón tells me your father was a brave man, one of the FBI's finest. It will be an honor to join my family to yours. You are welcome, *chicos*. I will love you as I love all my grandchildren. In time, my wife will do the same. She simply has a little growing up to do."

He softened his gentle rebuke by putting his arm around his wife. "Now, I smell something delicious and suspect all of you are as hungry as I am. Let's eat Alicia's wonderful cooking and spend some time getting to know one another.

Chapter Thirty-Three

As soon as his family got up from the table and Luis saw that Davie and Laura were comfortably engaged with their "cousins," he took Barbara's icy-cold hand and suggested a walk. "Let's take the path along the river; it will be pleasant this time of day."

Both were silent for nearly five minutes. "Barbara, I don't know what to say, how I can apologize enough for what you've just endured. I knew nothing about it, I swear to you."

When they'd walked several hundred yards farther down the path, Barbara pulled on Luis's hand, signaling she wanted to halt along the water's edge. "Who's this woman they talked about before dinner, Luis? Why is it I know nothing about her?"

If she'd spoken in tongues, Luis couldn't have been more confused. Why would Barbara bring that up?

"She's no one, at least no one important to me for years. We met in law school. Cristina was bright, dedicated to her family, and on a path that didn't square with mine. After a few months of being serious about each other, we both realized it wouldn't work. She went home to Oaxaca, and I joined the marines."

"You never once mentioned her or being in the marines, for that matter. It makes me realize I don't know anything about your past. Luis. My ignorance frightens me."

"You never asked. I suspect that's because you never considered me part of your future. As for Cristina, there isn't much to say. I'm almost thirty-four, and I certainly haven't led a celibate life, but Cristina's the only woman besides you I've been serious about. If you'd asked, I'd have told you about her, but I honestly didn't think she mattered."

"It sounds like she was everything your mother wanted for you."

"I am not my mother, Barbara. And I don't give a rat's ass what she wants. I left any desire to please her behind a long time ago."

"Why haven't you dated since our lives parted more than a year ago, Luis. You've already told me celibacy isn't part of your DNA."

Luis tugged playfully on Barbara's ponytail then left his hand tangled in her long hair. "This certainly isn't the conversation I thought we'd be having this afternoon. Okay, the truth is I'm more like my father than I'd guessed. Phil tried to fix me up with a couple of his wife's friends, and, sometimes, women I met or worked with flirted with me, but they weren't you."

"I still don't understand; you moved on from Cristina."

"She wasn't you, either. What you and I had and still have is different, Barbara. That's why I said I'm like my father. You know enough Spanish to understand the complexity of the word *mujer*. There's no real English equivalent. Once I made that commitment, no other woman was possible for me."

"You must think I'm a shallow person, then, for finding and loving Davis."

"No, *querida*, I don't think you're shallow at all—not now, anyway. I'll admit I was pretty ticked off at first. The more I learned about the man, however, the more I understood."

He kept his hand in her hair, stroking her ponytail absentmindedly.

"What are we going to do, Luis. Your whole family thinks we're getting married. This will be so embarrassing for you."

"I hate to break it to you, but you haven't met my whole family; that's still ahead for you. And it isn't just my family's expectations; it's Davie and Laura and Phil, and Wilma, not to mention Jim Corelle and half the FBI. None of that really matters. This is between you and me."

"Alicia accused me of lying earlier today when I tried to explain to her that I didn't return your feelings, at least not the same way.

Why does everyone think I'm lying, not merely to them but to myself?"

"*Bebe*, this is something you need to discover for yourself. I have my own theory, of course."

"Are you going to call me *Bebe* forever?"

"Until my dying day. Get used to it."

Giving her companion a long, thoughtful look, Barbara changed the subject. "Luis, do you miss making love to me?"

He couldn't hide his surprise. Nothing about this conversation was going the way Luis thought it would.

"Every minute of every day, Barbara. And you?"

"Sometimes—okay, more and more often. It makes me feel disloyal to Davis, and I hate feeling this way, despise myself for even thinking about betraying him."

"*Querida*, don't do this to yourself. Davis would want you to be happy, which means having the fullest kind of life. You're a normal, healthy woman."

"But you chose celibacy rather than be unfaithful to me—at least that's what you said."

Luis grinned. "Ever the academic, turning my own words back on me. But the two situations are different. I had no woman in my life who mattered to me before we met or after. Your situation was different. From what you admitted to me earlier, Davis and I shared a belief you hadn't stopped loving me even though you loved him, as well. If he could be part of this conversation today, he'd still say I mattered to you—just as he does. That's why I won't give up on you and why you still feel connected to me.

"You've insisted from the first," he continued, "that our connection was mostly a physical one, and I don't deny the sexual attraction between us. I'm feeling it right this minute. But I know it's more than that, was always more than good sex. We like each other, Barbara, and our characters are very much the same."

"How can you say we're anything alike? I'm cautious almost to a fault, and you're a thrill junky."

Luis's laugh startled her. "This from the woman who kidnapped two kids, learned to shoot a gun, and took on FBI bad guys, the Mexican Mafia, and some seriously bad gangbangers. You kept those kids safe and didn't spend one minute whining about it.

"And if you think I enjoy getting shot at," Luis continued, "you're wrong. I like winning, that's true enough, and when I only had myself to worry about, maybe I liked taking a risk now and then. Things are different now, *mi amor*. I have you in my life and Davie and Laura. Everything has changed."

"You really mean it? You're not just saying what you think I want to hear?"

"Barbara, have I ever lied to you? I'm not always the most open of guys though I'm working on that, but I'd never lie to you. I have no idea where my professional life is headed, but my days in undercover work are over."

"Oh, Luis, I'm so confused." She leaned her head against his chest, listening to the steady thrum of his heart before saying: "This feels good."

"It does," he agreed. "But I want more. I want to share your bed again. I think it's important for both of us. Let me make you a promise. I won't interpret your willingness to let me love you physically as a signal you're ready for marriage or any other kind of permanent commitment. You can take as much time as you need."

"But you think I'll marry you eventually."

"I do."

"Well, you might want to think again," she told him with sudden heat in her eyes. "I listened as your father ordered your mother a few minutes ago to stay silent the rest of the day, and I could see everyone expected her to mind him. I'm also remembering you just told me how much you're like your father. I would never submit to that kind of bullying."

Luis laughed until he began choking then pulled an annoyed Barbara to him. "Not once in my life, until today, did I hear something like that come out of my father's mouth. As difficult as Mamá can be, Poppy has always supported her. You might not see it yet, but he pampers her, would do anything to make her happy even after all these years. Surely, you'll forgive me if it happens to us no more than once and under the greatest provocation."

Barbara gave him a withering look. "I think you're more like your mother than your father. You always think you're right."

"Another trait you and I share. I can't promise we won't fight, Barbara, but this is part of living together and having strong personalities. Something about me puts the pepper in you. I'm sure you and Davis had a different kind of relationship.

But I want you to keep two things in mind. The first is that the most rousing argument you can imagine won't dent my love for you, and the second is that heated arguments make for great makeup sex or so I've been told. Our marriage, when we get to this point, won't ever descend to mere fondness. It will always be full-on love."

"We'd better get back. I don't want to leave Davie and Laura with strangers for too long."

"Ramón, Alicia, and their two kids aren't strangers, Barbara. And if I know my father, they're already calling him *abuelo*. By tomorrow night, it'll be one big happy family. You've already got my brother's approval. He told me I'd picked a juicy one, as if I didn't know."

The family had settled in the hacienda's large *sala* when Luis and Barbara returned. The children chose to divide themselves into two groups though Laura sat a little removed from the others, Lucky curled up in her lap. The older ones were watching television while the younger ones were coloring and pasting stamps into books. It wasn't the only division. The men had separated themselves from the women, which annoyed Barbara.

An amused expression on his face, Luis leaned in and whispered. "Get used to it, sweetheart. I don't see this changing anytime soon." It wasn't long before his joined his male counterparts.

Luis's mother maintained an ominous silence, but Barbara noticed her eyes were red-rimmed and her complexion blotched. When she accompanied Luis's sister, Catarina, to the kitchen for the snacks and wine the men requested, Barbara mentioned Amparo's distress.

"I don't want to drive any kind of wedge into your family, Catarina. I can see how close you all are."

"That's not going to happen, Barbara. *Mamá* is sad right now and a little shocked. *Papá* never disciplines her; he's too soft hearted. But Latino families stick together. All in all, I think that's a good thing. Alicia tells me you aren't too sure about marrying Luis. I think you should."

"You don't even know me. Why would it matter to you?"

"Because it matters to Luis. My brother is a good man even if he's too shy and private for his own good. However, I see how he looks at you. You might not be certain about marriage, but he is."

Barbara ignored the last of Catarina's words. She'd heard them too many times before. "Shy? You think your brother's shy? I think he's bossy, a borderline bully."

"Oh, he's that, too. I mean about his feelings. He finds it hard to share what's in his heart. My Arturo is the same."

"How do you deal with that?"

Catarina shrugged her shoulders. "Different ways. Sometimes, I ask him what he's thinking and ask again until he gets tired of my asking and tells me. Other times, I watch his eyes. My husband has what we call *speaking eyes*. They are the window to his heart.

And, once in a while, I just accept that he doesn't want to share his thoughts."

"I think you're a good wife. Arturo's a lucky man."

"I chose him because he was kind and because I knew he'd always put me and our children first. Now, I find it easy to put his wishes first. That's what happens when you love someone."

When Ramón suggested the children sleep in the barn's loft to give the grownups more room in the house, Barbara wanted to object. Davie's and Laura's delight in the adventure, however, made her hesitate. She found herself looking to Luis for a response.

"I don't know about this," he warned the children, including the two he thought of as his own. "Ramón loves to tell stories about *La Llorona*. You might be too scared to stay all night in the barn. I'll tell you what, I'll sleep in the loft with you," he volunteered. "The weeping woman doesn't scare me."

"I might as well," he whispered in Barbara's ear later. "I think my entire family is going to sleep with every bedroom door in the house open to make sure I don't sneak into your room. Well, to be more specific, the women will. My father, brother, cousin, and brother-in-law will be secretly cheering me on."

"Maybe, I should join you in the loft," she teased him.

Luis shook his head. "Not permitted," he told her. "Mine is a very traditional family."

"Do you intend to pass these traditional values on to Davie and Laura?" she challenged him.

"No, probably not. I think those two will be happier following their father's more casual ways."

"Maybe, we can do a little mixing and matching," Barbara reassured him, unaware she was treating her future and the children's as irrevocably linked to Luis's.

The children came inside the following morning stinking of straw and horses. Alicia orders baths or showers for all, followed by a gigantic breakfast that began with fresh fruit and ended with *huevos rancheros* and a side of more beans.

Only one child, Raúl's youngest daughter, had urged Luis to return her to her parent's room during the night. Since Lupita wasn't yet three, none of the other children teased her.

Laura took the rustic sleeping accommodations and Ramón's somewhat gruesome tale in stride, but Davie cuddled up next to Luis, his mouth opened wide, as he learned about the weeping woman who murdered her own children.

Still, he'd found more pleasure than stress in the outing. "Maybe we should live here at the ranch," he told Luis in the morning. "I like having lots of cousins. Everyone calls me *Dah vees*. It sounds almost like Luis."

"I don't know about living here, Davie, but we'll be spending lots of time here and on the other ranches. You've only met a small part of my family."

"For reals?" Davie asked, his eyes rounded.

"Yup, you'll have over fifty cousins someday soon. And everyone will expect you, as a male member of the family, to learn the *ranchero* way of life. I did, so did my brother."

"But not my sister?"

"Girls learn different things," Luis confided to his almost-son.

Davie frowned. "I don't think Laura will like that, or Barbara, either. Maybe, we can change the rules."

"I'm not sure I'm brave enough," Luis admitted to a surprised Davie.

"But you're brave like my daddy;' everyone says so."

"Some rules, especially in families, are hard to change, but I can promise you this. If it's important to Barbara or Laura, you and I will do our best for them. I think some of your cousins and uncles will help. After all, times change."

Shortly after breakfast, Luis's cousins on the Séguin side and his favorite uncle, Martin, began arriving to meet the newest members of the family. To everyone's surprise, Amparo took Davie and Laura, one in each hand, and paraded them from relative to relative. "It's about time my oldest son started his family. But you know Luis. He always has to do things his own way."

Davie confided his feelings about Amparo to Barbara later in the afternoon. "If Luis's father is my *abuelo*, then his mother is my *abuela*. That's how Spanish works. She's a little scary, Barbara—so bossy, not like Grandmother Anderson. Do you think she really likes me?"

"I'm certain she will in time. I'm pretty sure she's going to surprise you, Davie. Sometimes, it takes people a while to get used to someone new."

"Barbara?" Davis's son's voice was subdued. "Is Luis my dad now for reals? Everyone here says he is."

"Only you know what's in your heart, Davie. And I want you to trust your feelings. Luis will never try to take your daddy's place. He wouldn't want that, but he loves you very much and will do his best to protect you and make you happy."

"Isn't this what fathers do?"

"Yes, I suppose it is."

"Then, I think I'll call him *Poppy*. That's what J.R. calls Ramón. I think Daddy would be okay with it. Laura and I have been talking about what we should call you and Luis. Are you going to adopt us? Laura says we shouldn't give you special names unless you do."

"Do you want that? It isn't going to make any real difference, Davie. Family is more about feelings than blood ties or legalities."

"I want someone to be my mom and dad. *Guardian* just isn't the same thing."

"Have you told Luis how you feel?"

"No."

"Why not?"

"What if he doesn't want to adopt me?"

"Oh Davie, that's not possible. There is nothing on the planet that Luis wants more than to be your father. And even though you haven't asked, there's nothing more I'd like than to be your mom. Let's give a decision this important a little more time. It's something we should all decide together."

Chapter Thirty-Four

B arbara started the new year back on campus. Since someone else was handling her regular classes, she'd be teaching two Introduction to Sociology classes and a hastily arranged seminar on growing Native American participation in southern California's street gangs.

Somehow, she'd expected a more heartwarming return, a greater sense of celebration. Instead, everyone treated her as if she'd never been gone. Still, she breathed a sigh of relief to once again occupy her office in Loma Hall.

Luis returned to his duties at the FBI, much to Phil Reed's loudly expressed pleasure. He'd been carrying the load mostly alone for over six months and missed his partner. Everyone agreed there'd be no more undercover work for Luis Vallejo. He was too well known.

The shakeup at California's prisons, both state and federal, made national news and dominated the local news cycle for weeks. Roger Delvecchio left his job as the warden of Mendota and joined the prison population in nearby Idaho. Everyone agreed it wasn't safe for him to serve his time in California.

The wardens at Lompoc and San Pedro resigned under duress. They weren't accused of any specific wrongdoing, but their incompetence rendered them "unfit" in the eyes of the governing board. Then, the board itself went through a reconfiguration as politics reared its ugly head.

Even before Delvecchio's sentencing, Roberto Rodríguez lost control of *La EME* when the California State Board of Prisons approved his transfer to ADX Florence. The warden there assured everyone that Rodríguez would have no contact with his former lieutenants.

The Mexican Mafia's adjustment to a new power elite in their own ranks was almost instantaneous. Observing it, Luis decided to revisit someone he thought of as a friendly adversary—Martín Orozco.

"I see you healed nicely," Luis teased the man who'd been shot by his partner.

"Hurt like a bitch for weeks," Martín told the man whose life he'd saved. "But I got lots of sympathy from the ladies, and, more important for me, my badge of honor got me off the hook with Santiago. He's moved up to number one now with Roberto gone. You're looking good, by the way."

"No complaints, but I do have a request."

"Seems like I'm the one doing all the favors here," Orozco said dryly.

"What goes around comes around, Martín. I won't forget, and neither will my partner."

"What do you need, *hombre*?"

"I need to know that *La EME*'s interest in Barbara Allen has come to an end, the same for Davis Reynolds' kids."

"Yesterday's news, Luis. We got new problems and new opportunities. Your *mujer* is safe. You, maybe not so much. You've pissed off a lot of brothers, my friend. Others think you're okay for a Fed. You might want to rethink your lifestyle in the coming months."

"The same might be said for you."

"It's not the same. You can turn in your badge, and they'll throw you a going-away party. Me...it's a marriage for life."

"Until death do you part?" Luis asked, concern in his eyes.

"Something like that. I'm a realist, Luis, a businessman, which is why I stay away from the drug business. Besides, I have friends in the FBI, a kind of early warning system."

"Like I said, what goes around, comes around. You take care, Martín, and always remember that I pay my dues."

• • • •

When the Andersons requested a weekend on their yacht with Davie and Laura, Barbara felt she couldn't say *no*. Both children were excited about time on the water. More than that, some extended time with their grandchildren seemed a reasonable request from Barbara's perspective, and she had some things to work out with Luis.

Her plans focused on a frank discussion about his future with the FBI. Would he be happy with a desk job, for instance? Luis, equally delighted to have Laura and Davie gone for a few days, had an entirely different agenda. Time in the sack with his *mujer* pretty much dominated his thinking.

It'd been weeks since Barbara admitted her mixed feelings about sleeping with him. His feelings weren't ambivalent at all; it had been over a year since they'd made love. Their physical reconnection was long overdue.

When Luis showed up at her small home on 10th Avenue, carrying the same kinds of pizza he'd brought early in their relationship, Barbara didn't make the connection until he put the two pizzas in the oven on low and suggested a foot rub.

"Luis, really?"

Pleased that she'd remembered, he gave Barbara his best smile. "Yes, really. Only this time, I don't want you to fall asleep, at least not until much later when we're both worn out."

"We need to talk."

"We do," he agreed, "but not tonight. I miss the physical part of our relationship, *Bebe*; I need that closeness. If you're honest with me and yourself, you'll admit you miss it, too."

Barbara sighed, and both recognized it as a capitulation. "You might as well turn the oven off" she told him with her distinctive small smile. "I doubt either of us will be eating pizza tonight."

"Breakfast pizza is good."

She made a face. "You'd better be worth a missed dinner, Supervisory Special Agent Vallejo," Barbara warned him.

"Have I ever disappointed?"

"No," she shook her head, "you have not. I'm sure I would remember if you did."

"You know damn well I haven't." He took out his pocketknife, Martín Orozco's knife, and cut the elastic band from her ponytail, explaining: "I don't want to pull your hair."

Burying his face and hands in the hair that so mesmerized him, Luis lost his teasing tone. "I love you, Barbara, as every man should love his woman. It's forever, and it means everything to me."

It was so simply and sincerely said that tears filled Barbara's eyes. "Oh, Luis, I'm so sorry for all the pain I've caused you, and I know I have."

"Errors on both sides, *querida*. I can't speak for you, but I'm grateful for all of it. Without the pain of losing you, I'm not sure I'd ever have known how important you are to me or that I'd have the courage to admit it."

"I'm frightened, Luis."

"I know, sweetheart, but baby steps. Tonight, we'll reconnect in an important way, but I meant what I said months ago. When you're ready to make a leap of faith into forever, I'll be there to catch you."

· · · ·

Barbara feared she'd obsess about her future with Luis, but time intruded. Davie and Laura went back to school, doing their best to make new friends and adjust to new teaching techniques. Both needed her help with homework.

Luis came nearly every night, making his own demands on her time after the children were safely asleep. Her new seminar, one she'd never taught before, was a heavy time drain, as well. She picked Luis's brain, asking question after question about what he'd observed in the field.

The basics were already familiar to her—the breakdown of tradition, the growing trend to live much of their lives off the reservation, drugs and the big money they brought to a world of poverty. This she already knew.

Luis explained the increasing willingness of *Sureño* street gangs to grow their membership and power by including Native Americans in the gangs' economic activities. This, in turn, brought a new set of problems back to the reservations—guns, more drugs, and increasingly violent behavior.

Young Native American men in their late teens and early twenties became heroes to younger children on the reservation as they showed off fancy trucks and spread money around, further destabilizing the role of tribal elders. Both Barbara and Luis understood that solutions for these problems would be hard to find and implement.

Luis's interest in Barbara's work grew, and he shared his ideas with his partner. Both thought the FBI should expend time and resources to gather the hard data researchers like Barbara needed.

• • • •

Without mentioning it to Phil or Barbara, Luis put out some feelers for a career that would take his life in a vastly different direction. In early March, one of those feelers resulted in a quick trip to Flagstaff, Arizona. He was thinking about two possible positions rather than one.

Luis knew how much Barbara loved her university and the California lifestyle, so he continued his search in San Diego. Within two weeks, he'd gotten another offer. It was time to speak to Barbara. The decision would be hers.

Nearly two weeks went by before he made up his mind to act. Luis began with a casual suggestion. "Let's take a short vacation during your spring break, Barbara. I'm ready for a little R & R. I think the kids are, too."

"Where do you want to go?"

"There's a little canyon with a beautiful creek and some amazing scenery I like to hike. Don't worry; it's near a resort, so you'll have excellent restaurants and a comfortable bed."

"Sounds fine to me. Is it far from here?"

"An easy flight."

"We can't drive there?" Barbara had assumed until now it was somewhere close by in the mountains of southern California. "What's the name of this place?"

"Oak Creek."

"Like in Arizona? Are you talking about Sedona?"

"That's the place. Would it suit you?"

"Sure, I guess so."

Davie and Laura were delighted by his choice, insisting on a visit to Flagstaff, as well. "Maybe we can see our friends at Mountain School," Davie hinted. "I bet they're missing us."

Barbara didn't suspect Luis's ulterior motives until he suggested they dress in the only professional clothing they'd brought along for their trip to Flagstaff. Those suspicions intensified when the director of Mountain School greeted her two former pupils warmly and made it clear she expected them to spend several hours there.

Luis thanked her, gave Laura an affectionate pat, and took Barbara by the hand. "I know how we can spend the next few hours, *Bebe*. All I ask is that you keep an open mind."

The building housing the college of social and behavior sciences seemed familiar to Barbara since she'd visited the department of sociology several times while in witness protection. Apparently, the head of the department, a woman she'd never met, was expecting her.

"You come with excellent recommendations, Dr. Allen, both inside and outside our community."

"I don't think I know a single professor here, Dr. Winters."

"How quickly they forget." A dry British voice behind Barbara made her turn in surprise."

"Dr. Trask?"

"Hello, Barbara. It appears you aren't following the news in academia. I now head a new program called the Family Violence Institute here at NAU. That's why you're here."

"Well, not entirely," Dr. Winters objected. "It would be a joint appointment."

Barbara listened carefully, repressing a tide of different emotions, as the two professors explained the position they had in mind. It was a perfect match for Barbara's interests—familicide, work on several southwestern reservations, and teaching courses she'd already developed on family dynamics, the role of poverty, and rural communities.

"I'm interested, of course," she assured them, "but I have to be honest. This is the first time I've heard any of this."

"I find all of this rather amusing," Dr. Trask told her. "You always struck me as self-actuating. Still, the gentleman waiting outside made your case effectively."

Luis! He'd done all this without even discussing it with her—but why?

"Shall we invite him in?" Dr. Winters suggested. "He can tell you about the position he's been offered. It will keep the two of you in the same building if not the same department."

• • • •

On their way down to mountain to Sedona, Luis explained why he'd selected Flagstaff. It had more to do with Davie's attachment to the Mountain School and his neighborhood than anything else. Beyond that, there were Native American communities nearby, and he thought that important for Barbara. He'd had no idea Laurence Trask was on campus or even who Trask was."

"It struck me as icing on the cake, sweetheart. And I like the idea of being in the same building with you at least part of the time. I'll be doing more than just teaching criminology classes. They are interested in my idea of using specially designed educational programs to combat gang infiltration. I'll be working with NAU's education department, too."

"And you decided not to share any of this with me because ...?"

"Because there is another piece of the puzzle. We don't have to do this, sweetheart. I have an offer from the University of California, San Diego. It isn't quite as interesting as the offer from NAU, and we'd be on different campuses, but we'd be able to stay in San Diego. It's up to you."

"Pick NAU," Davie piped up from the backseat. Both children had been listening carefully to the discussion. "I like it better here."

"It snows in Flagstaff," Barbara objected. "I hate snow."

Luis laughed. "But it's almost five hundred miles to San Diego and nearly as far to San Bernardino. That means we'd have a lot more privacy as a family. We'd still be close enough to stay connected, but it would be on our terms."

"I'll think about it," she promised them. "This is a big decision."

The next morning brought a beautifully blue sky and perfect temperatures for a hike. Two hours into it, Barbara grew weary of Davie's inventive arguments for moving to Flagstaff and Laura's more subtle ones. Luis wisely stayed silent.

Zigging when they zagged, she wandered off a short distance from them, hoping for a few minutes of peace. Luis decided to give her the space she needed even though it still worried him to have her out of sight.

She could hear them gasping and laughing as they splashed in the icy creek. Their shrieks became irresistible, and she pushed through the bushes, following their voices.

"Barbara, stop!" Luis commanded her.

In her haste to join them, she hadn't noticed that she'd wandered onto a ledge overhanging the creek. She was a good fifteen feet above them. Luis took in the situation. It was doable.

"Jump, Barbara; I'll catch you," he promised. "Trust me; just close your eyes and go for it."

"Jump, Mommy, jump" Davie shouted in excitement. "Luis won't drop you."

Barbara looked down at the three faces she loved best in the world, hesitated a moment before kicking off her shoes and making the leap of a lifetime.

Epilogue

Barbara tapped the envelope that had been sitting on her desk for over two weeks against the fingers of her left hand—the one now sporting a small diamond band. It was time to open Davis's letter.

Dearest Barbara,

You'll never know how much I wish you weren't reading this letter. I didn't write it to make you sad, sweetheart, but to thank you for the gift of your love and to encourage you to be bold as you face all that lies ahead as you adjust to a world without me.

My world changed, became magical, the day you made the call I never expected and became part of my life. Right from the first, we had something few people achieve, a true partnering. You became my lover, my best friend, my conscience, and my soul. Among your many gifts was one I couldn't have anticipated—a second mother for my children. Knowing this almost makes leaving them behind bearable.

I know Davie and Laura are hurting, feeling lost and confused, but time and your gentle guidance will take them to a happier place. For that, I thank you. I hope with all my heart they help you heal, too.

Life is unpredictable and sometimes cruel, but it is all we have. I want you to live yours to the fullest. And this brings me to a part of this letter you might not welcome.

I knew almost from our first moments together that I shared you with someone else. In time, I learned his name—Luis Vallejo. Forgive me, but I did a little digging, wanting to know more about this man I knew only in a professional capacity.

I never understood completely why your relationship with him ended and didn't ask because I could see talking about him caused you pain. I knew from the first, however, that you hadn't let him go—not entirely. That's because you're an unusually loyal person, Barbara, one who doesn't make personal commitments easily but finds it hard to let go once you've included someone in your life.

If you can, if circumstances permit it, I'd like you to give Luis another chance. And if that isn't to be, promise me you'll move on and find someone else, a man who will love you as you deserve and take on another man's children, my children.

I love you, Barbara, and this love will always be there between us. Celebrate it often, hold on to our happiest memories even as you build new ones with someone else. One last thing—make new babies. I can't think of a gift I'd treasure more than brothers and sisters for the two I leave in your care.

Davis

A Personal Message from the Author

Now that you've finished *Hunting Barbara*, and I thank you for choosing one of my books, I'd like to ask a favor. Please visit one of the many readers' sites online and spend a few minutes writing a review. Authors need feedback, and readers need help finding good books. Love it or hate it, but let me and others know what you think. Blessings on you.

Diana León Clark

Meet the Author
Diana León Clark

Before beginning her career as a storyteller, a term she prefers to novelist or writer, Diana León Clark was senior editor at Northland Press in Flagstaff, Arizona. Later, she served as publications director for the Museum of Northern Arizona.

Her deepest interests, often the background for her stories, are Latin American political history and Iberoamerican culture. She is an enthusiastic supporter of preservation, both cultural and natural, and, like all of us, Diana also loves a good romance. These interests, too, often find their way into her stories.

Other passions include Latin American protest music (especially Nueva Canción), art—in all its forms, and life as an expat. She lives and works in Chapala, Mexico, on the shores of a mystical lake.

Her education includes a Bachelor's Degree from Western Michigan University, a Master's Degree in Latin American history from the University of Toledo, and a Ph.D. in American history/political science—emphasis historic preservation, from Northern Arizona University.

Other Books by Diana León Clark

Tapestries

"Sometimes, democracy must be bathed in blood." General Augusto Pinochet

A young Jesuit priest returns to Chile and a politically divided Catholic Church. After a violent coup, his bishop assigns Alejandro the task of guiding and protecting the women of a church-sponsored workshop.

At first reluctant to waste his time with lower class women, Father Saavedra soon discovers their extraordinary courage and unexpected wisdom. He also comes to admire the beauty of the *arpilleras*, or tapestries, they create to protest the violence of General Pinochet's brutal regime.

The themes these women use in their colorful creations come directly from the tragedy of their lives. Their work, merely art to many, depicts missing or detained family members, murder, the arrest and torture of husbands and sons, public protests against Pinochet, and the desperately poor conditions they live in.

The women of the Holy Rosary Workshop, brutally frank and disrespectful of all authority, gradually form a family with Father Saavedra and the three upper- class women who assist them in surprising ways. For nearly sixteen years, young or old, they share their personal stories, learn from each other, and fight against a government determined to destroy them, their loved ones, and their struggle for human dignity.

1077 Callaway Street

Mysteries, like great beauty, sometimes reveal themselves slowly.

Beauty starts within. That is the message Peter Vilaró gently delivers to young Lizzie Vitale, his troubled thirteen-year-old neighbor. Pere's faith in her future and his tender support for Lizzie, who is bullied at school and unappreciated at home, transcend his sudden death.

As she matures, Lizzie, now Liz, carries her warm memories of the old man with her to Chapel Hill, where she manages an international database. Her quick intelligence and skills as a researcher prove useful as she tries to discover what happened to her friend more than a decade earlier. Befriended by the old man's nephew, Lluc Toset, Liz gradually unravels the secrets surrounding her beloved Pere's death.

But this isn't the only mystery in Peter Vilaró's life. Lluc now knows why his famous uncle left Spain and where he went, but other questions remain. Unwilling to share his concerns with a woman he's come to love, Lluc returns to Spain to tackle his fears alone, leaving behind a grieving Liz.

Interlude in Las Alpujarras

"*Write what you know,* but what if that could get someone you love in trouble?"

Alexandria McCall has a problem. Everyone in her life knows exactly what her future should look like—everyone except her. Armed only with her mother's romantic nature and a small inheritance from her aunt, Alex flees a controlling boyfriend and her conservative Midwestern relatives, setting off on a quixotic trip to southern Spain.

When she encounters a reclusive and talented musician determined to change the course of her life, sparks fly. Now, she has a decision to make—continue on the path chosen for her or take a chance on a different life and a man she barely knows.

Dangerous Ground

"Money, Douglas, money and power, that's what oil and gas is all about. Why should I worry if a few lousy field workers get sick?"

Problems with radiation in the oil and gas industry are the last thing on geologist Cherylynn Rodgers mind as she begins her new job at the Museum of Northern Arizona.

All that changes when a brash field geologist seeks the advice of his former professor, a summer geologist-in-residence at the museum.

Despite her initial dislike for the irritating fieldman, Cherylynn soon joins the two Texans in a search for ways to make the lives of David Piper's men safer. It isn't long, however, before their own safety becomes a concern as Cherylynn learns just how ruthless powerful men with a lot to lose can be.

A Cottage in the Hamptons

"Trouble will follow you until you learn to face it head on."

Dina Marie Davis has a big problem—a powerful, vindictive professor determined to see that she washes out of her graduate program. Relieved when another member of Kent State's faculty successfully places her at Yale University, Dina soon learns that she's gone from the frying pan to the fire. Her options are limited. She can flee once again or accept the help of a reluctant ally, her remote, middle-aged seminar director.

Dina chooses to stay and fight growing increasing attached to Dr. Carl Rinaldi, who finds himself both embarrassed and delighted by his second chance at life. An unexpected tragedy puts Dina's life on a different trajectory, one with new challenges and even more danger.

Touchstone

"Three men, one confused young woman—what could go wrong?"

Lucy Clarke has given up on men after a disastrous affair with a manipulative professor. Still, she is lucky enough to have a "do over," a year in New Zealand courtesy of a Fulbright scholarship.

A cocky young American determined to win her, an upstairs neighbor who senses she isn't ready to give away her heart though he's lost his, and the man she thought she'd left behind forever in Ohio all challenge Lucy's desire to manage her own life. An unplanned pregnancy leads Lucy from New Zealand to the United States, Great Britain, and, finally, Spain.

Here, she finds herself and her life's work, creates an unconventional family, and centers her life around three men who have nothing in common except Lucy.

The Light of Hidden Flowers

"Rome cut off the heads of Christians and they continued to reappear. Something similar happens with Marxists." Augusto Pinochet

Arabella Davis, a young American scholar with romance on her mind, disrupts the settled lives of two wealthy Chilean brothers. The eldest, Diego, is appalled by Bella's brash behavior and does his best to discourage her outlandish adventures—even enlisting the aid of his CIA friend.

His younger brother, however, delights in her misadventures until a military coup, one backed by the U.S. government, makes any kind of acting out too dangerous.

From their family's hacienda, *Mil Flores*, Bella fights to protect her now-fragile husband and ensure his scholarly legacy. Her own work, five novels challenging General Augusto Pinochet's reputation, will eventually win her accolades in Chile and around the world. What it brings to Bella short term, however, is danger.

Now Available

The Light of Hidden Flowers

Diana León Clark

Enjoy your preview

Chapter One

Arabella Davis sat in her professor's deep, overstuffed guest chair, her feet dangling inches from the floor. Dr. Rojas was giving her instructions, yet again, for her upcoming research trip to Santiago, Chile.

"Remember, Bella, it's important to follow Chilean customs. Things are different down there. A single female on her own will not always be taken seriously as a scholar or respected as a person. You're not used to that. It means you must confine yourself to a group of like-minded students, at least one female besides yourself among them. And stay out of their politics. Have I been clear?"

Bella's dark eyes brimmed with mischief and a hint of impatience. She'd heard it all before—several times. "Yes, Dr. Rojas, I'll be careful; I promise."

Agustín Rojas groaned deep in his throat before glaring at his favorite graduate student. "I'm beginning to regret this grant already. I'm going to worry the whole time you're gone. It isn't just the unstable political environment in Chile; it's you."

Bella nodded though she couldn't understand her advisor's concern. Her life in Santiago would be full with researching and writing—not to mention attending classes and seminars. Besides, she'd never been one for political activism or an exciting nightlife. Her books had always been her lovers and best friends.

That's why she'd been delighted when Dr. Rojas found her a grant covering a whole year at the University of Chile and helped her get permission to use *El Mercurio's* archives and the Domingo Sarmiento papers in the university library. Grateful for all he'd done to make her trip possible, Bella didn't want her professor worrying about her.

"I won't get into trouble. I'll follow all your instructions, stick with other students, and stay on campus and out of Chile's politics, which really doesn't interest me anyway. Will you quit stressing out? I'm 25, you know. I can take care of myself."

She hasn't got a clue, Agustín Rojas worried once again. Bella was no beauty, but his favorite graduate student had bold dark eyes; a cute little figure he knew he shouldn't be noticing; and a sassy, sure-of-herself way about her he found oddly appealing. She was also a bit of a loose cannon, or *antojadizo*, as they said in his native Argentina.

"Here's your letter of introduction to Dr. Guzmán. I've encountered him a few times at conferences. He's a bit abrupt in manner but a good scholar. I want you to make every effort to get along with him. Don't even think about treating him like you do me." His eyes were stern as he finished his instructions but softened as he sent Arabella Davis on her way.

· · · ·

Bella's suitcases were neatly packed, and she'd put the papers she needed quick access to in her purse. Last night's conversation with her parents had been painful. They didn't want her to go and couldn't understand why she'd chosen such a backward place to continue her studies.

"Chile," her dad grumbled in disgust. "Who goes there? They're all Catholics and can't even speak English."

Bella didn't try to explain. The longer she'd been in school, the harder it became to relate to her parents. But she'd said everything proper, her mind already focused on the opportunities ahead.

The adventure she so eagerly sought began with a long, boring flight that took most of the next day. She flew first from Detroit to Fort Worth. Then, she boarded American Airlines for the Aeropuerto Internacional de Pudahuel outside Santiago. *Even the name sounds exotic,* she enthused, peering out of her airplane window as they finally landed. It was a brand-new facility, very modern but far from the city center.

Bella approached the nearest taxi, still stiff from her long journey. Two years of working with Dr. Rojas, three years of Spanish as an undergraduate, and a summer in Mexico made her confident she'd have no serious problems communicating in a Spanish-speaking country. That confidence lasted until her first conversation with the taxi driver.

The man didn't seem to have any trouble understanding her but spoke so rapidly, using what she thought must be some kind of dialect, that Bella missed most of what he said. As she listened to the other people around her, she realized she couldn't understand them very well, either.

This possibility hadn't occurred to her. Dr. Rojas was from Argentina, and she'd found his Spanish easy to follow once she adjusted to the Italian flavor of his speech.

Finally, the driver understood where she wanted to go, and they headed into the city. She'd spend the next two weeks at the Villa Ruiz, a modest inn close to the university. By the time her stay there ended, she hoped to find an apartment for the rest of the year.

The next morning, Bella got out her map and figured out how to get to the campus. She asked her taxi driver to drop her near the history building. The young man just laughed. "I have no idea where this building is, *señorita*, but I can get you to the university entrance." At least, that's what she thought he said.

Eventually, she found her way to Dr. Pablo Guzmán's office. The professor's door stood open, but Bella wasn't certain whether students in Chile could just walk in to their advisor's office or if they needed to make an appointment. As she stood there, hesitant, he looked up.

"Well, are you lost or just stupid? I don't have time to waste."

At least I can understand what he's saying, she thought ruefully. *Well, here goes nothing.* "I'm Bella Davis, Arabella Davis, from the University of Toledo. Dr. Agustín Rojas arranged for me to do my thesis work with you this year. He gave me a letter for you."

He looked at her impatiently. "Well, where's the letter?"

Bella handed it to him in silence, examining the older man's face while he read what Dr. Rojas had written. Looking him over, she couldn't imagine a greater contrast between two professors of the Latin persuasion. Dr. Rojas was a tall, handsome Latin male in his early thirties. Dr. Guzmán was far older, short and stout, and, to be honest, ugly. *Rude, too,* she decided in annoyance. The man totally lacked Agustín's easy charm.

"Well, my dear girl, according to him, I'm to consider you a competent scholar. We'll see about that. Most girls aren't worth my time or trouble. You Americans are the worst. Most of you come to play with the boys."

Bella's temper, usually reliably under control, began to sizzle. She remembered what Dr. Rojas said about getting along with her Chilean advisor, but that might not be so easy.

"Dr. Guzmán, please don't call me *dear girl.* I may be female, but I'm not a girl. If you're a fair man, I'm confident you'll find my scholarship more than acceptable. Dr. Rojas, wouldn't send me here unless he was certain I'd do well. I hope we understand each other and have a satisfying professional association. Just don't go all *macho* Chilean male on me. Judge me by my work, not my gender."

Bella was pretty sure she shouldn't have added that last part. To her surprise, Dr. Guzmán snorted in amusement then laughed out loud.

"Agustín said I'd find you tart tongued. We'll do just fine, Arabella Davis. See our department's secretary for your schedule. Classes start Wednesday. Don't expect me to coddle you, and never come to class unprepared. That's all for now."

• • • •

Over the next two weeks, Bella gradually adjusted to university life in Chile. The departmental secretary, Barbara Hinckley, helped her find a small, furnished apartment near the building housing the history department.

"The immediate neighborhood is safe," she reassured Bella, "but some of the surrounding ones aren't quite so good. Unless you're with friends, I'd stay close to home after dark."

Bella did her best to make friends on campus, introducing herself to a variety of students, including one young man who told her his name was Arturo Reyes. "I know your name," she told him. "I read it in several news stories about protests in Santiago. You've even been arrested, haven't you? You're braver than I am."

Arturo, who helped establish MIR as an important left-of-center political movement in Chile, was a tall, rangy young man with a mop of curly, dark hair. He smiled at Bella, his brown eyes flirtatious. "If you're interested in Chilean protests, *señorita*, I'll be happy to be your guide."

As he told her about an event scheduled for that day, Arturo placed a hand casually on her upper arm, his palm *accidentally* touching her breast. American girls, in his experience, had a well-deserved reputation for being receptive to Chilean males. Bella pushed his hand away and shook her head.

Although his eyes were amused, Arturo accepted her polite rejection, telling her instead about the roots of student protest in his country. "We're part of a worldwide phenomenon, of course, but we in Chile play a more important role. In fact, we are the strongest voice for change in our country.

"Part of it is rising expectations. Many of us are the first in our families to attend university. We expect a better future for ourselves and others, but we are not alone in this fight. Chile has strong labor unions, and the rural poor are organizing. Everywhere in Chile, the word *democracy* is heard and revered. Now, the elites must recognize what democracy means."

Bella returned to her small apartment, still energized by her meeting with Arturo. His was just one voice calling for change. She wanted to learn more, hear different voices, but that meant ignoring Dr. Rojas' advice. *It wouldn't be the first time,* she told herself cheerfully. *It's time to see what Chile is all about.*

· · · ·

Since one of the most popular off-campus activities for her classmates seemed to be attending rallies and political protests, Bella decided this might be the best way to make friends. Not only that, the cost of this entertainment, free except for a bus ride to the city center, fit right into her spartan budget.

She ran into Arturo Reyes again in the main plaza, where he'd organized a protest against the government's blatant disregard for Mapuche water rights. Taking her hand and pulling her close to his side, he began introducing Bella to some of his friends.

Although she remembered her former professor's warning to stay out of politics, Bella wanted to experience as much in Chile as she could. Besides, she welcomed Arturo's friendliness, finding herself a little lonely.

I'll be careful, she promised herself. *Besides, I've participated in protests before in Kalamazoo and Toledo. How different can they be down here?*

Protests and demonstrations had been popular in the United States during her undergraduate years, and Bella participated casually from time to time. It didn't take her long to learn the tone of protest was different in Chile. Here, people took to the streets because they had no other choice.

Chile's president, Eduardo Frei Montalva, was gradually introducing social and economic reforms, but it seemed too little and too slow for many Chileans crushed by out-of-control inflation and decades of repression.

The reasons for protest differed—indigenous groups being slowly starved to death, workers who couldn't find work to support their families, women banging on pots and pans because food was scarce and pricey, as well as all kinds of workers demanding better wages and working conditions. It impressed Bella, accustomed to a more individualized society, that people in one group often supported the demands of another.

This mutual support contributed to a sense of shared outrage and community new to her. After thinking about the differences between the two countries, she decided the Chileans got it right.

Page |